SOMETHING TO DO

1972

John M. Tallon

Something to Do 1972

(Revised and reprinted April 2015)

Copyright © John Tallon, 2013
Cover photograph, copyright ©
Clare Tallon 2013
Cover production John.A.Tallon

All rights reserved in all media. No part of this book may be used or reproduced without written permission, except in the case of brief quotations embodied in critical articles and reviews.

All characters and places are entirely fictitious. Any resemblance or similarity to persons living or deceased is purely coincidental.

Also by this author

Natural Born Skinhead 1971

Never a Dull Moment 1973

Find us on facebook @ John M Tallon

and

https://www.facebook.com/pages/Something-to-Do-1972/427764967346581?fref=ts

Dedicated to my beautiful wife, Clare

and my three incredible sons,

John, Adam and Paul

CONTENTS

CHAPTER 1 – Starry Starry Night **1**

CHAPTER 2 – All the Young Dudes **11**

CHAPTER 3 – Everywhere There's Lots of Piggies **46**

CHAPTER 4 – Ball of Confusion **79**

CHAPTER 5 – Instant Karma **100**

CHAPTER 6 – Move on Up **119**

CHAPTER 7 – Leader of the Pack **134**

CHAPTER 8 – Rocket Man **165**

CHAPTER 9 – Schools Out Forever **189**

CHAPTER 10 – Lean on Me **219**

CHAPTER 11 – War **242**

CHAPTER 12 – Living in a Broken Dream **272**

CHAPTER 13 – Ghost Riders in the Sky **297**

MUSIC (**end pages**)

Chapter 1

Starry Starry Night

Saturday, January 1st 1972

John Mack, better known to his friends and enemies as Jay Mac, finished lacing his boots and gave them yet another wipe with the soft polished-stained cloth that he always carried. The cherry red shine would have impressed even the sternest sergeant major but Jay Mac was still not satisfied that another combined coat of Tucson Red and Kiwi Oxblood, could not have improved the mirror-like finish further. Having attended to this most vital item of his apparel, Jay Mac carefully scrutinised his over all appearance. His dark hair had grown out considerably since his last ultra-short crop of the late summer of the previous year. The warm balmy days of July and August, when a 'Number One Perry Como' with obligatory razored trench was both fashionably de rigueur and comfortable, had long passed. The iron-hard frozen ground, bitter Arctic wind and accompanying flurries of bone-chilling sleet of a Liverpool winter, made the somewhat longer hair of the 'Suedehead' a more practical coiffure, whilst simultaneously satisfying the ever-changing whims of the youth culture fashion gods.

Jay Mac's dark blue-black *Owen Owen's* Crombie still looked sharp, considering its relatively moderate price and the escapades it had endured. The White Horse of Hanover, King's Liverpool badge on the breast pocket was barely marked, the faux red garnet stud, which held the neatly folded piece of scarlet silk cloth in place, also had survived intact. He fastened his Levi's denim jacket with bleached white collar but left his Crombie open because he liked the way it hung. Over his white Ben Sherman shirt, he also wore a colourful sleeveless v-neck Fair Isle jumper. A pair of neatly ironed eighteen inch parallel, hand-scrubbed Wrangler blue jeans, with half inch turn-ups, completed his ensemble.

He left the small stuffy living room with its permanent haze of nicotine smoke, produced by a combination of his chain-smoking aunt's cigarettes and his uncle's old briar pipe. Some inane variety show was playing on the small black and white television in the corner of the room. However, having spent the previous evening celebrating the New Year with other elderly relatives, neither of Jay Mac's guardians was really focused on what was happening either on-screen or in the room. His imminent departure was, as usual, almost unnoticed except for the appropriately named Patch, a white with large brown patches *Heinz 57* of a mongrel who bore more than a passing resemblance to a dishevelled collie dog. The former rescue pup, now aged twelve, had been Jay Mac's constant companion since he was four years old. He mumbled a cursory goodbye and stepped into the even smaller hall.

The door to the tiny adjoining bedroom was open and this gave Jay Mac one more opportunity to check his appearance, as the mirror on top of the old utility dressing table, was perfectly angled to reflect his gleaming red Airwair. Another quick wipe with the cloth then he opened the front door and stepped out onto the grey concrete landing. The youth quickly walked down the two flights of tenement stairs, to the main communal door that opened onto the street outside. The smell of strong bleach that struggled in vain to mask the pungent odours escaping from the tenants' bins stored immediately under the staircase, mixed with the even stronger odour of stale urine, from numerous opportunists who had taken advantage of a door accidentally left open on previous occasions, made him glad to step into the bitterly cold afternoon air.

Jay Mac quickly surveyed the landscape between him and the vandalised, old concrete slab bus shelter. 'No sign of the enemy,' he thought, as he crossed the road and entered the crumbling structure. The icy wind howled through window frames that had long since contained any glass. Various pornographic, biological and anatomically imaginative figures had been scrawled with felt pens on the grey precast concrete slabs and pillars of the shelter. Jay Mac was more concerned with the names of gang members of the Kings Estate Team, most recently daubed in paint both inside and out. Nothing specifically referred to *him*, other than the general propaganda statement, that the Kings Estate Team being the 'gunners' meant that the Crown Estate Team were clearly the 'runners' and the warning that the latter would be truly 'fucked' in their next encounter on the motorway flyover construction site that bordered both estates.

A bus finally appeared on the horizon at the brow of the rise that demarked the territory of yet another team, appropriately named 'The Brow'. When the vehicle arrived Jay Mac paid the ten pence minimal fare that satisfied the mutual requirements of both parties and made his way to the back of the lower deck. Previous, painful experience had taught him never to go upstairs alone, particularly in full 'uniform' on a rival team's bus. The short journey was uneventful, there were no sounds of stomping boots from the upper deck, no raucous laughter, or excessively loud swearing, clearly the previous night's festivities and the inclement weather, had dampened the enthusiasm of some of the other players. However, darkness had not yet fallen and that always provided tempting opportunities for entertainment.

Jay Mac reached his destination and alighted from the vehicle, at the stop facing the old bus terminal sheds at the edge of the Crown Estate. This collection of dilapidated buildings, where the corporation buses were garaged, repaired and cleaned, also served as an armoury for the gangs, with easily accessible supplies of munitions, principally in the form of aluminium support poles from the interior of the vehicles.

Making his way through the maze of streets, filled with tightly packed rows of small drab post-war economy housing, he looked for other members of his team. Apart from the usual motley collection of feral children and the obligatory odd stray dog that seemed to permanently roam the streets in all weathers, none of his usual companions were visible.

Passing the house of one of his former associates, Mal 'the Pig', Jay Mac's mind wandered and he considered how this would-be necrophiliac, séance-organising genuinely strange character, who had a penchant for continuously playing Black Widow's *Come to the Sabbath*, occasionally interspersed with selected tracks from Led Zeppelin or the Beatles White Album, had ever been part of his inner coterie. The gaily coloured nylon curtains covering Mal's bedroom window, the neatly painted façade and front door of the end terrace, gave no clue to the madness that raged within, inside Mal's disturbed and now mutilated head. Jay Mac entered the alley-way between the houses, which led to the waste-ground behind. His gaze once more wandered to the window that had burst open on that fateful sinister night late in the previous autumn. For a moment he thought he glimpsed the morose figure of Mal himself, standing staring with his soulless eyes into the evening gloom, silhouetted by the glow of a small bedroom lamp. He rarely left the house these days.

Mal Chadwick was not a Skinhead; in fact he was in many ways the antithesis of this particular youth movement. Shoulder length unkempt centre-parted mousey hair, hung over and separated to reveal an acne-scarred weasel-like face, with thin lips that barely concealed yellow and brown tobacco stained teeth. Small permanently blood-shot eyes were closely set on either side of a predominant long pointed nose - at least that was prior to the night of the accident. He dressed in the height of late Sixties Hippie fashion with his Paisley shirts, tie-dyed granddad vests, sleeveless faux fur jacket, or old air force surplus greatcoat, brightly coloured striped flares and 'desert wellie' boots of faded brown suede. Around his neck hung an array of assorted jewellery, including an apotropaic evil eye and a small cow-bell. His long fingers with their dirt encrusted nails, were adorned with an assortment of rings, set with different coloured paste gems and, an obligatory gold skull with red garnet eyes.

Mal was accepted by Jay Mac's group only because the lodger in Mal's parents' home, Tony Gregson (known as Tony (G)) happened to be a particularly vicious, street-fighting Skinhead, who not only dressed the part but more significantly, was the proud owner of a Lambretta LI175. This prime example of the ultimate mode of transport was resplendent with colourful red fly screen, multiple mirrors, Florida bars, an awesome air horn, extended aerial and that Holy Grail of all aspiring Scooter Boys, the word 'Outcrowd' emblazoned in gold lettering on the detachable red and white side panels, indicating membership of this exclusive club. With the kudos of such a house-guest, Mal had sufficient entrée credentials, to gain access to any group and he exploited this to maximum effect.

Jay Mac considered the irony, that it was Tony (G)'s electrical skill that enabled him to hotwire cars with ease. In fact on that fateful night of the previous November, he had 'started' a neighbours vehicle within minutes of the door lock being forced and provided Mal with another opportunity to test his driving skills. Jay Mac and two of his friends who were passing by at the time, seized the offer of riding around the city, in a warm car rather than tramping the bleak streets of the estate for another night.

Several hours later, after some 'wild' driving, a police chase and drinking numerous bottles of Double Diamond, they had returned to the estate. Jay Mac and his best friend Patrick O'Hare known by everyone as Irish, got out of the car to continue their drinking, in the Eagle Public House with the usual crew and two local girls were easily enticed away from outside the chip shop, to replace them in the vehicle.

A short time later the unmistakable sound of a terrible crash brought Jay Mac, Irish, and several others running from the pub. In a nearby road they soon found the wreck of the car mounted onto the kerb, smashed into a concrete lamppost. Smoke was coming from the engine; one of the girls was lying partially in the car, with her legs broken and her face scarred with dozens of glass splinters. Tony (G) and the other female passenger where unconscious in the rear of the vehicle, covered in blood, suffering from multiple fractures and internal injuries. Mal looked to all intents to be dead; he had been thrown through the windscreen and was partially lying on the crumpled bonnet, both his legs were broken as was his left arm and collar bone. His skull was fractured and the blood-soaked hair was matted to his mutilated scarlet face, the fleshy tip of what had been a prominent nose was sliced clean off, leaving two nasal cavities that led to the application of his new epithet of Mal 'the Pig', from that day on.

Jay Mac's thoughts returned to the present evening as he neared the house of Irish, his long-time friend. 'What would be on the agenda tonight he wondered?'

"What the fuck do you want?" asked Irish as he opened the door to the small, cramped terraced house where he lived with his mother, father, two brothers, two sisters and family dog, Toby.

"Happy New Year to you too, cunt," Jay Mac replied, "What's happenin' tonight?"

"Fuck all as usual, what do you think? It's fuckin' New Year's day," Irish responded, in his usual depressive, monotone manner.

At six foot he was slightly taller than Jay Mac's five foot ten, though physically he was very similar, with a rangy athletic build, dark hair and eyes. They had been friends since they first met, in the early days of their five year 'incarceration,' in a Christian Brother run hellish institution, known as *The Cardinals' School for Catholic Boys*. Both boys had the shared bond of being considered as the disappointing failure of their respective families.

Jay Mac being the illegitimate son of the alcoholic, feeble-minded daughter of a disenfranchised, exiled, large, Irish Catholic family was never really going to be anything, other than an embarrassment to his relations. Given the prevailing social and religious mores at the time and place of his birth in a mid-1950s closely-knit parochial community, he was fortunate that his mother had lost her nerve at the last minute and refused to proceed with a hastily arranged back-street abortion.

Irish's disgrace was perhaps more self-inflicted than Jay Mac's accident of unfortunate conception. As the second child of a hard-working but poor family, of similar Irish, Catholic origin, he was over-shadowed by a highly intelligent, industrious elder brother, plus subsequently two younger sisters and yet another brother of the same vein. Irish rebelled against everything, particularly his parent's stress of the value of study and application. His political argument that he cultivated from an early age, was that the system would always strive to keep the working class in their place, no matter how hard they tried to rise, resistance was futile, social mobility was a myth created by the bourgeoisie to keep the proletariat in thrall. The fact that he was lazy, workshy, took no pride in his appearance and infinitely less talented than his siblings, never really crossed his mind and he took solace in his conviction of the immovability and fixed hierarchy of the status quo.

"I'll just get me Crombie and me fags" said Irish as he disappeared back into the stiflingly hot living room.

Jay Mac waited in the doorway; he did not want to go inside and be forced to observe the conventional New Year exchange of greetings with Irish's family. It was not because he did not like them, or because he was 'too cool' to socialise with 'ordinary' mainstream citizens but primarily he was uncomfortable with situations that required physical contact and displays of emotion. He had long ago learned to remain detached and distant, too many painful memories of a love-less childhood and constant rejection, kept him tightly locked within his own personal space.

Irish stepped out of the front door dressed in his expensive Jackson the Taylor black Crombie. Although a much superior brand to that of Jay Mac, Irish normally 'hung it up' on his bedroom floor, therefore, it did not have the neatest appearance. Added to this Irish did not bother that his cigarette ash peppered the front of his coat, or that fragments of various meals could clearly be seen matted into the woollen fibres. Rather than a red or white silk, neatly folded, faux handkerchief, Irish just stuffed a regular brown checked fully functioning item with its contents, into his breast pocket. As a comb very seldom came into contact with his unkempt greasy hair, or even a dab of polish ever found its way onto his unconventional black Airwair, this made him the odd-man-out in the midst of a group of military pristine, fashion-conscious, generally clean-cut youths.

As they were about to leave, Irish's elder brother Dermot opened the door of the converted storage room that ran along the side of the house, where he tended to study and sometimes sleep. *Sweet Black Angel* from the Rolling Stones *Exile on Main Street* album could be heard playing inside as Dermot stood in the partially open doorway smoking a cigarette.

"Where are you two Charlies off to tonight?" he asked barely suppressing a sarcastic laugh.

"Piss off Hippie" Irish replied, as he reached the safe distance of the front gate.

"Wankers!" Dermot shouted, flicking the glowing remains of his cigarette after them, as they walked away towards the shops were the team usually gathered.

The shops consisted of an obligatory chippy, a laundrette ('the bag-wash'), a bookmaker (betting shop), a general store and occupying one complete semi-circular end structure, a library. Above this tired looking, vandalised, graffiti covered assortment was a local function hall. This was the venue for a variety of affairs, the one of primary interest to gang members and civilian youths alike, was the weekly disco on a Wednesday evening. Opportunities for peacock-like posturing displays of high fashion and testosterone, mixed with previously consumed cider, beer and, or whiskey-fuelled aggression, were virtually guaranteed. This made the event un-missable and the main players sought to reinforce their precarious status, by sporadic, explosive episodes of extreme violence.

Passing by the shops the two youths casually glanced at the almost undecipherable graffiti that camouflaged the steel shutters and doors.

"How many fuckin' years do you think people have been writin' on these shops?" Jay Mac asked in a rhetorical manner.

"Generations probably" Irish replied, "Its people communicatin', leavin' messages" he added.

Jay Mac looked at Irish sceptically and asked, "So kids drawin' fuckin' big cocks and tits is the workin' class makin' a comment on the key problems of society, is it?"

Irish did not reply, as they rounded the corner of the library building.

The shop area was deserted, the chippy was closed and even the large concrete, continuous windowsill of the library, the usual perch for their crew, was unoccupied. They continued on to a nearby friend's house, Billy Boyd known as Blue, or sometimes unkindly referred to as 'Blub/Blubber' because of his corpulent physique. Another of their associates Daniel Glynn, or Glynn, a tall blond haired Skinhead prone to displays of conceited arrogance, was also at Blue's. After a brief exchange of customary insults, all four set off looking for adventure on the frozen streets of the bleak estate.

Disappointingly for the four comrades it was one of those deadly boring nights that were in fact, the norm rather than the exception. The only adventure that night consisted of riding up and down in the filthy, litter-strewn tower block lifts, that also served as urinals for both humans and animals, as the need arose. After an hour or so of this desperate attempt to stay warm and find entertainment, the group decided to torment the occupants of the flats, by ringing doorbells and kicking doors then running away.

"Fuck this bollocks" said Glynn, "I'd rather 'ave stayed in Blue's and listened to some records, than do this shite." He continued in this vein, while the aforementioned Blue relieved himself by urinating through some poor unfortunate's broken letterbox.

"Hey Blue, watch out there's a little old woman livin' in there, she'll 'ave yer cock off" shouted Irish in mock warning.

"She'll think it's a fuckin' slug and put salt on it," quipped Jay Mac as Blue stepped away from the door, whilst still urinating.

"Listen she's screamin', cos she thinks a fuckin' snake's got in through the letter box," he responded, finally zipping up his Wrangler jeans.

The youths then set about scrawling the names of all four crew members, on every possible surface. This was followed by throwing some empty milk bottles off the top landing, into the entrance and street below. As there were no moving targets to focus their aim upon, they soon tired of this distraction too and vacated the flats.

"What a shit night, there's not even any birds about" Glynn began complaining once more.

"That's cos they're all shagged out from last night" Blue replied, smiling.

"Not if you had anything to do with it they're not," Jay Mac added.

The four team mates then proceeded to make their way back to the shops and eventually arrived at Blue's house. Irish decided to stay with Blue and Glynn, playing records, smoking cigarettes and drinking Blue's parents' left-over beer and spirits from the previous evening. Jay Mac said he would just have a couple of bottles of brown ale then leave, he never smoked. Whilst drinking he sat listening to some tracks from *Motown Chartbusters Volumes 3 and 4.* The Four Tops and the Temptations were his favourites, with *Still Waters* by the former firmly in his own top ten.

Time passed and Jay Mac realised it was probably too late for the last bus, particularly given that it was a Bank Holiday.

"Any chance of kippin' at yours Irish?" he asked.

"I'll ask me mam, you can crash on the floor in our room, if she says it's ok," Irish replied.

"Fuckin' great, all the comforts of home, Happy New Year 1972" was Jay Mac's tired response, as he sat back and took another swig from his bottle of ale. Letting the sound of the Temptations '*Runaway Child Running Wild*' wash over him, he began contemplating what the next twelve months may hold in store for him and his team mates.

Chapter 2

All The Young Dudes

Saturday 29th January 1972

Jay Mac sat slumped over his evening meal of fried eggs, fried sausages and deep fried chips. Four slices of heavily margarined bread to make the essential 'chip buttie,' smothered in red sauce, accompanied by two steaming mugs of tea and followed by half a dozen custard cream biscuits, left him feeling satisfied and perplexingly somewhat sleepy. The fact that earlier in the day he had already consumed four pints of brown mix at the Central Public House in London Road and a sloppy 'meat' pie, from one of his favourite eateries, 'The Pigeon Pie Shop', as it was popularly known, based at the Pier Head bus and ferry terminus, may also have contributed to his growing need for sleep.

In his aunt and uncle's small, cramped, one-bedroom, council flat, situated above a radio and TV shop, it was difficult to find anywhere to stretch out and relax. At night he normally slept on the couch or a small folding bed that was stored in a hall cupboard during the day. However, when his uncle was relaxing watching television, particularly his favourite *The Black & White Minstrel Show*, whilst smoking his pipe and his aunt was reading one of her Agatha Christie murder mystery novels for the hundredth time, smoking a twenty pack of Embassy king-size filter-tip cigarettes, there was no room for a comfortable nap. This evening having left the tiny kitchen after completing his meal, a flagging Jay Mac 'collapsed' into a small, well-worn armchair by the fire, Patch the dog immediately curled up on the floor at his feet. Even whilst sitting upright in an awkward position, with the sound of the television blaring in the background, tiredness and a full stomach eventually overtook the youth and he drifted into a deep slumber. His canine companion soon followed suit.

When Jay Mac awoke he glanced at his small collection of birthday cards on the mantelpiece. He had reached seventeen years of age a couple of days earlier and the meagre monetary gifts he had received, at least supplemented his pittance of a weekly wage. His uncle was singing along with the final show tune, as Jay Mac asked him for the usual chore. Jack feigned a protest but in reality was happy to oblige; an ex-military man, a professional regular soldier, who served throughout the 1930s, was subsequently a member of the B.E.F and then a prisoner of war for nearly five years after Dunkirk, he enjoyed keeping his own postman's uniform in pristine condition, as if waiting for his next inspection. He had no objection to Jay Mac's choice of youth fashion, in fact short hair, clean, neat kit and highly polished boots were to him, a massive improvement on the scruffy, long-haired effeminate styles most young men seemed to prefer. Jay Mac asked his uncle to iron his best two-tone trousers because he felt no one could match the razor sharp crease that he could produce. If neat almost invisible sewing was required, Jack was also his first choice.

"I'll iron your kecks but I'm not listenin' to this shite," Jack said with a grin as he stepped into the kitchen where Jay Mac had quickly set up the ironing board and placed the old flat iron onto the oven gas ring, to heat up

"It's Mungo Gerry, that," Jay Mac replied, "It's better than that Black & White Minstrel stuff... now that *is* shite," he added laughing.

"Hey, at least you can hear the words with the Black & Whites, who knows what's being said in that garbage" was Jack's retort "and they're not puffs, like those long-haired pricks you listen to" was his final comment, before spitting on the flat iron and setting about the task in hand.

Whilst ironing he was deliberately loudly whistling the show tune '*Swanee River*', to drown out Marc Bolan's '*Ride a White Swan*', which had replaced '*Baby Jump*' on the turntable of the Radio One Chart Show.

The seemingly easy, relaxed, relationship between the man and the boy, belied a more uncomfortable, awkward and often volatile association, simmering just below the surface. Jay Mac knew not to overstep the invisible boundaries. Good natured humour could easily be misconstrued; a chance comment or naïve statement may quickly lead to contemptuous ridicule, or menacing physical intimidation. On this evening the atmosphere was deceptively calm, with no obvious portents of the events to come. Jay Mac followed his usual preparation ritual and when he was finally satisfied that everything was in order, particularly his gleaming cherry red Airwair, he set off.

The gangs had been quite active in the past fortnight; there had been several skirmishes, conducted across the busy dual carriageway and central reservation of the broad main road that served as a man-made border between the two estates. Supporting structures for a motorway fly-over, that would eventually join the two warring factions' territories, were still in the early stages of construction, on both sides of the carriageway. As yet they served only to provide various building miscellany that could be used as impromptu weapons and as graffiti covered grey concrete rallying points.

Jay Mac was aware that he had been spotted several times by Kings Estate team members, particularly when he wore his distinctive, white parallel 'bakers' trousers. He knew he was playing a dangerous game, living on one estate and fighting for the other. It all added to the risk factor and the excitement for him, he felt in a sense that he had always been playing against the odds, since the accident of his birth. Jay Mac had attended school in the centre of the city, not the Kings Estate. He only lived there because, having run away from his drunken mother's house to his aunt and uncle's home, seeking refuge and sustenance on countless occasions, they had eventually agreed to let him reside with them, albeit on a long-term, temporary basis. His main friends from school happened to be from the Crown Estate, he visited them regularly and knew them and their families well. This began long before the violent conflict flared up between the two post-war, slum clearance, housing projects known as The Estates. The youth did not intend to stop visiting his friends; not now that he was at a time of life, when socialising with a group of his chronological contemporaries was his raison d'être.

The probability of a bad beating, if he was identified and caught by the Kings Estate Team was high, yet it was a preferable option to death by extreme boredom, as he viewed life, trapped in that same small flat with two ageing relatives, one of whom was lost in a 1940s world of memories and repetitive tales, of a daughter, who had long since grown, married and become a mother herself. Could he really stand to hear yet another rendition of how the aforementioned cousin and child prodigy, had during the war apparently been mistaken by a group of American soldiers, for an infant Shirley Temple? Or, the tale of how subsequently her own meteoric rise to stardom, on the boards of the local David Lewis amateur theatre, had been untimely halted by the shocking false allegation that she had drenched those very boards, with the physical consequences of stage-fright, causing her to flee in tears, mid-way through her solo performance of *'On The Good Ship Lollipop'*. No, the risk of serious physical injury was infinitely preferable to the mind-numbing consequences of even one more tale of the infant phenomenon in all her glory.

Jay Mac closed the sheet steel covered front door behind him and stepped into the freezing, moonless winter's evening. Despite the sub-zero temperature, he did not wear his denim jacket under his Crombie. He did, however, supplement his usual attire with his red and white striped, woollen Liverpool F.C scarf, as a tacit nod to the prevailing weather conditions. His reasoning was that even though it was deepest winter outside, the temperature in the public houses in the city centre would be sub-tropical. Added to this he knew the false beer-and-whiskey-induced sense of warmth, would mask the bitter cold of the night.

Standing in the darkness within the old bus shelter, dressed in his dark Crombie, green-blue two tone trousers, red Airwair and football scarf, he felt relatively safe. The longer he waited, however, the chance of his being 'spotted' increased considerably.

"Where the fuck is this bus?" he muttered to himself after an anxious half hour had passed.

For the last ten minutes or so, a group of youths had been gathering in and around the chip shop. They were now about fifteen to twenty in number, mostly males from the 'Anvil' crew, one of the Kings Estate's numerous teams. Apart from shouting, swearing loudly and throwing chips at each other, or unwary passers-by, they posed no obvious immediate threat.

Suddenly, two youths who were engaged in the chip-throwing entertainment, started arguing then kicking and punching each other. The scuffle spread out onto the main road, enthusiastically encouraged by the remainder of the group who quickly gathered around the two protagonists, with shouts of "fuck him" and "kick his fuckin' head in." The fight finished almost as quickly as it had started, with the loser slumped against the external concrete slab wall of the bus shelter.

Jay Mac stepped further back into the inner shadow within, losing his place at the front of the queue, which had now developed. He recognised the victor of the conflict as Danny (H), one of the main players of the Kings Team. They had faced each other recently, exchanging insults and missiles across the Lancashire boundary road. With a bus now on the horizon, Danny (H) who had turned away from his fallen adversary, ran back and delivered a bone-cracking boot to the head of the latter. A second kick quickly followed and the fallen youth's nose erupted in a burst of snot and blood. One of the other occupants of the shelter lit a cigarette as the bus was almost at the stop. In the brief light of the glowing match, Danny caught sight of Jay Mac.

"I fuckin' know you, cunt!" he shouted.

Jay Mac did not respond.

"Hey! There's a fuckin' Crown Skin in 'ere." he called to his colleagues, who were mostly engaged in casually sexually assaulting one of the female camp followers in their group. The team ambled across the road as the bus arrived at the stop; sensing the imminent danger the other would-be passengers quickly pushed their way onto the vehicle.

"You're not gettin' on any fuckin' bus, cunt" said Danny (H) as he stepped forward to grab Jay Mac by the coat.

"Ger 'old of 'im Danny!" the team shouted in unison.

Jay Mac knew it was time for decisive action, and produced a long, thin razor-sharp knife from his Crombie side pocket.

"Back off shit-head, or lose a fuckin' eye" he warned his would-be captor. Danny (H) saw the blade flash, in the light from the interior of the bus and quickly pulled out his own Stanley knife in response. In an instant Jay Mac leapt onto the vehicle and shouted to the driver "Shut the fuckin' door!"

As the latter complied, Danny (H) threw himself at the opening and slashed wildly with his craft knife. He caught Jay Mac a glancing blow just above the wrist, on the left sleeve but the damage was to the material only. The bus pulled away and Jay Mac threw down his ten pence fare to the driver.

Deprived of his victim, Danny (H) flew into an inconsolable rage and began screaming, "Do the fuckin' bus, do it!"

When the vehicle slowed to turn the corner of the junction, a few yards from the stop, the whole team threw every available missile at it. The driver who knew his route well and the nature of his passengers, calmly steered the bus into the main road, seemingly oblivious to the madness taking place outside.

"You're fuckin' dead, you Crown twat, fuckin' dead! I know you now!" were Danny (H)'s parting words, as he ran alongside the vehicle pounding on the windows, until it gained momentum and left him and his frustrated crew far behind. Jay Mac made his way to the back of the bus and sat down. He turned around to look out of the rear window and raised two fingers in a gesture of defiance, as Danny (H)'s enraged face faded from view.

Inside he was shaking, not because of the clumsy knife attack but through anger at his identification, he knew serious consequences would follow and began to consider rationally what the Kings Team may now surmise. They did not know exactly where he lived, or even if he definitely was from that area but one more sighting at that bus stop would probably remove any doubt they may have. From now on Jay Mac would have to time his run to the stop to perfection. Above all he did not want any trouble to find its way to his aunt and uncle's residence.

Whilst mentally reviewing the situation, he became aware of two tall Skinheads standing at the bottom of the stairwell, looking at him intently, having come down from the upper deck. They sauntered towards Jay Mac and one sat next to him, the other facing, after ousting an elderly man who formerly occupied that position.

"Fuck off granddad, we've got business here" said one of the Skins, as he placed a hand casually but firmly on the man's shoulder.

Jay Mac looked at them both in turn whilst assessing the possibility of a quick escape, through the emergency exit door. Both males were about nineteen he thought, the one next to him had a short crop and large sideburns, outlining a hard angular face. He wore a sheepskin coat over a checked blue and white Ben Sherman shirt, a pair of white bakers' trousers and the obligatory red Airwair. The seat usurper facing Jay Mac was smoking a cigarette, oblivious to the non-smoking signs on the lower deck of the bus. He was dressed in a dark Crombie, plain white Ben Sherman, blue Wrangler jeans with bleached half inch turn-up and red Airwair also. Slightly longer Suedehead style, dark hair and heavy stubble, framed a more rounded face, with two small brown eyes, a flat broken nose and a wide full-lipped mouth. The sheepskin wearer stared intently at Jay Mac, whilst the smoker began his questioning.

"Had a bit of trouble with Danny (H), 'ey?" he asked rhetorically, whilst blowing smoke into Jay Mac's face; though seventeen years living in a virtual nicotine fog meant that this gesture had little effect on him.

"Not really" he answered, "It was a gentleman's misunderstanding, he mistakenly thought he was first in the queue." Jay Mac forced a grin as he spoke.

"You're a cheeky cunt, aren't yer?" was the smoker's response.

"Yeah, a cheeky cunt" repeated the somewhat slower witted, sheepskin wearing echo.

"Balls" said the smoker, whilst studying Jay Mac's manner of dress.

The youth did not respond, he in turn was reading the signs himself. These were two original Skins, he thought from 1969 or shortly after, when the London originated, Hippie antithesis youth movement, first made its presence felt. Jay Mac had been a regular, non-descript, American comic-collecting fourteen year old boy at the time, bored, angry and looking for direction. He knew at once, as he read the first accounts in the *News of the World*, of crazed, Skinheads terrorising long-haired, acid-dropping, middle class, anti-establishment Vietnam War protestors in Hyde Park, that this was the way forward for him. Although the fashion was now nearing its final flowering, he and his mates held true to its original ethos and style.

"I said balls, are you listenin' to me?" the smoker asked becoming angry.

"Fuckin' listen" repeated echo.

Jay Mac still did not respond, something seemed to be on the smoker's mind and he wanted to be certain what it was, before he committed himself with a reply.

"You've either got fuckin' balls, or you're a mad cunt, if I'm right." The smoker pressed on, "You're a team player, I think... the question is... which fuckin' team? I know it's not the Anvil crew, that's for certain," he correctly surmised.

Jay Mac considered his response; he knew he was not far from his stop, at the corporation bus sheds. The moment he moved to leave the bus, they would know immediately he was part of the Crown Team.

"I'm not in a team, I just like the style," he lied.

The smoker looked at him quizzically. "All dressed up in yer best two-tones, where are you off to then?" he asked.

"I'm seein' a bird on the Crown Estate" he extended the lie further. In his mind he had a number of his friends' sisters' names ready and a composite description, should the inquisitor require more specific detail.

"Knobbin' a Crown bird, 'ey?" was the smoker's questioning response to this new information.

"How do the Crown Team feel about that and, how do you get through their estate, without gettin' fucked, dressed like that?"

"Er...she lives facing the bus sheds, so I don't have to go that far." was Jay Mac's quick-thinking reply. In fact one of his team mates lived on the very edge of the estate and he had a sister, even if she was only twelve years old. The bus was almost at Jay Mac's stop when the smoker asked his final question.

"Who do you know from the Crown Team then?" he leaned forward menacingly, watching Jay Mac's face.

"I don't know any of them, I just keep out of their way and mind me own business." Jay Mac lied again, motioning to stand up and leave the bus. The smoker looked at his echo; he seemed satisfied with Jay Mac's replies and gestured to his accomplice, to allow him to pass.

"Off y'go then, we'll be seein' you again" said the smoker.

Jay Mac stood up and calmly walked along the aisle of the bus, to the door at the front of the vehicle, he expected a missile to be thrown at any moment and didn't look back. The bus arrived at the stop and he waited for the doors to open, the smoker shouted from the rear.

"When you see Dayo (G), tell him Yoz said hello"

"I will do..." Jay Mac shouted back, and realised he had just enacted a scene from *The Great Escape*, when Gordon Jackson's character is recaptured by momentarily lapsing into English, in response to a German inquisitor's good wishes.

Now he knew who the smoker was. Yoz, whose name he had seen scrawled and daubed over most of the south sector of the Kings Estate for years, was the leader of The Engineers Public House Team. Unfortunately he had just inadvertently told this main player, that he was at least on speaking terms with Yoz's counterpart in the Crown Team. Dayo (G) was a gorilla-like, nineteen year old Skinhead, who was one of the original founders of the team. He was unofficially ranked in the ever-changing top five of fighters and despite vicious challenges from younger contenders, his own brutal responses maintained his position and usually, left his defeated opponent permanently scarred. Clearly if Jay Mac knew Dayo (G) to talk to, then he must be more than a minor player and certainly not a 'civilian', as he had stated. He realised that if he was to encounter Yoz again, there would be no misunderstanding.

Jay Mac considered the events of the evening, as he walked through the frozen streets of the estate, towards the home of Irish.

"What happened to y'sleeve" asked Irish whilst finishing lacing his unpolished boots, in his small untidy bedroom, which he shared with his younger brother.

Jay Mac briefly described his encounter with Danny (H) and then his meeting with Yoz.

"You're fucked if the Anvil crew see you again" laughed Irish after listening to Jay Mac's tale.

Jay Mac sat on the lower tier of the bunk-beds, which were somehow squeezed into the tiny box-room. Having removed his Crombie, he was examining the damaged sleeve. He did not notice at the time that he had dropped his prized knife, in its slender black lacquered case onto the bedroom floor.

"I don't fuckin' believe this" he said dismayed and becoming increasingly angry. "I'll 'ave to save up and get another one, this looks shite now." he continued. "I'm gonna cut that fuckin' Danny (H) cunt next time I see 'im on the Lancs."

"Sure yer are" said Irish amused by the incident and the improbability of Jay Mac's speculative threat. "When do we even get that close to those fuckers anymore? You know the rules; throw a few bricks and bottles, maybe a bit of fightin' with the poles, then run like fuck. We're always outnumbered now."

Jay Mac understood the way the game was played but he had also seen some spectacular individual clashes. He intended to extract a suitable revenge for the damage to his Crombie at the first opportunity.

One thing that he appreciated was the value of money. Having lived in the squalor of the old Victorian slum housing, in the Irish heart of the city as a child and regularly watched his mother squander the meagre means-tested benefits that she had virtually begged for, on drink, he had learned to take good care of any personal property that he managed to acquire. The more he concentrated on the 'flesh wound' to his coat, which he had saved for months to buy on his pitifully low wage, the more he determined that someone was going to pay.

A short time later after collecting Blue and Glynn, the four youths made their way to the bus stop nearest to the shops. Jay Mac recounted the events once again, for the benefit of the other two team members, much to their amusement. When the bus arrived, all four paid the basic ten pence fare, even though they were going all the way to the city centre several miles distant.

The bus drivers played their part in the game also. They rarely remonstrated with the Skins and they never issued tickets, they just pocketed the fares and drove their buses. Arguing over a monetary discrepancy, which might lead to a beating, or worse, including permanent scarring with a Stanley knife, was not worth their while, not for a minimal basic pay that kept them in penury and the bus company bosses in their big houses and expensive cars. The only or main perk of their employment, as they saw it, was the opportunities it provided for looking up the short skirts and dresses of their female passengers, which given the prevailing fashion for ultra-short micro-minis, did not require much effort on the part of the driver, either directly or via use of a strategically positioned appropriately named rear-view mirror. Delays often occurred in issuing fares to less stimulating passengers, whilst an over ambitious voyeur ensured he had not missed viewing any vital statistic of an unwary, long-legged female passenger, as she innocently loitered on the nearby staircase, waiting for the travellers in front, to move on.

"Where are you wankers off to?" was the question that greeted them, when they topped the stairs to the upper-deck of the bus. Loosely sprawled across the back seat and the next two rows, where eight members of their extended team from the bottom of the Crown Estate, the Heron crew. Their titular leaders were a triumvirate of three disparate characters, two of whom were present on this evening. Yad, the younger seventeen year old brother of Dayo (G), always assumed the position of sole commander, issuing orders as he saw fit. However, his status as everyone knew was largely maintained by his older sibling's ferocious reputation and his close friendship, with his psychotic sergeant-at-arms, The Weaver. Both of these dangerous individuals, where strategically positioned in the centre of the rear seats of the upper-deck. The third member of this unholy trio, Macca (G) was absent due to an injury sustained in a recent encounter with some of the Kings Team. He was considered the brains of the crew and had a particular penchant for sexually orientated sadism, whenever the opportunity presented itself. Of all three, Jay Mac and everyone else were in agreement that Weaver was by far the most dangerous. He was the classic textbook clinical, sociopathic, psychopath. Nobody ever knew where they stood with him, at one moment seemingly friendly, at the next instant a maniac capable of barbaric violence.

"We're goin' to town on the piss!" exclaimed Blue in response to the original question.

All four sat down amongst the randomly scattered crew members. "Jay Mac nearly got fucked by Danny (H)'s Anvil crew tonight," Blue continued, much to Jay Mac's chagrin and annoyance. Blue was a garrulous individual and could not keep any information to himself.

"Tell me more Jay Mac, tell me more. What's been happenin' in shitland tonight then?" asked Yad, as he gestured for Jay Mac to sit alongside him at the back of the bus.

This was not what Jay Mac wanted; he disliked Yad intensely, viewing him as a blustering bully, who owed his position entirely to his brother's reputation and his sinister associate. He would like to see Yad in action, rather than just barking orders. If his older brother ever fell from grace, he knew Yad's own plummet would be immediate and bloody.

"What d'yer wanna know Yad?" Jay Mac asked.

"Like I said, what's happenin' in that fucking shithole you come from?" Yad replied with a sneer.

He hated the Kings Estate and was not happy with Jay Mac freely wandering about, in *their* territory. He knew, however, that Jay Mac was popular with the other Skins and one of his long-standing friends from his schooldays, known as Terry (H), was his own brother's closest acquaintance.

"They still dress like fuckin' Mods up there don't thee?" he continued in his usual derogatory manner, drawing some weak laughter from his companions.

Jay Mac did not acknowledge Yad's intended insult. Instead he ignored him and addressed his comments to Weaver.

"All right Weaver? Could've done with you tonight. Your hammer would've been drippin' in blood, y'know what I mean?" He balanced his words to Weaver carefully; not too obsequious but flattering enough to acknowledge his prowess with his weapon of choice, a small solid steel toffee hammer.

"What happened, 'ey? How many was there?" asked the curious Weaver. Jay Mac recounted the events once more for the benefit of all assembled. When he reached the part of his tale where he had spoken to Yoz, he waited for Yad's reaction to the mention of his brother.

"Our Dayo took him on the Lancs Road the night the Kings Team had Mash and were doin' his face with bricks." Yad was referring to a 'famous' incident from a couple of years earlier.

The unfortunate Mash was a Crown Estate Skin, who was captured by a probing group of Kings Estate players, who were spraying their names on the walls outside the flats where he lived. They had dragged him across the boundary road, to the nearby flyover construction site and began shattering his facial features with pieces of broken brick. The agonised screams that managed to escape from the resulting mush of the unfortunate captive's face, brought a rescue mission mounted by Dayo (G). Legend had it that on that occasion he personally fought Yoz, the overseer of the torture, to a standstill using his favourite weapon, a heavy studded leather belt and as more Crown Estate reinforcements arrived, the small Kings Team retreated badly mauled.

"Next time you talk to y'mate Yoz, tell him Yad's gonna do 'im permanent." was Yad's boastful angry outburst at the end of his tale.

"Why not tell 'im yerself? I'm sure yer'll get the chance soon enough." Jay Mac replied staring at Yad, who looked like a younger cloned version of the gorilla-like Dayo (G), with a short, dark crop, thick black eyebrows that met in the middle of his forehead, heavy stubble and a large jutting lower mandible.

"I fuckin' will do, don't you doubt it *boy*." replied Yad angrily.

Jay Mac reached into the left side pocket of his Crombie, to reassuringly feel for his knife. He was not going to be called 'boy' by this prick, he thought. 'One more insult and, I'm gonna cut this fucker, whatever the consequences' he said to himself.

His movement was not missed by Yad.

"You thinkin' of doin' somethin'?" he asked grinning slyly. "You wouldn't like that would yer Weaver?" asked, Yad as he nudged Weaver with his elbow.

Jay Mac desperately felt about in his pocket for his missing knife, he knew Yad would be carrying a 'tool' and was certain that Weaver had his hammer and other assorted weaponry on him. Without any form of 'equaliser' he was wise enough to lighten the situation with some humour.

"I was lookin' for me snot-rag" he said, "You're not scared of that are yer?" Weaver stared at Jay Mac's hand, as he pulled out some toilet paper from his pocket and blew his nose. His small triangular-shaped, steel grey eyes and grim scarred countenance, surrounded by thick curly sideburns and short wavy dark hair remained expressionless. All the crew, including Jay Mac's three original companions, sat silently in the now tense, stale nicotine-smelling atmosphere at the rear of the graffiti covered bus.

"Scared of some snot, that's a good one eh, Yad?" Weaver laughed as he spoke and, as if it were a signal to the others, they laughed too.

"We're goin' into town for booze and birds" said Blue, thankful that the uncomfortable tension had been broken. "Any of yous wanna come with us?" he asked smiling.

As if telepathically connected Jay Mac, Irish and Glynn simultaneously looked at Blue, mentally commanding him to shut up. Nobody wanted any of this crew with them on a night out and certainly not the explosively psychotic Weaver.

The bus was by now close to another legendary meeting place for the local teams, The Bear public house.

"We're gettin' off here, come on" commanded Yad.

"What's happenin' ere?" asked Blue cheerfully.

'He still cant be quiet', thought Jay Mac.

"What do you think shithead?" Yad responded in answer to Blue's query.

"We're meetin' up with the Bear crew, goin' to stroll over to Ravens Hall and do them fuckers." he continued.

He was referring to more of their extended team allies, The Bear Public House crew, who they sometimes linked up with to increase numbers further. Their nearest rivals were a team, who lived behind the ten-foot high walls that enclosed the Ravens Hall Estate. This was yet another sprawling post-war housing project, that some condescending high-minded Le Corbusier inspired architects and a group of equally detached-from-reality civic planners, had decided would be ideal, uplifting towers in the sky, where former inner-city slum dwellers would give daily thanks for their good fortune.

The paradoxical reality was the usual dystopian landscape of drab towering concrete habitations, with litter and faeces strewn stairwells, covered in pornographic, boastful graffiti and containing the occasionally working lift, that also served as vertically mobile toilets. Broken lights both within the blocks and standing atop of precast concrete posts, like eyeless sentinels, allowed the denizens of the night, to carry out their work under the cover of darkness. The few garages that had been constructed in anticipation of the more thrifty factory worker, being able to scrape together enough funds for a deposit on a small motorcar, had long since been burned out. They now served as dark, foul-smelling, scorched dens for the gangs to use as shelters or convenient, if stinking venues, for perfunctory, not always necessarily consensual sexual encounters.

"You queers aren't invited!" shouted Yad, as he led his crew to the top of the stairs. "Ger into town and get bummed on Lime Street" was his final riposte. To the cheery responses of, "Fuck off arse bandit" and "Get fucked chimp face." Yad and the rest vacated the bus.

Weaver turned and looked up at the rear window where Jay Mac, who had now been joined by his three companions, was still sitting. Jay Mac saw the glint of Weaver's hammer, which he had produced from the inside pocket of his Crombie, then, as if in macabre portent of possible future events, Weaver gestured towards the head of his steel weapon and pointed to Jay Mac's face. He mimed an action as if repeatedly smashing an egg. Jay Mac took the inference to be fairly clear, although he told his colleagues, who also witnessed Weaver's act that he was only joking; he resisted the temptation to give him the usual two-fingered salute.

The remainder of their journey was uneventful, despite the fact that they passed through the territories of numerous other teams. Eventually the packed vehicle arrived in the city centre. The four companions stepped off the bus, into the bustling, loud, scary world of hard-drinking adults, looking for love, or casual sexual encounters, or oblivion at the bottom of a glass. Some of them were looking for one thing only... trouble. On their own estate territories, the youths were the big men; here amongst the thousands of Scouse adult, Saturday night revellers, they were four young boys.

Blue and Jay Mac were the eldest of the group, the former having reached seventeen the previous September and Jay Mac three days earlier in the current January. Glynn and Irish would not respectively become seventeen until June and August of that year. While they strolled along Lime Street, past the grand Empire Theatre and the magnificent Neo-Classical façade of St George's Hall, they shouted and whistled at girls and women who, despite the freezing weather, teetered in their highest heels, short jackets and even shorter mini dresses or hot-pants. They were circumspect in their choice of targets. Nobody wanted a man-sized fist in the face from a disgruntled boyfriend or husband. Liverpool had always been a place of hard men and a number of even harder women, who would not think twice at setting about, four cheeky youths barely out of puberty.

Soon they were comfortably seated, in the relatively plush parlour area of the Harp public house near the junction of Mount Pleasant and Ranelagh Street. This was a favourite haunt of the underage drinker, where they knew they were guaranteed to be served. As they sat drinking their pints of amber liquid, which happened on this occasion to be Double Diamond, they surveyed the crowded interior of the pub. Irish, who was a chain smoker, whenever he could buy or scrounge cigarettes, was adding his own contribution to the thick blue-grey haze and gave his usual, unappreciative assessment of the assorted characters gathered around them.

"Ugly women in 'ere" he stated emphatically, banging his pint glass down on the small round table in front of them.

"What d'yer expect" asked Jay Mac "It's a fuckin' dive, we only come 'ere cos we can get served." he added.

"Another pint and lets geroff" said Glynn, "Am lookin' for quality birds, not old bints."

"Me too." Blue added whilst greedily consuming his second packet of cheese and onion crisps.

"Blue, you're lookin' for anythin' that's got a pulse or owns a fuckin' chippy" Jay Mac said, laughing.

While the four debated, whether to have another round of drinks in this present hostelry, *Gimme Shelter* by the Rolling Stones, loaded onto the turntable of the nearby juke-box.

"I'll get them in" said Jay Mac, determined not to leave, while one of his favourite singles was being played.

"It's your fuckin' round anyway, *birthday boy.*" said Irish sarcastically, as Jay Mac, assisted by Blue, who was eager for more salted snacks to be purchased, made their way to the crowded bar. He did not respond to Irish's comment as they always tended to buy rounds of drink, in a chronological age-descending order, with Blue first, followed by Jay Mac and so on, he didn't need any reminder.

The cardinal rule and one of the few gems of drinking etiquette that his uncle had drummed into him from an early age was: "You must always stand your round, never be a man who accepts a drink and doesn't buy one in return." Some rules of male society were sacrosanct to the old soldier and Jay Mac acknowledged and respected the sagacity of the veteran of so many campaigns, both military and social. On this evening, prior to Jay Mac's departure, his uncle had surreptitiously slipped him some change without his aunt noticing, which amounted to fifty new pence or ten shillings in 'real' money, as Jay Mac still thought of it. His uncle had taken the opportunity to repeat this maxim once more, followed by his usual ancient joke of "Remember if you're not in bed by ten o'clock, come home."

Jay Mac tried hard to listen to the haunting, long introduction of the song but the noise and general clamour formed a loud disruptive cacophony of sounds. Deep-voiced males telling rude jokes, the shrill forced responding laughter of their female partners and the incessant clink of empty glasses urgently waiting to be filled, blurred the lyrical tones emanating from the electric music box. Every so often, the unmistakable shatter of breaking glass could be heard above the din, as a randy male customer casually groped a female member of the bar staff, who had bravely sallied forth to collect desperately needed 'empties', risking her honour in so doing. Cheers, raucous laughter, the sound of a slap and more raucous laughter usually followed sequentially.

Whilst waiting to be served, Jay Mac wondered why anyone bothered paying for a record on the juke box, when only extracts of the actual song could be heard. A boy amongst men and women, he followed the time-honoured rituals, trying to nonchalantly but in his case unsuccessfully, catch the attention of one of the bar staff, whilst tenaciously holding on to his place, at the seething bar.

"How old are you lad?" asked the hard-faced forty-something, surly barmaid, revealing her red lipstick stained, yellowing teeth, when Jay Mac was finally about to get served.

"It was his birthday a couple of days ago" offered the ever chirpy Blue.

"I'm not askin' you, short arse!" she stated, unkindly acknowledging Blue's not particularly shorter than average five foot eight, portly stature.

Jay Mac looked directly into her tired eyes, with their pale blue eye shadowed lids, edged with lashes covered in thick, tacky black mascara and announced:

"Madam, three days ago I reached the age of majority, where I can legally do anything, including partaking of your fine ales."

He always resorted to this manner, when responding to challenges from any petty authoritarian figure. In this instance he resented being questioned, in a known haunt of underage drinkers particularly by this Harpie sporting a beehive hairstyle.

'Piss-oles in the snow', he thought, as he continued staring into the eyes of the ageing Dusty Springfield fan.

"Listen love, I don't know what the fuck you're talkin' about and I don't care. Are you eighteen or not?" she snapped her questioning reply.

"I think that I have clearly stated, that I am" he answered firmly. 'She thinks she's a hard bitch', he thought, 'she hasn't gorra clue.' He was mentally conjuring up an image of one of his elder female cousins, the dreaded Theresa. Together with other siblings of her thirteen-strong family, she regularly assaulted and robbed merchant seamen from all nations, enticed by the promise of rough sex, in the alleyways behind the myriad pubs along the Dock Road. Compared to his familial, female robbery with-extreme-violence exponent, the bar maid was a novice he concluded.

"Listen, drink these and piss off, y'getting no more service in 'ere." was her final comment, as she passed them four more pints of 'Diamond'.

"I take it that a birthday kiss is out of the question?" Jay Mac asked rhetorically with a grin, before carefully stepping away from the bar holding two golden pints, avoiding the unthinkable crime of spillage.

"Worrabout me roasted peanuts?" said Blue, similarly balancing two shimmering pints and acutely aware that he had not eaten for several minutes.

"See a fuckin' doctor," replied Jay Mac unsympathetically.

When they had finally threaded their precarious way, through the sweating, heaving throng, they found the hapless Glynn standing clutching their Crombies.

"What the fuck's happened 'ere?" asked Jay Mac angrily.

"Irish had gone for a piss and these people made me move out the way" he replied sheepishly.

At this juncture, Irish returned wearing a suitably relieved expression, which quickly changed to a scowl.

"What's goin' on 'ere" he asked incredulously, echoing Jay Mac's sentiments.

Comfortably ensconced in *their* seats, were two large, stocky, late thirties-early forties looking males, with battered faces and heavily Brylcreemed, slicked-back, thinning D.A. style hair. On the banana-like fingers of their large meaty hands, they wore a selection of heavy gold sovereign and oversized coloured gem rings. Their swollen knuckles were individually tattooed with letters spelling L.O.V.E and H.A.T.E and on their leathery skin, between thumb and forefinger were faded blue-black swallows. Their female companions, sipped their port and lemons whilst their tall, badly-dyed, purple-black beehive hairstyles, quivered simultaneously without a single thickly lacquered hair ever moving out of place.

"Excuse me mate, we were sittin' there" Jay Mac said, stating the obvious.

"Were yer? And now we're sittin' here, so fuck off." Ex-Teddy Boy number one replied.

"No mate, that's where we're sittin,' so you need to move." Irish added, actively supporting Jay Mac. It was usually at this point of any confrontation that Jay Mac and Irish displayed their more aggressive nature, while Blue and Glynn faded into the background.

So it was now, as Irish continued "There's four of us and only two of you".

"Is he threatening you, Dave?" asked the female companion of the original speaker.

"Hold y'tongue woman, these are no fuckin' threat." Dave responded angrily.

Ex-Teddy Boy number two now spoke, "Listen *boys* do you wanna do anythin' about it? Cos we'd be happy to take the four of yer outside and kick the fuckin' shite out of yer."

He put his whiskey chaser down on the table and cracked his tattooed knuckles loudly. Faced with this standoff and cognisant of the fact that the silent Blue and Glynn had shuffled several steps away, Jay Mac looked at Irish and then finally responded.

"Keep the fuckin' seats, you need them more than us." He knew they were no match for these veteran brawlers with their ugly harridan companions.

"Piss off while yer still can." Dave said then turned his attention back to downing his pint of Guinness in a single swallow.

The four boys finished their drinks in silence, put their Crombies on and departed from the heaving pub. Roy Orbison's *'Only the Lonely'* was playing on the juke box, as they stepped from the boiling, smoke-filled interior and were struck by the sharp cold of the freezing night air.

Once they had crossed the road, at the bottom of Mount Pleasant and walked past the imposing frontage of the Adlephi Hotel, Glynn broke the angry silence.

"We'd have done them if they was on the Estate" he said unconvincingly.

"Yeah, they wouldn't have acted so hard then" added Blue, with similar lack of conviction.

Jay Mac could not bring himself to respond, he hated having to back down to bullies. Although he considered himself to be a coward by nature and always sought to avoid confrontation, in certain instances when the injustice was glaring, or a weaker individual was being intimidated or harmed, somehow against his self-preservation instincts, he found himself intervening. Accepting the *real politik* of the incident that had just occurred was unpalatable and he knew it would torment him for some time.

A few moments later, they were standing at the bar, in the splendid, architectural gem of the cocktail lounge at the rear, of the magnificent Orchard public house, on Lime Street. The Mansion, as this particular drinking establishment was colloquially known, was a personal favourite of Jay Mac. The spacious, expensively decorated interior contained a wealth of original features including; highly polished, dark red, solid mahogany bars, intricate plaster work and a magnificent glass domed ceiling. In Jay Mac's mind he imagined, well-heeled Victorian and Edwardian shipping magnates, leading industrialists and a throng of top professionals, standing at the bars or seated at the handsome carved tables, testifying to Liverpool's bygone wealth and pre-eminent status, as the second greatest port, within an empire that spanned the globe.

Tonight's clientele were somewhat different but the majority, were dressed in their finery, well coiffured and ready to spend their hard earned cash freely for a night's revelry in this more salubrious than usual, public house. Irish and Blue went to find seats, while Jay Mac accompanied Glynn to the bar.

"Why did we have to come into the fuckin' lounge? You know they charge more for a drink in 'ere than in the bar." asked the miserly Glynn.

"Stop moanin' you tight-arse cunt and get the drinks in." Jay Mac replied, studying the members of the queue waiting to be served, then glancing at the large selection of colourful, exotic-looking bottled liquids, stacked on the ornate shelves, behind the bar.

After several minutes had passed without the boys being served, Jay Mac began to feel they were being ignored because of Glynn's obvious youth. With his pimply-spotted, hairless face and short, blond side-parted hair, he looked more like a choirboy than an experienced drinker who knew his ales. As he considered this possibility, glancing along the bar once again, he spotted two unaccompanied older females. Both were smartly dressed, in similar short mini dresses of psychedelic print material, one wore purple knee-length suede boots over dark coloured tights and the other wore white shiny, wet-look, blue edged, Cuban-heeled shoes with gold buckles and tan tights. Their dark shoulder-length hair was back-combed and heavily lacquered; both wore broad coloured *Alice* bands and large dangling hooped earrings.

Jay Mac thought they had reasonably pretty faces and slim figures, they would be attractive except for one feature, they were both smoking king-size cigarettes. He loathed the smell of smoke on a girl's clothes and hair but his number one hate, was a girl with smoker's breath. Despite, or because of the fact he had lived amongst smokers virtually from the moment he was born, he always found the sight of women smoking, ugly and repulsive.

"Look at those two birds, Glynn," said Jay Mac already slyly forming a plan in his mind. "The one in the boots keeps eyeing you up," he added falsely.

Glynn's massive ego had been massaged and developed since an early age by a doting mother who, after the early departure of her feckless husband, produced numerous 'uncles' as possible substitutes. Most of these uncles did not remain for long, some only for a weekend, or just a night. The lovelorn mother lavished more attention than was healthy, on her sole progeny.

"Thee look about twenty five." Glynn said, already partially succumbing to Jay Mac's guile.

"No, I don't think they're that old," said Jay Mac. "Anyway, y'know what thee say about birds of that age?" he began.

Glynn's eyes widened as he listened and asked "No, what do thee say?"

"Once thee get that old, thee go all kinky." Jay Mac was now in full flow whilst Glynn listened expectedly. "Yeah, er, thee all do that, er, Kama Sutra stuff. Look at the one in the boots who keeps eyeing you, look at the way she's suckin' on that cigarette, d'yknow what I mean?" Glynn was firmly on the hook.

"Let's, er drift over and chat them up, y'know what the birds are like for you? Look 'Boots' has just piped you again." Jay Mac lied, once more perpetuating the myth. The vanity of Glynn had now been sufficiently primed.

The two youths casually strolled the short distance to their unsuspecting prey.

"Evenin' ladies." said Glynn, "Waitin' to get served are we?" he asked, stating the obvious. Unexpectedly to Jay Mac's complete surprise, they both turned and smiled at Glynn.

"Hello handsome" said the girl in the boots.

'What the fuck?' Jay Mac said to himself.

Glynn was now firing on all cylinders. "Yes, we often come in here, a much better class of customer, I find. Their prices are a bit more but it's worth it for the company, I say."

Jay Mac smiled at the other female, trying to mask his astonishment.

"Likes to spend his cash, does he, your mate?" she asked.

"Oh yeah, he's a regular big spender" lied Jay Mac in reply. Glynn was now well and truly ensnared.

"Maybe you'd like to buy us a drink." said 'Boots' to Glynn. "I like men who are generous." she added.

"Of course." said Glynn. "But the service is a bit slow in here tonight."

"We'll order, if y'like" said her accomplice.

"Sure, that would be great." sighed Glynn, now resigned to his fate. He was notoriously tight with his money and Jay Mac could see this was almost physically painful for him. In an instant the first female, managed to attract the attention of one of the smartly dressed barmen.

"Yes gorgeous, and what can I do you for?" he asked in a lascivious manner.

"Two Brandy and Babychams please, and make them large ones." she said smiling sweetly at the flirtatious barman. "What are you having lads?" she enquired generously.

Glynn still reeling from the shock, had seemingly lost his new-found loquaciousness.

"Better make it four pints of Diamond." said Jay Mac, adding "We're quick drinkers, y'see." He did not wish to reveal that their two associates were waiting for them nearby.

The barman returned swiftly with their drinks, hoping for an appropriately large tip. "£1.80 please" he said.

"What! Are you takin' the piss?" shouted Glynn momentarily forgetting his 'big spender' character.

"Is there a problem?" asked the boots wearing female, gently placing her well-manicured hand onto Glynn's arm.

"No of course not" he answered, fumbling desperately in the side pocket of his Crombie, to muster all the change he had, in order to pay the bill. Glynn handed over the exact money, much to the disappointment of the expectant barman.

"Well, thanks for the drinks lads" said the boots wearer. "Where are my manners? I'm Sandra by the way and this is Helen, and you are...?" she asked feigning a genuine interest.

Once again Glynn seemed to be unable to speak, as if the realisation of how much he had just spent had struck him dumb. Jay Mac provided a cursory response, as he clutched two of the pints, ready to supply his thirsty colleagues without further delay.

There was a short uncomfortable silence, then Glynn spoke, "So what are we doin' then ladies?"

Any naive hope that he may have had, was soon dashed by Sandra's reply. "I dunno what your doin' but we're goin' clubbin', when our fellers turn up. Anyway thanks for the drinks."

From the look on his reddening face, Jay Mac could see Glynn was rapidly approaching a paroxysm of rage. "Are you fuckin' jokin'?" he asked angrily. "What do I get for me money?"

His question drew a stinging response from Sandra, who stared Glynn in the face and said, "You love, gerra lesson in not tryin' to pick up women that you can't afford and, wouldn't know what to do with anyway. We like men, not little boys."

Almost instantly the scarlet faced Glynn thrust his left hand under the hem of the short mini dress of his 'teacher' and firmly grabbed her crotch.

'Fuck me this is gonna be good,' thought Jay Mac

The palm of Sandra's right hand, connected with Glynn's left cheek, just below the eye with a resounding slap that left Glynn with a perfect facsimile hand print, whilst discharging an inch of grey ash from her glowing filter tipped, king-size cigarette.

There were the usual cheers from the nearby male drinkers and one clearly failed marriage guidance counsellor shouted "Give her one back lad!"

The sharp sting of the slap made Glynn release, his nylon covered fleshy prey.

"You dirty little bastard!" Sandra screamed, "Wait until our boyfriends get here, your dead!"

Glynn placed the offending hand over his mouth and nose and breathed in loudly, then said "Thanks bitch, I'll be back for me change in a minute."

The boys turned and carried their drinks to the table that Irish and Mac had previously secured.

"Nice one Glynn, I'm impressed" said Jay Mac grinning wickedly.

Glynn and Jay Mac sat down and removed their Crombies as Blue and Irish had already done. They were seated at a small round table, in a semi-circular arrangement, looking towards the bar, where the assault had just taken place. Glynn now came into his own as he delivered in exaggerated, creative detail, every moment of the crotch grabbing incident.

"I'm tellin' yer, she had no knickers on." he lied, wafting the fingers of the offending hand under their noses, for their benefit.

"Fuck off, with yer fishy mitt," said Irish, who was seated on the right hand side of Glynn. Blue was next to Glynn with Jay Mac on his left; he always kept an eye open for trouble and was watching the bar, for the anticipated arrival of the boyfriends.

"She was wearin' tights, you lying fucker," he said, getting a little tired of Glynn's exaggerations, which had now advanced to a virtual finger penetration.

Irish had listened to Glynn's tale with some circumspection and his attention was also focused on the bar where two smartly suited, well-built young men were now standing with Sandra and Helen. A brief conversation ensued and then one of the young men marched towards the boys' table. He was dressed in a well-cut dark blue suit after the 'Mod' fashion, of narrow lapel and collar, two buttons at the waist, single vent and slim-fitting. Wearing a crisp white shirt and narrow dark blue and white striped tie; his shoes were expensive black Italian leather with a pointed toe.

"I believe you've just assaulted my girlfriend, you dirty little shit." he said angrily staring at Glynn, clenching his fists.

Jay Mac noticed a heavy silver identity bracelet had slipped forward on his right wrist, bearing the name *Steve* deeply engraved on its flat shiny surface.

"That's a nice suit mate, expensive was it?" Jay Mac asked before Glynn could make any reply to Steve's outburst.

"What are you, some sort of fashion critic?" he responded turning his attention towards Jay Mac.

"No, am just thinkin' you might not want to get it damaged," Jay Mac replied staring at Steve intently.

"Are you threatenin' me?" Steve said, as the pitch of his voice rose in anger.

"*I am*." Irish responded, producing a dirty wooden-handled craft knife from the pocket of his discarded Crombie and pointing it at Steve's groin. "If y'want to keep that tiny prick, which you're probably hopin' to try and push into yer bird's smelly minge, later tonight, you'd better fuck off while it's still attached." Irish warned.

Blue and Glynn also produced similar weapons and placed them on the table in front of them whilst calmly drinking their ale. All four youths were now staring at the boyfriend, no one was smiling. Steve retreated back to his companions at the bar and explained what had just happened.

The flirtatious barman approached next, resplendent in his red waistcoat, black bow tie, white shirt, black trousers and patent leather shoes, looking like a ship's steward on an ocean-going liner. He assumed his role of official delegate.

"We don't want your sort in here; finish your drinks and leave." he ordered.

"When we're ready," Irish stated in response.

"Listen, I don't want to call the bouncers over, leave your drinks and fucking get out." the irate barman now demanded.

"I don't particularly care for your tone bar-keep," said Jay Mac, "I'd thank you to keep a civil tongue, when addressing your betters. If you wish to call for assistance from your boyfriends, please do but I think we all want to avoid an ugly situation, don't we?"

Whilst speaking Jay Mac tried to recall, the last time he had seen any 'bouncers' or security in this pub. He felt fairly certain the barman was bluffing. The boys carried on drinking their pints until they had nearly finished, completely ignoring the barman.

"I told you to gerrout!" shouted the furious individual, conscious of the fact he was losing ground rapidly.

"Oh do piss off, you're becoming a frightful bore." said Jay Mac as the group laughed in unison.

It was the barman's turn to retreat to the relative safety, of his own territory, intending to call for assistance to remove the four youths. However, the boys now stood up, put their Crombies back on and prepared to leave. A wild and heavy shower of large hailstones battered the glass domed roof above. As they approached the bar to make their way to the exit, Steve, emboldened by what he sensed was a moral victory and wishing to reaffirm his previously challenged masculinity, could not resist a parting shot.

"Good night little boys, its gone nine o'clock, so hurry home to bed." His companions and the crest-fallen barman, laughed loudly.

Sandra joined in the merriment. "Look, this one's bringing his glass back, that's a good boy for mummy."

Sandra was referring to the pint glass which Glynn was carrying. If she had looked more closely she would have noticed it was still partially filled, with a mixture of amber liquid and mucus, the boys having poured all the dregs of their beer into Glynn's glass and added as much phlegm and catarrh they could produce at such short notice. The final ingredient of this exotic cocktail, were Irish's cigarette butts. Without any warning this unpalatable mixture was thrown into the smirking face of Sandra.

"'Ave another drink on me!" said Glynn grinning broadly.

Simultaneously Irish delivered a perfectly executed head-butt, which would have scored a winning goal in any match, with explosive force to the bridge of Steve's previously straight nose. The latter staggered against the bar with blood pouring from his now broken nose, like two red rivulets running down over his mouth and chin, onto his crisp white shirt.

Boyfriend number two shouted in panic "I don't want any trouble, please." Jay Mac stuck him with the palm of his hand on the chest and pushed him firmly back, into the brass edging of the mahogany surface. The barman now raised his level of threat, to that of calling for the police. The boys sauntered into the adjoining bar catching a brief snatch of *It's all in the game* by the Four Tops, which was playing on the juke box in that room.

"Good night all, safe journey home!" Jay Mac shouted back to Steve et al, before the door to the cocktail lounge closed behind him. "Excellent work Carruthers," he said to Irish, as they stepped from the cauldron of the bar into the frozen night. "I don't think our Steve or his oppo will be performing on the nest tonight, do you?"

They all laughed, turning up the collars of their coats against another squall of sleet and hail that danced around them.

The youths quickly made their way past the Scala and Futurist Cinemas. The frontage of the latter being particularly ornate, reflecting a by-gone golden age of picture houses in the city. Having tried the 'bad' and the 'good', they were now about to enter the 'ugly'. The States Bar on Lime Street was at the epicentre of the maudlin Scouser's universe. In a city filled with hostelries, where pained anonymous souls could easily drink themselves into oblivion, whilst crying into their beer unnoticed and unloved, the States Bar was perhaps the 'finest' example of these transcendental portals. Its location only minutes from a magnificent bustling Nineteenth Century national railway station, and moments from two lively electric picture palaces, in the heart of the thriving shopping district, somehow paradoxically added to its gloomy, dejected ambience.

Jay Mac and Irish found it well suited to their peculiarly dark sense of humour. Their five years 'schooling', trapped amongst sadists, sexual deviants, liars, thieves and other disturbed individuals, both masters and pupils, had given them each a damaged, distorted perception of life. Standing at the bar in the garishly lit interior of their present venue and dressed in their long dark overcoats, adorned with sparkling faux diamond or garnet studs on their breast pockets and colourful silk handkerchiefs at the ready, the four incongruous figures looked like Victorian philanthropists, conducting 'a study of the wretched drunkards of Old Liverpool.'

A change of tipple was called for here. "Four Newcastle Brown, when y'ready mate." Irish requested politely. This was his type of drinking establishment, he felt refreshingly reconnected with his Celtic, working-class roots.

The surly barman passed them their bottles of rich brown translucent nectar and four pint glasses with barely a word, other than to tell them the amount they owed. Jay Mac ordered four shots of whiskey as chasers whilst still at the bar, then joined his colleagues at a nearby table. All four sat with their backs to the partially wood panelled walls. Various badly printed posters, with stock images of New York's iconic buildings, juxtaposed with Irish landscapes and faded photographic portraits of local boxing legends whose prime had long passed, covered the ageing painted plaster walls, above the dado rail. The floor was constructed of old, tired wooden boards, not for affect as in later trendy, 'yuppie' wine bars but for functionality and cost. The one concession to the second half of the Twentieth Century, other than the electric lighting, was a glorious 1950s style juke box in the far corner opposite the bar.

The four youths sat with their Crombies folded next to them, idly chatting about the evening's events so far and watching the other occupants of the one-roomed bar, in between taking refreshing mouthfuls of their drinks. Irish and Glynn were both smoking cigarettes, the former to satisfy his craving, the latter for effect only. Glynn never inhaled and they were all amused by his clumsy attempts to 'look cool'.

"Slainte!" said Irish and Jay Mac one after the other.

"Cheers!" Blue and Glynn said together.

All four downed their whiskeys in one gulp and banged their shot glasses loudly on the table.

"A bit slow so far tonight," said Irish, looking about through the heavy nicotine haze that hung from ceiling to bar like a tattered grey veil.

"Give it time, Irish it's only mid-morning for some of these boys." Jay Mac answered, studying the spectrum of lone drinkers, arrayed about the narrow bar. They were mostly males, aged between forty to seventy, as far as Jay Mac was able to determine. Nothing distinguished one from the other, except varying degrees of shabbiness, their glazed and vacant eyes made them all appear to be citizens of a nation of the undead. The dulcet tones of Dean Martin's *Little Ole Wine Drinker Me* burst forth from the juke box.

"How goods that?" said Blue, smiling as he sat back down after making his selection.

They all applauded Blue's choice.

"I've put 'Frank' on next" he added, more congratulations followed.

"Blue you are a man of taste and discernment." Jay Mac said, fully appreciating Blue's gesture, it was the closest he would receive to an acknowledgement that it was his birthday. They all knew Jay Mac was an obsessive American popular culture fan. In fact all things American appealed to him and if he could have found a legitimate way to emigrate, he would have left on the next boat.

One of the solitary drinkers began to sing along with Mr Martin, using his own lyrics to fill any gaps. When Mr Sinatra launched into his classic rendition of *'New York, New York'* the discordant singer continued, getting louder with each verse. The four companions encouraged him enthusiastically and joined in each eponymous chorus. A large fat male drunk stood up and staggered over to the juke box.

"Who put this shite on?" he enquired loudly.

Not one of the youths replied, they were waiting to see what would develop.

"Turn this fuckin' shite off now!" he demanded of some invisible phantom which, from the direction of his pointing finger was standing somewhere between him and the far wall.

The singer was not impressed. "Sit down fat arse, and shut up!" he shouted whilst brushing his long, matted, dark greasy hair away from his face. He was one of the younger drinkers, possibly only in his early forties. Wearing a heavily stained light-grey suit jacket, over a faded primarily blue tie-dyed tee-shirt, grubby green jumbo cord trousers and a badly split pair of brown brogues, he looked in need of a hot bath and nourishing meal. The music critic now had a direction and physical persona, for the focus of his comments.

"Did you tell me to shut up?" he asked angrily, his filthy tattered gabardine overcoat flailing about, as he gesticulated to the singer. "Because no one tells 'JJ' to shut up" he continued, apparently unconcerned about the observation regarding his weight. The singer ignored him and finished the final bars of the song, with gusto.

JJ now leaned on the table of the singer. "I never liked your brother" he said randomly.

At this point the singer's mood changed and his vacant eyes suddenly gleamed, as they fixed upon the bloated, sweating countenance of the bald-headed JJ.

"You leave my brother out of it, you cunt" the singer demanded angrily. Much to the boys' disappointment however, JJ sat down and put his left arm around the shoulder of the singer. The mellow voice of Jim Reeves now began to sing *I love you because* as Irish, Jay Mac and Glynn looked at Blue; he shrugged his shoulders and said "It's nothing to do with me, I didn't put it on".

"That's fuckin' calmed them down," Irish said disapprovingly.

JJ now became singer himself and began delivering *his* discordant version of the song, directly into the face of the original singer. Whilst his serenade continued, without any warning a third solitary drinker emerged from the zombie ranks, crossed the floor and smashed a pint glass onto JJ's bald head. The sight of the blood streaming from the open wound of this unprovoked attack on his carousing partner, elicited a furious response from the original singer, he leapt up and threw himself at JJ's assailant. The table and its contents were upset, JJ was shouting in pain but used his right filthy meat-hook of a hand to grasp his attacker's tattered, woollen pullover, whilst clasping his left hand firmly over his gushing head wound. All three combatants now engaged in a grotesque spastic dance, as they wrestled to and fro at the end of the small room. Mr Reeves heroically carried on regardless, listing the reasons for his love one-by-one, until the three wrestlers fell against the prize juke box, momentarily jarring the unflappable artist.

The surly barman lifted the hinged wooden access flap, at the end of the pitted, stained bar, which separated him from his clientele. Casually dressed in a short-sleeved open-neck white shirt, dark trousers and black, steel toe-cap boots, the only item of clothing that distinguished him from the customers, was his stained, grubby off-white apron. A stocky, squat individual, with thinning dark hair and an unshaven round face, his brawny arms displayed a variety of classic tattoos; including a bloody dagger passing through a red heart on his right forearm and a ships anchor wrapped with a heavy rope on his left. He was armed with a short, dark wooden club.

"Pack it in you fuckin' bums!" he shouted, surprisingly calmly, thought Jay Mac considering the situation. Not prepared to be ignored, he set about striking all three participants in the swirling mêlée, as they revolved past him in turn, like a grizzly carousel of flesh, blood and tattered, smelly clothing. He had no favourites, as he struck legs, arms and torso in random sequence. The barman remained coolly dispassionate throughout; the damaged table and broken pint glasses and bottles, were his primary concern. A few of the other drinkers momentarily awoke from their beer and spirit induced comas, and began cheering loudly, while they watched the live entertainment. Others too far adrift from reality, lost in the canyons of the mind, remained oblivious to the whole spectacle. Some semblance of order was gradually restored, with JJ's principal assailant being ordered to leave at once, despite his whimpering protestations of innocence.

With shouts of "I love that feller, I love 'im, you don't know." he made a reluctant, tearful exit.

The four boys having finished their drinks and watching the floor show, firmly closed their coats ready to brave the outside elements and shouted farewell to the barman, while he dabbed JJ's head wound, with his filthy apron. The original singer now gave forth his rendition of the quintessential melancholic tune, *Oh Danny Boy*, the juke box in the corner remained silent, acknowledging defeat.

"Not a bad effort." said Irish, as they crossed the busy thoroughfare at the corner, by the splendid Crown Hotel, facing the art deco ABC Cinema. They were heading down Elliot Street past, the bland, utilitarian, relatively recent structure of St John's shopping precinct.

"It's been a game of two halves." said Jay Mac lapsing into football phraseology.

"Started shite, continued shite, like Everton, for much of the first half, then steadily improved throughout the second, with moments of brilliance, like Liverpool, in the closing minutes. Let's hope extra time produces a pleasing result."

"Fuck off," said Irish and Blue, the two Evertonians in the group.

They passed the shop fronts and doorways, noticing that in the entrance below 'Top Secret' *'Wig makers to the stars,'* an ardent pair of lovers undeterred by the inclement freezing weather, were locked in a passionate embrace.

"Give her one for me!" shouted Glynn.

"Haven't you had enough sexual excitement for one night?" asked Jay Mac smirking.

"Fuck off" said Glynn, echoing Irish and Blue's previous response and cognisant that it was Jay Mac, who had led him into the drinks' ambush, in the first place.

"What a night, 'ey? A few beers, a bit of live entertainment and Glynn gets his first sexual experience," Jay Mac responded quickly to Glynn's instruction.

"I've had dozens of shags, me." protested Glynn.

"Sorry Glynn, I don't know how to break this to yer but only the ones were there's another person involved, not just yer hand, count." Jay Mac replied, delivering his coup de gras. All four laughed, even Glynn as he muttered "Twat."

They had now arrived at their next port of call, outside Owen Owen's department store. Drawn by the pungent aroma of frying onions, similar to a bad case of body odour, Jay Mac always thought, they had located its source, the Hot Dog seller and were ready to eat their fill. In a time long before the arrival of fast food outlets, save for the sole American foray into the English market by Wimpey, which having failed to transfer any of its customer service ethos across the Atlantic, had become just another drab café chain, the Hot Dog vendor was the mobile eatery of the day, providing sustenance to countless drinkers and something solid other than 'carrots,' to bring up when the vomiting began.

A small queue of other revellers waited their turn, while the proprietor of the two-wheeled establishment, wiped his greasy hands on his soiled trousers, as a nod to hygiene procedure before preparing his next order. While they were waiting, the boys amused themselves by heckling members of the 'dirty mac brigade,' now forming an orderly, if conspicuous line, outside the Jaycee Cinema opposite. This was Liverpool's prime venue for supposedly adult films. These lonely, sad, wretched individuals, shuffled about in anticipation of masturbatory delight, though usually they were betrayed and rewarded only with grainy, badly dubbed, foreign studies of ugly beach ball throwing naturists.

"Wankers!" shouted Blue.

"Original." said Jay Mac to his colleague, not bothering to take part in the sport, considering the prey too easy a target. "I bet they've never heard that before."

Irish was annoyed that he could not find something to throw. When he mentioned this, Blue obliged by providing an empty Newcastle Brown bottle, which he had brought from the States Bar, to supplement his Stanley knife, in case of trouble. He happily passed this to Irish, hoping to see a good strike on one of the freezing perverts.

"'Ere, throw this at them fuckin' wankers, you're the best shot," Irish said to Jay Mac, acknowledging his prowess with missiles and legendary accuracy.

"No, fuck it, Irish... you throw it yourself, I can't be arsed." He was about to be served and was mentally getting into character, preparing his best American accent as he felt befitted ordering this imported US snack.

"Hi Hot Dog Man," he started with an attempted nasal New Jersey twang. "Yeah, I'll have a foot-long dog, with fries, ketchup, mustard, on a sesame seed roll and hold the onions."

The tired vendor looked at Jay Mac and said dolefully, "One hot dog, no onion, help y'self to red sauce and mustard, ten pence... Next."

Jay Mac paid the dishevelled, clearly freezing purveyor, while the latter reached into the pocket of the old Donkey jacket that he wore over his heavily stained, once white uniform. In between customers, he sneezed heavily into a dirty blue checked cotton handkerchief, adding to its already considerable infectious contents.

"Fuck off, what a shot!" shouted Irish triumphantly, as his well-aimed empty glass bottle, struck one of the queuing masturbators squarely on the right shoulder and fell exploding on the pavement at the target's feet.

The sad grey figure did not respond but merely rubbed his shoulder with his left hand, then shuffled away from the sparkling glass splinters that lay on the icy concrete ground.

When all four had purchased their food, including Blue's triple order, one of which he ate while waiting for the other two to be prepared, they casually strolled along Church Street in the direction of the Pier Head. It was their intention to catch the last bus home from the terminus at midnight but only three of the four companions would board that bus.

Chapter 3

Everywhere there's Lots of Piggies

Sunday, 30th to Monday, 31st January 1972

It was nearly half past eleven when the boys neared their intended destination. The chimes of the tower clock, from nearby Saint Mary and Saint Nicholas church, announced the arrival of the last half hour of that day. Echoing their baleful notes around the chasms between the tall office buildings, of this now resting financial heart of the city, they reminded the companions that they had but a brief time left before catching the midnight bus back to the barren estates from which they came.

Having wound their way along Church Street, across Castle Street and made a deviation down Brunswick Street, past the rear entrance of the spectacular India Buildings, they had halted in Drury Lane, by the motionless steel buckets of the functioning art installation, entitled 'The Fountain.' Now perfectly still, its constantly recycled water frozen in the concrete tiled pool at its base, Blue and Jay Mac, having climbed on to the top tower, were precariously perched whilst charitably making their own liquid contribution.

"It's fuckin' freezin' me dick off," said Blue, with the rising steam from his stream of urine, mixing with the cloud of his condensed breath.

"Yeah, but no one would notice any difference," replied Jay Mac.

Irish and Glynn had discovered a small red and cream moped parked outside a nearby office block. Whilst smoking their cigarettes, they were arguing about how to get the vehicle started.

"You need a fucking key" said Jay Mac, having joined them with Blue, who had finally finished his lengthy urination.

"No, you can bump start these little fuckers." said Irish, who fancied himself as something of an authority on these matters, his brother Dermot having a Kawasaki 125cc motorbike, at home.

Conscious of the short time they had left before catching their bus, and not wishing to pay anything towards the extortionate fee, that an enterprising taxi driver would charge them after midnight, to travel the seven miles back to the Crown Estate, the thrifty Glynn urged them to leave the bike where it was.

"Fucking leave this piece of crap and lets gerroff." he exhorted.

"I'm gonna get this thing started." insisted Irish.

Suddenly Jay Mac noticed something moving within the darkened interior of the office building. He and Blue were facing into the main entrance foyer and Irish and Glynn on the other side of the bike, had their backs to it. In an instant he realised it was the night watchman. 'This must be his bike,' he thought, as the glaring beam from the guard's torch picked out the silhouettes of all four youths.

"Fuckin' run, it's the cocky watchman!" he shouted, momentarily blinded by the flash of dazzling light, which caught him fully in the eyes.

The bike fell against Jay Mac's legs delaying his escape; the entrance door opened and the irate sentinel charged out.

"Come 'ere you fucking cunts, steal my bike would yer?"

Irish and Glynn had disappeared to Jay Mac's right, away behind the rear of James Street station. Blue, running just in front of Jay Mac, retraced his steps back up Brunswick Street. Jay Mac, who was renowned for his throwing ability, was equally famed for his running speed, having been a key member of his 'school' athletics and cross-country team. He took the opposite direction to Blue and sprinted down Brunswick Street, towards the Pier Head and the waiting final bus to safety. The security guard had chosen to follow him but the youth could hear his heavy breathing and knew he would easily leave him behind. At that moment a large, dark figure stepped from a parked car in the road of his escape route.

"Gerrout the fuckin' way!" Jay Mac shouted as the figure blocked his path.

They were the last words he could manage for some time. The force of the mighty punch from this weighty individual expelled all the air from Jay Mac's body, when his heavy fist made contact with the youth's stomach. Badly winded and doubled up on the floor, he heard the dreaded words…

"Police, you're under arrest, anything you say may be used in evidence against you, now get on your fuckin' feet, you little shit."

He was dragged by the collar of his Crombie, across the road and forcibly stood upright, only to be immediately bent over the bonnet of the arresting officer's car. The large plain-clothes policeman was then joined by an almost equal-sized, cigarette smoking colleague, who quickly and painfully handcuffed Jay Mac's wrists, after pulling his arms into the required position, behind his back. He took advantage of the opportunity, to bang Jay Mac's head loudly onto the steel bonnet of the vehicle.

"Hey, don't do that" said the first policeman "I don't want this car damaged, by that little cunt's head." They both laughed heartily.

The puffing security guard now arrived, "Hold 'im!" he shouted. "Let me give 'im a dig."

Happy to oblige this honest citizen, the officers quickly stood Jay Mac back up. "Not the face mind, not the face." said the helpful cigarette smoker.

The out-of-shape-guardian summoned all his remaining strength and punched Jay Mac as hard as he could manage, virtually in the same area as his original assailant. The youth doubled up again, even though he had managed to tense his abdominal muscles to receive the blow, which was not as powerful as the first.

"Can I give 'im another?" the balding fifty-something watchman enquired eagerly.

"Not here sir, perhaps later at the station, when you've given your statement." said the first officer, smiling.

"He *did* try to steal my fuckin' bike y'know?" the watchman added, as if this information may be sufficient entreaty, for another crack at Jay Mac.

"We'll meet you down at the Pier Head Station sir: if we get the chance you can probably give him a slap there, ok?"

Officer number two had decided to put an end to the conversation at this point. The handcuffed boy was then bundled into the rear of the vehicle and driven the short distance to the police station located at the Pier Head. The chimes of the nearby Saint Nicholas' bells confirmed the close of that day and as Jay Mac peered out of the passenger-side window at the rear of the police vehicle, he noticed the hands of the huge clock on the nearest face of the Liver Buildings concurred it was now midnight. How much the events of that last half hour of Saturday the 29th January 1972, would impact on his future, he had no comprehension of at that time.

"Trying to steal a working man's bike, were you? You little cunt." said the arresting officer seated next to Jay Mac, whilst his colleague drove quickly towards their destination.

"Bit of luck getting this little prick." he said over his shoulder. "I feel like a brew and I could really do with a good shite." He farted violently, as if to emphasise the urgency of his need.

"Put that fucking fag out, before we're all blown up," his colleague advised wryly.

Within minutes they had arrived at their destination and Jay Mac was marched into the small grey, utilitarian building and brought before the desk sergeant.

"What 'ave we got 'ere?" asked the grey haired, impressively moustached officer, without the slightest interest.

"Attempted taking away of a motorcycle, Drury Lane, complainant will be joining us shortly." answered the equally apathetic arresting officer, his colleague having gone swiftly to attend to his main priority.

After a cursory rough search for concealed weapons and contraband, Jay Mac confirmed his details and was formally arrested, then taken to an interview room. Once inside he was violently pushed into a grey plastic chair, in this sparse, dingy, windowless room. Apart from two other similar chairs and a grey Formica topped table, with dark grey metal legs, a shadeless low-watt bulb dangled by a cobweb covered plastic sheathed electric cable. Jay Mac was perturbed by the faded red stains, on the surface of the lower areas of the walls; they had been scrubbed but not fully removed.

"Open your legs wide" commanded the original detective constable.

Jay Mac complied, still sitting with his wrists handcuffed behind his back, he was uncomfortable and scared. The officer placed a toe of his black leather boot, between Jay Mac's parted legs and under his groin, the youth's discomfort increased considerably. Next he caught hold of Jay Mac's red and white striped Liverpool F.C. scarf and flung it onto the floor, spitting in disgust following the direction of his throw.

"I'd like to make a phone call please sir, I believe I'm…"

Before he could continue further, his mouth and chin were firmly clamped by the constable's right hand, whilst the index finger of his left poked Jay Mac firmly in the forehead, to emphasise his comments that followed.

"You… don't… fucking… speak… until I say, right?" His overpowering halitosis breath filled Jay Mac's nose almost making him want to retch, as he continued, "Right, the complainant says there were four of you little shites, trying to steal his bike and I can tell you that we were sat watching two of you taking a piss, so don't fucking say you were on your own."

He poked Jay Mac's forehead several times with more force after each statement.

"I fuckin' needed that; here's a brew for yer." announced his relieved colleague, the smoker, as he entered the room, clearly having satisfied both of his pressing needs.

"Hope you've washed your fucking hands," said the finger poking officer.

"Give me the names of the other three shits and their addresses and it might go easier for you." He continued with his interrogation along these lines and Jay Mac responded each time by saying he did not know the other boys but had met them by chance in town earlier that evening.

"Let me have a go at him." said the smoker, taking over from his colleague, to allow him to drink his tea. He assumed the same position but clearly favoured the use of the left foot. Instead of poking Jay Mac's reddened forehead, he grasped him by his hair and wrenched his head violently back and forth.

'I wish I still had a crop,' Jay Mac thought to himself.

His present tormentor then put his fat; sweaty face close to Jay Mac's and proceeded to blow a cloud of grey smoke which enveloped the youth's head. He was clearly disappointed that this drew no response from his victim.

"Bit of a heavy smoker are yer?" he deduced, using his finely honed detective skills to the full.

"No sir, I don't smoke sir." Jay Mac replied.

"Are you a little queer, then?" asked his interrogator, as if denying the one vice confirmed the other.

"No sir, I am not." Jay Mac responded firmly, his eyes fixed on the growing sweat stains adding to the earlier dried patches, in the armpits of the officer's Bri-nylon, yellowing shirt.

"Give me the fucking names of your mates, you thieving little cunt, or I will burst your tiny balls." he shouted, increasing the pressure under Jay Mac's groin with the toe of his boot.

"I met them earlier in town by accident, I don't know them sir." Jay Mac replied once again.

"Oh, so you *were* trying to pick them up, eh? You fucking queers make me sick." the smoker pressed on.

"I'm not queer, and I don't know them." Jay Mac responded, making a mistake of losing his temper.

"Don't you raise your voice to me, shit-head!" the officer bellowed, as he released his hair and removed his boot from under Jay Mac's groin, now placing it on the youth's stomach before kicking him backwards, whilst still seated, across the room. Jay Mac and the plastic chair parted company, as he fell heavily to the floor.

"You're from the Kings Estate aren't you?" asked the original interrogator, standing over Jay Mac whilst the boy lay on the hard floor.

"Yes sir, I am," he replied.

"Well fucking stay on your dump of an estate, don't come into the city for your thieving – right?"

Jay Mac did not respond.

The second constable now stood over Jay Mac also and spoke. "They're all fuckin' scum on that Kings Estate, aren't thee?"

"No sir they're not." Jay Mac replied.

"Are you calling me a fuckin' liar?" he snapped, dragging Jay Mac to his feet by his collar.

The youth looked into the glistening face of the profusely sweating officer and offered no response.

"I can't be arsed with this any longer." said the original arresting officer. Get a couple of 'uniforms' to run this little shite up to Cheapside."

Jay Mac's stomach turned over, on hearing the terrifying name of the notorious old Victorian Bridewell.

Moments later as he was marched out of the small, claustrophobic room, by a uniformed constable, the first officer stopped him, leaned across, removed the handcuffs and returned his scarf.

His final words of advice were "Never, ever grass on your mates lad." Then he slapped Jay Mac across the back of the head, as if acknowledging and supporting his refusal to identify Irish, Blue and Glynn.

Jay Mac passed back through the entrance area, rubbing his chaffed aching wrists and noticed the watchman was sitting, drinking a steaming mug of tea. Clearly he had not been anxious to return to his solitary duties in the icy-cold office block.

"Am I too late to give 'im another dig?" he enquired hopefully.

The uniformed constable looked at the sorry individual and said, "You are really, mate, unless you want to follow us up to Cheapside."

The tired security agent did not respond but smiled with morbid satisfaction, when he heard the name of Jay Mac's next destination.

The journey to the main Bridewell in Cheapside was slightly longer than the previous one, from Drury Lane to the Police Station at the Pier Head. Jay Mac wished it would have taken hours. While they travelled the short distance through the dark winter's night, it began to snow heavily.

"That'll stick with all this ice on the ground already." said the uniformed officer, seated next to Jay Mac in the rear of the small police Panda car, breaking the silence.

They were almost at their destination, when Jay Mac made a desperate plea.

"Is there any chance you could let me out? Y'see, me mum's getting on a bit and she always worries about me if I'm home late." There was no immediate response, so he continued, "Yeah, she's really quite ill and this'll only make her condition worse." He thought if he was going to lie about his relationship with his estranged mother, then he might as well make it a whopper.

A sharp elbow was thrust into Jay Mac's already sore ribs, as the officer next to him spoke.

"You should've thought about that, before you went out theivin' shouldn't you lad?"

Jay Mac said nothing further before the vehicle stopped and parked outside the grim structure of the archaic prison. The Main Bridewell, Liverpool's own Bastille, constructed of huge, solid sandstone blocks, blackened with the grime of ages and set all about with thick gauge, dark, ironworks, looked like an impenetrable and escape-proof Medieval fortress. The snowflakes swirled wildly about the dark-coated boy and his two similarly sombre-looking, uniformed escorts. With the constable on his left side, holding Jay Mac's arm and wrist firmly in a prescribed restraint position, he was led up the well-worn steps and in through the heavy reinforced wooden door.

Standing perfectly still on the large weathered concrete paving slabs from which the uneven floor was constructed, Jay Mac looked about him. He felt as if he had accidently, slipped through a rend in the fabric of time and was actually back in Victorian Liverpool. The receiving area for felons was essentially a high-ceilinged vault, with walls partially tiled in glazed dark-green rectangles and painted gloss cream above the mid-point. Several lights with brittle old shades, hung in strategic areas, casting radiant pools over the tall, aged, oak reception counter and the imposing figure of the desk sergeant. A good six foot four inches and heroically built, with a full head of wavy slicked-back, grey hair and a thick bristling moustache, he presented a formidable character; Jay Mac had already decided to choose his words carefully, when addressing him. Two other similar-looking constables, stood near the antique wooden reception counter. The officers who had escorted Jay Mac provided the sergeant with the appropriate paperwork, containing his details and, after exchanging a few observations about the inclement weather, made their way to the exit.

"They love young fellers like you in 'ere, don't fall asleep whatever you do, or you'll wake up with a nasty surprise." advised the rib-poking constable, smiling slyly as he opened the large creaking door and departed.

Jay Mac was told to stand in front of the wooden counter and one of the other loitering policemen, stood behind him. The towering desk sergeant began by asking Jay Mac to confirm his name, address and contact details. In desperation, conscious that his aunt and uncle did not have a telephone, he had provided the number of his cousin, their daughter and former 'infant phenomenon'.

"Would it be possible to ring my cousin, please sir?" Jay Mac enquired politely.

He was immediately struck across the back of the head by the large policeman to his rear. "Shut your fuckin' mouth!" he barked.

"All in good time, first things first." the sergeant said, appearing almost kindly Jay Mac thought. Next he gave the youth a verbal sequence of instructions to follow.

"Empty your pockets, take off your scarf, remove any braces or belts you may be wearing, take the laces out of your boots and remove that stud from your pocket – now!"

After Jay Mac had complied with these demands, he passed the items to the sergeant. The constable behind the youth pushed him sharply and he fell forward, catching the edge of the counter with his hands.

"Open your legs." the officer shouted and then proceeded to frisk him roughly and with relish, taking the opportunity to slap Jay Mac's testicles with the edge of his hand.

The sergeant then spoke. "What are you supposed to be? A little 'Skinhead' is it? No, hair's not short enough. I know, you're a 'Bovver Boy', is that it?"

"Sorry sir, I don't know what you mean, sir." Jay Mac replied as politely as possible. This drew the same response from the slapping policeman.

"No weapon, no little Stanley knife? You're not carrying a 'tool'? Are you a tough guy? Rely on your fists and big red booties do you?" the sergeant asked, continuing his informal questioning.

"No sir, I deplore violence in all its forms. I try to avoid trouble whenever I can sir." Jay Mac's answer led to another slap and a slight change in accompanying dialogue.

"Don't you answer the sergeant back, you little shit!" The constable added an extra slap to emphasise his warning.

"What 'ave we got here then? Are you a queer, a little Nancy boy?" asked the sergeant, following a similar line of enquiry as the two fat D.C's at the Pier Head Station.

"No sir, I am not." Jay Mac answered firmly but this time without raising his voice, remembering the response of his earlier interrogator.

The huge sergeant leaned forward over the counter and looked sternly at him.

"We've got a nice gentleman in the cells, 'Old George' who loves popping the arses of young boys. Picked him up tonight, hanging around the toilets in St John's Lane. Had his wrinkly old cock out, touting for business. Would you like to meet him? Should I arrange a date for you?" he asked without changing his dour expression.

"No thank you sir, its very kind of you to offer sir." Jay Mac managed to reply, feigning a confidence that had long since departed.

"Take 'im to cell number six Charlie, put him in with Old George, I think it will be a case of love at first sight, don't you?" The sergeant's suggestion clearly amused PC Charlie, who laughed loudly, dragging the reluctant youth towards an old black iron door.

"No thank you sir, I'd rather not disturb the old gentleman if he's resting." Jay Mac called back to the sergeant desperately, while the other loitering constable unlocked the door for both him and PC Charlie. The sergeant looked on dispassionately, as the weighty door was closed behind the youth and his escort.

Jay Mac felt faint and panic began to take hold. He was conjuring up mental visions of a crazed, elderly rué, who would molest anything that stayed still long enough. His escort led him along a dark, dank, narrow corridor that smelled of strong disinfectant. The sound of the constable's boots echoed in the cold, otherwise silent passageway. Suddenly prisoner and escort stopped in front of another heavy black iron door; evidently this was cell number six. As the gaoler searched for the appropriate key, other occupants of cells along the corridor heard the jangling of the metal bunch and their chain, which was attached to the officer's belt.

"Who's that, who've yer got there?" shouted one angry voice.

"Bring 'im over 'ere, I could do with some company." entreated another.

These shouts animated the other residents and, in a matter of seconds the corridor was filled with shrieks and howls, like the inside of a primate house at a zoo. Jay Mac was now in a state of near terror, as the door of the cell swung open.

He had been planning how he would deal with its deranged, perverted occupant, in various ways. A straight punch to the face, a kick in the balls and then strangulation, with possibly a bit of eye gouging for effect, he thought.

"Gerrin you little cunt, what are you waitin' for, a written invitation?" said the smirking gaoler, pushing Jay Mac firmly into the tiny room.

'Here we go, I'll do this old bastard,' he thought and sprang forward ready to do or die. To his grateful relief, the cell was completely devoid of other occupants.

"You bastards" he said out loud with a sigh, as the dark iron door clanged shut behind him.

The exterior flap covering a small observation hole was moved to one side by Jay Mac's escort. "Get to sleep and no playin' with yerself either, I'll send someone along later to keep you company."

With that he strolled away laughing to himself, adding to the tumult of terror that raged in the dark corridor.

"Shut up you fuckin' animals!" he shouted, finally exiting back into the relative sanity of the receiving area, to repeat his well-rehearsed double-act with the desk sergeant for the benefit of the next poor unfortunate arrival.

Jay Mac quickly scanned the cell for possible escape routes, even though he knew it was highly improbable that there was even the slightest hope of any such portal existing. The walls were roughly plastered and gloss painted in cream, similar to the reception suite. A number of patches of plaster had fallen away and the ancient sandstone brickwork was exposed, green algal bloom revealed where colonies of mould had made a precarious hold in these random gaps. The floor was made of old, crazed concrete and was stained in certain sections, from a variety of bodily fluids, discharged by previous tenants. In the far right corner facing the metal door, Jay Mac noticed a grubby-looking, off-white plastic pot with a similar coloured lid. Apart from this perfunctory toilet, there was one other item not part of the actual fabric; a thick wooden well-worn five foot long plank, about eighteen inches wide, firmly bolted horizontally to the left-hand wall on iron brackets. Above this multi-purpose item of furniture, was a window, the only source of light, apart from a half-round, iron-grilled storm lamp secured to the ceiling.

He climbed onto the sturdy wooden plank-cum-bed and examined the small window carefully. Rectangular in shape, if it had been filled with one piece of glass and no other restriction, it may have offered some possibility for a small child to pass through. However, a solid iron criss-cross framework was set within the borders of the window and each small section of this metal honeycomb, contained a thick piece of dirty, opaque glass. Two of these pieces were missing in this particular window, though Jay Mac could see that not even that same infant, could fit its hand through either of these apertures.

He took his Crombie off and used it as a make-shift blanket, trying to make himself comfortable on the hard, old oak 'bed'. The room was bitterly cold and he now wished he had worn his denim jacket and some extra layers, as he lay there shivering with cold and anxiety. A bone-chilling wind howled through the two non-glazed spaces in the small window, occasionally bringing accompanying clusters of frozen snowflakes or hail. Jay Mac desperately tried to sleep, even though the prevailing conditions were not exactly conducive and his mind raced with fearful images and dark thoughts.

Another inmate was screaming loudly and kicking the door to their cell repeatedly and with increasing force. Jay Mac realised the noise was coming from the next room on the right side of his. This disturbance continued for some time before he heard the rapid approach of at least two warders. The rattle of keys was followed by the creak of the heavy iron door and then the dull thud of repeated deliberate punches striking a fleshy body. These disturbing sounds had Jay Mac's full attention.

"Now shut the fuck up, you old perv or we'll come back and give you a proper kickin'… right?" shouted one of the gaolers rhetorically, clearly not happy with having his own rest disturbed.

Jay Mac wondered if his neighbour was the infamous 'Old George,' if so, he had clearly been capable of a vigorous display of rage. For the remainder of the night, however, after his beating, he remained silent.

The youth eventually drifted into a fitful sleep, only to have this rudely shattered, after what seemed to be a few short hours, by the clang of his cell door being thrown open. "Gerrup….get your piss pot and wait in the corridor… come on, fuckin' move!" shouted the warder, announcing the start of another new morning in the old Bridewell.

Jay Mac quickly put his Crombie on and grasped the partially filled plastic pot, then stood in the now brightly lit passage outside his cell. When his eyes had adjusted to the light, he saw he was in a line of at least ten other male inmates of various ages and physiques.

"Slop out!" Instructed the same warder and this order was repeated by several of his colleagues, who were also present. After entering an open washroom further along the corridor, each prisoner emptied his pot in turn into a metal sluice and then briefly made his ablutions.

"Move y'selves, you dozy bastards!" another warder shouted as the men were directed back along the same passageway. They were ordered to stop suddenly and, six of them, including Jay Mac were pushed into another small cell and told to sit down. The youth quickly sat on the concrete floor, near the metal door with his back pressed firmly against the wall and his head lowered. He did not wish to make eye contact with any of his new companions.

When everyone appeared to be seated, Jay Mac furtively looked about him, studying the other occupants and making mental assessments, as to who might pose the most likely potential threat. Almost immediately there seemed to be a minor dispute between a big overweight man in his early fifties, with a large stomach straining against his open-necked, white, long-sleeved, expensive-looking shirt and two wiry, smaller grey individuals. The latter were both seated on the wooden plank 'bed' in this room.

"Move your fuckin' arses, if you know what's good for yer!" the big man ordered.

One of the 'greys' complied immediately and sat down opposite Jay Mac, the other tried to offer a token resistance.

"Why should I? Who the fuck are you to tell me to move?"

On hearing this negative response, the standing inmate slapped the now sole bench occupier, hard across the face with his right hand. The smaller, weaker man's head turned violently with the force of the blow and he decided to join his colleague on the floor, facing Jay Mac.

"That's more like it," said the proud new possessor of the battered old piece of wood. Smugly satisfied with his minor victory, he let out a massive fart, as if confirming the legitimacy of his claim to his 'throne.'

Diagonally across to Jay Mac's right was a young man of about eighteen or nineteen, with a short blond crop, who was staring directly at him. Dressed in a sharp Prince of Wales check two-piece suit, pale blue Ben Sherman shirt and highly polished, though now scuffed, black leather Como shoes, Jay Mac instantly recognised another player. The young man stood up, walked over to Jay Mac and then sat down next to him.

"Alright Skin?" he asked, clearly acknowledging Jay Mac's membership of this violent youth group.

"Frank Jordan of The Swan" said the blond Skinhead, by way of a formal introduction.

"Nice one mate, Jay Mac from the Kings Estate." Jay Mac replied, studying his new acquaintance's battered face with a blackened eye, split lip and considerable bruising. He was sitting with his knees drawn up and his clenched fists resting on them. On the cut and grazed knuckles, of both hands, he had S.W.A.N tattooed in blue-black ink. Jay Mac knew the names of lots of key players from other teams across the city; he carried a mental catalogue of their acronyms or sobriquets and their battle-honour, conferred status. Like a surreal 'Who's Who' he also recorded whether they were currently active or 'away' and their weapon of choice.

'Jordo: Key player, the Swan, likes to use a short heavy metal club but will resort to glassing opponents if the opportunity arises, done some previous in Borstal.' He knew who this was and addressed him accordingly. "I've heard of you, Jordo, top man in the Swan Team, yeah?" he said, flattering his new friend.

"Not quite the top man yet." Jordo replied, then asked "What's your team?"

Jay Mac explained the situation briefly, about his residence on the Kings Estate but affiliation to the Crown Estate Team.

"You must 'ave balls, you mad cunt," Jordo responded in an equally flattering manner.

"When you two lovebirds 'ave got a minute, 'ave either of yer gorra ciggie?" asked the bench master.

Both Skins replied that they did not have any cigarettes, or other smokeable items.

"Worrabout you, kiddie fiddler?" he shouted at the solitary figure, who stood in the right corner opposite Jay Mac.

The elderly male was about five foot six inches tall, well groomed with thinning auburn hair and a blotchy red, heavily jowled face. Over his bespoke dark pinstripe suit, he wore a beige gabardine Macintosh. With his white shirt and blue with white polka dotted bow tie, he looked like a retired city gent, thought Jay Mac, except for his incongruous footwear, a pair of dirty, split, badly fitting, old tennis shoes, one of which had no lace in it.

"Ey you fuckin' turd burglar, I'm talkin' to you." the large white-shirted individual shouted once more.

His stinging remarks drew no comment. The old man merely tapped his chin repeatedly with his forefinger and muttered to himself "they took my shoes you know, they took my shoes, I only wanted a kiss, that's all."

The large fat male stood up and pushed the aged mutterer against the wall, then slapped him loudly across the face.

"Give me any smokes you've got, you fuckin' old perv." he demanded, then struck him once again.

"Please don't hit me sir, I don't wish to offend." was his tearful response.

At this point, Jordo removed his left shoe and threw it violently at the back of the tormentor's head. Both Skins leapt up as one and set about the cigarette seeker, as he turned to face them.

"You fuckin' cunts" he announced, shocked that anyone would have the audacity to attack him.

Jordo closed his mouth with a vicious straight right and Jay Mac caught him in his swollen stomach, with a powerful left hook, which bent him forward to receive a well-timed left cross from Jordo, which almost dislocated his jaw. Dropping to his knees, he then received half a dozen vicious kicks to the body, from the booted Jay Mac and his one-shoed accomplice. It was now the big man's turn to beg for mercy, as he whimpered, "Please no more."

Old George thought he had finally found his champions. The two youths sat down on the wooden bench and he shuffled across to join them.

"Fuck off, arse bandit," they both said and he shrunk away once again back to his corner. The two grey figures had sat silently watching the entertainment.

"I fuckin' hate bullies." said Jordo.

"Me too." Jay Mac concurred.

Any further conversation was suspended by the sound of a key turning in the lock and the heavy door being pushed open.

"Room Service!" shouted a warder, placing a plastic tray on the floor containing six enamel mugs filled with dark brown tepid tea and, a plate with six slices of bread and dripping.

"Ere, y'are, Jay Mac, catch these," said Jordo, as he dived forward like a starving animal and threw two pieces of bread, discus style towards his cell-mate. He then brought over two of the mugs of tea. While he sat drinking his beverage, Jay Mac realised that he had no idea of the time. It was still dark outside but as it was the middle of winter, this could indicate any hour up to 8.00 or 8.30am, he thought.

"How did you come to be in 'ere anyway?" Jay Mac asked, assuming that Jordo's cuts and bruises may have some bearing on his present incarceration.

"I had a bit of a disagreement with some cunt of a bouncer, at the Top Rank. Next thing I know the bizzies come steamin' in, I cracked one and I ended up in this shithole. Worrabout y'self?"

Jordo's question made Jay Mac feel a little uncomfortable. Compared to his cell mate's heroic exploits, Jay Mac thought his minor offence may sound comical and, considered whether to embellish the actual details or, exaggerate his role. He finally decided to just outline the facts and wait for Jordo's response. After he had listened to Jay Mac's story, describing the final events of the evening, from his arrival at the fountain to his arrest, Jordo gave his considered opinion.

"You shouldn't be in 'ere; this is a pile of shite. When you go up in front of the Mags, they'll just give yer a fine and a warnin' not to do it again. Don't even worry about it." His comments allayed Jay Mac's fears to some extent and he felt relieved.

"Thanks mate." he said. "I'll be glad to get out of 'ere, any idea when they'll let us get off?" Jay Mac asked, not fully taking into account, the gravity of Jordo's offence.

"I don't know when you'll get out but I'm not goin' anywhere for a long time, I'm a repeat offender, so it's Walton or fuckin' Risley for me." Jordo replied dejectedly.

Just at that moment the iron door opened once again. "John Mack, on your feet, come on hurry up!" the gaoler shouted.

"Looks like you're off mate." said the experienced Jordo, as Jay Mac sprang to his feet and made his way to the door opening, stepping over the 'greys', who had remained seated in their original position on the floor.

"See yer Jordo, take it easy mate." he shouted back.

"If you're ever in The Swan look me up, I'll be at the bar in the Painted Wagon." Jordo's final words only just escaped from the cell, before the loud metallic clang of the heavy door closing, sealed the five remaining occupants from any further communication with the outside world. Jay Mac was led briskly back to the receiving area.

"Your uncle is prepared to stand bail for you." said the original desk sergeant, still positioned at his counter.

Jay Mac's belongings were returned to him and then he eagerly signed a release document.

"Listen to me, you're clearly an intelligent lad, so take my advice, stop hangin' around with scum, they will only bring you down." was the sergeant's friendly advice. Jay Mac thanked him and as the door to the street outside was being unlocked, the sergeant added, "and change the colour of that fuckin' scarf, you may have better luck."

Jay Mac laughed as he stepped through the iron-framed portal and back into the twentieth century.

He walked slowly along the frozen pavement of Cheapside, which was partially covered with a light dusting of snow and frozen hail. The youth breathed in deeply, enjoying the cold morning air, as it filled his nostrils and lungs. The desk sergeant had countersigned his release at 8.30am, providing Jay Mac with a fixed bearing in time once again. The whole nightmare experience had lasted for nine hours; it would haunt his dreams for years to come. While he waited at the recently vandalised, modern, glass-panelled, bus shelter, avoiding the thousands of sparkling splinters on the icy ground, from one of those glazed sections, he considered what may lie in store when he arrived home. How he would face his aunt he did not know but how he would face his uncle, he did not even wish to contemplate. Eventually a bus arrived bound for the Kings Estate and Jay Mac leapt on, throwing down the customary ten pence.

"Are you going all the way to the Kings Estate lad?" the driver enquired.

"Yeah, I am." Jay Mac replied.

"Then it's the full fuckin' price, right?" the driver demanded.

'Trust me to get a cunt,' Jay Mac thought, throwing the remainder of the fare, down onto the small metal collection tray.

He made his way to the rear of the empty vehicle and sat warming his tired back against the graffiti covered seat, with the heat escaping from the engine. The bus sped along on its lonely, grey Sunday morning journey and after forty minutes, delivered the exhausted, anxious boy to his appointment with adult reality.

"Is that you John, you little idiot?" shouted his aunt, as he closed the door to their first floor flat, behind him.

He had barely made it to the living room, before he was struck with a hard slap across the face, by his elderly female guardian.

"You swine, you stupid, ungrateful swine!" she cried out, as the full force of her tearful rage enveloped Jay Mac.

Slapped, punched, smacked and pushed, he was continually pummelled, until his aunt exhausted and spent, stood back looking at him in disgust. He made no response, having learned in many previous situations that a still tongue was the wisest option. His uncle now entered the room; his face was contorted with rage and dismay, as he caught hold of Jay Mac by the front of his Crombie. He did not strike the youth, that was not his way, he just pulled and pushed him around the small room, swearing at the top of his voice, with the veins in his temples standing out and pulsing with anger. Finally, after his entire lexicon of expletives had been fully utilized, with one powerful push into Jay Mac's sternum, he forced the youth over the back of the old couch and onto its yielding cushions. His uncle looked down on him, as he lay there and spat at him.

"You fuckin' stupid little bastard! That's all you are nothing more, a stupid little bastard." He walked away into the kitchen and turned the radio on.

Nothing could hurt Jay Mac more than this choice of words; a physical beating was painless compared to his uncle's scornful affirmation of his lack of legitimacy.

Although he was ravenously hungry, he decided not to follow his seething relative, into the small kitchen. Instead he went into the bathroom, washed his face and brushed his teeth. As he finished his cleaning ritual, he could hear his aunt, crying in the bedroom nearby. Ashamed, he returned to the living room and changed his clothing.

After about an hour, hunger pangs increased in intensity and he decided to risk entering the kitchen. His uncle was standing at the sink, rinsing his false teeth under the tap, after removing them from their Steradent filled plastic beaker. Smoking his old pipe and staring blankly out of the window, he completely ignored the youth. Jay Mac helped himself to a bowl of cornflakes, added the milk and then poured a cup of dark brown, luke-warm tea from the glazed teapot standing on the metal grill covering the gas burners of the stove. Whilst he sat eating his late breakfast, his silent uncle, now seated at one end of the small plastic-topped, chipboard table, was reading his usual Sunday paper, the '*News of the World.*'

"More dickheads like you in 'ere." he announced, breaking the angry silence. "Causing trouble at the match, they need teaching a lesson they'll never forget." he continued in between taking long puffs from his pipe. '*Two Way Family Favourites*' was just beginning on the radio; his uncle stopped talking and began listening to another of his preferred programmes. At that moment his aunt appeared in the doorway and spoke.

"The shame you have brought to this house. Mrs Ashworth had to knock and tell me all about it, the shame of that."

Jay Mac realised that his cousin Margaret had rang Mrs Ashworth, as she was the only neighbour in the flats, with access to a telephone. He imagined the relish with which Margaret would have announced, that he had been arrested and, was being held in the notorious Cheapside Bridewell.

"Margaret told Mrs Ashworth all about your arrest and being charged with theft." his aunt said with tearful eyes.

"I bet she enjoyed that." was Jay Mac's response.

"You're a disgrace; you're no good, just like your father." she announced.

"I wouldn't know would I? I never met him." Jay Mac replied, pushing past his aunt and entering the living room. Patch the dog, who had retreated to her bed when the earlier argument raged, now sat wagging her tail as the youth approached.

"All right hound, what's happening with you?" he asked rhetorically, addressing the old dog, as she stretched out on the faux fur rug, in front of the two-bar electric fire.

A short time later Jay Mac put his denim jacket on over a plain knitted dark blue, woollen jumper. He was also wearing his usual Wrangler jeans and once he had energetically polished his red Airwair, he finished fastening their laces, preparing to leave. Instead of his Crombie over his denim jacket, he decided to wear a dark blue zip fronted, bomber style jacket, with red and white elasticated collar and cuffs. The final item of his partial disguise was a close-fitting black woollen hat.

"Where do you think you're going?" asked his aunt, opening a new twenty-pack of Embassy king-size filter tip cigarettes.

"Out!" was Jay Mac's one word reply, before he stepped into the hallway.

"Don't bother coming back." were her final words.

Jay Mac had been carefully observing the movements of the buses over the past half hour. He quickly ran down the stairs, opened the sheet-metal covered front door then locked it behind him, and sprinted across to the stop, just in time as the bus was arriving.

The short journey to the Crown Estate passed quickly and Jay Mac soon arrived at his destination. He walked briskly through the almost deserted streets, on this bleak winter's Sunday afternoon. The sky was light grey, tinged with pink and laden with the promise of heavy snow to come. Jay Mac's eyes were drawn to the sad sight of a small old black dog, with a white blaze on its chest, lying supine, frozen dead on the icy pavement next to a low buff coloured brick wall. At least he was at last freed from his desperate search for his callous master, who had long since abandoned the once cute pup, Jay Mac thought, entering the road where Mal the 'pig' resided.

"Alright Jay Mac, how's it goin' mate?" shouted Tony (G), Mal's apprentice electrician house guest.

"Ace, Tony, are you alright mate?" Jay Mac replied, happy to be distracted from his sombre thoughts.

The two youths passed a brief exchange of updates, whilst Tony (G) continued his maintenance work on his splendid Lambretta LI175.

"Yer'll be alright in the Mags." advised Tony, echoing Jordo's earlier heartening words, after Jay Mac had provided a cursory outline, of the events of the previous night. Jay Mac thanked his fellow team-mate and moved on, towards Irish's house, located further into the estate.

"Fuck off quick, you shouldn't 'ave come here." was Irish's hasty advice, on opening the front door to Jay Mac.

"Is that John Mack? I want a word with him." shouted a stern female voice from within.

Too late to run, Jay Mac was confronted by the formidable Mrs O'Hare, the mother of Irish. A tall, heavily built woman, in her early fifties, she had short chestnut, permed hair, set atop of a long pale face, containing a pair of piercing dark brown eyes, a sizeable pointed nose and a fleshy lipped mouth displaying a number of overshot uneven teeth of different hues. Jay Mac liked her a lot, because of her integrity and directness. Unfortunately, on this occasion, he was on the receiving end of her perceptive intelligence and barbed tongue.

"What is the meaning of this?" she asked angrily, producing Jay Mac's knife from her permanently attached apron and, holding it in her right hand.

"Our Sean found this under his bed. He could have cut his throat with it, or took one of his eyes out. He could have stabbed Patrick while he was sleeping, or murdered us all."

She continued in this fashion for some minutes, pausing only occasionally for breath and then each time escalating the possible crimes the six-year old Sean, could have carried out, with the deadly weapon in its black lacquered sheath. Jay Mac waited for the right moment to interject with a suitable reply, before the infant's wildly spiralling trajectory of misdemeanours, found him practically accused of starting a nuclear holocaust.

"It's only a toy replica y'see, Mrs O'Hare, I bought it in the old curio shop by our school about a year ago, for my collection." Jay Mac replied, partially truthfully.

He had in fact bought the knife from the shabby junk shop, located in the road behind the boys' school. The sign above the door declared that they were 'Specialist's in House Clearance', with their one display window filled with assorted bric-a-brac and militaria. Jay Mac's keen eye had spotted the miniature replica of a Samurai Sepuku dagger, amongst the detritus of rusty old medals with faded ribbons and tarnished belt buckles. At three shillings and sixpence it was just within his price range, unlike the Waffen SS dagger, minus its black casing, bearing the legend *'Meine Ehre heist Treue,'* on the steel blade, or the Kriegsmarine officer's sword with scabbard, priced respectively at twenty one shillings and £2.00. Despite lengthy grovelling attempts to convince his uncle that these were truly classic items, he was unable to secure the necessary funds and his own mythical collection, remained at one item.

"I'll give it back to you but you must promise me, that you'll never bring it out of your house again and, I will be speaking to your aunty about this, next time I see her." Mrs O'Hare had delivered her judgement.

Jay Mac promised never to remove the knife from the fictional display cabinet, where he supposedly kept it and, as he knew it was highly unlikely that his aunt and Mrs O'Hare would come into contact in the near future, he acquiesced on this point also.

"Now go away, I don't think I want Patrick, hanging around with someone who carries a knife with them. Heaven forbid!" Sentence was passed.

Jay Mac walked away exiled and disconsolate, with the door of his best friend's house firmly shut behind him. A few moments later, he was surprised to find Blue and Glynn, sitting on the concrete windowsill, which spanned the large bay window, of the library. They were chatting to a number of other peripheral members, of their team and some younger females, eager to become camp followers themselves. Jay Mac was not in the mood for any small talk or pleasantries with these others. He wanted to speak to Blue and Glynn alone without the possibility of indiscrete listeners, overhearing what he had to say.

"Been let out by the bizzies, 'ave yer Jay Mac?" said one of the anonymous girls, barely out of puberty.

"Excuse me, do I know you?" Jay Mac asked politely.

"No, I don't think so, my name is …"

Before the girl could continue, Jay Mac snapped, "Then shut the fuck up!" He turned his back on the stunned, silenced female and faced Blue and Glynn scowling.

Blue then spoke, "When the pigs had yer, they let that security man give yer a dig, didn't they?" He had apparently stopped running due to exhaustion and, concealed in a doorway part way along Brunswick Street, watched Jay Mac's arrest.

"Yeah, they did why?" answered Jay Mac, wondering in which direction, this line of questioning was proceeding.

"Yer didn't grass us up, did yer?" Blue asked, looking up at Jay Mac.

The pent up rage from his treatment by the police and his guardians, exploded. In a flash, Blue's Suedehead style hair was grasped by Jay Mac's right hand and the podgy head that it was attached to was violently banged against the large plate-glass window. The four-inch blade of the slim knife, deftly unsheathed by Jay Mac's left hand whilst still in his pocket, a movement he had long practiced, was now levelled across Blue's flabby neck.

"Do you want your fuckin' fat head to stay connected to your fat cunt body?" he asked, seething with black anger. He momentarily glanced to his right, where Glynn was sitting with his hands in his Crombie pockets.

"Don't even think, about gettin' that fuckin' Stanley out Glynn," Jay Mac warned.

Nobody moved as he lightly nicked Blue's neck with the razor-edged blade and then released him. Jay Mac stepped back and stood facing Blue, the blade still in his hand. He was waiting to see if his team-mate, wanted to pursue the matter further. Blue looked down at the floor and covered his injured throat with his right hand. Glynn almost choked as he accidentally inhaled some smoke from his cigarette.

"Don't ever call me a grass, ever." Jay Mac said coldly, backing away from the youths, still watching them all closely.

"Fuck it!" he exclaimed, turning and walking towards the nearby main arterial road of the estate.

"You mad cunt!" shouted one of the other male players.

"Yeah, I fuckin' hate you anyway, wait till I tell my brother!" screamed the girl, with too much to say.

Jay Mac ignored them; Blue and Glynn remained silent.

While the fuming Jay Mac walked along the central road that connected most parts of the inner estate, he was suddenly surprised by the sound of a scooter's air-horns, being blasted loudly behind him.

"Alright Jay Mac, want a ride?"

The youth turned to see Tony (G), riding towards him on his Lambretta scooter. "Too right mate." Jay Mac replied and quickly jumped on the back of the ultra-cool machine.

Tony was dressed like Jay Mac with jeans and boots but was wearing his black well-cut Crombie and his distinctive stars and stripes white-peaked 'Centurion' helmet.

"There's a spare lid on the back!" he shouted to Jay Mac, gesturing toward a similar, though plain white, black-peaked item of headwear. Jay Mac clipped on the plastic cupped chinstrap and they took off at speed.

"Just finished sortin' her out and given her a good polish." Tony (G) announced proudly.

"Are you talkin' about yer scooter or yer bird?" Jay Mac replied, as they sped along the main road.

Tony (G) liked Jay Mac. Even though he had been lapsing in and out of consciousness, he knew it was Jay Mac who had pulled him out of the smoking wreck of the previous November's car crash and, had stayed by them all until the ambulance arrived. Now, fully recovered from his injuries, he felt he was in Jay Mac's debt, even though they never discussed the fateful incident.

No stranger to motorbikes and scooters, Jay Mac was in his element, as he proudly rode pillion, on this superb machine, with his friend the driver, fully looking the part. Charlie Lowe, the husband of his cousin Margaret a.k.a 'infant phenomenon', was a tinkerer with all things two-wheeled. Many times during Jay Mac's dark 'childhood,' his favourite lighter moments had been those spent, riding on the back of Charlie's old BSA, or

Triumph, or as a passenger in the side-car of his Sunbeam scooter, accompanied by Charlie's crazy red and white English Bullterrier, 'Champ.'

'Cars are great but this beats everything', Jay Mac thought, while the bitter wind mixed with the smell of two-stroke petrol assaulted his senses as the Skins raced along through the now darkening afternoon. Passing the row of shuttered, dilapidated shops at the bottom of the estate, exact replicas of their counterparts in the centre, except for the absence of a library, Jay Mac spotted Yad and his Heron crew, sitting on the low wall outside the closed chip shop.

He tapped on Tony (G)'s helmet and shouted "Let's buzz these fuckers!"

Expertly, Tony (G) bumped the speeding scooter up onto the pavement and shot towards the assembled youths. Those who were standing, quickly leapt to one side, or jumped over the wall, as twin air-horns blasted out a triumphal warning. Yad, who had fallen backwards over the brick barrier, losing his cigarette in the process, leapt to his feet gesticulating and swearing loudly as the scooter-borne rider and passenger dismounted the pavement and shot away, back onto the main road.

"Who the fuck was that with Tony (G)?" he shouted, recognising the distinctive bike but not the partially incognito Jay Mac.

After riding around the estate for a while, Tony offered to take Jay Mac back to his aunt and uncle's home. He gratefully accepted, 'this was travelling in style, compared to using the grotty bus', he thought. A short time later when they entered the Kings Estate it was fully dark and it began to snow once again. The sole headlight and the additional spotlights cast their brilliant beams through the swirling white storm that quickly blew up. They turned the corner of the junction leading into the road where Jay Mac lived above the shops, which were laid out in virtually the same order as those on the Crown Estate.

Danny (H) and some of his team were busy vandalising the small Methodist Church that was situated on the opposite side of the road to Jay Mac's guardians' flat. The remaining windows of the building were boarded and the doors covered in sheet steel, though surprisingly the plain rendered walls of the structure still had available spaces for the painting of names and slogans. Danny (H)'s accomplices had lit a fire outside the church entrance and were adding to its roaring flames by the minute. Their leader was creating one of his masterpieces of graffiti, this time without a spray can but armed with a large stolen brush and tin of red paint. They all turned and looked as the scooter roared into the deserted road.

Tony (G) saw them at the same instant as Jay Mac and instead of slowing down to stop, increased his speed driving off up the rise towards the brow About a hundred yards further on he stopped and Jay Mac jumped off, returned the spare Centurion helmet, then thanked his friend. The scooter driver turned his vehicle around in the road and sped back down past the Anvil crew, still diligently engaged in their vandalism. As Tony (G) slowed once again at the junction, Danny (H)'s eyes fixed on the scooter's near-side panel, underneath the existing golden legend 'Outcrowd', Tony (G) had recently added 'Crown Skins.'

"Brick him, brick that cunt!" Danny (H) screamed and his crew threw anything that came to hand, at scooter and rider. Their aim was poor; Tony had already turned the corner and was increasing his speed when the first missiles passed by him, or fell short onto the frozen pavement. Jay Mac, having sprinted through the back streets behind the main road housing, had already climbed up onto the ledge of the communal backyard, behind his residence and heard the defiant blast from the twin air horns of Tony's scooter as he rode out of the estate. After a quick vault over the rusty iron railings, he ran towards the brightly lit kitchen, of his aunt and uncle's flat and banged on the window.

"I've forgotten me keys, can yer let me in?" he shouted to his uncle, who was ironing his Postman's uniform, in preparation for the next day.

After several agonising minutes, his uncle came round and unlocked the backdoor to their block. He did not speak to Jay Mac but just muttered "stupid child," then locked and re-bolted the reinforced door.

Jay Mac thanked his uncle and, once inside the warm kitchen, swiftly ate a large slice of steak and kidney pie, with potatoes and garden peas that had been left for him on a plate in the oven. He took his mug of stewed tea into the living room, where his aunt was sitting as usual, silently smoking a cigarette and reading a lurid murder mystery. *Songs of Praise* was playing on the small black and white television in the corner to the largely indifferent audience of Patch the dog.

Jay Mac parted the closed curtains slightly and looked curiously, to see what Danny (H) had been working on, with his brush and paint. To his horror he saw the words "CROWN ESTATE TWAT WILL DIE" in two foot high, bright red letters. He closed the curtains, sat down and tried to gather his thoughts, in preparation for tomorrow's dreaded court appearance.

Monday 31st January 1972

The narrow, cold, dank corridor, with its whitewashed walls, was almost filled to capacity; Jay Mac sat on a long wooden bench, with his fellow potential prisoners. It was almost midday, according to the old brown, wooden-framed clock, with its age spotted cream face and tired black hands that was fixed to the wall opposite the youth. While he watched their agonisingly slow journey to each new point, set around the clock's circumference, marked by large Roman numerals, he wondered when those hands would summon him to appear before the magistrates, seated on their own bench in the forbidding Victorian chamber above.

Jay Mac had presented himself at ten o'clock sharp as required, to the officer stationed at the front desk. He was promptly led down to the cells below the court and re-arrested. Following this, he was photographed, both in frontal and profile position, had his fingerprints taken, asked to confirm the presence of any identifiable birth defects, marks, scars or tattoos and, told what the charges against him would be. That sequence of required procedure, took approximately thirty minutes in total. Jay Mac, who was positioned midway along the well-worn seating amid a varied assortment of males, some of whom were handcuffed, was experiencing the paradoxical dilemma of wanting the proceedings over and done, whilst wishing it would never be his turn.

"John Mack, gerrup, move to the steps, quickly." the nearest warder shouted. Jay Mac's stomach began to churn and he felt dizzy as he ascended the ancient steps, which led him up from the subterranean holding area and into the dock. He suddenly became tunnel-visioned and felt unable to look about him; instead he focused his gaze upon the three elderly male magistrates, positioned directly in front of him, seated behind a tall, highly-polished mahogany desk. Despite previous verbal assurances from his recent acquaintance Jordo and, his friend Tony (G), the austere imposing physical actuality of his situation, now induced a deep sense of foreboding.

The charge was read by the Clerk to the Court. "Attempted taking away of a motorcycle without the owner's express consent."

The three magistrates had been studying Jay Mac, while he stood in the dock facing them. Dressed in his blue-green two-tone suit, with white shirt and slim black tie, borrowed from his uncle and, wearing his brushed-clean, dark Crombie, except for his red Airwair polished to a glass-like finish, which were fortunately not visible to the magistrates, he looked like a respectable, young, trainee stockbroker or articled clerk. He had Brylcreemed and side-parted, his Suedehead length dark hair for added effect.

The central figure of the three grey, sombre-looking males spoke, whilst adjusting his gold, half-rimmed pince-nez, spectacles, perched almost on the tip of his crow-like beak of a nose.

"Why is it, that *your* type, feel that they are entitled to steal the legal property of gainfully employed, respectable citizens?"

Jay Mac attempted to respond. "I don't think that I…" he started but was abruptly stopped.

"Be quiet! You have not been asked to speak." snapped the pince-nez wearer.

"We have the arresting officer's statement and that of his colleague, in addition the vehicle owner, by whom you were formally identified, has confirmed that the principal architect of this disgraceful incident was indeed you. Do you have anything to say, before we consider an appropriate sentence?"

'That's it', thought Jay Mac, 'nothing more, just like that, I'm guilty and sentence is about to be passed'.

He summoned his wits about him and made a concerted effort to speak in his own defence.

"Thank you for allowing me, the opportunity to respond sir. I think there has clearly been some misunderstanding. As I explained to the arresting officer and his colleague, during my interview, I was merely an onlooker, while three other boys that I did not know, attempted to start the motorcycle."

The central magistrate, having conferred with his colleagues on either side, raised his hand to signal to Jay Mac that he had heard enough.

"Typically you *people* always lie when confronted with the awkward truth and seek to place the blame on their supposed friends, for their own crimes. I would advise you now, not to make any further negative assertions, with regard to the veracity of these long-serving officers' statements."

Jay Mac sensing the magistrate was drawing to a close and about to pass sentence, blurted out...

"I'm sorry sir, but I'm afraid that I must insist that there has been a misrepresentation of the facts and, that I was *not* the perpetrator but in fact, an innocent bystander."

The judicial trio looked aghast and were momentarily rendered speechless.

"That's it Jay Mac, you tell 'em lad!" shouted a voice from the public gallery, followed immediately by another. "The bizzies always lie!"

Jay Mac recognised the distinctive accent of Irish and turned to see to his horror, his three companions in the tier above.

"Quiet! If I hear one more such outburst, from the public gallery, I will have it cleared!" shouted the outraged pince-nez wearer then he turned his attention towards Jay Mac.

"I have never heard such an outrageous, scurrilous attempt by a blatantly guilty party, to extricate themselves from a predicament which was a direct result of their own felonious nature. Society must be protected from your sort and, it is my duty to impose a custodial sentence."

Jay Mac grasped the brass bars, surrounding the top of the dock, in order to steady himself. He was unable to comprehend the enormity of what had just been said, then he heard a familiar voice cry out...

"Please sir, may I approach the bench?" It was his uncle, who had also made his way to the court and was present in the public gallery.

The magistrates looked at each other and then at Jay Mac's uncle in his immaculate dark blue with red piping, postman's uniform. For a brief moment they made no response and then, for whatever reason, they summoned the old soldier forward. The youth's guardian produced certain documents and, what appeared to be a hand-written statement. He also spoke earnestly and imploringly, to the aged custodians of the law. Some unspoken acknowledgement passed between the three sons of privilege from the officer-class and the once impoverished child and, former rank and file artillery gunner.

"Based on this gentleman's testimony and representations, I am on this occasion, prepared to be lenient. A custodial sentence of thirty days will lie on record and be suspended for twelve months. However, should you appear before this court, or any other, within that period, this present sentence will be added to any subsequent sentence. Is that clear?" asked the leading magistrate.

"Yes sir it is, thank you very much." Jay Mac replied with considerable relief and, was immediately taken back down the stairs, to be formally released.

Minutes later he found his uncle at the front of the building and walked towards him to offer his sincere thanks. Jay Mac extended his right hand and spoke.

"I don't know how to thank you but…"

His uncle ignored the outstretched hand and looked Jay Mac directly in the eyes then spoke…

"That's you and me finished." He turned and marched away back to his place of employment, without a backward glance.

"Alright Jay Mac, fuckin' nice one!" shouted Irish who was then joined by Blue and Glynn, both of whom then offered their congratulations also. Blue was apparently unconcerned by his neck wound, which now bore a small flesh-coloured plaster.

"You really showed them fuckers." he said obsequiously.

Jay Mac asked them how they knew he was due in court at that time. Irish advised that Tony (G) had called to see him on his return to the Crown Estate and urged him to attend in support of his friend. The four reunited companions walked along Dale Street in the direction of Jay Mac's employment, a shipping office at the bottom of Water Street, where he held the lofty position of office junior. He had to return to work by one o'clock, or lose a whole day's pay.

Irish then spoke. "Hey, seeing as we're already in town, let's go on the rob in the shops. Y'know how well that knock-off Brut sells in the Eagle."

Jay Mac stopped and looked aghast at his long standing friend.

"Are you fuckin' mental? I've just walked free from that shit-hole and, you want to go theivin'. Fuck me, you *are* cracked."

With that he walked away briskly and left his team mates to their own devices. Confused and angry, at that moment he was determined to change his ways, however, the ineluctable path that nature and nurture had set him upon would not prove easy to leave.

Chapter 4

Ball of Confusion

Friday 25th to Sunday 27th February 1972

The heavy rain had finally stopped, when Jay Mac, Irish, Blue and Glynn arrived at their destination Our Lady's Youth Club. Once they had passed through the small gateway between the neatly painted wooden fencing, they crouched down to avoid being seen by any of the occupants in the small, prefabricated, single-storey building situated in the centre of the immaculate manicured lawns. Carefully peering through the condensation-covered window, they spotted their prey.

"That's 'im, the cunt." said Blue, "Look at 'im, trying to steal my bird".

He was referring to a seventeen year old youth, with a mop of black hair that looked like it had been dropped onto his head from a great height. With an angelic face and cherubic mouth, he looked more like a young novitiate, than a potential girlfriend seducer, as he innocently played table-tennis with a pretty, dark-haired girl in a plain knee-length skirt and sensible shoes.

"Are yer fuckin' sure this is the right lad?" asked Irish, surprised and a little disappointed, at their fairly ordinary-looking intended victim.

"Never mind 'im, are yer sure this bird's worth the effort? She's not exactly a stunner." Jay Mac asked, echoing Irish's surprise.

Blue was not happy with any criticism directed towards the object of his desire, "She's just dressed like that tonight, because of the fuckin' penguins, y'know what they're like." he said angrily.

The 'penguins' that he was referring to were the nuns who ran the youth club, attached to the local Catholic girls' secondary school. Ferocious when roused, they could prove more dangerous than any number of strutting young males. Sister Gertrude, was the Head nun who ran the school and the club with a rod of iron and thought the only really safe sex for any couple, was for each of them to sleep in separate countries. She constantly gave the girls one piece of contraceptive advice 'Always keep your legs firmly closed.'

"I've been wantin' to shag Quirky's sister, for months and I know she's up for it, the way she looks at me when I'm collectin' the milk money." said Blue

Julie Quirk was the younger sister, of one of their senior team players, Georgie Quirk, known as 'Quirky.' Jay Mac thought Blue was making a bad mistake, even fantasising about this particular girl. Quirky was yet another slightly unhinged character and would not take kindly to any advances towards his sister, made by a fellow team member.

"What are you boys doing there?" shouted an irate nun, on discovering the four youths peering in to the side window.

"We were thinkin' of joinin' Sister and we wanted to see what was on offer." said Jay Mac quickly.

The Sister looked at the four boys in their dark Crombies, jeans and heavy boots.

"I don't think that you would like it in *this* club. It's not your sort of place." she observed.

Irish wasn't happy with this response and immediately adopted his usual truculent stance.

"How would you know what's *our* sort of place? What do *you* know, other than prayin' and lookin' down yer noses at people?"

The Sister had had enough "Get off this property now, before I call the polis!" she shouted.

"Thanks, that's *really* Christian; then again, I wouldn't expect anything else from one of your sort." Irish was now in full flow.

Although he and Jay Mac were both baptised Catholics, Irish had developed an intense hatred for his religion and any of its representatives. Jay Mac, once devout as a child, had become entirely indifferent and no longer attended Mass or received Holy Communion. However, he could not tolerate rudeness to a nun.

"Alright Irish, leave it, the Sister has asked us to go, let's gerroff." he said, trying to ameliorate the situation.

They were about to leave, when the nun spoke again.

"Do you have a sister in this school?" She had noticed, Irish's distinctive accent and recognised his striking resemblance, to the elder of his two sisters, Dymphna.

"Why? What the fuck has it got to do with you, if I have a sister in your school or not?" he shouted back at the shocked nun, stood in the doorway of the youth club dressed in her black habit and white wimple.

"Get out! You creature of the Devil!" she screamed at the top of her voice.

Some of the youths inside rushed to her aid, including the unlikely seducer and his potential victim. They began shouting that the Skins should 'leave the poor sister alone.'

The four youths, retreated to the nearby flats to avoid any further embarrassment. Strong, icy winds now blew, clearing the heavy rainclouds and revealing a large, radiant full moon.

Half an hour passed and then suddenly, just before nine o'clock, the lights went out across the whole estate. It was a power-cut, one of several that had occurred recently, as the intransigent unions and the obdurate government, continued to fail to resolve their differences. Watching from the entrance area of the darkened tower blocks, the four companions observed the youth club occupants file out into the road.

"There he is, come on!" shouted Blue, seeing the young male in the middle of a group, making their way to a bus stop farther along the road. The four youths darted across towards the group and positioned themselves in front and on either side.

"Hey you fuck face, I want you!" Blue shouted, pointing directly at the angelic faced youth.

Although there were nine members of the youth club party, including three girls, one of whom was the object of Blue's affection, they stopped as ordered and stood in nervous anticipation, of what was about to happen.

"My name's Kenny, I don't know what you think I've done but I don't want any trouble." he replied bravely.

"I'll hold y'coat." said Glynn, while Blue carefully removed his Crombie and called his unwilling adversary out.

"C'mon cunt, me and you now." he said, gesticulating with his left hand and all the while keeping his right behind his back.

Earlier that evening, when Jay Mac had called for Blue, they had planned the way the fight would go.

"Keep the belt in your Crombie pocket, then just before yer start, take yer coat off, get the belt and wrap it round yer hand. Make sure, yer hand stays out of sight, until yer bang him." advised Jay Mac, acting as Blue's trainer and second, should the need arise.

Kenny 'the unsuspecting' stepped forward, having removed his blue-grey R.A.F greatcoat and prepared to do battle, by raising his fists Marquis of Queensbury fashion.

"The rest of yer, keep the fuck out of it, or we all jump in, right?" instructed Jay Mac, continuing his second's official duties.

"C'mon, come on," said Blue smiling.

Then, as the victim moved into range, Blue caught him with a terrific right hook to the left temple, with his fist wrapped in its metal-studded, leather binding. Kenny collapsed, like a crumpled marionette, whose strings had been cut, the side of his face pouring with blood. Blue stood over him and viciously booted him hard in the stomach, then fully in the saintly face. The youth lay on the ground moaning and bleeding in equal measure. Blue looked away triumphantly in the direction of his 'beloved'; only to be punched hard in the testicles. The angel clearly knew a few dirty tricks of his own.

As their comrade dropped to his knees the Skins watched the bloodied Kenny grapple him to the ground. He seemed to be trying to get Blue, into some sort of hold, Jay Mac thought. Blue was desperately throwing ineffectual punches to the body, whilst his adversary struggled to get a headlock on him. The youth club crowd sensed that their man was gaining the upper hand.

"Go on Kenny, use your Judo skills on him!" one of the males shouted.

"Oh shit, that's all we need." said Glynn to Jay Mac and Irish, while they looked on astonished.

Blue was struggling to breathe, now firmly clamped in a choke hold by the surprising Kenny.

"Fuck this crap" said Jay Mac looking at Irish.

Then in an instant he bent down, snatched hold of the mop of hair, above Kenny's bloodied face and produced his slender blade, which flashed in the no longer artificially polluted light of the full moon. Irish and Glynn had drawn their craft knives also, although Glynn's hand was clearly shaking.

"Any of you fuckers move and, this cunt loses an eye." said Jay Mac using one of his favourite stock threats. Everyone stood perfectly still.

"Right you, let go of 'im now, or yer won't be blimpin' any other birds... ever." he said to the prone Kenny, who was slowly squeezing the life out of his friend.

Not getting the immediate response he wanted, Jay Mac drew the razor edge of the blade across Kenny's already blood spattered forehead, leaving him with a permanent reminder of the night. Screaming in agony, he released the choking Blue.

Jay Mac helped his team mate to his feet. "Your mate had a good go back, that's it... ended. Take him and fuck off."

The youth club crowd, assisted the bloodied, formerly angelic looking Kenny to stand, and then shuffled away in their anoraks and duffle coats. The three armed Skins, never took their eyes off them.

"Look at that," said the slightly dazed Blue, rubbing his neck and taking in gulps of air.

The object of his unrequited love looked over her shoulder and smiled, as her group reached the nearby bus stop, which in this case was merely a rough-cast ten foot concrete post, with a small metal sign fixed about a foot from its top.

"She's fuckin' smilin' at me; I told yer that she wanted me." Blue announced jubilantly, though only partially correct.

"Come on" said Irish "What are we doin' standin' here? All the lights are off across the estate and, it's only early. What we need is some mindless vandalism."

With that, they ran back across the main road and into the maze of streets, looking for stones or milk bottles to throw at windows, front doors, cars and even the now resting street lights themselves.

From the general wild noises emanating from different parts of the estate, ranging from angry residents' shouts, wailing police and fire-brigade sirens and, the desperate screams of an unfortunate female being dragged into one of the stinking burned out garages, it appeared others had already had the same thought as Irish.

While they busied themselves, hurling bricks through windows and striking out the dead glass eyes on top of each lamppost, Jay Mac spoke to Blue.

"Next time yer fancy a bird; why not just try speakin' to her first? I'm not sure the direct caveman approach, of tryin' to kill yer rival, is really working for yer."

Blue the recipient of Jay Mac's wisdom replied optimistically in a hoarse voice. "Y'saw the way she looked at me Jay Mac? She was sayin', 'you're the big man, any chance of a shag?'"

"More like fuck off tit!" said Irish laughing.

They whiled away the happy hours, until finally targets, ammunition and all four youths were exhausted.

"What's the chances of gettin' me head down at yours Irish?" asked Jay Mac, half in jest.

"Yeah, why not? Tell yer what, wake our Sean up and, give him yer fuckin' knife as well.., piss off!" was his firm reply.

"You can kip at ours Jay Mac, if yer want?" said the quieter than usual Glynn.

"Good man." Jay Mac said, gratefully, pleased not to have to catch the last bus and risk the possibility of running into the Anvil crew once again.

As they passed the shops, before Irish and Blue entered the road where they both lived, Irish spoke directly to Jay Mac. "What was all that about tonight?" he asked, "That business with the knife, that's not you. You're losin' the fuckin' plot."

Jay Mac carefully listened to what was said, then replied, "Thanks for that mate. I think I've just got too much shit goin' on in me head, anyway, take it easy, see yer."

With that he strolled away along the main road, accompanying Glynn towards his house.

Ever since his arrest and police interrogation, Jay Mac's mind had been troubled by dark thoughts and anxiety. An oppressive foreboding now seemed to overshadow his every waking moment.

When they arrived a few minutes later, the two youths noticed a dark blue K registration, Ford Escort, parked outside Glynn's small terrace residence.

"Looks like one of your 'uncles' has called round, Glynn. He must have a few bob, that's a nice new car. Keep yer fingers crossed, yer could be well in here, dependin' on yer mum's generosity." Jay Mac said, cruelly.

"Fuck off! Do you wanna stay over or what?" Glynn snapped angrily.

They entered the small hall, then opened the living room door. Mrs Glynn, positioned on the three-seater couch, sprang up quickly and hurriedly fastened the buttons on her white see-through blouse.

"I didn't hear you come in dear." she said apologetically, whilst fixing the hem of her skirt, which was considerably higher than its intended knee length, revealing fully the dark tops of her black stockings. Seated next to her, in the boudoir-like glow of several candles, was a large male with dyed black hair, previously combed over from one ear to the other but now in disarray. He was seated side-on to the boys and did not look at them.

"I didn't know that you had fuckin' kids," he said, clearly annoyed at some perceived deception.

"I don't.., I mean... only the one is mine." Mrs Glynn said reassuringly, to the fitted floral shirt and matching kipper-tie wearer.

Jay Mac could see that he was sweating profusely, as he studied the large expensive, gold medallion, hanging on its heavy chain, ensnared in a forest of grey chest hair, revealed by the open-necked collar and the lurid tie, hanging at half-mast.

'That's a bad choice of shirt', Jay Mac thought, 'with that size of paunch'.

"Jay Mac's stayin' over, alright." Glynn stated, growing increasingly embarrassed in front of his friend.

"Yes, of course dear, now go straight to bed." the accommodating Mrs Glynn replied.

"We're havin' some toast first." Glynn shouted brusquely as he and Jay Mac walked into the kitchen.

Fortunately the oven and grill were gas powered. The boys sat in the kitchen and ate copious amounts of toast, by the blue light of the gas flames, which Glynn had deliberately turned up fully as some form of defiant gesture. An uncomfortable almost oppressive silence hung in the air, only interrupted by the odd giggle, or coarse laugh from the adjoining room.

"We're going up," announced Glynn, in the general direction of his otherwise occupied mother.

"Me too, hopefully," said the sweaty medallion man, without a thought for the son's feelings.

Glynn's room was well decorated, with quality wallpaper and fittings, though largely obscured by a variety of posters, including the obligatory twin classics of Brigit Bardot stretched out suggestively on a motorcycle and Raquel Welch, in her *One Million Years BC* risqué fur bikini. Whereas Jay Mac cramped his five foot ten frame onto a small couch most nights, or experienced the exquisite luxury of an old folding camp bed, with several missing springs, Glynn had been granted the extravagance of a solid wood bunk bed. Depending on his mood, he could choose to sleep in the top or bottom tier. To Jay Mac this was opulence of the first order.

"Got any new wank mags, Glynn?" Jay Mac asked hopefully, having exhausted his friend's existing collection on previous stays.

"No I haven't and there's no fuckin' light to read them by anyway." Glynn retorted.

"I don't wanna *read* them, prick, anyway it'll save me from going blind, I suppose. Hey, d'you think they have fuckin' Braille porno books for those poor sods?"

Glynn refused to dignify Jay Mac's question with an answer and soon drifted into a sound sleep.

Unlike his team mate, Jay Mac could not get his brain to relax and lay on his back playing over recent images, in his private mental cinema. Mrs Glynn had been twenty one years old when Glynn was born and, as his friend was not yet seventeen, Jay Mac calculated that she could not be more than thirty seven or thirty eight. Although this was virtually ancient to his just-seventeen years of age perception, he could not help thinking about the way she had looked that night, in the flattering light of the numerous candles. He began to have a growing desire to see her again and in more detail. Visions of her ample, rounded breasts and deep cleavage, barely concealed by her awkwardly fastened, transparent blouse and her nylon-clad legs, kept tormenting his mind, playing over and over again.

He had not heard the sound of anyone on the stairs, or of a car leaving and he concluded that the ill-matched couple must be doing the deed at that very moment on the straining sofa in the living room. While Glynn snored contentedly, Jay Mac unable to find relief from his torment, decided to investigate. Wearing a white short-sleeved T-shirt over his straining Y-fronts, he stealthily crept down the stairs and silently opened the door, to the small, previously candle-lit chamber. He peered through the opening and was instantly rewarded with the disturbing sight of a large, sweaty, hairy arse rising and falling erratically, like a steam-hammer that had been set to a random sequence of strokes. The curtains had been partially opened and the room was now bathed in a pale moonlight, replacing that of the extinguished candles.

Jay Mac lost all sense of caution and stepped into the stuffy room. His gaze fell upon Mrs Glynn's legs which were wrapped around the waist of her heaving lover. She still retained one black, patent leather stiletto shoe; the other had been lost in the heat of the moment, as had her discarded blouse. Her rounded breasts had been released from their retainer and, were receiving the full attention of the 'medallion man'. While Jay Mac looked at Mrs Glynn's glistening face, with her smudged red lipsticked mouth, heavy dark eye shadow and mascara, he began to see her as an attractive older woman and no longer his friend's mother. Her half-closed eyes suddenly opened fully and her gaze fixed on Jay Mac, travelling rapidly down his firm, lithe body to his growing erection. She let out a loud sigh. Her tiring lover was spurred on, by this apparent acknowledgement of his prowess.

"I told you I was good on the job." he grunted. "You're fuckin' lovin' it aren't yer?" Sensing his ecstatic partner, was approaching climax, he increased his pace to ramming speed.

Mrs Glynn kept her gaze fixed upon the youth who was now feverishly masturbating himself.

"Oh God, please, oh please!" she shouted, erupting in a wild orgasm and physically shaking her already spent lover.

"No need to thank me darlin', just doing what I do best." he mumbled arrogantly and a little surprised at the results of his efforts.

The agonised youth came at about the same instant as the grateful older woman and he exited the room as silently as he had entered. Much relieved he returned to his sleeping friend's room and soon was snoring loudly himself.

Sunday 27th February 1972

It was a typically boring, grey Sunday afternoon, and the team were sitting on the concrete sill of the library, discussing recent events. Jay Mac, Irish, Blue and Glynn had been joined by three more of their usual crew; Brian 'Brain' Dent, an apprentice panel beater; Joey 'Tank' Turner unemployed and, Stevie 'Johno' Johnson, a farm labourer. Standing not far from the seven youths, who looked in part like a motley metamorphic group of undertakers above the knee, in their dark Crombies and, factory workers in their blue jeans and industrial boots below, were four young girls, who were practicing a favourite dance routine, desperately trying to catch the attention of the team. One of the dancers was the girl who had 'too much to say'.

Apart from the non-smoking Jay Mac and Blue, the latter of whom indulged sometimes similar to Glynn for effect, the other Skins were all rapidly, disposing of a twenty-pack of John Player Special filter tips 'lifted' earlier from the local newsagent's shop, whilst the owner's attention was distracted. When each youth had almost finished his cigarette, they either flicked the glowing butt at the young chorus line, or offered to barter them in exchange for sexual favours.

There had been little activity on the Lancashire Road 'battle zone' recently and, therefore, the team had spent the previous Saturday evening drinking in the Eagle, until their funds were entirely depleted. Jay Mac had decided not to stay at Glynn's that night, after his Friday night's experience and thought it best to let some time elapse, before he did so again.

"Look, 'ere she is now," said Blue, excitedly. "That's some leg," he continued.

All seven boys looked in the direction of Blue's lustful gaze. Two females were approaching the dark blue van parked off the main road in the street facing the library, which served as a mobile shop for out-of-hours purchases of a wide range of essentials, at exorbitant prices. The girls wore short bomber jackets with elasticated waists and cuffs and almost indecently short, checked miniskirts over dark tights with a leaf motif up the outside of each leg and Cuban heeled, moccasin style shoes. They both had shoulder length dark hair surrounding quite pretty faces, masked by heavy makeup.

"Who the fuck are you talkin' about?" asked Jay Mac, curiously.

"Julie Quirk, who d'yer think?"

Jay Mac looked more closely and realised that one of the females, now out of her prim and proper disguise, was in fact Blue's intended paramour. A chorus of whistles and shouts greeted the girls' simple act of walking up the four wooden steps to the open entrance at the rear of the van, revealing their choice of underwear to the assembled, appreciative crowd. The four young dancers ended their impromptu routine, acknowledging defeat at the hands, or rather legs and bottoms, of their elders.

"Come on Jay Mac, you do the talkin'." Blue requested.

"Fuck off Blue, take Glynn, he's the bird bandit." replied a tired Jay Mac, mindful that Julie Quirk's deranged older male sibling, Quirky, lived not far from where they were presently seated.

After more impassioned pleas, from his team mate, Jay Mac acquiesced and strolled over to the static vehicle with Blue. The girls who were merely wanting to be served, where stood in front of the small wooden counter in this cramped one-bulb lit emporium. Phil 'the Robber' as he was less than affectionately known was subjecting the disinterested females, to his usual well-rehearsed seduction patter.

"So my lovelies, is there anything else I can offer you? Don't be shy ladies, if you've seen something that tickles yer fancy, I'm yer man."

The girls looked at each other slyly then Julie said, "If those lollipops are goin' free, we wouldn't mind one each."

Instantly two large, transparent red lollipops were thrust into their waiting hands.

"Provided yer eat them here, they're free of charge." the 'robber' said, already forming small beads of perspiration, on his brow.

"Why not?" said Julie's equally coquettish accomplice.

At this moment, the two Skins sprang onto the top step.

"Any chance of us squeezin' in there and gettin' a bit of service?" asked Jay Mac both cheekily and pragmatically, conscious of the limited customer space within.

"Can't yer see that I'm busy?" said the disappointed 'robber', one hand out of sight under the counter, adjusting the small change in his trouser pocket.

"We're goin' anyway" said Julie, taking a long, lingering lick of her red lollipop.

"That'll be fifteen pence for the ciggies." the frustrated 'robber' reminded the girls.

"I'll pay for them for yer, Julie." Blue offered, generously.

Once he had handed the shop keeper the required amount, the smiling Julie spoke.

"Thanks for that lad, I'll tell me Mam yer paid for her fags, she'll be made up." Then, as she squeezed passed the waiting boys on the stairs with her friend behind her, she looked directly at Jay Mac.

"Nice to see *you* again Jay Mac."

With that the girls departed, leaving a lingering aroma of their cheap perfume, as a reminder of their presence and a memento of what might have been, for the deflated shopkeeper and confused Skins.

"What did yers want anyway lads?" asked the 'robber', ever mindful of his profits.

"Fuck all, I've changed me mind," said the crest fallen Blue.

"What the fuck just happened?" Blue asked as they returned to their seated crew.

"I don't know Blue, do I?" said the equally surprised Jay Mac.

"Are either of you two, goin' to knob Quirky's sister?" the direct talking Tank asked.

"You dirty bastards!" shouted the young girl who always had too much to say, who having moved closer to the team, was listening to their conversation with particular interest.

"Not you again." Jay Mac said recognising the eaves dropper. "Listen little girl, I don't know yer name and I don't wanna know it. It's nearly five o'clock and it's gettin' dark, so as it's way past your bedtime and yer mum's probably got the bizzies out lookin' for yer, fuck off home now."

The young girl didn't reply but glowered at Jay Mac, then smiled knowingly, as she turned and departed with her fellow hoofers.

"Are we goin' to see this film or not?" Irish asked, directing his question to his three usual companions.

"I'm not in the mood anymore." said Blue quietly.

"I've got no cash." answered Glynn, lying, having received a whole pound note from his most recent 'uncle' before he departed, satisfied and proud of his previous night's work.

"Yeah, I'm up for it, if we can scrape enough together, for a pint and a pie later," replied Jay Mac who never had any desire to go home, before the night was ended.

Irish advised that he had 'borrowed' some money earlier from his older brother Dermot's wallet and, confirmed that they should have sufficient funds. Further conversation was abruptly cut short, by the unwelcome arrival of Yad with some of his 'Juniors' in tow. The latter were prospective members of the Heron crew but as they were not yet sixteen, could only have auxiliary status conferred upon them. As such they had to perform any task given to them by Yad or his two other commanding counterparts. Appearing with him this evening was 'Peza', 'Nat' and 'Tomo,' poorly dressed, scruffy excuses for would-be team members.

"We had a fuckin' good night on Friday, didn't we boys?" announced Yad halting any other talk.

"Yeah, fuckin' ace," answered the dirty-faced, tattered denim jacket and 'monkey boot' wearing Nat.

"My cock's still sore," laughed the equally dishevelled Peza through his alternately missing yellow-toothed mouth.

"Mine too," said Tomo always the last to respond, as he stood there in his greasy, stained, maroon bomber jacket, drawing the right sleeve of the already shiny garment across his bubbly, green snotty nose."

"Been wankin' each other off again, 'ave yer?" asked Johno, the tall, fair-haired and immensely strong farm labouring Skin.

Yad did not respond directly to this slur, he felt Johno was just crazy enough to forget about his older brother and, he did not fancy being on the receiving end of one of his legendary punches, or trapped in his trade mark unbreakable headlock.

Instead he turned his attention to Jay Mac, "Alright Jay Mac, mate. I heard you was dead, yeah, bummed to death in Cheapside, and *you* fuckin' loved it."

Jay Mac looked directly at Yad and then replied, "No, yer heard wrong. Funny enough, two really old queers in there mentioned you by name, thee said to thank yer for suckin' them both off in the bogs in Lime Street Station."

Everyone laughed even Yad's three apprentices. The outraged Heron leader's right boot slammed swiftly with a dull thud, into Jay Mac's stomach but his Crombie and denim jacket underneath absorbed most of the impact. Before he could withdraw his leg, Jay Mac quickly grabbed Yad's ankle in both hands and stood up.

"Shall we have a little dance Yad?" Jay Mac asked, pulling his enemy around in a circle, making him hop in an undignified manner for one of such status. "D'you wanna sit on yer arse for a bit, instead of just talkin' through it?" Jay Mac asked his second question then quickly booted the ankle of Yad's supporting leg to one side, making him fall solidly onto the chewing-gum patterned pavement. "I don't wanna drag yer round this fuckin' shitty ground Yad, so if yer promise to be good, I'll let yer go, what d'yer say?"

For a few tense moments, Yad sat in this ungainly position, with Jay Mac firmly holding his ankle. He looked at Jay Mac and then at his six companions, who were all staring at him intently. Yad knew that in reality he was not a popular leader, whereas the charismatic Jay Mac was well liked by most of the team. "Yeah, c'mon, we're all mates here aren't we? I was only jokin' with yer." Yad replied, appreciating that he was not on his home ground in front of the Heron pub and, knowing his three stooges would be useless against this seven-strong crew.

Jay Mac released Yad, who stood up, brushed the dirt off his Crombie with his hands and without warning pulled out from his coat's right-hand side pocket, his own particular weapon of choice, a double-edged Royal Marine Commando knife. He pointed it at Jay Mac and his friends as if it were a loaded gun. "You're fucked you shit! Your time's runnin' out, and I'm gonna bring it to an end! Watch yerself boy, if yer go anywhere near the Heron patch, it's over."

With that and a quick command to his minions he walked away, making sure not to take his eyes off any of the seven.

"Like Irish said, are we goin' to town, to see this fuckin' film or what? I could do with a bit of light relief" asked an alleviated but shaken Jay Mac.

There was some half-hearted laughter as the two youths stood up to cross the road and catch the approaching bus.

"*Midnight Cowboy* is re-showin' on the Odeon, if anyone fancies it!" Jay Mac shouted a final invitation over his shoulder, as they strolled across to the stop.

No one replied, they all knew Yad was deadly serious and that Jay Mac was now a marked man.

"Not enough shagging, for an 'X' Certificate," said Irish, critically, whilst successfully blowing a perfect smoke ring after several failed attempts. He then took another drink of his glass of Guinness and, waited for Jay Mac's response to his assessment of the film they had just seen.

"I don't think that was the director's main concern, Irish. He was dealin' with certain themes and takin' us on a journey.

Fantastic performance from Hoffmann and Voight, don't yer think? It's definitely goin' in my top ten of films."

Jay Mac's reply amused Irish, who knew that his friend was almost as passionate about film as he was about Americana.

"Go on then, where does this one rank with fuckin' *El Cid* and *Ben Hur*, or *Zulu*?" he asked, waiting for the usual list to be enumerated by Jay Mac.

"I'm not sure yet, I'll have to adjust the rankings now but, as *The Graduate* is already in there, Hoffmann is definitely chasin' the 'masters'." Jay Mac was referring to his number one favourite film, *On the Water Front* and the towering performances delivered by Marlon Brando and Karl Malden.

The Skins were comfortably ensconced at a corner table, in the bar room of the 'Mansion' having been denied access to the more plush lounge bar because of their attire. "No Work Wear Allowed" read the black and white sign, by the entrance to this cosy imbibing chamber and, this was rigidly enforced by the vigilant barman, at least on this occasion.

While they were discussing the relative merits of certain films, their classification by the British Board of Film Censors and, the performances of the actors starring in them, the youths were slowly drinking the four bottles of Guinness and eating the two packets of cheese and onion crisps they had managed to purchase. They were saving some residual funds for their minimal bus fares and the obligatory meat pies, from their favourite Pier Head dining establishment.

Jay Mac poured the last of his two bottles into his half pint glass and nodded to Irish.

"Have you clocked this character mooching around?"

He was referring to a tall, thin 'female' dressed in a long, gaudy floral print dress, wearing theatrical heavy make-up and sporting a lofty braided, black wig. The bar was only half full at most, this being a dismal, wet Sunday night and the thirsts of the drinking hordes having been slaked sufficiently, if only temporarily, on the previous two nights of wild indulgence.

After accosting a number of the other drinkers without success, the bizarre, wandering figure now arrived at the boys' table.

"Would either of you two young gentlemen like to buy a lady a drink?" the 'pantomime dame' enquired, pulling up a chair and then sitting in front of them.

"Yeah, of course" said Jay Mac, "d'yer know where I could find one?"

The 'lady' smiled next at Irish, "Just a port and lemon, thanks dear."

Jay Mac's friend looked at the sad character and spoke, "Listen Widow Twankey, or whatever you're supposed to be, we're havin' a quiet drink 'ere, so piss off."

With that rebuff, he flicked his glowing cigarette butt at the pathetic figure's improvised bust. The tragic creature lowered its purple, eye-shadowed lids, turned down the corners of its bright red lipsticked mouth and looked as if it were about to cry.

Jay Mac offered some advice, "Mate, don't take it too bad, yer just need to shave that stubble off and work on yer act a bit, ok? Now fuck off and find the other Ugly Sister."

Just at that moment the current barman went for his break and was replaced by his colleague, the flirtatious cocktail lounge server. He clearly had a good memory for faces and angrily approached the boys' table.

"You two are barred from 'ere, so gerrout now," he demanded.

Having already finished their drinks, the two Skins and the 'lady' stood up. Jay Mac quickly caught hold of one of the large, hairy hands of their would-be guest and placed it on the forearm of the barman, as he stood facing them.

"There y'are, you've copped off, *he'll* buy yer a drink, because you two sad cunts belong together." With that he and Irish pushed past the odd couple and left.

Outside the still, large pools of rainwater, that had collected on the pavement, testifying to an earlier torrential downpour, reflected the amber glow of the street lamps, as the two youths made their way along Lime Street.

"Just think, that was somebody's son once." said Jay Mac with a degree of sympathy.

"Yeah, well we both know how they get started off, don't we?" replied a perceptive Irish.

Neither of them spoke another word but in the ensuing silence, they visualised shared nightmare memories of some of the horrific torments, they had both witnessed being carried out on other helpless, terrified pupils at their former, all boys, educational establishment. The name of 'Denny', an asthmatic, vicious, sadist, who spent five years 'pretending', to rape other pupils, whilst they were being held down by his grinning, moronic associates, was top of their respective lists of apprentice torturers that they had encountered. 'Mitch' an expert in cutting the heads off live pigeons, throwing cats off the top landing of tower blocks and, as he proudly announced on one occasion, deflowering a struggling captive female, with a dirty milk bottle, was probably the nearest rival to the aforementioned 'Denny', the boys concurred. They both well understood from first-hand experience, how a once normal, innocent child, could be corrupted and perverted by the deliberate, self-gratifying cruelty of others.

While they meandered along their route to the Pier Head, they eventually arrived at 'The Fountain' the site of Jay Mac's recent arrest.

"You was unlucky." Irish gave his verdict on the unfortunate outcome of that night.

Jay Mac accepted that really there was no other reason or excuse, he had chosen the wrong escape route and that was it. He realised that sometimes in life, people chose the wrong path, or made an ill-judged decision and then paid a terrible price for their error.

A short time later they were in the queue at the 'Pigeon Pie Shop'.

"Meat pie and a mug of tea, thanks" said Jay Mac, when it was his turn to be served.

Irish was already attempting to devour a red-hot pie, of similar non-specific meat variety and taking sips from his heavily stained, once white cup of scalding dark brown tea. Although they enjoyed people watching in the States Bar, or one of its equally melancholic rivals along London Road, the Pier Head Bus and Ferry Terminus approaching midnight, was perhaps, they thought, the ultimate gathering place for the widest spectrum of disparate individuals and groups. Tonight they were not going to be disappointed.

Walking through the glass-panelled cloisters of the temporary resting place for most of the city's buses, they stepped over numerous tramps, who having forsaken all hope, or drunk too many intoxicating fluids, had slumped semi-comatose onto the damp, litter strewn floor. Some of their more animated rivals approached each passer-by and asked for either a cash donation or a tobacco offering. One particularly persistent dishevelled male, who reeked of spirits and urine, fell against the rail on which the boys were leaning, staring into the dark distance beyond, towards the Liver Buildings, whilst finishing their evening repast.

"Two pence lads, that's all" he said, trying unsuccessfully to stand up straight, desperately clutching on to the metal rail for support. Getting no initial response from the dispassionate youths, he tried again.

"Only two pence, c'mon lads. Me fuckin' wife's threw me out, gorra new fella, the fuckin' bitch. Only two pence to get a bit of food."

Irish had a small piece of rock hard crust left and some inedible gristle, Jay Mac had similar items that he had chewed but was unable to swallow. The boys placed these 'tasty' morsels into one silver, tin-foil pie case, and poured the dregs of their now tepid tea into one cup, then offered these to their new dining companion.

"Here y'are lad, have your dinner on us." said Irish.

In the absence of a monetary contribution, their guest snatched the unpalatable remnants and devoured them, then swigged the tea in one gulp.

"Two pence lads, only two fuckin' pence," he began his familiar litany once again.

Just then a woman's piercing scream was heard from outside the bus shelter, clearly coming from nearby. The boys ambled along to where the sound was emanating from and then took their place with other curious spectators, who had already secured a vantage point.

"Please somebody help us!" shouted a hysterical, attractive blonde woman in her mid-twenties. "Please help him! Help my husband, someone!"

The boys peered through the dirty glass panel, like voyeurs behind a transparent screen and were faced with a surreal tableau. The woman who was about five foot three inches tall and dressed in a dark red mini dress and waist length leather jacket, was desperately struggling with a grinning dwarf, who had one hand lodged firmly up her dress between her legs and was clinging to her right leg with the other. As she struggled to free herself from her diminutive assaulter, a few feet away her husband was valiantly engaged in a desperate boxing match, with four other similar sized individuals.

"You couldn't make this stuff up," said Jay Mac to Irish, while they stood leaning on the aluminium support rail, like two Victorian toffs watching a grotesque side show.

"This evening, for your entertainment and delight, we present the pageant of the brave knight and his lady in red, as he fights five evil dwarves to defend her honour."

Jay Mac continued in this vein, whilst other spectators enjoyed the ill-matched contest, placing bets on who would triumph. The desperate woman tried to reach her outnumbered husband but was hampered by the groping dwarf, attached limpet-style to her leg. Meanwhile the battered husband was now bleeding from numerous facial cuts, having previously slumped back against the rear engine compartment of a green Atlantean bus, after being punched with considerable force in the groin.

"Please, God, somebody help him!" the screaming woman implored but it was too late, her husband's fate was sealed.

Reduced by the groin strike, to a similar height level as his assailants, the four set about him with increased vigour. Punched, kicked and occasionally head-butted, he lost his footing and, as he slipped was dragged out of sight of the spectators, behind the back of the parked vehicle.

Even in this perilous position he managed to shout – "Someone help my wife, get that dirty little cunt off her!"

He was finally silenced by a torrent of vicious kicks and punches, whilst the distraught woman, stood weeping, apparently no longer concerned about the investigating hand of her pint-sized tormentor.

"Someone should get the police" said one of the onlookers half-heartedly, when the show reached its finale.

"Fuck it, let's gerroff" said Jay Mac.

"Those dirty little bastards are fucking nuts." replied Irish, as they strolled away from the scene and around to their own bus stop.

While sitting on the upper deck of the late bus, they recalled the events of a similar evening of the previous summer. Both boys had been approaching the Pier Head, after a night in town, when they saw a forty-something woman being punched and dragged around by her hair, by a similarly aged male. The woman was screaming for help and claiming that the man was trying to 'murder her'. Without hesitation, the boys ran to her rescue and leapt upon her attacker. However, the screaming woman then took off one of her shoes and began battering the youths with it, all the while calling for the police, with shouts of "Please somebody help us, these Skinheads are trying to rob me husband, call the police please!" The boys made-good their escape and vowed never to get involved or assist anyone ever again.

"Not a bad night Jay Mac" said Irish, trying to repeat his trick of blowing a whole ring of smoke, as they travelled through the rainy night.

"Yeah, a pantomime dame and five of the seven dwarves. I wonder what the other two little fuckers were up to?" he asked lazily.

"Probably at home, knobbin' Snow White" replied Irish with a sly smile.

Chapter 5

Instant Karma

Thursday 16th March 1972

It was a Thursday night and nearly seven thirty.

"Turn the fuckin' sound up mate." Tank shouted to the distracted barman behind the counter, in the crowded lounge of the Eagle pub.

The volume control knob was adjusted slightly as a minor concession and the opening theme tune of *Top of the Pops,* could almost be heard above the general clamour and, the sounds of the juke box in the corner nearest to the door, currently playing *'He's Gonna Step on You Again'* by John Kongos.

Thirteen of the core members of the Eagle crew including Jay Mac and his three usual companions, were seated in a large semi-circle around the lounge. Other older semi-retired players, who may now have a steady girlfriend, or wife, or both, were also present and, in addition several members of the general civilian population were dotted around the room.

The lounge was the slightly more comfortable and, marginally better decorated bar of this two-room drinking establishment, in contrast to the sparsely furnished, bare, floor-boarded and paint-peeling walled, bar itself. That room was the domain of the professional drinker; he or she had not come there for the ambience, or the convivial conversation. Drink, either spirits or beer, in large quantities served with the minimum delay or exchange of words, was what they sought and the space to unwind after a hard day, or to forget after an even harder life.

The team were in a good mood on this particular evening, as one of their top players had returned after an enforced absence.

"Cheers! Tommy lad, welcome back!" shouted a smiling Johno, acting as unofficial toastmaster.

A chorus of similar, genuinely warm greetings, echoed around the semi-circle of Skins. Tommy Southern known as

Tommy (S), the object of the spontaneous felicitations, was seated in the centre of the group, like a medieval baron amongst a company of his loyal knights. During a night out the previous summer, the then seventeen year old Tommy (S) and two other Crown crew members had been attacked by several unwise Kings Estate players outside the Cavern Club in Mathew Street. In the ensuing battle one of the Kings Team was partially blinded, losing an eye, another received a punctured lung and a third ended the night with serious head injuries. Apart from cuts and bruises, the Crown Team trio emerged virtually unscathed.

When the police arrived, however, the walking wounded survivors of the Kings Team broke with established protocol and gave up the names of their victorious rivals, without any inducement from the officers of the law. Found guilty of numerous charges, including affray; aggravated assault; unlawful wounding; battery and grievous bodily harm, the convicted Crown Team members, received varying degrees of sentence. The youngest at the time, Terry Harper, known as Terry (H) served three months in a borstal, Tommy (S), nine months of a twelve month sentence in Walton Jail and the knife wielding Skin, viewed correctly by the judge as a danger to the public, Sean Devlin known as Devo, was still in the early stages of a three year stint in Risely Jail.

Jay Mac who was sitting three places to the left of Tommy (S), with Irish, Blue and Glynn in that order on his left, thought their newly returned leader was the right man for the job. Having seen Tommy (S) in action on several occasions, he had personally witnessed his legendary fighting prowess with head, hands and feet. Weapon of choice when required, in this case was a short, heavy, steel-linked dog lead with leather handle, used either like a medieval flail or Roman gladiator's cestus. With or without this devastating implement, Tommy (S) had speed, strength, deadly accuracy and, in Jay Mac's opinion, that most vital quality for a leader of young aggressive males... heart.

After the customary exchange of insulting banter and a few cautious half-hearted jests, impugning the sexual orientation of prison warders and some of their guests, the jokers all the while ensuring there was no accidental slur on Tommy (S)'s own heterosexual preference, the leader looked about the group and spoke.

"What's with the fuckin' haircuts? I've only been away nine months and you've all gone back to originals."

He was referring to the recent Number One crops with razored trenches that nine of the group, including Jay Mac were now sporting.

"Blame that mad cunt." said Johno pointing at Terry (H), who was seated immediately on Tommy (S)'s right.

"Yeah, I just said everyone's talkin' about fuckin' Suedeheads and Boot Boys, like Skinheads were over, so I asked these lads who's up for bein' real Skins again?" Terry (H) offered by way of explanation.

Tommy (S) once again surveyed the assembly and gave his judgement. "I like it, looks like a proper team again. I'll be in *Tony the Barber's* tomorrow gettin' a Number One meself. Yeah, Terry lad, yer right, I think the whole crew should get done."

Everyone laughed but Jay Mac was certain that by tomorrow evening, Tony the Barber would have had his busiest day in a long time.

"Here they are, look at them birds move." shouted an unusually excited 'Brain', as Pan's People made their eagerly anticipated weekly appearance, on the otherwise tired, contemporary music programme.

Whilst the crew and the other male drinkers of the lounge bar studied form carefully, a heated debate raged amongst some of the youths, as to which member of the female dancing troupe would prove to be the best private performer.

"Can you fuckin' wankers shut up? I'm tryin' to listen to this." said Tommy (S)

"Yer mean yer actually listenin', not just tossin' y'self off." asked Terry (H), laughing.

"Hey mate, I've just come out of the fuckin' nick. There's only two things to do in there, weights and wankin'. I've done both until I can't do no more." replied the grinning leader.

While the crew downed numerous pints and the obligatory accompanying whiskey chasers, the conversation volume grew and the content became less coherent, by equal measure. The small tacky room, with its badly stained, cigarette-burned threadbare carpet and worn, red leatherette, graffiti covered seating, was stiflingly hot and the cream gloss painted walls, ran with nicotine hued condensation. Suddenly, the frosted glass half-panelled lounge door swung open, allowing some of the thick smoky haze to escape into the night outside and, a momentary gust of fresh, cold air, to cut a brief swathe through the stale atmosphere within. The bloodied face of Peza was the focus of the entire crew, as he staggered into the room and blurted out:

"The fuckin' Kings Team, they're 'ere, they're doin' the Heron now!"

Denim jackets and Crombies were hastily put on and as many empty ale bottles as possible were stuffed into the pockets of each garment by the departing Skins, for use as ammunition. Nobody ran but the relief column progressed at a quick march pace, with Tommy (S) leading the van. If anyone had a spare pocket, it was quickly filled, with an empty glass milk bottle, taken from any convenient doorstep, as the team passed en route towards the bottom shops and Heron public house.

"How many of them was there, Peza?" asked Tommy (S), of the bloodied Junior, while the boy wiped his face with a sodden bar towel, borrowed from the Eagle.

"Twenty or thirty probably, they just ran through from behind the Heron and started twattin' everyone with bus poles and bricks." The boy was almost running to keep up with the lead Skins and kept dabbing at the scarlet gash on his forehead.

Shortly they arrived at the row of shops, ending with the Heron pub standing in its small, low-walled, permanently empty, expectant car park. The large, frosted plate glass window, with the word 'Saloon' etched into its surface, lay in thousands of glittering fragments on the grey-black pitted tarmac floor, outside the front of the pub. Stretching across the whole frontage of several of the shuttered, shop windows, were the words 'KINGS SKINS RULE OK,' in fresh black paint. This, more than anything else, seemed to incense the Crown Team leader.

"Where the fuck is Yad and the rest of your crew?" he shouted at the worried looking Peza.

Some of the older drinkers had emerged from within the Heron, clutching their pints and smoking their Capstan full strength, non-filtered cigarettes. These were mostly hardened veteran ex-soldiers, or sailors, or merchant marines, either now retired or working out their few remaining years, as dock labourers or factory hands, they were not impressed by the young Skins.

"Not much fuckin' use are yer?" said one elderly curmudgeon, moving the top palette of his false teeth around with his tongue, as he spoke.

Another gentleman, wearing a greasy flat cap and tattered old donkey jacket, added; "Fuckin' Jessies, that's all you are. Those Kings cunts walk in here and do what they want." He spat a considerable volume of phlegm, onto the floor in front of him to emphasise his scathing assessment.

Tommy (S) glared at the veterans, with his barely visible steel-grey eyes but kept his thin-lipped mouth tightly closed. Gradually, in answer to the Crown Team leader's original question to Peza, the various members of the Heron crew began to emerge from their hiding places, in the alleyways behind the rows of terraced housing and tenement blocks. Yad and Weaver approached the seething Tommy (S) and his twelve companions.

"Alright Tommy? Glad to see you're out mate." said the smiling Yad.

The leader looked at Yad, then Weaver and then at the ten other members of their crew now present.

"Apart from your three Juniors over there and this little fuck, who ran into the Eagle, how come none of your team have got a fuckin' mark on them?" he asked casually in a seemingly disinterested manner.

"It was the way they came at us, dead fuckin' sneaky like. There was too many of them Tommy." Yad replied nervously, as his gaze moved around the Eagle crew until it fixed on Jay Mac. "What the fuck is that Kings grass doin' here? He's the one Tommy; he told them where to find us."

Before he could say any more, Tommy (S) caught hold of him by the throat, with one of his large, broad hands. "Listen to me shithead, Jay Mac is part of the Crown Team, right? He's never let us down. Don't make me forget your brother is one of the originals and a mate."

He squeezed Yad's throat tightly then released him, turning his attention next, to Weaver. "I thought you had bottle, you're supposed to be tapped in the head, aren't yer?" Tommy (S) asked of the grinning psychopath.

"No chance to use me hammer, Tommy. Too fuckin' many of them." Weaver replied honestly then added, "When thee'd done the shops, thee just got off back to their side of the Lancs Road."

The Crown Team leader grabbed Weaver's Crombie collar and pulled the youth towards him. "You fuckin' moron, you're tellin' me that you shitbags watched them paintin' those shops?"

No one answered Tommy (S)'s irate question.

"They haven't gone anywhere, they're just sittin' in the field lightin' a fire!" shouted an excited anonymous Junior, returning from an urgently needed al fresco urination, behind the Heron pub.

On hearing these words, both crews raced to the road that ran along the back of the lower part of the estate and separated it from a large overgrown field on their side of the main thoroughfare, which passed between the estates. One after the other they entered onto the weed-infested ground, through several small openings in the rusty, old, iron-railed fencing. The stinking, polluted river meandered its haphazard route, unseen in part, through the field and, the youths stopped at this natural boundary to observe their enemies encampment.

A couple of small fires had been lit by the Kings Team raiding party, on their side of the main road and, it appeared these were located in front of the same river that also made its way through the field, in their territory. There was no sign of movement in their camp but it was difficult to see clearly, with the tall weeds and grass obscuring any activity, under the dark cloak of the cold night. Following Tommy (S)'s direction, all the Crown Team leapt across the slow flowing river at a point where they knew the banks were closest. As they approached the main road boundary, where they could now clearly be seen illuminated by the tall overhead carriageway lights, several old bricks, some still attached to their original mortar, landed with a crack onto the central reservation.

'That was some throw.' thought Jay Mac, the Crown Team's own missile-throwing marksman.

"Show yerselves, yer fuckin' wankers. Stop hidin' like little bitches!" shouted Tommy (S).

On the other side of the road, the curtain of tall, dark grass parted and a stocky, shoulder length haired individual, wearing a denim jacket with bleached white collar and pocket flaps, stepped out. On his head was a '*Clockwork Orange*' style black bowler hat, as even though none of the teams' members had yet seen the recently released notorious film, they were all aware of its content and, from stills recognised the distinctive garb of its principal characters. The youth now facing them, was Brian Monaghan, known as Mono, an apprentice street paviour, with phenomenal upper body strength and a taste for the theatrical.

"Well, if it isn't Tommy the puff!" he shouted in response. "I thought you were still suckin' cock in Walton." Mono did not wait for a reply but pressed on, "We've got somethin' of yours. Show them lads!"

He gestured to two accomplices waiting in the dark grass behind him. They emerged holding onto a dishevelled youth with fair hair and a bloodied face. Jay Mac recognised him even in this condition, as Peter McCoy, known as Treky (P) the younger brother of one of his friends from his original infant and junior school, in the centre of the city. He shuddered at the sight of his friend's brother held by these vicious captors and at the thought of what they might do to him. Mono waited until the impact of his revelation had been fully absorbed, then spoke once more.

"Ah, tell yer what I'll be generous, yer can have what's left of him back, when we've finished with him. That's if yer still want him?"

With that, he disappeared back into the grass 'curtains' and was gone. The stunned Crown Team stood silently for a few moments, until the sickening screams began.

"Let's get over there now and get Treky back!" shouted a distressed Jay Mac. Even though he had no desire to run into a mob of Kings Skins, in the dark, on their territory, he could not bear the sound of his long-standing friend's young brother being tortured.

"No one's goin' anywhere, right?" Tommy (S) said firmly.

"That's right Tommy, you tell 'im. We're not gonna risk any of our team, for that little prick. Fuck him, it's his own fault for gettin' gripped." said a relieved Yad, who did not want the night to get any worse.

Tommy (S) turned and stared directly into Yad's face. "You fuckin' cunt, that kid is one of your Juniors isn't he? You're supposed to look out for them, not fuckin' leave them if they're in trouble. Stand there and keep that tart's mouth shut."

Turning his back on the chastened Heron leader, he then spoke to the combined crews and Juniors. "Right, this is what we're gonna do. So Johno, Jay Mac... you're the fastest runners, I want four others to go with them. Who's up for it?"

Irish hesitated for a moment, then stepped forward, Blue and Glynn made no response.

"We're in." said the older of two gifted, amateur boxer brothers, Bobby and Liam Anton, who were popular members of the Eagle crew and, because of their small stature were known as 'the Ants', distinguishing themselves as 'Ant One' and 'Ant Two'. Then to Yad's further embarrassment, his co-commander spoke.

"I'm fuckin' in. My hammer is bone dry, it needs wetting." shouted Weaver, whose rage was clearly boiling inside him.

"Give them yer bus poles, yer don't need them." Tommy (S) instructed Yad and his crew, who were each armed with the gleaming four foot hollow aluminium tubes.

"Ok, these six are gonna take off an get across into the bus grounds, then over the wall into the field. Yous wait until it kicks off 'ere, then grab the kid and get away. Everyone else comes with me."

The five members of the six-man snatch squad, who were carrying ale or milk bottle 'ammunition,' passed these to the diversionary group, then sprinted across the dual carriageway and into the grounds of the corporation bus depot. Once there, they chose a point where they could see the fires of the Kings Team and quickly scaled the low wall surmounted with iron railings. Crouching in the dense tall grass and weeds, they crept towards the sound of the captive boy, who was now sobbing loudly and, halted.

"Mono! You fuckin' little queer! I am calling you out, come'ed, me an you now! Take yer dress off and stop hidin' behind yer team of shits!" Tommy (S) shouted at the top of his voice.

He and the rest of the feint group, had positioned themselves about two hundred yards further along their side of the main road, from where Mono had originally appeared. Several bricks and stones landed in the road near the Crown Team, narrowly missing speeding vehicles that swerved to avoid being struck by, or passing over the debris. While the crew watched, gradually at least two dozen Kings Skins emerged from the grass screen; Mono was not with them. Like a row of stone throwing automatons, they discharged a volley of missiles at the assembled Crown Team, some of which struck the youths, now being in range. Tommy (S) gave the command and the Crown Skins, returned a devastating salvo of glass projectiles, striking their enemy on the head, shoulders, or chest.

The waiting rescue squad took this as their signal in the absence of any other more obvious alert and sprang forward. Within moments they arrived at the torture site. Three of the Kings team, where kneeling over their prostrate victim, cutting his exposed chest, abdomen and forearms with Stanley knives and a broken bottle. They were so absorbed in their task, of trying to engrave the Kings Skins emblem into the boy's flesh, they were momentarily stunned by the speed of their rivals' attack.

"Fuck off cunt!" shouted an incensed Jay Mac striking one of the torturers hard across the side of the skull with his bus pole, then followed with half a dozen more wild strikes to the head and body.

Weaver leapt onto his victim and repeatedly hit him violently about the head and face with his solid steel toffee hammer, whilst screaming his usual oath…

"I'm Weaver, remember it was me that done this to yer! I'm Weaver!"

Blow after blow rained down on the unfortunate focus of his wrath and very soon blood poured from numerous wounds, covering the scarlet head. The third member of the torture trio managed to scramble to his feet and turned to threaten Irish with his engraving weapon, a broken, jagged, glass bottle. It was a futile gesture, Irish's aluminium bus pole cracked him hard across the nose and then again across his open mouth, splintering his front teeth and splitting his lips.

"Johno, get hold of Treky (P) with me and let's gerroff!" Jay Mac shouted to the tall Skin, as yet without an opponent. The wounded, bleeding boy was hauled to his feet and dragged a couple of yards, before the rescuers were halted in their tracks.

"Where d'yer think you're goin' ladies?" asked a smiling, bowler hatted Mono, standing in front of the Crown Skins, with four of his crew, armed with Stanley knives.

"Jay Mac, grab hold mate!" shouted Johno, letting go of the barely conscious wounded youth, before leaping onto Mono without a moment's hesitation. The wildly grappling pair fell to the ground and rolled through the tall grass and weeds, flattening a crushed dark green path under them.

Both 'Ants', disarmed their knife wielding opponents in seconds and then expertly dispatched them, with perfectly executed punching combinations of straights, crosses and hooks. Weaver was engaged in a staccato dance, with his terrified Kings Team opponent, who had realised he was facing the infamous psychopath. Thrusting his Stanley knife wildly in desperation, he caught Weaver's left arm, cutting his Crombie sleeve and nicking his Skin. He paid a heavy price for his minimal success, when Weaver's blood stained hammer hit him first in the temple and then proceeded to devastate his facial features, with accompanying sickening cracks and screams. The fourth youth, threw his Stanley knife at Irish, then turned and ran. Irish, though not as fast as Jay Mac, partly due to his heavy smoking, sprinted after the Kings player and hit him hard across the back of the head with his bus pole, dropping him to the ground. No mercy was shown to any of this team and Irish booted and struck his fallen victim repeatedly, as he cried out.

They ran forward towards the main road, no need for any further stealth or to return via the bus depot.

"Kings Skins, come on, over here!" screamed a desperate Mono, momentarily disengaged from his wrestling contest with Johno.

As the artillery cohort of the Kings Team, raced the two hundred yards back to their beleaguered companions, Jay Mac shouted to Irish and the 'Ants' "Can you get Treky back over to our side? I want to find Johno, then me and him can easily sprint it!"

Without replying, Irish and Ant One, grabbed the rambling youth and Ant Two covered their exit onto the brightly lit thoroughfare. Jay Mac darted back through the tangle of grass and weeds, leaping over one of the battered fallen Kings Team and on in the direction, from where he had heard Mono's recent rallying cry. He did not know where Weaver was and he did not really care. Almost running over the edge of the unseen riverbank, Jay Mac skidded to a sudden halt and looked about him.

The dark night sky was momentarily lit up with an eruption of glowing red sparks, as Jay Mac saw his comrade crash into the dying embers of one of the Kings Team's fires, still grappling with his equally determined opponent. Rolling through the flickering flames they arrived at the lip of the bank and then fell over the side into the foul waters below. Mono had gained the advantage in the accidental descent and was sitting on Johno's back, straddling him whilst employing his awesome arm strength to force the Crown Skin's head into the dark brown liquid with his hands. Jay Mac leapt down the muddy bank to where the two combatants had arrived.

"Mono! You fuck!" he shouted, raising his aluminium weapon back behind his left shoulder with both hands, as if preparing for a powerful home-run baseball strike.

The now bareheaded Mono turned and grinned at Jay Mac, "Do it shit!" he said defiantly.

Jay Mac brought the pole down in a descending arc, with all his strength. The locus of its path could have been calculated by the imprint it left on Mono's face, running from the right of his forehead, across the bridge of his nose and onto his left cheek. Falling awkwardly backwards, he landed on the stinking mud at the water's edge.

"Johno, c'mon mate, this is no time for washin' yer fuckin' hair!" Jay Mac shouted, as he grasped his friends Crombie collar and pulled his head out of the stagnant stream.

They scrambled up the slimy bank as quickly as they could, then ran with all their speed to the edge of the main road. Racing towards them, directly from their left were the returning two dozen strong Kings artillery crew. The front runners were only yards from Jay Mac and Johno, who was still slightly dazed from his drowning. Suddenly, from out of the dark grass leapt the crouching Weaver, he was armed with his hammer in his right hand and a discarded bus pole in his left.

The nearest Kings runner was struck across the shins with the pole, then hammered hard full in the face, as he dropped to his knees. Almost immediately the second Kings sprinter, was hit on the side of his skull, with the aluminium lance and then in the testicles with the hammer. The sight of their forerunner comrades so effectively dispatched, now kneeling in the grass moaning in pain, whilst the crazed hammer and pole wielding psychopath stood screaming his intimidating eponymous oath, slowed the pace of the other Kings runners.

"Throw everything at them!" shouted Tommy (S), leading his team onto the central reservation and parallel to the Kings Skins.

Any remaining bottles, accompanied by half bricks and other building debris, taken from the nearby flyover construction site, were thrown at their rivals as they were approaching Jay Mac, Johno and the screaming Weaver.

"Come on you mad fucker!" shouted Jay Mac to Weaver, who had just closed on his third victim and began his tandem assault.

After Weaver had dispatched this opponent, he sprinted towards the lone Jay Mac waiting on the edge of the highway, Johno having already managed to dodge the speeding cars and reach the relative safety of the central reservation and the Crown Team missile throwers. Weaver was only feet from Jay

Mac when the first brick hit him in the middle of the back, the Kings Team pursuers having chosen to change tactics, stopped running and began directing their fire towards the two remaining Crown Skins, on their side of the road. A second missile hit Weaver in the left leg behind the knee, causing him to falter, stumble and fall.

"We've done Weaver! He's down!" shouted jubilant members of the Kings team.

Encouraged by this success, a hail of stones, pieces of brick and even sods of earth, rained down upon the fallen Weaver, as he tried to raise himself on one knee.

"Fuck it!" shouted Jay Mac, running across towards the beleaguered maniac. A sharp edged stone caught Jay Mac on the right temple as he bent down to assist his stricken team mate.

"C'mon crazy arse, you can't take them all." Jay Mac caught Weaver under the right arm with his left hand and helped him to his feet, before another shower struck them.

Tommy (S)'s team also renewed their throwing efforts, in an attempt to cover their two companions' escape. Shouts of "Jay Mac run lad, run, c'mon!" and "Weaver move y'self!" could be heard from the cheering Crown Skins who were now under fire themselves from the entire stationery Kings Team.

After dodging through the fleeting outward bound traffic, Jay Mac and Weaver reached the central reservation and then the whole team, darted between the speeding inward bound vehicles, which were heading towards the city centre. When they had all arrived safely on the dark green grass and weed covered field on their side of the road, they halted and rallied around their smiling leader. The Crown team turned and jeered at their Kings Team rivals, then moved towards the crossing point on the nearest bank of the meandering, polluted river. Almost everyone was pleased with the outcome of the rescue mission and congratulated the members of the snatch squad. A seething Yad chose not to speak.

Over on the Kings side of the dual carriageway the disappointed Skins, gathered together their injured team mates and prepared to depart. The tall grass curtains opened once more and the now scarred, bleeding Mono stepped out onto the road and watched the departing Crown team, then spoke out loud, "I know that fucker that hit me. I'll see him again."

"I thought that prick Mono, was gonna fuckin' drown me" said a smiling, relieved Johno, as he told the tale from his perspective, of what had just transpired. "Next thing I know, the Kings cunt is lyin' on his back in the mud and *this* nutter is standin' there, with a bus pole drippin' in blood." he continued, exaggerating details as he saw fit.
"I don't think it was exactly drippin' mate." Jay Mac said, trying to encourage his friend to keep to the facts, having no desire to be presented in any way as a hero.
"Who's tellin' this fuckin' story?" said Johno laughing.
The whole team with the exception of the Juniors, who had been assigned the duty of conveying their wounded colleague, Treky (P) to his parents' home for them to deal with, were now seated more or less, in their original positions around the circumference of the Eagle lounge bar. Generally the atmosphere was positive and the members of the 'rescue squad' and, the 'artillery corps' were pleased with their respective actions. Yad remained sullen but thought it best, not to directly criticise Jay Mac, at least for the moment.
"It's funny how y'get people who can fight and other people who can run, if y'know what I mean?" he began, then continued, "Yeah, some lads can stand their ground and fight but others like, thee run about everywhere and when it comes to actually fightin' they're shite, y'know what am sayin'?" Yad casually glanced at Jay Mac as he spoke, to see if his words were having any effect.
"Are you fuckin' talkin' about me there, you cheeky cunt?" asked Johno angrily, rising to Yad's misdirected bait. "Cos I can do both an I'll show yer if yer want."
The blond Skin, never took his eyes off Yad as he spoke. The Heron leader had his crew with him, minus his Juniors but declined Johno's offer. He knew he was no match for Johno and in their current location, of the Eagle crew's home ground, with the prevailing climate also in their favour, he wisely decided to withdraw.

"No! Of course I'm not talkin' about *you*, Johno. Forget it, I'm just sayin' that's all, it'll keep."

My Brother Jake, a firm favourite of the whole team, was now playing on the juke box and this required everyone's attention in order to join in the title chorus. Jay Mac knew full well what Yad was implying and in part he agreed with him. He did not consider himself in any way a skilled fighter, having seen too many of them throughout his childhood and school years, to even contemplate such a notion.

Whilst drinking his brown mix, he mentally visualised blurred images of long passed incidents, where he had stood up to a belligerent bully and taken a beating for his impudence. Everyone acknowledged Jay Mac had heart but he knew he lacked the necessary ability required to enter the successful fighter ranks, instead he remained consigned to scrappers' limbo, permanently fixed between victors' heaven and vanquished hell.

Naturally gifted with phenomenal running speed and a deadly accurate throwing arm, these two talents had been honed by environmental nurture, from an early age. Having been born in the largely Irish Catholic descent sector of the Everton district, his earliest memories were of being taken by older boys, to throw stones at the Orange Order parades, while they processed loudly along Shaw Street, through his area, from their Irish Protestant descendent heartland of Netherfield Road, just a few hundred yards further west, also in Everton. Escaping from their enraged, sectarian rivals, after an impromptu missile throwing assault, required all the speed his young legs could muster. No one wanted to be battered by men, women, boys, or girls, dressed in mock seventeenth century costumes and wearing loose curled black wigs, or worse, stabbed by the legendary sharp dirks, visible in the 'Scots' bandsman's gaiters.

"Anyone fancy some chips, or a couple of dozen chop suey rolls!" shouted Blue, who had been uncharacteristically quiet since the rescue mission episode.

Tired of the public house fayre of salted crisps and nuts and, having expended a degree of energy whilst engaged in the missile throwing cover duty, Blue needed to refuel with copious amounts of deep fried sustenance. It was nearly ten o'clock and

Something to Do 1972 • **115**

even though there was an hour's drinking time left, before last orders were called, the whole team and, more importantly its leaders, concurred with Blue's proposal. For the second time that night they departed from the Eagle en masse.

When Jay Mac stepped outside the Skins' favourite watering hole, Weaver approached, leaned into him and spoke quietly, "You know before, when you helped me get up?" he paused for a moment as Jay Mac listened expectantly for a grateful acknowledgment, "If you ever put your fuckin' hand on me again, I will kill you." he said with a cold menace, then rejoined his crew, Jay Mac wisely offered no response.

The whole team were now strolling down the central main road that led to the chip shop at the bottom of the estate, located at the end of the row of shops next to the Heron pub. Even though there was a similar establishment facing the Eagle pub, everyone agreed that Mr Li's 'Golden Diner' where the team were now heading, was the superior eatery. The proprietor Mr Li, was a Chinese gentleman, whom the youths all respected because of his ferocious nature and his lightning dexterity with the gleaming steel meat cleaver, which appeared to be permanently attached to his hand. They made sure not to insult him, either deliberately or by accident.

While they were travelling towards the bottom row of shops, where the Kings Team had earlier been painting their logo undisturbed, Tommy (S), who was accompanied by Terry (H) and in close conversation with his associate, called Jay Mac over to them.

"Good effort by you tonight Jay Mac." Tommy (S) said, warmly.

"Thanks Tommy. I'm glad it all worked out well for the team."

"Y'know if y'could scrap as well as you can run and throw, you'd be a main player" the leader advised.

"I try me best, Tommy." Jay Mac replied, honestly.

"Yeah, yer keep tryin' and yer keep endin' up on yer arse." Tommy (S) acknowledged smiling.

"Its cos he's got no arl fella." offered Terry (H), Jay Mac's senior school acquaintance. "Every lad needs an arl fella." he continued philosophically.

Jay Mac recalled how he and Terry (H) had been wrestling in a mock fight in a class room, whilst waiting for one of the disinterested teachers to finish his cigarette and cup of tea in the staff room and finally arrive to deliver the lesson. Terry (H) had got Jay Mac into a tight headlock and would not let him free, until he was prepared to say that he 'liked it up the arse'. However, as Jay Mac continually refused to comply, it soon became obvious, by the changing colour of his face he would not last much longer.

Irish had realised that his friend, was in a desperate position and blurted out, "He's got no dad, Terry, he doesn't know how to break a headlock, no-one's ever showed him!"

Terry (H) immediately released his victim and apologised, saying he didn't know about Jay Mac's sole parent situation. To Terry (H), who idolised his own unlicensed boxing champion father, Jay Mac's lack of a paternal role model and guide, was unthinkable. From that time on in his own way, Jay Mac's former school-mate looked out for his interests when he felt that interference was warranted. So it was now when he offered Tommy (S) this piece of background information, much to Jay Mac's embarrassment.

"I didn't know that Jay Mac, sorry to hear it lad. You've got fuckin' balls mate." With that the leader fell silent, as did the whole team, on arriving at the junction facing the shops.

There was an ambulance parked outside Mr Li's chip shop and two uniformed males, were lifting a stretcher borne casualty into the rear of their vehicle. Two police panda cars were also positioned in the access road in front of the shops. The police officers were engaged in taking statements from various onlookers, who had arrived, either from the nearby Heron, which now had a wooden boarded front window, or from the small terraced houses directly opposite the shops. Mr Li was even more animated than usual and appeared to be giving a graphic eye-witness account of what had occurred.

"What the fuck has gone on here?" asked a curious Tommy (S), echoing the sentiments of the other members of the team.

Suddenly Mr Li spotted the youths and began shouting. "Stupid boys, this your fault. You do this, stupid boys!"

One of the police officers turned towards the team and spoke. "Do you know anything about this?"

Tommy (S) replied for everyone, "We've been in the Eagle all night officer, ask anyone. We only came down 'ere for our supper, cos it's gettin' late."

The young police officer looked at the Skins in disgust.

"Typical of you boys always talking tough with the smart mouth but keeping out the way when there's any real trouble. Now move away from here, or we'll do you for unlawful assembly."

Out of the crowd stepped a small grey man, who had clearly left home in a hurry, as he was still wearing his slippers. Holding back the tears, he approached the ambulance and looked in at his unconscious, barely breathing son. A shudder ran through his body and he visibly trembled.

Before entering the rear of the vehicle, he turned to the team and spoke, "Why did you make this happen, why? My boy is not like you, he's good, he studies. You're scum the lot of you, not my boy!"

He took his seat in the ambulance and the doors were closed. The alarm bells rang loudly as the speeding vehicle departed out of the estate and onto the main thoroughfare, the scene of the earlier confrontation between the rival teams.

While the Crown Skins had been celebrating in the Eagle and retelling their own versions, of the night's actions with advantages, Mono and his Kings team had decided not to depart but instead once more entered into the Crown Estate. When they silently approached the row of shops, they were disappointed to find them deserted, until they spotted a lone youth, standing in the chip shop waiting for his father's fish supper, which he had volunteered to collect, on his tired parent's return from a late shift in a local factory.

As many of the Kings crew as possible, who could fit inside Mr Li's establishment, attacked the innocent, unsuspecting 'civilian' youth. Once he had been felled, he was repeatedly kicked, stamped and, struck with the discarded bus poles that the Crown team had left on their own field upon returning to safety. Numerous Stanley knives were produced and a frenzy of angry, frustrated cutting began, with blood spurting from each new gash. At that moment Mr Li cleared the counter in a single vault and leapt into the mob like an avenging Chinese dragon. Using the legendary meat clever in his right hand, more as a weapon of intimidation, with his empty left hand and both of his feet he struck, punched, kicked and chopped the astonished Kings team players. Intending to drag their unconscious prey outside for a continued assault, instead the bloodied youths fled from the shop as Mr Li crouched protectively over the broken body of the innocent boy.

Months later different members of the Eagle and Heron crews, would stop and say hello to the once gifted athlete and formerly highly articulate student, as he sat in his wheelchair in the doorway of his distraught father's small terraced house, barely able to mutter a garbled response. Nobody could ever look the boy or his father in the eyes again.

Chapter 6

Move on Up

Tuesday 16th May 1972

It was a warm late spring afternoon; the city centre was crowded with shoppers and office workers. Jay Mac was taking a late lunch, which meant that he had to be back in the shipping and forwarding office where he worked by two o'clock at the latest. He was making his way along Church Street with Timothy Murphy, one of the other office juniors from his place of employment. Timothy was a few months older than Jay Mac and the very antithesis of his own youth style. On that particular day he was dressed in a long, grey-blue R.A.F greatcoat, a flowery silk shirt with an extensive penny-round collar and dark blue loon trousers, barely revealing his mustard coloured suede boots. Timothy moved his light brown, shoulder-length curly hair, out of his eyes and wiped his sweating brow.

"Its hot today, don't you think Jay Mac?" he said, adjusting his heavy coat to allow some air to circulate around his thin, frail body.

"No wonder *you're* fuckin' hot, with all that Trog's shit gear on." Jay Mac replied unsympathetically.

In reality he actually liked Timothy, even though they were polarised opposites in so many ways but he was embarrassed to be seen with him, by any other Skins, as they walked through the city's main shopping district. On a couple of previous occasions he had experienced uncomfortable moments, when a passing group of his own youth movement, had shouted and whistled "All right Skin? Who's yer fuckin' girlfriend?"

"I hope we don't run into Josh and his boys" said an anxious Timothy, who had been constantly bullied by a particularly nasty sadist, during his five years in school. Unfortunately this torment had continued almost from the start of his working life, as the principal bully and some of his craven associates, happened to work in another nearby office.

"Fuck them shit bags, Tim, they're no-marks. Don't worry about them." Jay Mac replied, trying to reassure his co-worker.

Following an earlier incident the previous summer, when Timothy was being forced to hand over his weekly luncheon vouchers by the bullies and Jay Mac had intervened, there had been a number of nasty reprisals. The Skin knew the way these matters inevitably escalated and that a display of excessive force was going to provide the only effective resolution. He was confident that if it came to a showdown he could rely on some of his Crown Team allies to assist in bringing about a swift and bloody conclusion.

"Jay Mac alright man, come over here!" shouted a familiar voice, coming from the direction of a cluster of women's dress and shoe stores nearby.

After crossing the busy main road, Jay Mac made his way through the throng of mostly female shoppers, with Timothy in tow and arrived just in front of Chelsea Girl and Dolcis. Standing in the middle of four tall, black youths, was an acquaintance of Jay Mac's from the Crown Estate known as Floyd. The eighteen year old, six foot two, auburn haired Francis Lloyd, always reminded Jay Mac of a young James Coburn. In Jay Mac's view Floyd was the embodiment of 'cool'.

Today he was casually posed and immaculately dressed in a cream polo-necked sweater, calf length soft black leather coat, blue Levi jeans and spotless white Converse All-Star basketball boots. His four companions were similarly attired, with the exception that one of the youths was wearing a well-cut black Crombie, instead of the varying shades of dark brown leathers, of the other three. All the black youths had Afro hairstyles of different sizes, chin length sideburns as did Floyd and two were sporting thin moustaches and goatee beards.

"What's happenin' Jay Mac?" asked Floyd, affecting his best American soul singer drawl, then casually taking another drag on his slender brown cigarillo.

"It's all good." replied Jay Mac, slipping into his own version of a similar generic figure.

"You know the brothers already man, don't you?" Floyd asked, continuing his role.

Jay Mac nodded to Delroy, Kenny (D), Frenchy and Kelvin. He had met them on several occasions, either strolling through town with Floyd, or in the Moonstone pub in St John's shopping precinct.

"What's happenin', Jay Mac?" asked Kenny (D), who was always the most loquacious of the cool quartet.

"Yeah, it's good Kenny. You been kickin' ass again my friend?" asked a curious Jay Mac, having observed Kenny's swollen left eye and knowing how capable a martial arts exponent he was. As Kenny laughed, Floyd focused his gaze on the diminutive, puny Timothy.

"What the fuck have you come as boy?" he asked smiling.

Before the nervous five foot six office junior could reply, Jay Mac nudged him with his right elbow and spoke, "Ok kid, I'll see you back in work later. Have a coffee waitin' for me... see yer."

Timothy looked quizzically at Jay Mac then asked "On my own, Jay Mac? What if I meet Josh and his crew, what'll I do then?"

An embarrassed Jay Mac, quickly and cruelly replied, "Get the fuck off now, yer little shit, before yer get a slap."

Floyd and his friends laughed, as the clearly upset, tousle haired boy, turned and shuffled away. Jay Mac instantly felt sick and ashamed, watching the pathetic figure struggle through the bustling crowd.

"What did yer want anyway Floyd?" asked a guilt-ridden Jay Mac.

"Got some nice gear here my man." Floyd opened a plain white plastic bag that he was holding, somewhat incongruously with his sharp attire. Inside was an assortment of different brands of bottled aftershave and Jay Mac realised immediately what Floyd wanted, having acted as his 'fence' a number of times previously.

"There's a dozen bottles in there Jay Mac, some of them are Brut and you know how well that sells. Get fifty pence a bottle and I'll drop you a note later, ok?" asked a smiling Floyd, who was used to getting what he wanted.

Jay Mac knew it was futile arguing with his thieving acquaintance and replied, "I'll sell what I can to the office crowd and I'll give yer what's left later, yeah?"

While Floyd and Jay Mac were discussing sales projections and, negotiating Jay Mac's commission, Floyd's colleagues, who worked with him as apprentice chefs in a sea food restaurant in the city's financial sector, admired the numerous and varied female shoppers, as they passed by.

"So much pussy man" said Kelvin appreciatively.

"I have got to get me some of that fine snatch tonight." observed Frenchy enthusiastically.

"You ain't gettin' any action tonight, boy, unless it's from Sally the manageress and that pussy is rank." a smiling Delroy advised. They all laughed, at the very suggestion of this apparently unsavoury union.

Conscious of the time, Jay Mac took the bag from Floyd, said farewell to the students of female form and set off to return to work.

"Jay Mac my man, call round tonight, late, yeah?" shouted the lugubrious Floyd, before settling back into his arduous task of observing women and girls as they passed, offering propositions to the lucky few and occasionally getting a positive response.

Briskly making his way through the crowded shopping area, Jay Mac could not help but mentally play the theme tune from *Shaft*, on his internal stereo system.

◇◇◇

That evening Jay Mac was sitting on the concrete sill of the library window, with Irish, Blue and Glynn, all trying to decide what activity they should engage in, for the remainder of the night.

"It's either, we have a few pints in the Eagle and make them last as long as we can, or we get some fish and chips and stroll round the estate with them." said Irish, having calculated the combined disposable income of all four, based on the amount each youth said they had in their possession.

Jay Mac had deliberately lied to Irish, as he was carrying Floyd's aftershave profits and could have used some of that money, if he chose to. However, although he enjoyed an amicable relationship with Floyd, he knew he was not a person to be crossed and would not appreciate any shortfall, in his anticipated returns. Heavily influenced by Blue's urgent entreaties, the crew decided to opt for a visit to Mr Li's Golden Diner.

After a relatively short casual stroll they arrived outside the chip shop, at the end of the bottom row of shops. When they approached Mr Li's they found Nat, Peza and Tomo with some other scruffy-looking Juniors, tormenting a frightened girl of about sixteen or seventeen, who was attempting to leave the Golden Diner.

"Let girl pass, you boys!" shouted Mr Li angrily.

However, as the Juniors felt they were at a reasonably safe distance, the group continued with their 'game'.

"Come back for more 'ave yer?" asked a grinning Nat, trying to put his arm around the waist of the clearly distressed girl.

"It's me she wants, isn't it girl?" said the dentally challenged Peza as he leaned across the object of his lust and tried to kiss her.

"Please leave me alone, please" the terrified girl said, quietly.

"Fuck this." said an enraged Jay Mac grabbing hold of Peza by the back of his denim jacket collar and wrenching him violently to one side.

Irish immediately slapped Nat hard across the face with the back of his hand. "Move out the fuckin' way, you dirty little shit!" he shouted angrily.

Blue and Glynn, taking their cue from their two friends, also began kicking and slapping Tomo and the other leering Juniors. The distraught dark haired girl kept her head down and quickly made her escape through the temporary opening, that the four companions had created.

"Wait till Yad hears about this" said Tomo, before Peza added, "Yeah, he said if Debbie Gill ever comes down here, we should keep hold of her."

Jay Mac did not know what these youths were talking about but he noticed that his three companions seemed to fully comprehend the meaning of their comments. The disgruntled

Juniors walked away disappointed and took up their respective positions on the low wall outside the Heron pub. Jay Mac curiously followed with his eyes, the soberly dressed girl's progress up the main central road until she disappeared from view. He somehow felt that he had seen her before, although there was nothing striking about her ungroomed appearance or her clothing, of a long dark gabardine Macintosh and blue jumbo cord trousers with flat black shoes.

'Why were the Juniors so determined to stop her?' Jay Mac wondered. He did not ask his three companions immediately but waited until they were eating their various meals from Mr Li's, whilst strolling back up towards the shops in the middle of the estate. "What's the score with this Debbie Gill kid?" he asked casually, breaking off a piece of steaming white, golden-batter covered fish.

"She's the one, y'know, that Yad and the Juniors done in the garages, when those power cuts was on." Blue replied smirking.

"When was that?" asked Jay Mac who did not like Blue's callous attitude, to what must have been an horrendous ordeal.

"Remember when Blue sorted out that Kenny Goodwin prick, by the youth club? Well it was on that night." said a helpful smiling Glynn, in an equally dispassionate manner.

Jay Mac looked at Irish and wondered why his friend had not told him about this incident. Because the others lived on the Crown Estate, they were privy to the latest gossip and rumours, most of which were falsehoods, or wildly exaggerated versions of minor events. "What happened there then, Irish?" Jay Mac asked quizzically now intrigued.

"It was really bad Jay Mac, yer know what that bastard Yad is like. Our Dymphna is in the year below that Debbie Gill in school, that's how I know about it". Irish began his detailed reply and provided Jay Mac with a grim synopsis of what had occurred on that night. "Yeah, her brother was supposed to meet her at the youth club when it closed at about half nine but it shut early because of the power cuts and she went home on her own. She was runnin' through by the flats behind Central Road and Yad and the Juniors ran after her."

Something to Do 1972 • **125**

Irish left out any further graphic details but he was clearly angry and upset on completing his disturbing narrative. He had two young sisters of his own and could not bear to think of either of them in the clutches of Yad and his vile crew.

Now Jay Mac knew where he had seen the unfortunate girl before. She was another of the table-tennis playing, innocent youth group and he recalled how, while they watched Kenny Goodwin and friends depart, he had also seen a lone figure run across the road, not far from where they were positioned. Jay Mac cursed himself, even though he knew there was nothing he could now do to turn back time and assist the girl.

"I wouldn't have minded a piece of that meself" said a leering Glynn, as he finished the last of his sausage dinner with gravy and, began licking his sticky brown fingers.

Jay Mac stared at his team mate in disbelief and then to further compound matters, Blue added "Yeah, me too, they say she was a virgin until Yad and the Juniors broke her in."

Jay Mac looked at Irish then back at Blue and Glynn. "Can yer believe what yer hearin' from these two sick fuckers?" he asked angrily.

Blue suddenly responded before Irish could speak. "Don't call us sick, who the fuck are you? You wanna watch that mouth Jay Mac!" Blue's face flushed with anger as he spoke.

Jay Mac stepped in front of his seething team mate and stared into his eyes. "Make your move, Blue, whenever yer feel ready."

While he spoke he remained perfectly still, with his clenched fists hanging loosely on either side of his hips. For a few tense moments there was no further conversation, or movement from any party.

Glynn decided to break the silence and spoke, "Look Jay Mac, Blue's just sayin', we've got our view and you've got yours, y'know what I mean?"

Blue, relieved that a third party had intervened, quickly added "Yeah, that's all I was sayin' Jay Mac."

The moment passed and the four youths continued on their brief journey to the central shops and their library 'perch'.

Johno and a number of their crew, where already seated on the concrete sill when they arrived. After a brief exchange of insults and another count of available funds, they decided that their best option was to wander around the estate, engaging in some mindless vandalism for the remainder of the night.

A couple of boring hours were passed in this pursuit, until eventually the group tired of throwing stones at passing buses, trying to blind the few remaining working street lights and smashing empty milk bottles in the main road. The Skins eventually drifted away, home to their respective abodes but not Jay Mac, he remained standing on the corner of the road where Irish and Blue lived, talking to his friend.

"You're gonna miss the last bus mate, if yer don't move y'self," warned Irish, smoking his final cigarette of the night."

"I'm hangin' around for a bit, I'm not bothered about the bus tonight" Jay Mac replied, not wishing to reveal his real purpose.

Irish was curious as to why his long-standing friend was lingering about on the estate after midnight, considering the fact that he had to go to work the following day. He also knew that there was one of their acquaintances, who usually began his business activities around this time of night.

"Are you meetin' that cunt Floyd, by any chance?" he asked, correctly assessing the situation.

Jay Mac was aware that Irish did not like Floyd, particularly as he had previously been arrested for shop lifting after Floyd had passed him a bag full of stolen goods, shortly before a pursuing security guard pounced. Irish had received a minor caution from the police and a major beating from his father on that occasion; he swore that he would have no further dealings with Floyd.

"I've got some business with him, that's all." Jay Mac replied.

"You're fuckin soft in the head, if yer get involved with that rat." Irish responded, flicking the glowing butt of his cigarette into a nearby neighbour's garden, before walking away.

A few minutes later, Jay Mac rang the specified doorbell of the two on the front of a brightly painted end-terraced house, with its neatly trimmed small front garden, surrounded on three sides by an equally small neatly clipped hedge.

"Come in Jay Mac my man." said a smiling Floyd, after opening the front door and pointing to the narrow staircase leading to his first floor bedroom.

Once inside Jay Mac sat down on one of the two comfortable leather swivel chairs in Floyd's room and looked around admiringly at the cool opulence on display. He had been here before but it appeared Floyd had redecorated once again since then. A variety of posters covered the white painted walls, mostly depicting females in differing stages of undress, interspersed with film advertisements in Italian or French for works that Jay Mac had not previously heard of. There was no bed visible but rather a dark brown, leather two-seater couch, which folded out to serve that purpose when required. Against one wall was a small cocktail cabinet, with a selection of colourful bottles on its top and a stereo record player. Above this item of furniture was a pair of shelves containing an extensive collection of black soul music, of which the names of some artists Jay Mac had never encountered.

"Fancy a cold beer Jay Mac?" Floyd asked, opening the small fridge, at the opposite end of the room and taking out two dark brown chilled bottles of ale. After he had passed Jay Mac his drink and lit a small cigar for himself, he placed a recently acquired album onto the record player.

"These brothers are too cool man," he announced, then sat down onto the remaining leather covered swivel chair.

The smooth sound of the *Chi-lites* filled the room and mixed with the grey-blue swirls of smoke from Floyd's cigar. The contents of a red lava lamp incongruously situated on top of the small fridge, seemed to fluctuate and reconfigure with the tempo of the music.

"You got my money?" Floyd asked casually.

Jay Mac passed Floyd the profits from the aftershave sales and received a pound note as his commission in return.

"What is it y'wanted tonight, Floyd?" Jay Mac asked warily.

"I've got some jobs need doin'. I'll make it worth your time, ok?" Floyd replied, taking a draw on his cigar and relaxing in his comfortable chair.

"Now first things first my man, are you gettin' any pussy, cos you look fuckin tense?" Floyd inquired, smiling.

"Not unless yer count me own hand." replied Jay Mac "Why? Are yer gonna fix me up with some brown sugar?"

They both laughed, then Floyd, who was notorious for the wild house parties that he frequented in the south end of the city, spoke, "Now Jay Mac if I took you to the parties I go to and hooked you up with some black pussy, I wouldn't be doing you any favours man."

Jay Mac knew what was coming next but continued, "Why's that Floyd?"

His lugubrious business associate stretched out casually and replied, "Everyone knows Jay Mac, once you go black, you never go back."

Jay Mac was tempted to ask the androgynous Floyd if he was referring to a female or male partner, when he made this statement but decided to err on the side of caution.

"Is that from yer own personal experience, Floyd? Or just some shite yer read on a cornflakes packet?" he said smiling.

"Don't knock it until you've tried it man" was Floyd's final response as he finished his cigar and swigged the last of his bottled beer.

"Ready for some business, Jay Mac?" he asked, then slipped on his long dark leather coat, over his black polo neck sweater and dark jeans. Floyd also added a pair of black leather gloves and threw a similar pair to Jay Mac, then pulled on a tight fitting woollen skull cap.

"What the fuck are we on to Floyd?" Jay Mac asked fearing that some major felony was about to occur.

"Just a bit of redistribution my man, that's all." said Floyd motioning to Jay Mac to follow him downstairs and out into the dark night. "No noise, Jay Mac, don't want me dad wakin' up do we?" Floyd laughed ironically, as they silently closed the front door behind them.

Floyd's father was a long serving police officer and all the Skins appreciated the joke that the biggest thief on the estate was the son of a dedicated law enforcer. Once outside he opened a heavy padlock securing the door to a storage area that ran along the gable end of the house. He reached inside and flicked on a light switch, then passed Jay Mac two dark green, heavy canvas holdalls. The youth could see inside under a protective tarpaulin, the outline of a Lambretta scooter with its fly screen and pillion back rest.

"Is that your famous SX200, Floyd?" Jay Mac asked curiously.

"It is my man. You'll be riding home in style later tonight, on the 'dream machine'." Floyd replied smiling.

Everyone on the estate knew Floyd, even though he didn't really associate with the crews. He never used public transport and travelled everywhere either by taxi, or on his ultra-cool Lambretta SX200, with its distinctive silver side panels, bearing the title *'Cloud Nine'* in red letters on each. On occasion Floyd would be seen riding through the estate at speed with a female companion apparently randomly selected, according to his particular desires for that evening.

The prospect of travelling back to the Kings Estate via any means other than one of the potentially dangerous, green Atlantean buses, the arrivals of which were keenly observed by Danny (H) and his waiting crew, was welcomed by Jay Mac. He was concerned, however, with what Floyd had planned for the night ahead.

They quickly left the eastern side of the estate where Floyd lived, facing the old uncultivated and overgrown farm fields. Within minutes, Floyd had spotted his first target, a Ford Escort, parked in a nearby road. He carefully produced a metal ring of keys from the inside pocket of his leather coat and opened the front passenger door.

"Ok Jay Mac, open y'bag quick," he said quietly but firmly.

Two detachable headrests and the contents of the glove box were swiftly removed from the stationary vehicle and dropped into Jay Mac's holdall. There were not many cars on the estate but those that were unfortunately targeted by Floyd, were easily accessed and rapidly stripped of any re-salable items.

"Ford takeaways, is what I'm mainly lookin' for Jay Mac, they're just too fuckin' easy man." Floyd advised Jay Mac, as he continued his rapid pilfering progress through the adjoining streets, coolly and randomly taking whatever caught his eye, like a human, eclectic thieving magpie.

After about half an hour engaged in this task, Jay Mac's large canvas holdall was almost full and he slung it across his back for ease of transportation.

"Floyd, I'm nearly loaded mate, I'll lift the gear now and you can carry this sack ok?" he suggested to his associate.

"No man, that's not the way I work. I know what I'm lookin' for, you don't. So just start fillin' the next bag and leave the 'borrowing' to me." Floyd's reply was delivered with one of his usual ingratiating smiles but in a tone firm enough for Jay Mac not to pursue the matter further.

Just after one o'clock in the morning both holdalls were full to capacity and the redistribution duo were about to close business for the night, when Floyd spotted an expensive-looking man's gold watch, with its gleaming plated strap, clearly visible for all to see, in another nearby vehicle. Try as he might none of the varied keys that he possessed, would open this particular vehicle. Suddenly Floyd reached into the side pocket of his leather coat and produced a heavy metal knuckle duster. With one deft punch he shattered the passenger side window and unlocked the door. The semi-precious watch was quickly and securely placed into his inside breast pocket and Floyd was about to exit the vehicle, where he was crouching inside, when the youths heard a noise behind them. A large stocky man in his late forties dressed in striped pyjamas and tartan slippers, had just opened his front door and was standing with an empty milk bottle in his hand.

"What the fuck are you shits doin' there!" he bellowed then sprang forward and quickly crossed the tiny grass strip of a lawn in front of his house. He dropped the milk bottle in his haste and it shattered with a loud crash that echoed around the silent street. Other lights came on in the bedroom windows of the terraced row.

"Come here you cunt!" he shouted trying to grasp hold of Jay Mac, who was encumbered with the heavy load on his back. The youth punched the man in his pyjama covered stomach but this had little effect.

"What the fuck's goin' on there?" shouted an angry voice from one of the brightly lit windows.

The stocky male now had a firm hold of Jay Mac by the shoulders and was screaming for someone to call the police. The Skin stamped as hard as he could with his right boot onto the man's left slipper-encased foot and punched him in the gut once again. Releasing his grip for a moment, the man shouted in pain and then stumbled against the car.

Other front doors were opening and someone advised "I've called the police, their on the way."

At that moment Floyd, who had been unable to extricate himself from the car because of Jay Mac's struggle with the owner, which was blocking his exit, emerged and with a devastating powerful right hook, encased in the heavy metal knuckle duster, hit pyjama man fully in the face. With blood spurting from his mouth and nose, he dropped against the open door and fell awkwardly onto the pavement.

"Let's fuckin' go man!" Floyd shouted unnecessarily before both he and Jay Mac sprinted away along the street, with their heavy cargo filled bags slung across their backs. A couple of the fallen man's neighbours made a brief pretence of a chase but quickly abandoned their half-hearted pursuit and the youths vanished into the enveloping night.

"Fuckin' close Jay Mac?" a breathless Floyd said, while they crouched hiding in the cover of the long grass, in the uncultivated farm field near his house.

Their bags were lying on the ground alongside them, as the youths watched for any signs of a police patrol car. They waited for several minutes then sprinted towards Floyd's house, keeping low all the time. Again they waited and watched the road that passed between the edge of the field and the row of terraced housing. In the distance they heard the discordant two-note alarm call, of a panda car and knew it would probably not be long before it would pass by them as part of a perfunctory search and then move on. To their surprise it appeared more vehicles were now arriving at the nearby crime scene, one of which had a different tone and was clearly an ambulance. Then suddenly they heard the noise of barking dogs.

"Shit! This doesn't sound good." said a worried Jay Mac

"Come on man." Floyd shouted and signalled to his colleague to run towards his residence.

The heavy padlock was again quickly opened and the two bulging holdalls were placed inside at the rear of the long thin vestibule. Floyd pulled the thick tarpaulin, off the SX200 and threw it across the bags. Moments later the scooter was wheeled out and the door to Floyd's own 'Aladdin's Cave,' relocked.

"Grab these, Jay Mac!" Floyd shouted and passed him two empty glass milk bottles off the front door step. As he did they heard the deep growling and excited barking of dogs not far distant.

Just as they rode away from the end terrace, two police officers arrived at the field further along the road, at the junction of the adjacent street; they were leading two large German shepherd dogs.

"Police! Hey, you two, stay where you are!" one of the officers shouted, leaning forward and unleashing his hound.

Floyd pushed his vehicle to its limits and raced for the corner of the road. Both dogs were now loose and in hot pursuit, barking wildly as they closed on their prey. Jay Mac looked over his right shoulder and could see the exposed white teeth of the snarling lead dog; his four-legged colleague was not far behind him.

"Sorry lads it's either you or me." he said with the cold pragmatism of self-preservation, before reluctantly throwing both milk bottles one after the other into the path of the charging animals. Exploding in a mixed burst of splinters and shards, these glass caltrops were sufficient to stop the canine pursuers in their tracks.

The scooter-borne youths raced down the main central road, then along past the bottom row of shops and out of the Crown Estate onto the dual carriageway, heading towards the Kings Estate.

Jay Mac shouted to Floyd, "What was all that about? The bizzies don't even usually turn up."

Floyd didn't reply but concentrated on making good their escape, constantly checking his array of mirrors for any pursuing police vehicles.

When they finally arrived outside Jay Mac's tenement shop-fronted block, the road was completely deserted and it was close to two o'clock in the morning.

"I'll drop you some cash when I've got rid of the gear Jay Mac." Floyd advised.

"I wouldn't go back to your place, Floyd, if I were you." Jay Mac warned his associate, as he dismounted from the scooter and strapped the spare Centurion helmet onto the pillion back rest.

"Man, d'you think I'm fuckin' crazy? No my friend, there's a hot, wet pussy waitin' for me in the south side, I won't be goin' nowhere for some time. Move on up Jay Mac, move on up!" With that he rode off towards his destination.

Chapter 7

The Leader of the Pack

Wednesday 24th and Thursday 25th May 1972

The sun was still visible in the clear blue evening sky and the warm air of the day had not lessened by any appreciable degree, there was not the slightest breeze. For the past half hour the Skins and their female counterparts, had been gathering in groups of varying number near the shops in the middle of the estate. Some of the Eagle crew, including Jay Mac, Irish, Blue and Glynn were already seated in the lounge bar of the eponymous establishment. Fresh from an en masse visit to Tony the Barber's tonsorial parlour the previous day, the majority of their crew were sporting number one crops with razored trenches and looked like a cohort of new army recruits. Everyone was dressed in their best kit and looking forward to a night of sex and violence in any order or permutation. The Wednesday disco at Central Way Hall was always alive with the potential for old scores to be settled, new rivalries to erupt, hierarchical positions to be challenged and random, spontaneous, torrid sexual encounters.

"Nearly half seven lads." said Tommy (S) who was as usual sitting at the centre of the crew on this evening. "Shouldn't you youngsters be gettin' your little dicks over the road and rubbin' up against some under-age pussy?" he asked smiling slyly, before taking another drink of his brown bitter.

Being a little older than most of the crew, Tommy (S) and some of his chronological contemporaries, felt the specified fifteen to eighteen age range of the usual disco crowd, was a bit too juvenile for them. They normally tended to stay in the pub drinking and then may at some point, make a casual but conspicuous appearance, to reaffirm their status and select suitable females to bestow their favours upon, for that night at least.

Jay Mac was dressed in his best short-sleeved, red white and blue check Jaytex shirt, half inch wide red clip-on braces and cream twenty-two inch parallel trousers. His obligatory red

Airwair were at their polished best. In the inside pocket of his well-scrubbed blue Levi's denim jacket, with bleached white collar and pocket flaps, emblazoned with a selection of sewn on badges, including the classic stars and stripes hand giving a victory salute and, an American bald-headed eagle with thunder flashes in its talons, Jay Mac kept his small polish-stained cloth. Like most of the other Skins that evening, who were dressed in a similar fashion, Jay Mac was carrying his jacket rather than wearing it. Whilst in the Eagle he kept his coat folded on the window ledge behind his head, with his slender knife securely hidden inside the garment, most of his team mates observed the same practice.

"We'll drop these pints and get over there, hey lads?" suggested an anxious Blue. He was still clinging to a vain hope that Julie Quirk may reciprocate his feelings, or at least acknowledge his existence. All the crew were aware of this and, as a consequence, Blue was subject to merciless derision.

"You worried Quirky's sister might be gettin' knobbed by somebody else before you get there, Blub?" asked a smirking Yad, who had recently arrived with Weaver and the now fully recovered Macca (G). The accompanying Juniors, were consigned to waiting in the doorway of the pub, or chasing each other around the empty forlorn, litter strewn car park outside.

"I might just poke that bitch meself." added Macca (G), whilst watching Blue's reaction.

"You might wanna think about how her brother Quirky is gonna feel, when he hears about this, boys." advised Tommy (S) coldly, without bothering to look at Yad or Macca (G).

"Are the Kings Team comin' over tonight, Jay Mac?" asked Yad, slyly.

"I wouldn't know Yad, would I?" Jay Mac replied cautiously.

"Its just I thought, you probably told them we're all here, so it would be safe for them tonight. Cos, y'know what shit bags everyone is that comes from the Kings Estate." Yad concluded, watching Jay Mac carefully.

"I didn't know you lived there, Yad?" was all that Jay Mac said in reply, then he stood up to leave with Irish, Blue, Glynn, Johno, Brain and Tank.

"'Ave I said sumthin?" asked a grinning Yad but no further response was forthcoming, only a brief remark from Tommy (S).

"Y'know Yad, sometimes you're about as welcome as a fart in a diving suit."

The crew of seven Skins left the Eagle and strolled across towards Central Way Hall, which was situated above the row of shops, facing the pub. The downstairs, sheet-metal covered doors were opened and the queuing crowd began to be admitted.

"Look at the birds waitin' for us." said Glynn, as they crossed the road and approached the packed entrance.

At least several dozen females where standing in the line of prospective disco revellers. A similar number of males were also present but they didn't register with the enthusiastic Eagle crew and may as well have been invisible. The majority of the girls were dressed in miniskirts or, dresses of varying lengths ranging from ultra-short to almost obscene. A few adventurous spirits had opted for skin-tight hot pants, either of velvet or satin, worn over dark tights and complemented in some cases, with knee length boots. Rarely were the girls' legs obscured from appreciative view, however, there were isolated outbreaks of the all-encompassing new fashion statement, the maxi skirt or 'passion killer,' as the boys referred to this particular garment. They girls were all wearing excessive amounts of makeup, including false eye lashes, heavy dark eye shadow, ruby red lipstick and as much foundation or concealer as was needed to cover any teenage blemishes, or untimely prominent spots.

The two forty-something council employed males who collected the door receipts, issued tickets and, theoretically checked the age of each youth as they entered, were unable to give these tasks their full attention, as their gaze was constantly drawn to the array of giggling girls, while they ascended the stairs to the hall above and revealed their choice of underwear for the evening.

There were a small number of females, who had opted for their version of the male Skins' attire and wore, short sleeved checked or plain Ben Sherman shirts, scrubbed blue denim jeans with bleached turn ups and highly polished red Airwair or oxblood brogues. These girls were not looking for emotional entanglements, they were instead hoping for the opportunity to display their own fighting prowess and as such the other females avoided them, as did the majority of the boys.

If for any reason, the police had wished to arrest the hardcore members of the different crews, that comprised the Crown Estate Team, then this would have been the perfect venue. Skins from the Eagle were there in force, as were the Heron crew and the Hounds, with the Unicorn and the Bear also well represented by their own eponymous crews all dressed in their sharpest kit and primed for action.

"Fuckin' hell, it's packed in 'ere." Irish observed, as they topped the metal railed concrete stairs and entered the heaving, stifling, cauldron of the dance hall and were engulfed by the sounds of Harry J. All Stars' *Liquidator*.

Immediately their senses were assaulted on at least three fronts. The room was in semi-darkness, lit only by a number of revolving glitter balls, which reflected and bounced the colourful beams of the disco lights, in myriad rays and directions. Occasionally this illumination was reduced even further when strobe lighting was substituted, to accompany a particular record and a surreal staccato motion animated the movements of the dancers and onlookers. An overpowering aroma, concocted of heavily dowsed cheap perfume and Brut or Old Spice aftershave applied in equal strength, filled the limited air as it struggled to circulate about the clammy room. The pounding beat, ear-splitting pitch and deafening volume of much of the musical fayre on offer, made it difficult enough for individuals to hear their own internal voice, so conversations with others were virtually impossible and consisted mostly of one word questions and responses.

"Drinks?" Blue asked, while the four usual companions made their way to a small window opening, from where plastic cups filled either with diluted orange juice or watery Coke, were being dispensed.

"Sorry love." repeated a grinning Glynn numerous times, as he 'accidentally' groped the bottoms of different girls, whilst supposedly struggling to make his way to the drinks counter, with his friends.

"I fuckin' love it in 'ere when it's this packed." he shouted to Irish, Blue and Jay Mac.

Though hardly any of what he said was actually heard, his smiling face and physical gestures, managed to convey his delight more effectively than any words ever could.

Once they had consumed their drinks of pale orange liquid and their vision had sufficiently adjusted to their surroundings, they took stock of the assembled crowd and assessed the available talent on display.

The Four Tops' *I can't Help Myself (Sugarpie, Honeybunch)* was currently playing, as the boys observed the line of girls dancing nearest to them. In accord with contemporary convention, the females tended to dance either in small groups around their handbags, which lay on the floor at their feet, or they formed into extended linear troupes. An anthropological study could have been conducted detailing the cultural mores and rituals that the young males and females used prior to selecting a mate, either for a single, temporary coupling, or as a long term partner. Some boys were brave enough to approach these gatherings alone and risk the ridicule of a blatant rejection, others preferred the relative safety of joining one of the parallel lines of males, that quickly formed, depending on the record being played, facing those of the girls. Here, although individual conversations may be initiated with members of the opposite sex, it was as if the whole group were dancing together and when the music ended, there was no compunction for either party to continue further, unless they particularly wanted to.

While the Skins studied the female forms displayed temptingly nearby, they made casual comments about various prominent anatomical features of individual females.

"Look at those tits bounce," said an appreciative Blue, whilst staring at a particularly well-endowed dark haired girl, dressed in a tight fitting mini-dress.

"There's so much leg, it's hard to choose." Irish observed, attempting to excuse his reticence to make an actual approach to any one of the girls.

"Fuck blimpin' the legs and tits, look at some of those arses!" shouted Glynn, watching the ridiculously short skirts and dresses ride up, with the energetic gyrations of the dancers and reveal all for his pleasure.

"Hey Blue, is that your bird?" Jay Mac shouted to his team mate, as a new line of dancers took to the floor, to the sound of The Supremes' *Floy Joy*.

"Yeah it is," Blue replied, delighted. "Dive in with us lads, before someone else gets in front of them." he pleaded.

"Come 'ed, let's do him a favour." said an obliging Jay Mac to Glynn and Irish. The latter reluctantly acquiesced and all four quickly but as casually as possible, positioned themselves in front of Julie Quirk and her friends.

"Alright Julie, how are yer?" asked a nervous Blue, now standing facing his beloved.

"Yeah, great," she replied apathetically, turning her head and looking to her right, where Jay Mac was trying to engage a pretty blonde colleague of hers in basic conversation.

"D'you fancy a drink, when this dance is finished, Julie?" Blue enquired hopefully.

Julie turned and looked fully at Blue, while the love struck youth gazed at her in awe.

"D'yer mind if we change places lad?" she asked rhetorically, then quickly moved to where her friend was dancing, facing Jay Mac.

The pretty blonde now appeared in front of the deflated Blue, after Julie had asked her to do so.

"Alright Jay Mac? Haven't seen much of you lately." Julie said smiling sweetly.

"I've been keepin' a low profile, y'know what I mean?" he replied honestly.

Since the last eventful episode with Floyd and the subsequent police investigations, seeking to apprehend the *'two violent youths involved in a vicious assault on a local man, whilst protecting his property,'* as it was reported in the city's press, he had decided to curtail his usual evening visits to the Crown Estate for a while.

Although he was slightly bemused at first, as to why Julie Quirk had changed places with her friend, the more he looked at the smiling brunette, he found himself becoming surprisingly attracted to her. When their dance ended, the girl moved closer to Jay Mac and spoke into his ear, lightly brushing her soft lips against his cheek, filling his nostrils with the fragrance of her perfume.

"When the slowies start, I'll be lookin' for you, don't leave me waitin'."

She caught hold of his left hand with her right and squeezed his fingers, before leaving the dance floor with her giggling friends.

The four youths also rejoined the crowded ranks of onlookers.

"What the fuck is goin' on with you and my bird?" asked a furious Blue.

"Listen mate, I dunno what's happenin' either but if there's a chance of some action, I'm not gonna miss out, ok?" Jay Mac replied firmly.

Before any further conversation could occur, everyone's attention was drawn to the corner of the room where the disc jockey was positioned. Wild screams, loud swearing and the sound of hard punches striking flesh advertised a violent struggle taking place between several females. The group of Skinhead girls that the boys had only given a cursory glance to, when studying the prospective partners in the waiting crowd earlier, had come with a specific purpose in mind. All music and dancing was now suspended whilst several other girls, uniformly dressed in Travera blue-green two-tone suits of jackets and skirts, punched, kicked and head-butted their jeans and boots wearing opponents, as they surrounded one lone female, attempting to batter her into submission.

The dispassionate DJ, who was also another forty-something, long serving, council employee and well used to sporadic outbreaks of violence at these weekly functions, announced in his best monotone voice, that the police would be called if the fighting did not stop at once. Cheers and shouts of encouragement from the boys almost drowned out his warning.

Then the tide of conflict began to flow in one direction only and it soon became clear, that the suit wearers were gaining the upper hand. The main object of the Skinhead girls' attack emerged from amidst the press of her enemies and became visible to the crowd. Punching accurately to face and body, like a skilled boxer she dropped her biggest opponent to the floor with several powerful combinations. Her rescuers then kicked and stamped the fallen girl with their heavy brogues or moccasins, fitted with metal heel and toe protectors in the soles. Flight was now the only option for the remaining Skinhead girls and they desperately struggled to reach the exit, whilst being spat at and having any possible missile thrown at them. The victorious boxing girl adjusted the short skirt of her purple-blue two tone suit and sat across the chest of her bleeding fallen assailant, whilst she lay on the dirty floor.

Those onlookers nearest heard the winner shout, "Here's a little reminder for yer, you fuckin' bitch!" as she deftly nicked the right and left cheek of her downed opponent's already bloodied face, with her Stanley knife.

"Now gerrup and fuck off while yer still can." she ordered then stood up with her reddened craft knife, still firmly held in her right hand.

The wounded, battered Skinhead girl stumbled through a similar gauntlet to that of her friends and finally escaped from the hall. Satisfied that some semblance of order had been restored, the DJ resumed his duties and, began to play *Double Barrel* by Dave and Ansell Collins.

"Who is that fuckin mad bitch?" asked Jay Mac, who knew most of the male crews by sight, if not necessarily to talk to but was unfamiliar with their female counterparts.

"Keep it down Jay Mac" said Irish "That's Jackie (M), she runs the Hounds' girls' crew and yer already know her fella." he advised.

"Yeah" added Glynn, "You were talkin' to him in the Eagle earlier, y'know, Tommy (S)."

Jay Mac appreciated this information. He had heard of this violent female and had watched a couple of spectacular fights, where the Hounds' females had battered some other misguided rivals, in front of the pub of that same name but he had never seen Jackie (M) in person before, or witnessed her considerable fighting skill. Jay Mac made sure that he studied her now and committed her appearance to memory for future reference.

Jackie (M) was a fairly ordinary looking girl of about five foot four inches, with short jet-black hair, she was not particularly stocky but she had been a keen athlete and swimmer whilst at school. Her face was not unattractive yet there was a coldness behind the stare, of her small, dark blue eyes and her thin lips appeared cruel, even when she occasionally smiled. In many ways, she was the perfect partner for Tommy (S). He was a dispassionate, unemotive fighting machine, admiring strength, prowess and courage above all other qualities. A shrinking violet, or a simpering doting girlfriend, who could not hold her own in a violent brawl would have been a hindrance or a liability to him, while he strove to maintain his prime position in the top ranks of street fighters.

The evening moved on, the boys danced with several different girls and practiced their best chat-up lines, receiving varying responses. Towards the final hour, after much encouragement from the crowd, the DJ acceded to their demands and began to play some records of a slower tempo; he also delivered a number of cryptic messages, to accompany specific requests, but never once changed the dull tone of his announcer's voice.

"Now then, boys and girls, this one is for Jay from JQ, she says, 'Don't fight it baby', whatever that means." he said in his best generic Disc Jockey attempt.

Have You Seen Her? by The Chi-lites began to play on the turntable, when Jay Mac turned to Blue and spoke.

"Alright Blue, no hard feelings mate, I'm steaming in, ok? Why don't yer grab another bird?"

Blue did not reply but watched, while a smiling Julie gestured to his team mate to join her on the dance floor.

"Sounds like they're playin' our song." Jay Mac said, placing himself in front of the waiting girl.

Julie didn't waste any time with small-talk, she flung her arms around Jay Mac's neck, drew him close to her, then nestled her head onto his shoulder. Putting his arms around her slim waist and holding her tightly, they slowly moved to the mellow Chicago Soul sound. He glanced to his immediate right on the packed dance floor and saw that Glynn was already passionately kissing the pretty blonde, who had earlier changed places with his present partner. Jay Mac leaned his face into that of the slender female and followed Glynn's example.

"Took you long enough." Julie said breathlessly when they finished their kiss, again resting her head on Jay Mac's shoulder.

The smell of her perfume and the touch of her soft skin and luxuriant hair, intoxicated Jay Mac's senses and his usual, cold detached persona began to melt. He drew her closer to him and kissed her again, her full lips parted eagerly. Their brief dance was almost over and they had hardly spoken a word.

"Don't go, Jay Mac, wait for the next record, will yer, please?" Julie asked as the final notes were played.

Jay Mac was more than happy to comply, his rising passion made him feel embarrassed to move away. The DJ appeared to sense the prevailing romantic mood and decided to give all the prospective 'lovers' a little longer to embrace, before resuming his more lively music selection. Diana Ross' dulcet tones were heard next, beginning *I'm Still Waiting* and an almost palpable sigh, emerged from the swaying couples, legitimately continuing their passionate clinches. Jay Mac and Julie held on to each other like two star crossed lovers, who knew the fates must separate them shortly and, that these few brief tender moments would be all they would ever share. They kissed again and their lips lingered as Julie gazed at Jay Mac through half closed lids.

"When the disco is finished, I'll meet yer outside, ok?" she whispered in his ear then kissed him again.

Jay Mac knew he was playing with fire and that if Julie's psychopathic brother, Quirky, became aware of their liaison, he would now have a seriously dangerous enemy on the Crown Estate.

"How will I find yer in the crowd, without yer being seen?" he asked Julie, when the record ended.

"Don't worry, I'll find you." she said, then kissed him on the cheek and turned away.

Jay Mac and Glynn re-joined their friends and discussed the recent developments.

"Fuckin' hell, Jay Mac, that Julie Quirk was all over yer. Are y'gonna knob her or what?" asked Glynn, somewhat indelicately.

"Listen Glynn, keep it on the low mate, ok?" Jay Mac asked his friend.

"Got yer Jay Mac, I won't say nothin' to no one. By the way if yer need a Johnny, I've got me pack of three with me." Glynn offered obligingly.

"Thanks mate. I'll remember that, if the chance comes up." Jay Mac replied, as his attention was drawn to the doorway of the hall.

Two large males, who looked as if they were in their late twenties or early thirties, had just entered. The door keepers normally left their station towards the close of the evening and returned after a quick pint in the Eagle, to dismiss the youths and lock up the premises, so no one had been present to challenge these two over-age intruders. Jay Mac and some of the other teens stared at the adults, who clearly had been drinking heavily and were making their intentions blatantly obvious.

Both men had thick moustaches, one was almost totally bald, the other had thin, long, greasy, unkempt hair. The taller male was about six foot two, the other approximately six foot. They wore short-sleeved, plain tee-shirts, revealing numerous tattoos, depicting stock figures of anchors, hearts, bare-breasted mermaids and black swallows. Their dark blue flared trousers barely concealed their heavy black industrial boots. Jay Mac always studied physiques, particularly if there may be potential trouble. These two characters he concluded, were heavily built, manual workers of some sort but were both out of shape and their tight-fitting tee-shirts, revealed considerably developed paunches.

"Any birds in here want a good hard shag?" the balding male shouted loudly, staggering about, leering at the multitude of young girls in the room.

"We're in the Merch y'see, so we've been all over the fuckin' world, right? And we've fucked everything!" his mate declared in an equally loud bellow.

The DJ, who was ostensibly also supposed to keep good order, if necessary, suddenly acquired acute deafness and kept his head down, attending to the task in hand. *Tears of a Clown* by Smokey Robinson and the Miracles was now playing and he knew that in another ten records at most, the evening would be over.

'Anyway,' he thought, 'these fuckin' kids all think they're hard, so let them sort it out, it's not my problem.'

Jay Mac and his nearest crew members glanced at the two tables by the door, where their denim jackets lay folded, with their weapons secured within.

"Come on girls, who's havin' a dance then?" the long-haired merchant seaman asked positioning himself in front of a line of girls, who turned as one and retired from the floor.

"Ah, c'mon girls, we only wanna fuckin' dance and a little kiss." said the balding drunk, reaching into his back trouser pocket and retrieving a small, flat, half empty glass bottle of whiskey.

Watching the haphazard direction of their progress around the room, Jay Mac could see that, as fate would have it, shortly and inexorably they would reach the spot, where Julie and her friends were standing engaged in some deep conversation. What he did not notice, was that at the same time, Jackie (M) and her two-tone clad entourage, were rapidly moving from the opposite direction toward the same area.

Johno, Tank and Glynn were nearest to Jay Mac, when he said, "C'mon lads, let's get over there before these cunts do."

Johno accompanied Jay Mac as they briskly crossed the dance floor but Glynn and Tank somehow got delayed. The taller, long-haired drunk, was already standing in front of Julie as Jay Mac arrived.

"Alright darlin', let's have a nice dance hey, you and me?" he said leaning into the girl and then belching loudly.

"Sorry there was no drinks left." said Jay Mac wedging himself between the drunk and the girl. "Nearly missed our song there, c'mon there's still time." he added, catching hold of Julie's hand and attempting to lead her onto the floor.

"Just a fuckin' minute there, you little cunt! This is my bird, she wants to dance with a man, so fuck off!" the tall drunk ordered, leaning across Jay Mac and reaching for Julie's other hand.

Johno had removed one of the girls to relative safety, as the balding drunk now also closed on his friend.

"I'll just finish me drink and then I'm gonna teach you a fuckin' lesson, boy." he advised, before greedily swigging the remaining amber liquid from his bottle.

"Back away quick." Jay Mac said urgently to Julie, then turned around to face her original dance partner. "No mate, you've got it wrong. The over thirty's night is Saturday. So come back then and there'll be loads of old birds of yer own age to have a waltz with."

Julie had moved further away whilst Jay Mac was talking and she now backed into Jackie (M) and her crew, who positioned themselves immediately behind Jay Mac.

"Brought your fuckin' whores to help, have yer?" asked the long haired drunk before slapping Jay Mac hard across the face with the back of his hand, as he made the mistake of momentarily looking away to see who his assailant was referring to. The youth staggered backwards from the force of the blow and almost lost his balance. The DJ decided not to put another record on and for a split second there was almost complete silence.

"I'll dance with yer." said Jackie (M), stepping in front of Jay Mac to face the belligerent balding sailor, motioning to one of her crew to make a similar offer to his long-haired companion.

"That's more like it, all nice and friendly like." Jackie's partner said, taking to the floor with the formidable female. He and his merchant marine friend with their two young female partners were now the only couples on the dance floor, when the DJ began to play *Israelites* by Desmond Dekker.

"Put somethin' slow on after this you cunt, or else!" shouted the balding drunk to the DJ, whilst leering at the expressionless female in front of him.

At that moment, Jay Mac noticed Irish entering through the main door and wondered where he had been. Most of the Skins were getting their jackets and beginning to leave the hall, Julie and her friends were with them. By the time the record ended, apart from Jackie (M) and her crew, there were less than a dozen males left, leaning against the walls around the room. Whether it was intentional or accidental irony, the DJ's closing record choice was *My Gir'* by the Temptations.

"That's better" said the long haired drunk to his friend, moving in to claim their prizes, hoping to rub themselves against a young female form and grope away the depressing thoughts of long frustrating nights at sea, confined in cramped quarters, with an entire crew of sweaty, farting males as their only company.

Jackie's partner leaned forward, to put his arms around the smiling girl, hoping to engage in a passionate embrace. Without the slightest hint of her intentions, other than her barbed smile, the female leader swiftly brought her right knee, violently into contact with the lecherous man's testicles. Stooping low, with the gut wrenching pain of the unexpected blow to his unprotected, dangling privates, his stubbly slack jaw, now came into the range of Jackie's awesome left hook, causing him to bite the tip of his tongue sharply. Crouching in agony, holding his groin with one hand and with blood running out of his mouth from his punctured tongue, he still managed to throw a desperate punch, which caught the girl a glancing blow in the stomach, before she stepped out of range of any further strike.

His long-haired ship-mate, however, ignoring his own dance partner on seeing his friend assaulted, hit Jackie with a similar back-hand blow, that had caught the off-guard Jay Mac earlier. The girl's lip split and she defiantly spat blood at her attacker. He in turn reached for something in his back pocket but was immediately surrounded by the remaining Skins, who had all retrieved their weapons from their jackets.

"If you've got somethin' in that pocket shithead, you'd better fuckin' leave it there" warned a deadly serious Johno, holding his own blade at arm's length, directly facing the drunk.

Before the youths or the merchant sailors, could speak or act further, the music stopped abruptly and the main lights of the hall were switched on, momentarily blinding all the occupants.

"Right! I've fuckin had enough of this shite! That's it; the job doesn't pay enough to put up with this. I want you *ALL* out of here now and, I am callin' the police!"

With that angry warning, the furious DJ shouted for assistance from his colleagues, whom he presumed had returned to their station at the main entrance downstairs.

When they entered the room, the two doormen found one girl bleeding from the mouth, being led towards the exit by her friends and a balding drunk kneeling on the floor, also bleeding from a mouth wound, in the process of rapidly voiding his stomach contents. His friend was unsuccessfully trying to assist him in standing. The remaining group of boys were putting their denim jackets on and preparing to leave, whilst continuing to stare at the two merchant men.

"What the fuck's happened here?" asked one of the door keepers, surveying the scene.

"Sea sick." advised Jay Mac, "That baldy cunt on the floor can't get used to dry land, he fell over and banged into one of the girls, his boyfriend's trying to help him up. It's fuckin' tragic really."

The crew laughed as they strolled down the concrete stairs with the bloodied Jackie and her friends in front of them.

They had all by now received Tommy (S)'s message conveyed by Irish, who had earlier crossed the road to the Eagle and advised their team leader, of the presence of the drunken sailors. Whilst continuing to calmly drink his pint and whiskey chaser, sitting in the company of his peers, Tommy (S) had considered the situation and then delivered his instructions.

"Keep them there till the end of the disco, nobody do anything but wait outside the doors. No one is to get off."

Irish had returned to the hall to deliver the message. Tommy (S) meanwhile, conferred with his old guard about how the drunks would be disciplined. The off-course sailors had earlier that evening drifted into the bar of the Eagle and had been shouting about falling asleep on a bus, missing their intended port, The Standard, a public house on Breck Road and, subsequently finding themselves rudely awakened, marooned at the bus terminus on the Crown Estate.

When Jay Mac and the crew members stepped through the main doors of the hall into the street, they found a huge crowd of youths assembled outside. They quickly took their places in the ranks and Tommy (S) approached from the Eagle, his drinking companions positioning themselves at strategic points, to cover any attempted flight, by the as yet oblivious sailors. Jackie (M) crossed to her partner and informed him of what exactly had just happened. Once he was fully briefed, the leader spoke to the crowd.

"When these fuckers come out, no one touches them until I say. If they try to run, just block them, nothin' else." he said standing facing the doors, in the centre of the large semi-circle that had now formed.

The sound of an argument could be heard from inside the main entrance to the hall, then the sheet-metal covered doors opened. When the two men stepped out into the street, they were immediately illuminated by the stark, white light of a security storm lamp, situated above the entrance. From within the doormen locked and bolted the only possible escape route behind the drunken sailors before leaving the building by the small rear exit, into the filthy alley at the back of the row of shops. Greeted by the spectacle of this teenage throng, the long-haired drunk, who was still assisting his bloodied friend in standing, looked about curiously and then spoke.

"What's this? Some sort of fuckin' kids meetin'?"

His friend now stood up fully, began to take stock of the situation and rapidly sobered.

"Gerrout the way or I fuckin' promise you, some cunts are gonna get badly hurt."

He couldn't have known then, how prophetic his words would prove to be.

Tommy (S) stepped forward and stood in front of the two men. "Who wants it first?" was all he said, never taking his ice-cold stare off them, whilst loosening the heavy metal shank, dog chain, with its thick leather handle, held in his right hand behind his back.

The balding male couldn't believe what he was hearing and immediately advanced towards Tommy (S).

"Fuck off boy!" he shouted painfully with his damaged tongue.

In one lightning-fast strike, Tommy (S) whipped the heavy chain around the man's balding head, with the steel clasp catching his right eye, almost blinding him. Within an instant the man had been battered again by the flailing chain, even as he howled in pain from the first agonising blow. Using the metal lead as a whip, the youth drew the man towards him, then leapt into his face delivering a bone crunching head butt like a powerfully thrown house brick, fully onto the bridge of his nose. A ferocious flurry of devastating punches then struck the wounded sailor in the body and face, as he stumbled about bleeding from the mouth, broken nose and blinded eye.

The flail-wielding Skin momentarily stepped away from his now erratically moving target and watched for the next opening. Half crazed with the pain of multiple injuries, the desperate man lunged forward, trying to grasp the tormenting youth that his blurred vision incorrectly positioned directly in front of him. A hard crack on the top of his skull with the heavy steel clasp at the end of the whip-like chain was his reward for this error of ocular judgement. He slipped, fell and collapsed onto one knee, immediately receiving a vicious rising boot under his already badly bruised jaw, snapping his head back violently. Reduced to a kneeling, moaning, bloody wreck, the previously belligerent drunk tried to mouth an impassioned plea for mercy. Springing forward, with the heavy chain now wrapped cestus-like tightly around his right fist, Tommy (S) delivered a sickening coup de gras punch, straight into the gaping maw of the already crimson-spattered face.

In the few minutes that this total destruction had taken to deliver, the long-haired seaman had stood rooted to his original position, frozen by terror and shocked disbelief. As his now silent, battered shipmate, slumped and fell face down onto the hard concrete paving, he tried to issue a final warning.

"Don't come near me, you little bastard, or I will fuckin' gut you!" he shouted nervously, then produced a shiny, black-cased flick knife from his back trouser pocket.

The steel blade flashed as it sprang open and, holding it in his right hand, the sailor crouched over stabbing wildly in the direction of his ruthless enemy. Suddenly and in direct contravention of their leader's original orders, there was some crowd interference. One of the estate's few remaining metal rubbish bins was snatched from its tubular steel cage support and flung over the heads of the mob, onto the extended forearm of the knife-wielding merchant marine, causing him to drop his weapon. Johno, the bin thrower, did not advertise his act when he heard Tommy (S)'s warning statement.

"I don't know who the fuck threw that but I'll say it again... don't touch these cunts, until I say." Then he turned to the stunned sailor and spoke. "Pick up your fuckin' blade and make your move."

The man grabbed his knife from the floor and instantly rushed towards the sporting youth, hoping to catch him off guard. It was a misplaced hope, as the Skin deftly side-stepped his lunge and wrapped the chain lead, around the wrist of the knife-holding hand. Tommy (S) wrenched the captive arm to one side, bringing his right knee sharply into contact with the elbow joint of the ensnared limb. The loud crack as the arm broke was audible to the entire crowd, some of whom now cheered, finally lifting the veil of almost total silence, that had lay across the proceedings so far.

This second matelot now stumbled and fell but, as he did he managed to sweep his left arm around Tommy (S)'s legs, unbalancing the youth who fell onto his back. With his remaining strength, the injured man threw himself onto the boy and began punching him in the face as hard as he could manage with his one functioning fist. Lying on the floor receiving a flurry of punches, the Skins' leader made no reaction, as if impervious to the pain of the blows, then he struck the momentarily triumphant man a tremendous right-hook with his chain-covered fist, to the left side of his face. A howl of pain escaped from the sailor's mouth, as his jaw bone shattered and he fell to his right side, releasing the youth from underneath him. Tommy (S) instantly sprang to his feet and kicked and punched his stricken adversary while he desperately attempted to stand.

Relentlessly pummelled, the bleeding sailor tried to scramble into a shop doorway but the steel shutter left little room for any shelter. Like a kicking machine Tommy (S) rained blow after blow onto the man's body and head. With jaw and nose broken and bleeding profusely, the sailor lapsed in and out of consciousness, whilst his remaining front teeth were kicked in. Finally the sweating, triumphal leader stepped away from his human punch bag and surveyed the carnage, his expressionless face revealed no hint of any emotion. He casually spat into the bloodied pulp of the long-haired sailor's face, then walked over and repeated the gesture onto the back of the balding head of his first opponent who lay unmoving on the pavement.

"Anyone who wants to throw in a few digs, help yerself." he said coldly, stepping through the throng, without a backward glance.

The Alpha male was joined by his female companion and they took up their positions seated on the low wall, outside the Eagle Public House across the road from the Hall. Whilst they sat and calmly discussed the evening's events, the pack now released and excited with a blood lust, took their share of the 'kill'. Both male and female members eagerly leapt onto the fallen sailors, kicking, punching and clawing their helpless prey. Boot after polished boot, struck the motionless figures, while the feeding frenzy raged and rival crew members were united in their sickening desire. Finally, when the two limp, bloody rag dolls offered no further sport and, the packs' carnal appetite was sufficiently sated, a chill calm settled over the scene.

Jay Mac stood back and caught his breath, then laughed nervously. His laughter was infectious and other relieved crew members followed suit. As quickly as the mob had formed and their rage had gathered momentum, so now it dissipated and they drifted away. Tommy (S), the old guard and Jackie (M) with her two-tone clad warrior maidens, were soon gone from the middle estate shops and heading back towards their own sector.

Yad, Macca (G) and Weaver who had been conspicuous by their absence during the disco, left with the Heron crew and Juniors, making their way down along the central main road to the bottom shops where they dwelt. Jay Mac had noticed that, unusually Weaver had not chosen to use his trade-mark toffee hammer or even issue his eponymous statement of intent, whilst repeatedly kicking the senseless pair of matelots. Perhaps, Jay Mac thought, a part-share of a kill was not worthy of the psychopath's usual theatrical efforts.

His mental speculations were suddenly interrupted, when a small stone hit him on his back, as he aimlessly wandered past the dank alley-way behind the shops, with several of the Eagle crew, including Irish and Blue. Quickly looking over his left shoulder, he saw a figure standing at the entrance, to this foul brick-lined corridor.

"I'm just goin' for a piss, I'll catch yer up." he announced, then darted into the alley to join the waiting Julie.

Stepping carefully over broken bottles, the remains of previously disgorged fish suppers, stinking heavily soiled discarded female sanitary wear and other assorted reeking detritus of a throw-away society, the excited couple made their way into one of the rear shop doorways. Jay Mac put his arms around the girl almost lifting her towards him. Julie responded eagerly and she clung tightly to him, with her slim arms about his neck. Soon they were both locked in a passionate embrace, sharing long lingering kisses, whilst their hands caressed each other's bodies tenderly. Jay Mac could feel the warmth of her soft skin and her shapely figure, through the thin material of her short, mini dress. Julie's hands roamed over his hard muscled athletic form and she breathed a sigh of delight into Jay Mac's ear, as they momentarily disengaged from their kissing.

Emboldened by his partner's apparent pleasure, he placed his hands on her curved, pert bottom, lifting her dress in the process. Julie thrust her tongue into his mouth and then repeating his action, squeezed the firm cheeks of his rear. Pleasantly surprised by Julie's enthusiastic response Jay Mac pressed on, sliding his left hand smoothly, between her nylon covered thighs and rubbed it firmly across the front of her tiny, white panties, which she was wearing over her dark tan tights, following the prevailing underwear code of the time. While he squeezed and massaged her most private place, through the thin yielding material of her lingerie, Julie put her head back against the sheet metal covered door behind her and moaned softly.

She opened her half closed lids, looked at Jay Mac and asked "Have you got anything?"

Jay Mac cursed himself for not accepting Glynn's generous offer earlier. "No, I haven't, sorry." was all he could manage to say, as a rapid deflation began to overtake him.

"Go and ask your mate next door, quick." Julie continued, much to Jay Mac's surprise and relief.

The excited youth hadn't realised that other amorous couples, aroused in part by the evening's entertainment, were also taking advantage of the al fresco facilities. As fast as he could physically manage, Jay Mac darted along to the next rear shop doorway, where he found Glynn with his right hand working feverishly, inside his earlier dancing partner's panties and tights.

"Alright mate, sorry to bother yer while y'busy like, any chance I could borrow one of your Johnnies," a desperate Jay Mac asked his sweating team mate.

"Fuck off, Jay Mac, you're out of luck." was Glynn's unsympathetic reply. Just then his partner, the now somewhat dishevelled pretty blonde, caught hold of Glynn's wrist immediately above the rim of her flimsy nylon panties and spoke.

"Listen lad, if he's out of luck so are you, so give him a fuckin' Johnnie now."

Glynn hastily searched the inside pocket of his denim jacket with his free hand, quickly produced the vital prophylactic, in its shiny foil jacket and threw it to a grateful Jay Mac.

"Don't ask me to put it on for yer." Glynn shouted, laughing, while his friend raced back to his expectant partner.

Quickly resuming their passionate clinch, Jay Mac pushed his hand down inside Julie's panties and tights and explored the warm moist thatch between her legs. The girl's hips involuntarily rose and pushed forward, to meet his firm invasive fingers.

After a few minutes of this stimulating, penetrating massage, Julie moaned softly and said, "Put it on Jay Mac, I'm nearly coming."

Eager to comply, Jay Mac opened the front of his trousers, pulled down his straining underpants and released his throbbing erection. As deftly as he could manage, in the near darkness of the alley, he rolled the gossamer thin rubber sheath over the head then along the shaft of his engorged member. Julie was equally nimble, in rolling her underwear partway down her thighs, then turning to face the door, she pushed her pert bottom towards the salivating male.

"Do me from behind Jay Mac, I love that." Julie announced, adding even further to his surprise and delight.

Jay Mac pressed himself against the burning flesh of the waiting girl and a shudder ran through her body. Fumbling at first to find the correct orifice, he used his hand to feel for her moist, fleshy entrance and inserted the tip of his tool into her quivering vulva. Slowly but deliberately, he pushed the entire length of his iron hard rod, up and inside the ecstatic girl and she pushed herself back onto him with equal determination. Once he was fully and firmly mounted he placed one hand onto the front of her downy thatch and teased her further.

His other hand was unable to gain ingress through her tight fitting mini dress, which had ridden up above her waist, so he squeezed and rubbed her small, firm breasts, through the thin, clinging material of her garment and teased her prominent nipples with his fingers. The young male increased the pace and strength of his movements until he was pounding the slender appreciative girl with greater momentum and intensity on every stroke. He knew that he could not last much longer, at this rate and was grateful when Julie began moaning loudly, then cried out in orgasmic delight.

"I'm coming, oh fuck, I'm coming."

Jay Mac reciprocated and exploded in a wild orgasm of his own, pumping his member until he was completely spent. He collapsed sweating and breathing erratically against his exhausted, grateful partner. After a few post coital, tender moments of mutual inertia, Jay Mac withdrew himself and threw the well-used condom, into the pile of collective filth on the floor of the alley behind them. Julie pulled up her panties and tights, then turned and kissed Jay Mac on the mouth.

"You know that we can never see each other again, don't you Jay?" she said with a genuine sadness.

"Do yer mean because of yer brother, Quirky?" he asked rhetorically, already knowing full well that this was the reason, for their one-off dangerous liaison.

Julie did not answer but instead she advised "You leave first, Jay Mac, I'll wait for Sue, I think your mate probably got more than he expected there."

Jay Mac adjusted his clothing, then kissed Julie passionately once more and furtively left the reeking alleyway, with its foul midden of mixed waste.

He didn't wait for Glynn, following Julie's cryptic message and set off to find the rest of his crew.

'What a fucking ace night,' he thought to himself and, with a beaming smile on his face he strolled along the road, past the old concrete bus shelter, diagonally opposite the scene of his recent sexual exploit. If he had even glanced at the heavily vandalised, pre-cast structure, he might have just caught sight of his fellow team mate Blue, crouched watching the alleyway entrance, from where Jay Mac had just emerged. Kneeling in the shadows within, Blue's rage was all consuming. Jay Mac had now lost a fickle friend and gained a determined, spiteful enemy.

Thursday 25th May 1972

At seven o'clock the following evening, Jay Mac arrived at the library in the middle of the Crown Estate. Blue, Glynn and Irish were seated on the concrete sill, with four other crew members, including Johno, standing nearby engaged in some mock fighting. Everyone was in good spirits, except Glynn, who sat sullenly smoking a cigarette and staring into the distance. Jay Mac quickly realised that Johno was acting the part of Tommy (S) and the others were variously pretending to be a trio of drunken sailors, in an improvised version of the previous night's drama. The tale was already beginning to grow and a new urban legend had been born.

"Alright Jay Mac, take a seat mate." said a warmly smiling Blue, much to Jay Mac's surprise. He squeezed in between

Blue and Glynn, then turned to his silent team mate and asked him if there was a problem.

"It's me mum; I don't know what's wrong with her." Glynn said quietly to his friend.

"How d'yer mean, is she sick or somethin'?" asked Jay Mac slightly concerned.

"I got home last night and she was just sittin' there in the kitchen, smokin' a cigarette and cryin'. She looked really rough, hair and makeup all messed up and yer know me mum's never like that Jay Mac." Glynn finished speaking, took a drag of his cigarette and actually inhaled fully.

"Did *you* 'ave a good night Jay Mac?" Blue asked with a grin.

"Can't complain Blue, can't complain." he answered, a little disconcerted by Blue's unexpected friendliness.

While they were talking and the mock sailors, who were now all stretched out on the pavement and being 'whipped' by an invisible dog lead, supposedly held by the triumphant Johno, who was enthusiastically entering into the spirit of his role, three scooters, each with rider and passenger rode by. They slowed down as they passed the library and one of the scooter-borne Skins, seemed to look directly at Jay Mac, he thought. At that moment from the opposite direction, a police panda car arrived. The scooters took off rapidly and were gone before the police officers stepped out of their vehicle.

"Evening boys." said a tall slim policeman, moving toward the eight members of the crew.

"Alright officer?" they replied in unison.

"Two young men were violently assaulted outside Central Way Hall last night and now they're in hospital in a bad way. You don't know anything about that do you boys?" the officer asked.

Jay Mac acted as spokesman for the group, before Irish could say something controversial. "Officer, if we were aware of any unpleasant incident of that nature, we would be the first to contact yourselves."

The second policeman, who was a more squat and heavy built individual, now stood in front of the crew and studied them carefully.

"You're funny little fellers aren't yer?" he began. "You play around here every night, pretending to be tough but y'don't even know what tough is."

When he had finished speaking, he stood directly in front of the seated Jay Mac, leaned over him and, prodding him in the chest with his right forefinger, said "I think you're the type of little cur, who would kick an injured man, when he was down, am I right?" He watched Jay Mac carefully for a few seconds then straightened up.

"Like I said sir, we don't like violence and we wouldn't ever be involved in causing harm to anyone." Jay Mac stared at the squat officer and smiled as he spoke.

The tall policeman clearly decided any further questioning would be pointless and returned to their vehicle, motioning to his colleague to do the same.

Just before he entered the car, he turned and looked back at the boys "Carry on with your little play." he said to them all, before speaking directly to Johno "By the way, was that supposed to be a dog lead, you were whipping your mates with? It was very good, very convincing." He said no more and got into his seat.

"Be seeing you, very soon." the stocky officer said smiling, joining his colleague, before they drove away.

"Fuck me," said Johno, "those pigs aren't as fuckin' stupid as they look."

◇◇◇

Jay Mac was feeling reasonably well off, having received a fair payment from Floyd, as his share of the proceeds from the sale of their recent haul.

"It's nearly half seven, time for Top of The Pops, in the Eagle and, a couple of pints. I'll get the first round in" he offered generously.

"Hang on a couple of minutes Jay Mac, there's no rush is there?" Blue said, once again surprising Jay Mac and this time the whole group.

"Hey Blue, you didn't get a fuckin' bang on the head last night, did yer?" asked Tank and they all laughed.

Just then the familiar sound of scooters was heard once again. The three Lambrettas decked out in the usual array of multiple mirrors, an assortment of gleaming chromed bars, colourful fly screens and small pennant flags fluttering on tall aerial wires, turned the corner of the central road and bumped up onto the kerb, then came to a stop by the library. The drivers and passengers all dismounted and removed their Centurion helmets. Dressed uniformly in denim jackets and jeans with obligatory red Airwair, they looked exactly like the eight Eagle crew members already present, only slight differences in the badges they wore or the specific bleaching of pocket flaps, collars and turn-ups, would enable the discerning observer, to separate them as individuals. Jay Mac tried to quickly study these new arrivals and considered them as being a little older than his crew.

His observations were interrupted almost at once, when Blue shouted, "This is him, Quirky, right 'ere next to me, like I promised!" He caught Jay Mac by the left arm to emphasise his identification and, to hamper any possible flight.

"Grab hold of that fucker, lads." ordered one of the scooter crew. "The rest of you keep out of it, right?"

Immediately, Jay Mac was surrounded and dragged from his seat by four of Quirky's accomplices. The youth looked at the older brother of Julie Quirk and felt a sickening wave of fear, run though his entire body. Quirky stood in front of Jay Mac and studied him for a moment, then spoke.

"So you're the little shit who thinks he can rape my sister and get away with it?"

An astonished Jay Mac looked at his accuser and considered his response carefully. "I don't know what yer talkin' about mate," he said nervously.

Georgie Quirk, at just nineteen years of age, was six foot tall and heavily built. He shaved his head daily and consequently only ever displayed the merest dark stubble on top of his meaty face, which contained two piercing dark eyes under a virtually eyebrow-less prominent ridged forehead. From the right side of his small broken nose near the tip, running across his cheek and ending just before his ear, lay a deep badly healed, disfiguring scar. The different coloured flesh of the wound increased its visibility and added credibility to Quirky's claim that he received it whilst engaged in a deadly struggle, during his most recent incarceration at Her Majesty's pleasure.

"Hold this rapist cunt still." he repeated angrily, as Jay Mac tried to struggle free from the grasp of two of Quirky's equally stocky henchmen.

The other three members of his crew stood facing the Eagle youths to ensure there was no interference, while justice was meted out to Jay Mac.

"You're not a bad lookin' kid are yer?" Quirky asked, smiling. "Let's see what we can do about that."

Drawing his heavy head back, he dropped it with all the force that his thick muscled neck could develop, onto the bridge of Jay Mac's nose. Already possessing a deviated nasal septum from a much earlier conflict during his formative school years, the youth's nose cracked and broke fully, issuing forth a scarlet stream.

"That's better" said Quirky, apparently pleased with his initial efforts, then followed the head butt with two straight short range jabs to Jay Mac's mouth. Feeling the tremendous force of these blows, he ran his tongue over his teeth, inside his closed split lips, to feel if any were loosened. The keen eyed Quirky noticed Jay Mac's facial movement.

"Oh, checkin' to see if you've still got any teeth are yer? Don't worry, we've got lots of time to break all of them."

Two more powerful punches to the stomach came next and Jay Mac could feel his fried tea of bacon, eggs and sausages, churn about in his aching gut.

"Here's a new one, you might not have seen this before." announced Quirky, warming to his role of public torturer, as he stepped away, a few feet from his victim.

Immediately turning to his side, he delivered an awesome thrust kick with the edge of his boot, directly into Jay Mac's already heaving stomach. The youth's mouth opened and he let out a gasp, followed by the partially digested contents of his recent meal.

"Yoko Geri Kikome, thee call that one, learned it in the nick, Shotokan Karate, yer can't beat it. What do yer think boy?"

Something to Do 1972 • **161**

Jay Mac was unable to answer Quirky's question but the deranged psychopath pressed on.

"Now, tell me why yer raped me sister?"

Jay Mac forced a reply through his bloodied, food stained mouth. "I didn't rape her." he mumbled.

"Wrong answer." was all Quirky said, then sprang forward and dropped his brick of a head once more onto Jay Mac's already smashed nose. The agonised youth winced in pain as more blood ran over his mouth, down his chin and onto the plain white T-shirt, he was wearing under his denim jacket.

"Are you sayin' then that my poor virgin of a sister, actually let you do her? Are you sayin' she's a fuckin' slag?" Quirky demanded leaning into the bloody mess of Jay Mac's face, releasing his whiskey and beer tainted breath with a loud belch.

"No, she's not…, she's a nice girl." Jay Mac could manage no more and began to fade in and out of consciousness.

Two more solid rights and a hard left pounded his rapidly emptying stomach, then Quirky stood back and looked at the helpless Jay Mac.

"How am I doin' boys?" he turned and asked his friends.

"Your're doin' great Quirky, fuckin' ace", they replied grinning broadly.

"Now here's the situation. I came in last night and I heard our Julie cryin' upstairs. When I ask her why, she won't say nothin' but today, our little Jenny comes to me and tells me about this cunt forcin' himself onto our Julie, she's been told this by our friend 'ere, Blue. When I had a word with *him* this afternoon, he's told me the fuckin' lot and promised to have this piece of shit waitin' for me 'ere tonight."

Irish and Glynn looked at Blue in disgust and disbelief. Glynn, who was nearest to him, said, "You fuckin' cunt. You know that's a pile of shite."

Blue kept his head lowered, then said in a quiet voice "He had it comin', takin' my bird."

Irish could stand it no longer and shoured "You shitty little cunt, it was Jay Mac who got that Kenny Goodwin lad off yer, when he was fuckin' choking yer to death." Then he turned to Quirky. "Listen mate I went to school with this lad, I've known him for years and I've got two younger sisters meself. Do yer think I'd have him in my house and have him stay over, if I thought he was even a bit like that? Just let him go will yer?"

Quirky looked bemused at Irish's impassioned plea. "Are you his fuckin' boyfriend then?" he asked, looking about the crowd and laughing, not noticing that one of the Eagle crew was missing. "In the 'Nick' there's only one way to deal with a nonce, even if you're not sure that he is a nonce. A bit of castration is what we need 'ere. In there lads." he motioned to his minions and they dragged the barely conscious Jay Mac into the reeking alleyway, the scene of the previous evening's passion. The youth was thrown onto the same pile of assorted filth, where he had discarded the semen filled condom and then held down forcibly. Realising what was about to happen, he kicked and thrashed his legs wildly causing Quirky to call for further assistance.

With Jay Mac now restrained by four of his crew, Quirky bent down, unfastened the youth's jeans and began to pull them and his underpants down.

"It's only a little prick, hardly worth the bother really," he mused, whilst reaching into the inside pocket of his denim jacket. Quirky then produced a bone-handled cut-throat razor, which he opened very carefully.

"Here's my tool, it's a beaut isn't it, does *lovely* work." he said, pointing to his own facial scar. "It only cost the previous owner an eye and then he let me have it. Hold still, this is goin' to hurt you a shitload more than me."

With his eyes watering from the pain of his injuries and, blood spattered from his hairline to his throat, Jay Mac just managed to see the gleaming blade, as it reflected a shaft of evening sunlight, which briefly penetrated the foul den.

He heard Irish shout "C'mon Quirky, he's had enough for fuck's sake!"

With the last vestige of his strength, Jay Mac drew together as much blood and saliva as he could manage and spat the sticky mixture into the eyes of his tormentor. At that instant, there was a terrific splintering crack and suddenly the oppressive weight of Quirky was gone, as he dropped to one side onto the stinking, litter-encrusted floor. Jay Mac's four remaining captors stood up slowly then he rubbed his eyes to see what had happened. Standing behind the fallen body of Quirky, was Tommy (S), not armed with his trade-mark dog lead but the remaining handle and part shaft of a broken wooden baton, in his strong right hand.

"Put that fuckin' little prick away, before a mouse has it off." he said almost breaking a smile.

Irish and Glynn helped their friend to his feet and he saw Johno, standing rooted to the pavement, with Quirky's other accomplice firmly clamped in his unbreakable headlock. Jay Mac offered his thanks as best as he could manage, through his injured mouth.

Tommy (S) explained how he had been in the Eagle with his peers, briefing other team members on what to say if questioned by the police when Johno had burst in. Knowing who he was about to deal with, he obtained the barman's disturbance-clearing wooden baton and sprinted across to the shops with his old guard in tow.

The temporarily stunned and silenced Quirky was helped to his feet by his companions and then Tommy (S) addressed him directly.

"Listen Quirky, you mad cunt, I've known yer a long time and you know me. This is a good kid, he's no fuckin' rapist. And from what Jackie has told me, your sister was all over him. So yer've given him a beatin' for knobbin' her, that's fair enough. I've got a younger sister and I'd probably do the same but that's as far as its goin' ok?"

When he finished speaking, he passed Quirky his weapon, which had been picked up by Irish and given to him. Rubbing the back of his head where an egg-sized lump was rapidly developing, Quirky and his crew returned to their scooters and prepared to leave.

As if nothing had happened, he shouted to Tommy (S), "I'll see yer at the match, in the Kop, next season, alright?" Then he turned to Jay Mac, "You even look at my sister again and your fuckin' balls are comin' off."

The three Lambrettas with their riders and passengers then sped away.

Jay Mac leaned against the steel mesh-covered library window and forced a pained smile, "Have we missed Top of the Pops or what?"

"Never mind that shite, you need a fuckin' ambulance mate," said Johno.

"I'll just have a pint first" Jay Mac replied.

The whole crew made their way to the Eagle with Irish and Glynn supporting Jay Mac.

Blue decided not to bother and went home alone, seeking comfort from a hastily purchased fish supper. Jenny Quirk, the fourteen year old sister of Georgie and Julie, the girl who always had too much to say, had just finished an impromptu dance routine in the front room of their house. She watched the television and mimicked the moves of Pan's People, whilst her tearful older sister sat silently imprisoned, in the escape proof cell of her over possessive, jealous brother's paranoia. The keen amateur dancer didn't know, or care, what consequences her lies had caused that night.

Chapter 8

Rocket Man

Wednesday 24th May and Saturday 17th June 1972

Sylvia Glynn looked hard and long into the mirror on the dressing table in her small, lonely bedroom. At thirty nine years of age she was, she thought, still an attractive woman. Her figure was more rounded perhaps, her once sparkling eyes may have lost some of their captivating glint and the full lips that pouted so provocatively appeared thinned and puckered but her vivaciousness remained undimmed. Nineteen years ago her longed for Prince Charming, had arrived and made her dreams come true, for a while. Once they were married he stayed for a few painful months after the birth of his son and heir, then he found a younger princess, leaving the heartbroken Sylvia alone and afraid once more. Now fearful of the dreaded rapidly approaching landmark fortieth birthday, she began to feel that she would never find another love and her search was becoming increasingly desperate, as were her sexual desires.

The random partners that she had chosen in the last few months had failed to provide the satisfaction that she craved. She had found her only recent fulfilment in watching her son's young friend frantically masturbating himself, whilst voyeuristically observing her, engaged with a flaccid, heaving mate. Time and again she replayed that image on her internal cinema screen, allowing her own hands to provide the pleasure that her greedy, self-satisfying paramours could not. It was during one of these precious interludes, that she was suddenly disturbed by an untimely knock on the front door. Quickly throwing on a thin silk dressing gown over her bra and panties, she went downstairs and opened the door, to find an androgynous, rakish young man of a similar age to her son's friend, standing on the step.

"Hello Missus, sorry to bother you but could I have a bucket of hot water, please," said a smiling Macca (G), part way through his window cleaning round on this unseasonably warm May afternoon.

Sylvia studied the youth as he leaned into the doorway, dressed in his fully open, short-sleeved shirt and blue jeans. The six foot tall Macca (G) was a rangy athletic figure, like many of his team mates but where he differed conspicuously was his hair, which was shoulder length, thick, black, wavy and never cropped.

Returning quickly from her kitchen with the required bucket filled with warm soapy water, Sylvia decided to make a tentative offer.

"When you've finished would you like to come in for a glass of juice, or a cup of tea? I mean, with it being such a warm day."

Macca (G), who worked part-time for his uncle helping him with his window cleaning round, smiled even broader than before. He was pleased to receive the tempting invite but even more smug that his plan had worked exactly as he had hoped. His uncle Sammy constantly talked about which women on the estate were potential lays and bragged about how many he had personally helped to fulfil their potential. Mrs Glynn was well known to the local gossips who spread their poison freely around the small community, exaggerating wildly the number of 'uncles' who had stayed overnight at her home, with every telling.

Old Sammy hoped to be added to that list of familial lotharios but never quite managed to get his foot over the lonely woman's doorstep. His nephew had earlier that day, bet him that he would prove more than capable and boasted that he would even bring him a trophy as proof. While an excited Sylvia stood hidden behind her net curtains, watching the lithe youth lathering then rinsing her front windows, she had no idea that she was the subject of a cruel wager, or of the terrible forfeit her son would pay.

After running his wet hands through his hair and moving it back away from his face, the anticipatory Macca (G) knocked once again on his customer's front door.

"I've finished all your windows, I've done yer front and back," he said with a cheeky grin.

Sylvia invited the young man into her kitchen and poured a cold glass of diluted orange juice for him, then returned the jug to the fridge. Both parties knew why they were present in this small room. Macca (G) sat on a chair by the highly patterned Formica topped table, drinking his juice and allowing his lustful gaze to slowly wander over the woman's voluptuous contours, barely concealed by the thin material of her dressing gown. Whilst the youth had been completing his window cleaning duties outside, Sylvia had hurriedly applied a full face of makeup and energetically backcombed her deep auburn hair.

After some brief dialogue concerning the unusually warm weather, an uncomfortable silence hung between the trembling woman and the excited youth. Fiddling nervously with the loosely tied silk cord that held her short gown closed, she decided to abandon any further caution. Sylvia undid the bow with her right hand and casually let the garment fall open. The seated young man murmured an acknowledgment of approval, as his eyes fastened onto her ample breasts only just contained in her transparent black bra, then his gaze travelled down over her rounded belly, to the dark thatch clearly visible through her small matching panties.

In a single bound Macca (G) closed the short distance between them and grabbed hold of the expectant female. He kissed her roughly on the mouth then moved onto her slender neck, whilst his moist hands squeezed her rounded breasts firmly. Sylvia quivered involuntarily when Macca (G) pushed one hand inside her panties and began exploring between her legs. With his other hand the youth eagerly struggled to unfasten his Wrangler jeans and unzip himself, intending to mate the willing woman against the fridge, or over the kitchen table, or on the floor, without any further ceremony.

Suddenly she stiffened and caught hold of his forearms with her hands, "Stop, stop!" she said urgently, "Listen, it's my son Daniel at the door."

The fully erect, frustrated youth now heard his team mate knocking on the front door, then shouting through the letter box.

"Mum, it's me! I've forgotten me keys, open the door will yer."

Quickly closing her gown and trying to adjust her ruffled hair, she shouted "Ok dear, I'll be there in a minute, hold on."

Macca (G) having managed to contain his desire, zipped up his jeans and moved toward the back door.

"I'm sorry, honestly I am," Sylvia said, then added hesitantly "If you like, you could come back this evening; my son will be out at the youth dance with his friends."

An evil smile lit Macca (G)'s face, as he turned and slyly answered the accommodating lady. "I'd love to; we'll have a real good time later, see yer."

With that he made his escape out through the rear alleyway and collected his ladder, bucket and leathers from where he had left them at the gable end of the terraced row.

Glynn the unsuspecting son, pushed passed his nervously smiling mother and ran up the stairs to the bathroom, "I'm burstin' for a piss!" he shouted.

"Oh Daniel, please don't use that language, you sound like one of those rough boys off the estate." his mother warned.

While Sylvia spent the rest of the afternoon preparing for her evening tryst, taking a leisurely bath, choosing her best outfit and most enticing underwear, her intended lover, Macca (G), sat in the front room of Yad's parental home with his two fellow commanders, describing with relish every detail of the older woman's curvaceous body.

"Don't say any more will yer, or I'll 'ave to have a fuckin' wank" said an excited Weaver.

"Calm down mate, yer'll need all yer've got for this one. We're goin' to give it to her alright... fuckin' hard." Macca (G) smiled wickedly as he spoke then continued shuffling a deck of cards that he was holding.

"Right Yad, choose yer card," he said holding out the splayed deck like a fan in front of him.

"Fuckin' shit, a four of diamonds. Am not havin' this, why can't we just all jump her at once?" A sulking Yad turned away with his low value card, like a truculent child.

Weaver was next to draw and when he saw that his chosen card was a Queen of Spades, he shouted with confidence "I'm up first and she won't even notice your two little pricks, after I've finished with her!"

Macca (G), the originator of the idea of the draw, picked a two of clubs, which cheered the peevish Yad but led to a call for a change of precedence, with lowest card first.

"Fuck it anyway, we'll all dive on her, once I've let you's in. Now remember give me about ten minutes to get the stupid old bird worked up, then I'll say I'm goin' for a piss an I'll put the front door on the latch for yer."

After outlining his plan once again, he then added, "Don't forget to lock that fuckin' door and bolt it, once yer in. We don't wanna be disturbed, do we?"

Around the time that Yad was receiving Tommy (S)'s observation, about how unwelcome his presence could be and Glynn was appreciating the females lined up in the queue outside Central Way Hall, the unsuspecting Sylvia was making the final adjustments to her make up. The malevolent trio left the Eagle, once the disco had started, in Central Way Hall, with evil intent on their minds. While Macca (G) knocked on the door of the waiting Sylvia's house, his two smirking associates took up their observation positions, in the entrance of the tenement block across the road.

Once he was inside, Macca (G) grabbed hold of the excited woman and pinned her to the wall in the small hallway. Kissing her roughly, his exploring hands began to open the expensive blouse that she had spent so long in choosing and then searched under her knee-length skirt, feeling the tops of her nylon stockings and suspenders.

Momentarily breaking away from his ardent embrace, a breathless Sylvia said "I thought you might like a drink first?"

Macca (G) smiled slyly and replied "Why not, you're right. We've got the house to ourselves, no need to rush things."

The woman and the youth were soon sitting on the same couch that had seen so many previous encounters and, each drinking a glass of red wine, which Sylvia felt added a touch of class to the proceedings. Quickly finishing his drink, Macca (G) said he needed to use the toilet and, as he passed the front door, before stepping onto the stairs leading to the bathroom, he silently unlocked it, flicking the metal catch down to ensure that it stayed open, for his evil accomplices.

Glynn and his friends were standing in front of their respective dance partners, when Yad and Weaver stealthily entered his home and burst in on his unsuspecting mother. Instantly realising that she had been cruelly duped, the terrified, desperate woman screamed for help and struggled vainly, while she was carried up the stairs and dragged to her own lonely bedroom. One more scream on an estate where the golden rule and key to survival was 'mind your own business,' attracted only the momentary interest of two elderly females, who were hurrying home before darkness had fully fallen.

"Hey Vera, sounds like Mrs Glynn, has got one of her male friends round again," said one of the ladies to her friend.

"Yeah, the lucky bitch." her friend replied while they scurried on, laughing to themselves.

When Jay Mac and Glynn were enjoying their slow dances with their two willing partners, Mrs Glynn had already had her expensive blouse ripped off, her flimsy bra torn in half and thrown across the room and, her carefully chosen matching panties, violently pulled off, in a concerted attack by the three Heron crew leaders. Repeatedly raped, buggered and subjected to other sexual assaults, by the time the two merchant seamen were approaching Julie Quirk and her friend Sue, Sylvia no longer struggled offering no further resistance, as she was dragged from one to another of the youths, who howled with laughter.

"Fucking bitch, keep struggling!" shouted a furious Macca (G), forcing himself once more into the exhausted woman.

Jackie (M) had just kneed her lecherous dance partner in his privates when the three raping team mates, finally tired of their victim and put their spent members away, before sneaking out of the front door, letting it lock shut behind them.

When an equally spent Glynn arrived home later that night, pleased with his own amorous performance and his partner's energetic, enthusiastic, sexual proclivities, he was surprised to find his dishevelled mother sitting in the kitchen crying, with half an inch of grey ash precariously attached to her smoking, king-size cigarette.

No amount of questioning could illicit a response from the traumatised woman, while she continually sobbed, wiping the heavy mascara stains from her moistened face. She drew her long, thick winceyette dressing gown, normally reserved for deepest winter wear, tightly around her. The spoilt boy abandoned his quest for answers and went upstairs to bed. Eventually the mother forced herself to do the same. Sitting on the edge of the heavily semen-stained double bed, Sylvia Glynn took a long, hard look in her dressing table mirror and wondered why life had to be so cruel. She broke down and cried uncontrollably like a little girl.

◇◇◇

The following day, in the middle of another warm afternoon, only a few hours before Jay Mac would receive a major beating from the paranoid Quirky, a smug Macca (G) was standing in the back yard of his uncle's terraced house, helping him put away their ladders and window cleaning equipment. Old Sammy was eager for a full account of Macca (G)'s encounter with Mrs Glynn. He had always been the main inspiration for the youth and regularly told his nephew of his own alternative war time 'exploits,' exaggerating the extent of his conquests for the benefit of the young, impressionable listener.

During the war, somehow the young Samuel Mackenna had managed to convince the authorities that he was unfit for active service. He did his own bit for king and country, by bravely continuing his window cleaning round, providing a regular service for the lonely wives and girlfriends of the absent troops, satisfying their needs, either with goods from his black market dealings, or in person. His nephew Gary Mackenna, also known as Macca (G), provided conclusive proof that the apple did not fall far from the tree.

Sylvia's ripped panties which had been roughly dragged from her were now thrown into the smirking face of his appreciative uncle.

"You jammy bastard." he said as he held the trophy over his mouth and nose, breathing in deeply. "Tell me all the filthy details, while I get you a pint in the Heron." He took another long inhalation then placed the tattered underwear into his jacket pocket.

"Sammy, it's gonna take more than a pint to hear all about this fuck." Macca (G) said wickedly.

"That's my boy, that's my boy," his uncle replied, with more than a hint of possible truth.

Saturday 17th June 1972

It was a hot, sunny Saturday morning and the soundly sleeping Jay Mac, was suddenly awoken by the strains of Elton John's *Rocket Man*, blasting out from the record player, in his friend Glynn's bedroom.

"What's happenin,' where am I?" said a groggy Jay Mac, who had been drinking heavily the previous evening with his regular companions, including a chastened Blue now readmitted to the fold after making profuse apologies.

"Shit, I've had another nose bleed, sorry mate." Jay Mac said, looking down at the dark red dried blood stains on the previously white pillow case.

Since the violent assault by Quirky, Jay Mac had been suffering from regular headaches and prolonged nosebleeds. He had been referred to hospital and had X-rays taken of his head, followed by an extremely painful, manual attempt to adjust the break in his nose. Jay Mac's aunt and uncle, who now had even less contact with him said that this latest incident, which Jay Mac had described as an unfortunate accident, was a portent of far worse events to come.

Glynn was wandering around the room loudly singing his own off-key version of his current favourite ditty, much to Jay Mac's annoyance.

"Alright mate, I know where I am now, so shut the fuck up will yer."

It was Glynn's seventeenth birthday and he was in good spirits, despite his growing concerns at the increasingly dark moods that his mother was displaying.

"D'yer fancy some breakfast before we get off into town?" Glynn asked whilst studying his appearance in the bedroom mirror and admiring his new short-sleeved, checked Ben Sherman shirt.

A few moments later the two youths were sitting in the small kitchen, where Macca (G) had previously enjoyed his first encounter with Mrs Glynn and formulated his evil plan. When they had both finished their bowls of cornflakes, Glynn made copious amounts of hot buttered toast and they greedily devoured these also.

All the while *Rocket Man* had been playing repeatedly on the large stereogram in the adjoining living room, the scene of the shocking prelude pounce by the three Heron leaders, on the unsuspecting terrified woman.

"Glynn, you must know every fuckin' word of this song, put somethin' else on will yer?" Jay Mac asked his team mate, who was now attempting to sing the lyrics once again but this time hampered by a mouthful of golden toast.

Suddenly the record abruptly stopped with a screech and a furious Mrs Glynn entered through the open doorway connecting the two rooms.

"What the hell is *he* doing here?" she screamed glaring at Jay Mac. "Get out of my house now, I don't want any of your sort in my house again!"

Jay Mac stood up to leave and looked aghast at the dishevelled woman, with her unkempt hair, which no longer regularly dyed deep auburn, was heavily streaked with grey and had returned to her natural mousey-brown shade. Her pale skin looked haggard and her blood-shot eyes were underscored with dark ringed lower lids.

The woman caught the boy's gaze and drew her food-stained, heavy dressing gown tighter about her. Jay Mac was a core part of Sylvia's recurring nightmares, a causal link between her innocent, erotic fantasy and the horrific reality of her violent gang rape. Glynn tried to remonstrate with his irate mother but Jay Mac could see this was futile, with Mrs Glynn seeming entirely detached from her surroundings, as if she could not even hear her son's words.

"I'll see yer in a couple of minutes." Jay Mac shouted grabbing his denim jacket off the back of the chair, where he had been sitting and hastily exited the house.

The youth made his way to Irish's home and as he passed Blue's residence en route, he decided to call for him. The chirpy Blue answered the door with his mouth full of food, having just started ploughing into half a dozen bacon sandwiches that his doting mother had made for him.

"Here y'are Jay Mac, drop one of these mate." he said, spitting particles of food everywhere and passing Jay Mac a moist sandwich packed with warm bacon, dripping with tomato sauce and melted margarine.

Blue was theoretically Glynn's closest acquaintance within their crew and Jay Mac asked him if he knew what was wrong with his mother.

"All I know is she hardly ever comes out of the house and when she does, everyone who sees her says she looks fuckin' mental."

After they had collected Irish, they strolled past the row of shops facing the Eagle and took up their positions on the library windowsill, whilst waiting for Glynn to join them.

"Fuck me, I only just got out, me mum's goin' wild in there, smashin' plates and stuff." said a slightly concerned Glynn, when he arrived at the library and joined his friends. "Here's a bus comin' - let's get on before the mad bitch comes out after me."

He appeared more worried about his planned birthday celebrations being spoiled, than the mental turmoil of his distraught mother. The four youths ran across the road and leapt onto the crowded bus heading for the city centre. It was almost half past twelve and they had a long day's drinking and female spotting ahead of them.

A little less than an hour later, all four were comfortably seated in the upstairs lounge bar of their favourite hostelry on London Road, The Central Public House. Blue had just returned from the bar with four pint glasses, half filled with bitter and the four accompanying bottles of brown ale, required to complete the mixture. As usual he had also purchased a variety of packets of crisps and salted peanuts for the crew. While they sat leisurely drinking their pints and eating their savoury snacks, listening to Elvis Presley's *Viva Las Vegas* on the juke box, blaring away in the bar just a few wooden steps below, Blue began talking to Jay Mac, who was sat on his immediate right.

"Listen mate, I know it's all sorted but, er, y'know what I'm sayin'," he began his preamble to his formal apology. "What I'm sayin', like, is I'm sorry mate, I don't know what the fuck came over me."

Jay Mac continued drinking his pint but nodded in acknowledgment of his team mate's gesture. "Birds mate, once they're involved, y'fucked. Yer head goes up yer arse and yer don't know whether yer comin' or goin'. Anyway forget it, yer know what they say about women 'you can't live with them and you can't live without them'."

Glynn, the birthday boy joined in, "Do yer think birds ever fight over lads?" he asked somewhat niaively.

"Fuckin' hell Glynn are you seventeen today or seven?" asked an astonished Irish. "Look at some of the crackin' scraps that we've seen outside the Hounds. Birds tearin' each other's hair out and, kickin' the fuck out of each other."

Glynn quickly interrupted Irish while he was in full flow "...and rippin' their clothes off, and showin' their knickers!" he added, excitedly, more like his old self, thought Jay Mac.

"Yeah Glynn and throwin' blimps to everyone but that's not me fuckin' point is it?" He stopped for a moment and looked sternly at Glynn, to ensure that there was no further interruption. "What I am sayin' is, birds probably get into more fights over fellers, than anythin' else, ok?" When he had finished speaking, Irish returned to sipping his pint and his usual game of trying to blow smoke rings.

Jay Mac looked around at his companions then said "Fuck me, its Irish the expert in women's matters now is it?"

They all laughed, even Irish, then Jay Mac continued, "Listen to Marjorie Proops, the agony aunt, yer'll be gettin' letters next – *"Dear Marjorie, can you help me? My boyfriend's knob is too big and I don't know what to do with it – signed 'Worried of Liverpool'."* Jay Mac pressed on – *"Dear 'Worried of Liverpool', thanks for your letter, don't complain, a bit extra always comes in handy, I'd be happy to help. Marjorie. PS, have you got any photos?"*

"Piss off arsehole" said Irish laughing. All four youths then began considering the serious business, of making plans for the afternoon and evening.

When Glynn had left the room to use the toilet, Jay Mac expressed his concerns about their friend and his mother, "We need to keep an eye on him, y'know what I mean? His mum's crackin' up."

A few minutes later Glynn returned from his ablutions and Jay Mac quickly changed the subject, "I was just sayin' Glynn, we'll have to start callin' you Rocket Man, the amount of times you've played that fuckin' record."

Glynn appeared pleased with this suggestion and said "Yeah, I like that Jay Mac that's a good one."

It was Jay Mac's round and when he had bought four more pints of brown mix and some crisps, he placed them on the small, round table, in front of his friends. A few moments later the barman unusually left his counter and brought a tray with another quartet of pints and brown ale bottles to them. He pulled an additional table toward them and put their drinks onto this.

"Er, mate I've just got the round 'ere, what's all this?" asked a bemused Jay Mac.

The tall, heavily built barman, who knew his regulars well and never asked any questions, nodded in the direction of a group of five older males, seated around a table in the adjoining parlour. "Compliments of the 'Gerard Boys'," he said, then shuffled away.

Jay Mac and his team mates looked over at their hosts, and raised their glasses, in acknowledgement, "Thanks lads, cheers!" they said smiling warmly, at this menacing looking group.

"Good luck to yer boys, *slainte*." they responded in turn, as one of the males gestured to Jay Mac to join them.

Already experiencing a sinking feeling, when he heard the infamous 'Gerard Boys' team name, as he approached the men and could see them more clearly, his worst fears were confirmed. Three of the five-strong group, were his cousins, brothers of the notorious Theresa, female mugger extraordinaire and all round violent character.

"Alright lads" Jay Mac said, as a small stool was pulled over for him to sit on.

All five of the early thirties males, were dressed in sharp tailored suits of either dark blue or pale grey material, that had a certain sheen and expensive black or dark brown leather shoes. With their narrow silk ties, fixed with gleaming bars or garnet studs, they could have been businessmen enjoying a working lunch. In fact they were business associates of a sort. However, their broken noses, battered faces and meaty fists, adorned with heavy gold sovereign or colourful gem rings on each finger, suggested that their occupations may not necessarily follow conventional hours.

Niall, Francis and Tommy Mack, were three of the eight sons, that Jay Mac's mother's older brother, Joseph had possibly fathered to his terrifying Harpy of a wife, Sheila. Jay Mac's uncle Joseph had moved to Liverpool from Ireland, with his wife and five children of his subsequent thirteen total, shortly after the end of the Second World War, consequently the older male siblings had been born in Eire and considered themselves Irishmen, who happened to be living in Liverpool, not in any way English. Jay Mac looked at the three sons of Erin and their two companions, whom he did not know. Their hair was almost uniformly dark in each case, heavily Brylcreemed and slicked back, in the earlier Teddy Boy D.A. fashion. Elvis was still their king, although they accepted other members of his royal family, including Dean Martin, Tony Bennett and of course Frank Sinatra.

"Haven't seen you in the Gardens, in a long time John," said a smiling Niall, the oldest of the three brothers present this afternoon, fixing Jay Mac with his dark brown eyes. "Seen yer Ma though, she still gets up in the Crescent or the Tug Boat and gives a song, in between collectin' the glasses. Keeps her in drink I suppose, good luck to her I say."

Jay Mac fully understood the meaning of his words and did not reply. They knew his background, in some ways better than he did himself.

Francis then joined in, "Yer never knew yer arl feller, did yer John?" he asked slyly and then continued, "He was another fuckin' piss head but he could scrap with the best of them."

Jay Mac waited for the final assault from Tommy, the youngest of the three. "Sure, he took a good kickin' when we caught up with him, after he left y'ma up the duff and fucked off. We couldn't let that go now could we? Not with us being family."

Whilst speaking, all three brothers watched Jay Mac's facial expression for any change but he was too practiced in this routine to let any show of emotion betray his inner thoughts and feelings.

"Nice talkin' to yer lads, thanks for the drinks, I'll see yer."

Jay Mac made to rise and leave but Niall caught his wrist in a firm grip with his tattooed left hand, "Hold on John, we've hardly spoken to yer. We've not long come back from the States, Chicago. We've got a few things goin' on there."

The youth made no reaction but continued looking at his older cousin, remembering how, when they had visited his childhood home where their sister Theresa, was a permanent, uninvited, rent free lodger, they had tried to drown the infant Jay Mac whilst he sat in the old tin bath in front of the coal fire. He knew them for what they were really like and always avoided them.

"Yer lookin' a bit scuffy there John, in y'jeans and workin' boots. Could y'do with a few bob maybe?" asked Francis.

"No thanks Francis, am doin' alright." Jay Mac replied carefully.

"Are y'now, maybe you could give *us* a loan then." Francis continued then laughed, "I'm only fuckin' jokin' with yer John but seriously, we could always put a bit of work your way now and then, what d'you say?"

Jay Mac knew he was outflanked and in a no-win situation, as Tommy joined in, "Any of those lads with you handy, are thee useful like?"

Before he could reply, Niall gave his assessment of Jay Mac's three companions, "The scruffy one with the tatty head might have a go, I think. I'm not sure about the young blond feller but your little podgy man, hasn't got a hope in hell." He had obviously began to tire of their exchange and decided to dismiss Jay Mac. "Y'had better get back to yer wee friends there, thee look worried." Then he reached into his trouser pocket and took out some change, "Here y'go cousin, here's a few bob for yer."

'As easy as that,' Jay Mac thought, 'I'm trapped.' He knew he could neither refuse nor accept without consequence and reached over to take the loose cash, which Niall placed in his hand.

"We might need yer for somethin' soon. Don't worry if we can't find yer, we can always leave a message with yer Ma."

Jay Mac looked into his hand, as he walked back to his friends' table. There it was, some mixed coin, not even thirty pieces of silver and he had sold his soul to the devil.

"Let's drop these pints and gerroff," he said barely containing his rage.

"Who the fuck are they?" asked Blue.

"Family." was all Jay Mac would say, before downing his pint in a series of rapid swallows.

When they had all finished their drinks, they descended the small staircase to the main bar and exit. Jay Mac stopped and ordered five whiskeys to be sent up to his cousins and their friends, it cost him a lot more than the handful of change that Niall had given him. He knew the rules of this game perfectly; it would have cost him more than mere money, if he had not returned the gesture.

After leaving The Central, the youths spent the rest of the afternoon, roughly following a route around the city's main shopping area that they had agreed upon earlier. Their meandering path was intended to ensure, that they could observe as many women and girls as possible. Deviations were only tolerated if pursuit of an individual female or giggling group appeared to promise the reasonable probability of a worthwhile return, such as names, addresses and telephone numbers.

Apart from this core objective, the Skins had only two other secondary targets, scooters and food. Leaving the latter until they reached their sorties end, at the Pier Head bus and ferry terminus pie shop, they went through their usual practiced routine of posing as prospective customers, in two of the city's main motorbike and scooter retailers, Victor Horseman and

Cundles. Once they had sat on several Lambrettas of different cylinder capacity and pretended to be driving them wildly around the estates, their raucous performance was usually sufficient for them to be asked to leave.

Jay Mac, who was not his normal ebullient self, only played a disaffected role in these proceedings, until he saw a gleaming Triumph Boneville 750cc motorcycle, proudly displayed in one of the main showrooms. Leaping on to the magnificent machine and grasping the handle bars firmly, all thoughts of being a Skinhead were banished. Now he was magically transported to the endless dusty roads of Arizona, speeding through Monument Valley, leading a cohort of Hell's Angels, wearing their colours with pride and being borne along, by their roaring hogs.

"Alright lad, are you buying that bike?" asked the security guard, placing a firm hand on Jay Mac's shoulder.

The youth turned to the frowning man and smiled, "That's a good question my man, would you recommend such a purchase? You see I have several of these vehicles, in my extensive collection and wonder if one more might appear a little brash. What do you think?"

A few moments later, Jay Mac and his three companions were standing outside the shop, protesting their innocence and proclaiming their supposed wealth, having been rapidly ejected.

Finally, they arrived at the Pier Head and consumed several 'pigeon-seagull' pies which were washed down with steaming mugs of brown tea. Unable to find any other opportunities for entertainment they eventually boarded the bus which led back to their own desolate territory. On this occasion they chanced using a Kings Estate bus, feeling it was fairly safe in the late afternoon to do so, although being cautious they chose to remain on the lower deck. Forty five minutes later Jay Mac's three companions, leapt off the vehicle at the corporation bus depot and he carried on alone to his stop. The remaining journey and his arrival home were uneventful and Jay Mac was looking forward to a good Saturday night out later in the city centre, away from the bleak estates.

"I met some of uncle Joseph's lad's in town earlier today." Jay Mac happened to mention in passing, breaking the uneasy silence while he sat finishing his evening meal, of steak and kidney pie and chips, with his aunt and uncle in the small kitchen of their council flat.

"Don't have *anything* to do with them; they're all rotten to the core," advised his aunt, as she lit another Embassy filter tipped cigarette and began clearing away some of the plates and cutlery.

His uncle had turned the small transistor radio on and was busily adjusting the station dial. "That's more like it, Max Bygraves, you can't beat Maxie, *he's* a proper entertainer." He looked at Jay Mac as he spoke, then joined in the chorus of *You Need Hands.* "You didn't take any money off them did you?" he asked knowingly.

"No, of course not." Jay Mac lied, wondering briefly whether his uncle had telepathic powers.

"Good, 'cos if you ever do, they think they fuckin' own yer, even you're not stupid enough to fall for that, I hope."

When his uncle had finished speaking and rejoined his harmonising with Mr Bygraves, Jay Mac tentatively asked him if he would iron his legendary sharp creases, in his new petrol-blue, twenty-two inch parallel trousers.

"Set up the ironing board and put the flat iron on the gas stove, while I light me pipe. You'll have to learn to do this yerself y'know." he agreed whilst feigning his usual reluctance.

Once this task was completed, Jay Mac changed into his evening attire and studied his appearance, first in front of the living room mirror and then via angling that which stood atop of the dressing table, in his aunt and uncle's bedroom. His dark hair had grown out a little from his most recent crop and his face bore only slight traces of his beating from the deranged Quirky, apart from the noticeable deviation in the path of his nose.

Tonight he was wearing a pale green Ben Sherman shirt and petrol blue parallel trousers, both items immaculately ironed by the old soldier, black half inch elasticated braces and his gleaming red Airwair boots. Jay Mac slipped on his black Harrington jacket, gathered together his remaining cash and then prepared to depart. His uncle appeared to have softened to him once again, having reflected on Jay Mac's childhood circumstances, after the mention of his criminal cousins and, as he was leaving put a handful of loose cash into Jay Mac's hand.

"Don't forget, always stand your round and never borrow money off anyone." he advised; then returned to the kitchen to smoke his pipe and listen to the radio in peace.

A few minutes later after timing his short sprint to perfection, Jay Mac leapt onto the waiting bus, just before the doors slid shut and shortly was conveyed past the old sandstone bridge that marked the original boundary of the two formerly tranquil, ancient farming communities. Soon he was briskly making his way to Irish's house, for his first stop of the evening. With his long-time friend accompanying him, Jay Mac next quickly marched up to Blue's front door, rang the bell and waited for their chirpy team mate to appear.

"Are we in a rush or something?" asked Blue, hurriedly following Jay Mac and Irish past the shops and around to the library.

"Let's get off this fuckin' estate and into town, as soon as we can." Jay Mac replied without offering any further explanation.

"Must be planning some serious drinkin'." Irish conjectured, watching for any sign of Glynn's approach.

Finally just as a bus bound for the city centre was about to arrive at the stop facing the library, Glynn came running up the road from his house, he arrived only moments too late for them to catch the green, Atlantean double decker.

"Sorry lads, it's me Mum." Glynn said breathlessly.

"Throwing stuff all over the place again like a nutter is she?" asked a tactless Blue.

"No you fuckin' knob, she's not, she's back to just sittin' in her bedroom, starin' in the mirror and sayin' fuck all." Glynn replied angrily

Jay Mac and Irish asked if Glynn wanted to forget about going into the city on a major pub crawl. The spoilt boy may have had some concerns about his mother but they were not sufficient, to make him consider postponing his eagerly anticipated birthday celebrations.

"No, fuck it, I don't know why she's acting mental but it's not my problem." Glynn adjusted his dark blue Harrington jacket and callously dismissed his mother's breakdown.

Blue, who was wearing a deep maroon version of this ubiquitous Skinhead garment, cream parallel trousers and red Airwair boots that matched Jay Mac's in brilliance, suggested they have a quick pint and some bar snacks in the Eagle, before the next bus arrived. Jay Mac was reluctant but gave way to the favourable majority view.

A few moments later they were all sitting at a table in the lounge bar of the Eagle, which was only sparsely occupied at this point early in the evening, although the actual main bar appeared to be hosting a sizeable poker game, with several members of the 'old guard' amongst the players.

"Happy Birthday Glynn, again." said Jay Mac as Blue passed him his pint, to commence their proposed night of drinking.

Ruby Don't Take Your Love to Town by Kenny Rogers and the First Edition was playing on the juke box and the youths, including Jay Mac, began to relax and lose any sense of urgency, about catching the next bus. Johno, Brain and Tank then arrived and joined their crew members. While the four original drinkers were deciding whether to have another pint or leave, the lounge bar doors swung open and Yad, with Macca (G) and Weaver, sauntered in. A crew of Juniors were with them and took up their usual loitering positions in the doorway vestibule and the ever-empty car park.

"Fuckin' great, we just needed these dickheads." Jay Mac turned and said to Irish, sitting on his left.

"What's goin' on girls? All dressed up hey, waitin' for yer fellers are yer?" Yad began his usual jibes.

Blue, who despite everything that had happened recently, had still not learned when not to speak, said "We're havin' a drink for Glynn's birthday, then gettin' off into town." With that he unwittingly sealed his friend's fate.

Yad positioned himself in front of Glynn and leaned on the small table where the pints had previously stood. "Well, little Glynn's birthday is it? Sorry lad, I've forgotten yer card."

He stood up and turned smiling broadly to Macca (G) and Weaver, "We've forgotten our nephew's birthday, what sort of uncles are we?"

His two grinning generals now approached, carrying their own pints and one for Yad. All three stood by the table, looking down at Glynn seated to the right of Jay Mac.

"Happy birthday Glynn, from your uncle Weaver and your uncle Macca and me, good old uncle Yad."

As they clinked their pint glasses together in mock good health, Jay Mac glanced to his right, watching his friend's reaction. Something seemed to be dawning on Glynn, as if missing pieces had now been added to complete a horrifying, mental jigsaw image.

Macca (G) blatantly forced the final segment into position, "What a great night that was. I tell y'what, she's a fuckin' goer alright, what do you think Weaver?"

The volatile psychopath then joined in the fun. "Too right Macca, I've hardly needed a wank since we done her."

All three laughed loudly at this final torment.

Yad then bent down once again and leaned into Glynn's face, placing his own pint on the table, then patted him on the head "Happy birthday nephew," he said with a broad grin.

The mouthful of ale that Glynn had just swigged, now sprayed violently into Yad's face and open mouth, the normally timid youth leapt up tipping over the table in front of him and its contents. Instead of striking the surprised Yad with his near empty pint glass, he dropped this and grabbed him by the front of his denim jacket.

"You fucking cunt! I'll kill yer, I'll kill yer now!" Glynn shouted wildly, before a delighted Yad caught hold of his wrists in a strong grip.

He steadied the crazed youth then spoke. "You all heard him, he's just called me out in front of everyone and I'm accepting, ok?"

A knowing Jay Mac looked at his desperate friend Glynn. He understood there was no choice for Glynn but wished he had delivered a decisive opening strike with his pint glass, rather than just letting it drop to the floor. Now the die was cast, unless there was some miraculous intervention, or it transpired that Glynn had secretly been hiding an awesome fighting talent for years, very soon he would receive a vicious beating, from the supremely confident Yad.

In the few seconds remaining, before Yad named his choice of venue, whilst he was still holding onto Glynn's wrists and grinning at him, the barman cracked his new dark wooden baton, down hard upon the heavy counter's surface.

"Right! Fuckin' take it outside to the car park, I'm havin' no more trouble in here."

Yad looked around at the different members of both crews and said, "There it is then, in the fuckin' car park, now."

With that he released Glynn with a shrug and threw him backwards. All the youths and some older drinkers, keen for a bit of free entertainment, made their way to the pitted, badly tarmacadamed, empty car park, situated to the right hand side of the main entrance to the pub.

The 'birthday boy' looked like a sacrificial lamb standing with his friends receiving last minute well-intentioned advice.

"Don't close with this fucker," said Jay Mac. "Bang him, then step off, watch for an opening."

Johno who had briefly tangled with Yad once before in the past, over a minor disagreement and, on that occasion they both became aware of each other's strengths, then added, "Glynn, this cunt can't take a hard dig but he is a strong grappler. Like Jay Mac just said to yer, twat him hard and get out of the way, don't let him get a lock on yer."

With those words of warning struggling desperately to reach his fevered brain, that was seething with vile, unbearable images of his mother in the hands of the three grinning Heron leaders, Glynn stepped into the human circle that had now formed.

Yad smiled as he came forward. Dressed in his scrubbed blue jacket, jeans and grubby red Airwair, with his heavy stubble and thick single eyebrow that spanned his forehead, he looked like a denim-clad gorilla about to slaughter an angelic choirboy. "I think am gonna enjoy this, even more than pokin' yer Ma," he laughed, turning for approval from his supporters.

Glynn's tremendous left hook, caught the unawares Yad, fully on the right side of his face and spun his head violently.

Stepping back awkwardly, a stunned Yad spat blood from his mouth and he was immediately struck in the gut, by an equally powerful right from his enraged opponent.

Shouts of "Move back, Glynn! Get out of his range!" rang out from his fellow crew members.

Glynn heard nothing other than his mother's screams and sprang forward again. Yad now had the measure of his opponent and had felt his best shots. Quickly side-stepping Glynn's lunge with a straight left, Yad brought his knee up in a rising arc with lightning speed and drove it into the boy's unprotected stomach. Even as Glynn doubled up in pain from being winded, Yad darted in front of him, seized his lowered head by the ears and smashed it repeatedly down onto his knee, banging it hard into Glynn's face. Yad stepped back a couple of paces allowing Glynn to straighten.

The bloodied youth stood up fully in front of his beaming enemy; Yad sprang forward and delivered a two-pronged assault, with a ferocious kick to the groin and a thumping straight right to the face. Despite all this Glynn tried to remain standing and once again lunged at Yad, throwing a number of ineffectual punches which completely missed their dodging objective. "Down yer go shithead," shouted Yad, kicking the boy in the shin, then tripping him up.

Glynn stumbled then fell onto his knees, before receiving a powerful boot in the sternum, which bent him backwards. Now sitting on his own legs trapped beneath him, Glynn became a fixed immobile target for a flurry of punches and kicks to the head and body, as Yad increased the ferocity of his brutal attack. Then suddenly dropping to hisown knees behind the battered Glynn, Yad threw a vice-like headlock around his neck with his arms.

"Now then 'nephew', tell everyone how much yer Ma loved it and how she keeps beggin' for more, again."

Glynn's bloodied face, which was already covered in scarlet streams, running from numerous cuts and gashes began to turn purple, as Yad increased the pressure on not receiving the response that he wanted.

"He's had enough! Leave him alone!" shouted Jay Mac, Johno and several other members of the crowd.

"I'll say when he's had enough, nobody else!" Yad screamed back in response.

Glynn looked as if he was losing consciousness and Yad became even more determined to make him cry out. He released the youth from the headlock, threw him fully onto the hard floor then sat astride his chest. Leaning over the prone, stricken Glynn, Yad again grabbed hold of him by the ears and began smashing his head into the ground. "Say it, say it, you little fuck!" he repeated, whilst constantly slamming the back of Glynn's skull against the grey-black tarmac surface.

Others in the crowd now began to shout out for Yad to stop, including some of the older veterans.

Unable to bear the distressing sight of his friend, who had started his birthday morning so happily, being pummelled and tormented by the merciless Yad, Jay Mac ran forward, threw Yad to one side and flung himself over the unconscious boy.

"The queer's jumpin' in, Heron crew all in!" shouted the malevolent Macca (G), as he and Weaver broke out from the audience and rained a flurry of kicks into Jay Mac's body and head.

Yad joined in with relish while the Juniors began to push their way through the onlookers, hoping to share in the kill. At that moment Johno and Irish grabbed hold of Weaver whilst Brain and Tank restrained Macca (G), with other crowd members thwarting the Juniors, attempting to reach the fallen Glynn and his human shield Jay Mac.

"Come 'ere, you fuckin' little shit," shouted a stern voice, as Yad was wrenched backwards into the throng. "What 'ave I told yer? When they're down and out, it's over." It was Dayo (G), Yad's older brother and founding member of the Crown Estate Team.

He had been enjoying his drinking and poker game in the bar, as one of the card school members, when he and his friends were rudely disturbed by the commotion in the lounge. Having watched the ensuing fight with the rest of the crowd, he had been fairly pleased with his brother's performance and, to see that he had used some of the unarmed combat techniques, that their ex-Royal Marine Commando father, had trained them in since an early age. Dayo was not prepared, however, to see a defenceless opponent in Glynn's state, beaten to death and, primarily for the sake of his family's reputation, he had decided to intervene and end the show.

With the announcement that an ambulance had been called for the unconscious Glynn, the crowd rapidly dispersed; no one wanted to be present when the accompanying police arrived and began their questioning. Irish and Blue stood looking down at their bloodied, battered friend with Jay Mac kneeling on the ground beside Glynn's unmoving body. 'Rocket Man' had been brought to earth with a crash, his 'timeless flight' had lasted barely a day.

An unknowing Sylvia had already opened her bottle of sleeping pills and swallowed a handful, before her son threw his first enraged blow at one of her tormentors. By the time the boy had slipped into unconsciousness, the woman was already wandering through a long, dark corridor, towards a faint dot of light in the distance.

Jay Mac accompanied their stricken friend to the hospital in the ambulance, while Irish and Blue went to inform Mrs Glynn of what had happened. Unable to gain any response after repeated loud knocking and shouting, they were joined by a concerned neighbour, who said he had not seen Sylvia in days, and together they forced entry into the house.

The disinterested hospital Accident and Emergency clerk recorded two Glynns as being admitted on that evening, one mother and one son. Sylvia could hear a voice calling to her, as she neared the welcoming glow of the now brilliant light. Not far away in another ward, her unconscious only son, drifted towards a similar luminescence and cried out for his mother.

Chapter 9

Schools Out Forever

Saturday 12th August 1972

Jay Mac and the rest of his Crown Team associates who happened to be Liverpool Football Club supporters, were standing in the middle of the tight press of pre-match drinkers, in one of the Red Army's favourite watering holes, The George public house on Breck Road. This was the beginning of the 1972-73 season and today would be the first of two consecutive clashes within three short days, with Liverpool's arch rivals Manchester City and Manchester United. Although the former fixture of the two was keenly anticipated, this was more related to actual, legitimate interest in football matters, whereas the second encounter had a far greater range of expectancy, way beyond genuine soccer speculation. Today most of the disparate Skinhead crews, who followed Liverpool FC, had come with the intention of watching the game and supporting their choice of the City's two top-flight teams. The following Tuesday, when they met Manchester's other premier club, United, the match and its result would only be of secondary importance. Both clashes, however, offered the chance for some off-the-pitch explosive violence and the Crown Team wanted to be sure that they were part of it, when it ignited.

Johno passed Jay Mac a pint of bitter and he in turn moved this onto Brain as best as he could manage in the throng, packed into the small smokey bar room. Two more similar pints followed by two brown bitters, meant that finally the five Crown Team members each had a drink in their hand.

"Fuckin' hell, you've got no chance of gettin' served in here today!" shouted a profusely sweating Johno to his companions, who were struggling to maintain their position and take a drink without any spillage.

"I'll try and get another round in a minute, otherwise it'll be last orders before we get served and we'll have missed the fuckin' game," one of the long absent Crown Team star players, James 'Treky' McCoy, answered in response.

Treky was a deckhand who served on the Isle of Man boats, which regularly sailed between Liverpool and the independent island. At five foot ten he was the same height as Jay Mac but of a more stocky build with a rounded face and almost bald ginger crop. He was also the older brother of the tortured Junior 'Treky' (P), a fact that Jay Mac had been acutely aware of on the night of the youth's capture. Instead of returning to his parent's home on the Crown Estate after each voyage, Treky preferred to stay in lodgings on the Manx island, where he was believed to be enjoying the hospitality of his accommodating landlady.

Also with the crew on this occasion, was a new member, Morris 'Crusher' Tierney, whose family had recently been relocated to the desolate housing estate, on the northern outskirts of the city. The heavily built six foot Crusher was a formidable looking character and tipped the scales at fifteen stone, considerably more than the usual, average weight of eleven or twelve stone of the rest of the crew members. Where his family's council flat was located within the Crown Estate, bordered Eagle and Heron crew territory and both were keen to recruit the powerful seventeen-year old. As yet he remained undecided and only happened to be with the Eagle youths, because they were Liverpool FC supporters like himself.

"Crusher mate, is it true how yer got that name?" asked Brain, before taking a long drag on his cigarette and sipping his pint.

"I don't like to talk about it lad, it was a fuckin' accident, that's all." Crusher replied, clearly uncomfortable with any reference to the incident, where he was supposed to have sat on his sister's pet hamster and killed it, forever changing his original nickname of Moby to Crusher.

Unfortunately Brain was not the most sensitive soul and he unwisely pressed on, "So was it just the hamster or the fuckin' cage as well? I'm just askin' cos that's what I've heard, like."

Crusher stared at the expectant youth, who was casually smoking his cigarette, then said, "Do yer want me to take yer outside and show yer how I did it?"

Even the tactless Brain had enough sense not to pursue the issue any further and said no more, the rest of the crew laughed and carried on drinking.

After finishing their next round which Treky managed to obtain fairly easily, despite the even greater density of the clamouring crowd at the bar, they set off towards the hallowed ground of Anfield. On the way Treky, who never travelled any further than his regular short crossings but somehow managed to sound as if he had circumnavigated the globe, single-handedly several times, began to expound about his own league table of different football supporters' fighting capabilities.

"Now yer Manc is a hard cunt, make no mistake about it. They are probably next in line to yer Scouser when it comes to scrappin' that's because they're northern types, y'know what I mean?" He momentarily paused to ensure that all were benefiting from his wisdom. "Yeah, y'Manc and some of the other woollie-back twats, like Leeds supporters for instance, they will have a go and they'll get stuck in, yeah?"

Jay Mac who had been a friend of Treky long before he acquired the sci-fi television show related sobriquet, chose to draw him further on this subject, "So what about yer Geordie caveman?" he asked.

"Yer right there Jay Mac, they are fuckin' cavemen, that's true. They're hard cunts and can go around all through the winter in just a fuckin' vest but they're like Scousers, they like a laugh, unlike y'Southern Jessies, they're all miserable fucks.

Crusher could see the pattern of play and decided to join in. "Aren't there some hard Southern bastards though mate, what about the Chelsea Skins, they're a bad team aren't thee, always tooled up and ready for a scrap?"

Treky realised that his friends may actually have views of their own but carried on regardless, "I'm not denying that am I? Yer genuine Cockney is as hard as fuckin' nails but how many of them would y'find in London now? They're a dying breed. There's probably some real Cockneys runnin' around with all the London crews, Arsenal, Tottenham, even West Ham but they're not the same as y'Northern types, except for y'Millwall nutters of course, I think it's the fuckin' weather."

The farm labouring Johno teased out some further enlightenment from their mentor, "So are the Brummies harder than y'Southern tarts?"

Treky looked at his questioner in stunned surprise, "Y'Brummie is a good lad, yeah? But he's just fuckin' dozy, gobby but harmless."

Jay Mac now asked the key question, "Who would win in a scrap between any Northern crew and the Jocks?"

Once again Treky appeared almost physically staggered by the incredulity of what he had just been asked.

"Fuckin' hell, Jay Mac are you alright in the head? Don't even get me started on the Jocks mate, they'll head butt yer in the mouth just to say hello. Thee fuckin' razor each other all the time for a laugh, that's yer weather again, y'see in Jockland it never stops rainin', its fuckin' freezin' and the sun never shines and that's just in their summer. Not only that thee eat shite. So no wonder they're always pissed off. Why d'yer think the Romans built a fuckin' great big wall to keep them out?"

As Treky ended his fascinating talk on regional characteristics, traits and propensities, the crew arrived at the ground and joined the huge queue of waiting supporters that snaked along the main road, all the way from the turnstile controlled entrance.

The Crown Team youths observed their numerous rivals standing in the packed line-up and they too were studied by those same crews. Jay Mac and his associates including Crusher but not Treky, were all wearing the latest fashion prerequisite amongst the ever style-conscious Liverpool teams; Flemings' twenty-four inch parallel jeans. In a similar way that military fashions change, so too did the uniform of the Skins. Not to appear on parade and ready for action in the newest kit, risked social censure, even possibly the application of the term 'ancient' or, uncomfortable questions being asked about your Scouse ancestry, as well as suggestions that you could be of dubious origin. Treky became a little self-conscious, standing there in his twenty-inch white parallel baker's trousers and aware of his singularly unique, outdated appearance. Naturally he responded by seizing the fashion moral high ground.

"What's with the fuckin' clown kecks anyway? One strong breeze and yer'll all be blown up in the air?"

Jay Mac provided Treky with an explanation, "Y'know with you being away at sea for long hours at a time? Well, you've lost touch with what's happenin.' These strides are from Flemings' shop in Walton, all the crews wear them now."

Treky listened with interest and made a mental note to get himself appropriately attired, before he returned to his Manx love interest.

Once they had all paid their admission fee and passed through the turnstiles, they quickly made their way to the concrete terraced tiers of the Kop. Pushing in between the tightly packed crowd already assembled, they finally reached their designated sector, where the Crown Team members regularly gathered, immediately behind the goal half way up the rows of steps and almost in the centre of the famed supporters' enclosure. Several members of the old guard were already present, including Tommy (S), standing with Dayo (G), Yad's older brother, who both nodded hello to the youths and, a number of their own contemporaries, notably Tank and the two Ants. Jay Mac noted with some relief, that the crazed Quirky was nowhere to be seen and couldn't recall a time when he had been aware of Quirky's presence previously at the match.

Other teams had also taken up the positions that they too had claimed as their own and, when Jay Mac looked about, he could see various home-made banners displaying their different symbols and names, all bearing the iconic Liverpool FC Liver Bird crest, or declaring *'Established 1892,'* confirming their affiliation to the Club. Compared to some of these huge gangs, such as the Speke Estate or Breck Road Team, the Crown's membership was insignificant and was positively dwarfed by that drawn from the three sprawling territories that comprised the Kings Estate. The latter mob was so numerous, that their presence dominated the last few top tiers of the terraced enclosure, positioned just under the rafters of the roof. Their large flowing red banner, emblazoned with white letters which read "Kings Skins" and their incessant repetition of their one-word chant *"Kings, Kings, Kings,"* made everyone aware of their presence and who they were. In addition they enjoyed throwing pieces of pie, or whole items, chewing gum, the occasional dart and if in season, fireworks, particularly bangers, randomly down amongst the crowd and sometimes at specific targets.

All local rivalries between the teams were temporarily suspended, when the sizeable contingent of Manchester City fans, clearly visible with their sky blue and white scarves and woollen bobble hats, in the opposite terrace, began booing and jeering the Liverpool squad as they entered onto the field. The whole Kop erupted with a spontaneous burst of *"You're gonna get your fuckin' heads kicked in,"* as a suitable deafening riposte.

Jay Mac laughed to himself, considering how quickly, when faced with a common enemy, the usual hostilities were forgotten and a unified front was presented to the foe malign. He thought about Treky's rambling regional assessment of fighting prowess and felt that he may have stumbled on to the core reason for the staggering historical military success of the British and how they had forged a global empire. Everyone on this tiny sceptred isle hated everyone else both regionally and within their own local neighbourhoods, therefore, on the occasions when this endemic anger found a national focus against a suitable foreign foe an unstoppable behemoth, suckled on patriotism and xenophobia, was unleashed. Standing in the centre of the Kop, screaming for Mancunian blood, swearing, chanting and singing the communal anthems, Jay Mac imagined himself at Agincourt, Blenheim, Trafalgar or Waterloo and he loved it.

While the Liverpool players darted about completely dominating the opening minutes of the game, their bright red strip contrasted starkly with the vibrant, verdant green of the immaculate pitch, which had been repaired, lovingly tended and manicured by the ground-staff during the off season. In the third minute after the referee had blown his whistle to signal the kick-off, Brian Hall rocketed the ball into the back of the Manchester City net, drawing an agonised groan from their disciples and a mass roar of exultation from the Anfield faithful. Jay Mac and his companions leapt into the air along with everyone else and then struggled to regain their footing as the tidal surge of the massed ranks swept all before it.

The Kop was the great egalitarian melting pot to Jay Mac, all were equal and all equally subject to its rules and conditions. It made no difference if you were a doctor or a docker, bin man or barrister, once you took your place in the heaving, swaying, tightly packed mob, individualism was surrendered and the red and white leviathan moved as one.

After the initial excitement of the early Liverpool goal, the match then settled into a struggle for possession of the ball with little effective progress being made by either side once this was achieved. During periods of less than dazzling football activity, certain members of the Kop amused themselves by throwing an assortment of missiles at random, virtually un-missable targets in the packed throng. A saliva-covered mouthful of chewing gum struck and then stuck in the thick collar-length hair of a heavy-weight bruiser, in front of Jay Mac and he turned around to confront the youth.

"Did you fuckin' spit some chewy at me lad?" he asked, exposing his awkwardly positioned, badly decaying teeth.

"Mate, I'm not that fuckin' soft. Some Kings cunt up there at the back probably did it, they've been lashing bits of food and other shite down 'ere, for the last half hour" Jay Mac replied diplomatically, sufficiently placating the large forty-something male, who decided to accept his explanation and wisely chose not to remonstrate with the huge Kings Team, clearly visible under their massive crimson banner.

It was close to half time and the rivulets of urine that constantly ran down the terraced steps were increasing in volume, as members of the crowd felt the pressing urgency to relieve themselves was too great to bear any longer. The pungent aroma arising from this alcohol-rich urea, mixed with strong body odour and a multitude of noxious farts, violently discharged at will throughout the first forty-five minutes, created a unique, almost overpowering fragrance that probably would have proved toxic if the stadium had not been open-roofed, allowing the foul incense to rise to the heavens above.

An impromptu chant of *"Come on you Reds"* was echoing around the Kop, when suddenly across in the Anfield Road enclosure opposite, a disturbance broke out. It soon became apparent that a lone Liverpool fan was wildly battling with a group of City supporters, near the lower tier, immediately behind the advertisement covered barrier. A buzz of excitement now animated and united the disparate team members in the Kop.

"Go on Skin, fuck those Mancs!" they shouted in unison, as the stocky youth in full Skinhead garb, smashed all about him with some sort of cosh that was barely visible from their distant vantage point.

The professional players calmly carried on without even glancing in the direction of the incident, while the part-time stewards struggled to restrain the violent sole scrapper, after a group of City fans, bleeding from head and face wounds, forcibly ejected him from their area.

"It's fuckin' Quirky, the mad bastard" announced one of the Crown Team from behind Jay Mac's group.

"Run you crazy cunt, run!" more of the crew began to shout and this exhortation rapidly spread across the assembled teams, only Jay Mac remained silent.

Finally overcome by sheer weight of numbers, including a police officer, Quirky was handcuffed and frog-marched from the field. As the Crown Team senior player disappeared from view into a nearby exit, the referee blew his whistle to end the first half.

Fifteen minutes later a suitably refreshed Jay Mac and the crew, returned to their central location and waited for the two football teams to re-emerge from the players' tunnel for the match to recommence.

"Y'know what? I'm sure that lad who sells the pies, gets them from the same place as the feller at the Pier Head," Johno said, spitting a large piece of gristle onto the back of the unsuspecting and oblivious fellow Kopite, standing in front of him.

The youths had just enjoyed their usual half-time mixed feast of pies and sausage rolls, smothered in red or brown sauce and washed down with mugs of steaming dark brown tea, at the refreshment stand located by the ground floor entrance.

The second half was a more disappointing lack-lustre affair than the first, with generally pedestrian performances from both sides, only sporadically lit by flashes of brilliance from individual players. Jay Mac's two favourites were both present on the field today and probably could not have been more diametrically opposed.

Tommy Smith the 'Iron Man of Anfield,' steadily moved about the pitch upsetting their opponents' run of play by deliberate hard tackling, which usually resulted in his target crashing to the turf wondering what had hit him. On occasion a suicidal rival player may risk life and limb by clattering into the legendary stalwart, only to find himself decked by the tremendous force of the rebound from striking such an immovable object. While Mr Smith stalked and challenged the foolhardy; Ian Callaghan 'The Terrier', raced about tormenting and stripping dazzled opposition stars of the ball, as if they were Sunday morning pub team amateurs.

To spur on their heroes the Kop choristers maintained a steady canon of classic up-lifting anthems, each merging into the other. With the last quarter hour now entered, the whole assembly joined in a rendition of the all-time favourite with interchangeable team names, set to the patriotic tune of *Land of Hope and Glory*. *"We hate Man United, we hate Everton too, we hate Nottingham Forest but Liverpool we love you."* All the while that the Scouse male voice choir were performing their number, the Manchester City fans punctuated each line with a constant repetition of "Shite! Shite! Shite!" which rose in intensity and volume from the opposite terrace.

Jay Mac pictured himself in a scene from one of his favourite films, *Zulu*, standing with his Twenty-Fourth Foot comrades at Rorke's Drift, trading martial chants with the enemy horde.

In the eighty-fourth minute of the game, Mr Callaghan's perfectly struck shot, tore into the back of the Manchester City net, crushing any hope of their team being victorious, or even managing a respectable draw. With the Mancunians falling silent, the Kop and even the more genteel supporters seated in the stands, erupted in jubilation, which was quickly followed by a heartfelt rendition of *You'll Never Walk Alone*. Jay Mac wondered if the original writer, who composed the song for the musical *Carousel*, could ever have dreamed that a bleak two-fisted, Northern European seaport's football club, would adopt and resound with this iconic ballad for generations to come.

After the addition of a couple of extra minutes of injury time, the match ended and the delighted Liverpool fans left the ground, ready to resume their drinking in celebration of a great victory. The dejected Manchester City fans sullenly made their silent procession to their exits and the waiting coaches, or private cars parked not far away. It was during this march of defeat that the assembled Skinhead teams struck. Avoiding the considerable police presence, in particular the mounted unit, like prowling hyenas waiting to pounce on a herd of weary, forlorn wildebeests, they chose their victims and leapt forward. The objective was to cull a small number of rival fans and subject them to a ferocious battering, before the 'herd' could assist, or the police intervene. Jay Mac and the rest of the Crown Team were busily kicking and punching half a dozen stragglers who had been corralled.

"Get their fuckin' scarves!" Tommy (S) shouted, while he repeatedly booted an already downed, bleeding thirty-something male.

Johno had wrested one City scarf from a beaten youth and was now assisting Jay Mac in the acquisition of another for his own collection from a wildly struggling, mid-twenties, civilian type.

"Give it up yer fuckin' dickhead, it's only a rag" Jay Mac snarled as he kicked the crouching man hard in the face and wrenched the blue and white item from around his neck.

"Fuck it's the Mancs, they're havin' a go back," Brain warned urgently, when a crazed mob of City fans charged back to aid their stricken comrades.

Tommy (S), Dayo (G) and other members of the old guard now ran towards them and began striking out, as the two opposing forces crashed into each other. Jay Mac and his Crown Team contemporaries made good their escape, with their scarf 'scalps' as tangible trophies to support their subsequent boasting, for the benefit of the 'Blue' half of their team who were not present. This was what separated the leaders from the carrion fowl, the former sought the actual conflict, the latter only the prize with least consequences.

Two mounted police officers then rode up and quickly dispersed the melee, separating friend and foe alike. In these situations everyone knew the procedure, escape first and regroup later. So it was on this day, when Jay Mac, Johno, Crusher and Treky found themselves hastily making their way towards their own particular bus stop.

As they approached the junction of the road that they were presently travelling along and the main shopping thoroughfare of Breck Road, Jay Mac spoke to his three companions, "Have you clocked that crew opposite, they've been keepin' alongside us all the way from the ground?"

Johno and Crusher acknowledged that they too had observed the dozen-strong gang, dressed in full Skin kit, that had been following the four Crown Team members for some time, Treky appeared unconcerned.

"'Ey you fuckin' Crown cunts you're dead!" was all the warning the crew received before the attack came.

"Straight into them!" shouted Treky darting forward between the virtually stationary traffic, trapped in the post-match gridlock.

Without enough time to allow his natural cowardice to become dominant, Jay Mac followed suit, with Johno alongside and the heavyweight Crusher bringing up the rear.

Treky smashed the lead attacker in the face with a powerful straight left but he remained standing and the two youths exchanged punches toe-to-toe. When another pair of Breck Skins weaved through the vehicles to reach Treky, Jay Mac leapt onto the boot of a car and then on to them, all three collapsed awkwardly in a struggling heap in front of a small delivery van. Johno was busy grappling with a large Skinhead and trying to crack his skull against the roof edge of a packed car, whose occupants were none too pleased. Another assailant jumped onto Johno from behind and threw a headlock around his neck.

Lying on the floor punching and being punched, Jay Mac was at first unaware of the shouts of encouragement from some of the previously impartial pedestrian spectators, who watched in awe, as the powerful Crusher picked up one youth and threw him bodily across the roof of another stationary car. Whilst the Crown Team juggernaut grabbed hold of his second potential victim, Treky was fighting like an enraged tiger with a new foe, having despatched his first opponent with a sequence of devastating punches.

The lights at the junction had changed several times without any vehicular progress; however, the traffic now began to slowly move forward. Irate drivers and their passengers shouted urgently to the struggling youths, to get out of the way or risk being struck.

With their multiple attackers calling for reinforcements, screaming "Breck, Breck, get over here!" Jay Mac suddenly felt one of his punching adversaries being dragged off him and he succeeded in regaining his feet before the second youth could rise. He immediately seized the opportunity to viciously boot the kneeling Skin in the gut then punch him hard in the face, as Crusher flung the other youth into the side of another passing car.

"Fuck, here's the bizzies!" someone shouted, as a pair of mounted police officers approached, anxious to get the traffic moving and clear any obstruction; dispersal by any means was their intent.

All the Skins, both from the Breck and the Crown Team scattered, nobody wanted to be trampled or kicked by one of the towering, immaculately groomed dark chestnut horses of the police and then be arrested by the constables following on foot.

The four companions rallied together and scrambled between the slow moving procession of supporters towards the green Atlantean bus that they could see approaching their stop, less than twenty yards away. Without looking at the number or destination on the front of the double decker, they forced their way onto the packed vehicle. As the upper deck was filled to capacity, with passengers even standing on the stairs, the crew squeezed into the lower deck and moved towards the rear.

"I never thought I'd say that I was glad to see the fuckin' pigs," said Johno, wiping his slightly bloodied face with the sleeve of his denim jacket. "How hard did *you* get hit Jay Mac?

Look at the state of yer face," he continued, turning to his friend who was once again bleeding profusely from his broken nose.

"Shit, one of those Breck cunts caught me on the beak and started me off, it looks worse than it is," he replied, whilst taking out his polishing cloth and attempting to stem the scarlet stream.

"You done well Treky," Johno acknowledged generously.

Treky, the stocky Skin, who was an American comic fan like Jay Mac said, "'Ey, never mind me, what about this fuckin' mad arse? It's like havin' the Incredible Hulk with yer."

They all laughed, even Crusher, who appreciated that Treky's observation was meant to be a compliment, although he had no idea who, or what his companion was referring to.

Just then as the vehicle passed their usual junction without turning, the huge youth turned to his friends and asked, "What fuckin' bus is this anyway?"

An elderly male wearing a cap and Liverpool FC scarf, looked up from his seat and said, "It's a number K1 lad, goin' all the way to the Kings Estate."

Upstairs they could hear the stamping of boots and the all too familiar one word chant of "Kings, Kings, Kings!"

Jay Mac looked at his friends and smiled, "Say nothin', no one's even noticed us and we can dive off at the corporation bus depot when we go past the Crown Estate. Now, who's goin' upstairs to tell them noisy fuckers to be quiet?" he asked laughing.

None of the adult lower deck passengers, who were enjoying discussing and dissecting their team's two-nil victory over their Manchester City rivals, even glanced at the four youths. The black outlined crowns bearing the word 'Skins' in their hollow centres, drawn with indelible marker pens on the backs of three of the crew's denim jackets, that had attracted the Breck team's attention, were not even noticed and, were meaningless to those who did happen to glimpse them.

Speeding along through the old Victorian and Edwardian terraced lined roads, then on to the 1930's suburban housing expansion districts, the overcrowded vehicle was making good time. With almost all the packed passengers bound for one destination only, the huge grey Kings Estate, there had been virtually no stops during the journey and consequently less than half an hour passed before the Crown Team quartet reached the corporation bus depot and garages, where they surprised the driver by asking him to pull over and let them off.

Quickly alighting from the bus they attracted the curious attention of the crowded upper deck Kings Team players, who began swearing and spitting out of the small window openings when they saw and instantly recognised the glaring Crown symbols displayed on the back of the youths' denim jackets. Realising that they had missed a golden opportunity on having four of their Crown Team rivals actually in their midst, the incensed Kings Skins carried on hurling abuse and anything else they could manage to fit through the narrow window apertures, even after the vehicle had sped off from the bus stop. All four Crown Skins gave enthusiastic, vigorous two-finger salutes to their howling enemies, as they disappeared along the main arterial dual carriageway.

Once they had crossed over the central reservation to their side of the road, they sprinted along to the building site where the enormous concrete stanchion supports were nearing completion and where they expected to find the rest of their team armed and poised for action.

"Any Manc fucks been through yet?" asked Johno, when they joined their comrades, after climbing up the gradiated slope leading to the top vantage point.

"Only a few cars with their shitty scarves hangin' out the windows. We done most of them but there's been no decent crashes yet." advised Macca (G), who despite their best efforts, was clearly disappointed at the lack of any major traffic accident so far. "We need this cunt for gettin' the cars," he admitted, acknowledging Jay Mac's deadly throwing accuracy, pointing towards the expressionless youth.

Yad turned around from his lead position at the very pinnacle of the concrete mound, "We don't need this Kings twat for nothin'. I can lash anythin' just as good as him."

At that moment an excited Junior lookout shouted "Here they come, here's their fuckin' coaches!"

Everyone took up their positions making sure they were loaded with as much ammunition as possible.

Four large coaches festooned with sky-blue and white scarves hanging from every window, packed to capacity with disappointed Manchester City fans, who were mostly consoling themselves with numerous bottles of ale, packs of cigarettes and in some cases engaging in high stakes card games, now came rolling along the Lancashire Highway. The supporters in cars always managed to get away first, even with the congestion and they presented a more difficult moving target but the slower moving coaches had to wait until everyone was on board and were usually ensnared by all the post-match delays, giving even those crew members who attended the game sufficient time to return for the ambush. Diagonally across the broad carriageway from the Crown Team artillery battery, a rival Kings troop had positioned themselves at the top of their man-made mound and were fully armed in readiness.

The traffic lights at the corporation bus depot changed from red, amber to green and the small convoy of coaches moved forward. All the drivers were experienced men, they knew what to expect and they hated this part of the journey. On the inbound route there was usually some sporadic missile throwing, anything from eggs to house bricks could be hurled at them as they passed the grim tower blocks on the western edge of the Crown Estate but the return journey, on the outbound side of the carriageway, brought them into the barren no-man's land that both warring teams claimed as their own and between the two grey concrete modern pillars of Hercules. Their carriage company bosses had complained to the authorities repeatedly and this resulted on some rare occasions, in a limited police escort to the northern boundary of the city, today they were unaccompanied and alone.

When the lead vehicle came into range of their grey reinforced concrete, siege tower position, the Kings Team let lose a tremendous salvo of bricks, stones, pieces of rock and handfuls of coarse aggregate. The deafening noise could be heard radiating out from the epicentre of their attack, across both sides of the disputed territory, as the windows, roof and left side of the coach were repeatedly and simultaneously struck by the hail of different gauge projectiles. Watching eagerly across on the slopes of their pillar, the Crown Team battery, which had to throw a greater distance to reach their target, discharged their light fire mixture of pebbles, stones and builder's ballast, directly onto the roof and at the driver's side of the coach. Both rival gangs shouted and howled wildly as they carried out their assault. The nerves of the leading driver held, as did his reinforced windscreen, which though badly cracked and crazed in part, remained whole and he successfully passed through the deadly corridor, with only the loss of a number of passenger windows and a badly dented roof.

Coaches number two and three tried a team effort, hoping to at least dissipate the ferocity and resulting damage of the twin-pronged barrage. Seeing a gap open in the other outbound traffic using the middle lane, the driver of the third vehicle quickly signalled his intent and swerved into position coming alongside his colleague in the second, thereby shielding his left side and the driver's side of the other coach. Outraged by this unexpected and, as they viewed it, underhand manoeuvre, which may deprive them of some of their prey, both teams increased their efforts, taking out most of the windows on each of the exposed sides of either vehicle. Again these two coaches passed through without collision or careering off the carriageway. Now only the fourth driver had to navigate between these 'clashing rocks' and the whole convoy would escape, if not unscathed at least without serious injury.

Mark Thompson was up for the task that faced him. At thirty five years of age and not long discharged from the army transport corps, he had been a soldier since he was eighteen, having served in numerous theatres, including two tours of duty in Northern Ireland. Mark had experienced worse things than stones being thrown at him and the vehicle he was driving. Unfortunately a small car cut in front of him, as coach number three pulled out, leaving a gap that an impatient motorist felt had to be filled and thereby exposed Mark's windscreen, which had previously been shielded by the larger vehicle, fully to the Kings artillery.

Mono's huge block of masonry encrusted in concrete, was thrown with all his street pavior's might and shattered the strengthened glass into countless, sparkling splinters, dozens of which burst into Mark's unprotected eyes. Blinded and with blood streaming from the sockets of his punctured, sightless orbs, he still managed to draw on his soldier's trained resolve and raw courage, to steer the vehicle just beyond the pillars to a safe halt, then collapsed at the wheel. As wild screams of triumphal jubilation rang out from the Kings Team, that were even echoed by their rivals, who rejoiced at the image of the stricken coach, now reduced to a stationary target, the front doors opened and a number of burly male passengers sprang from the vehicle armed with clutches of ale bottles.

"You fuckin' Scouse shitbags, you've blinded driver!" the lead male bellowed, after he and his colleagues ran to the rear of the parked coach and began throwing their brown glass ammunition in a futile gesture of defiance. Nobody returned their fire and both teams stood looking down laughing at the group of ten Manchester City supporters, while they hurled the last of their empty bottles, which fell hopelessly short of their intended targets.

"Come down 'ere and scrap, you little Jessies, c'mon!" shouted the large male at the forefront of the group.

Again the tormenting youths laughed at this ludicrous suggestion, they knew they were facing men who, for the most part, were toil-hardened manual labourers and factory hands, used to long shifts of strenuous activity, no one wanted to engage them in a close-quarter physical contest.

"Watch this," said Yad, stepping toward the edge of the Crown Team's throwing platform, "I'll drop this Manc cunt."

Then he hurled a piece of broken brick towards their challenger below. His missile sailed past the irate man and this would normally have drawn derision from their Kings rivals, except for Jay Mac's shot, a well-chosen perfectly rounded pebble the size of a large egg, which immediately followed Yad's failed attempt and struck the angry male right in the centre of his forehead. Staggering awkwardly for a few moments with his heavy hand clutching his bleeding wound, he stumbled and fell backwards into the uncultivated field of overgrown weeds and grass. For a split second there was absolute silence and then both teams erupted once more cheering wildly.

Danny (H) from the Anvil crew of the Kings Estate and his counterpart, the bowler-hatted Mono, of the Coopers crew, stood conferring together as they studied the successful thrower.

"Nice shot, you fuckin' Crown twat! Not long now and we'll be knockin' on your front door!" a sinister Danny (H) warned.

Jay Mac was sure they were bluffing, if they knew exactly where he lived, they would have already paid him an unwelcome visit. Their false claim was greatly appreciated by a slyly smiling Yad, who gave the signal for the Crown Team to recommence their barrage of missiles, as did their Kings rivals across the carriageway.

The fallen Mancunian male challenger was being aided by his friends, who were trying to conduct him back to the relative safety of the immobile coach, when the devastating torrent of stone showers began once again, only the flashing blue lights and blaring alarms in the distance, promised any hope of rescue. On both sides of the main highway, the teams of youths stopped throwing and quickly scrambled down the steep slopes of their artillery bases and ran as fast as they could manage through their respective fields to safety, before the police patrol cars arrived. As Mark Thompson was lifted into the ambulance, he ignored his terrible pain and focused hard on the comforting image of his wife and infant daughter that he held in his mind, he knew he would never see them again.

Once it appeared safe to emerge from their various boltholes, the members of the Eagle and Heron crews reconvened outside the bottom row of shops, where Mr Li's eatery had now opened for the tea-time and evening trade. Johno, Jay Mac, Irish, Blue and Treky where standing in the long queue of hungry diners and discussing the day's events so far. Irish and Blue were Everton supporters and usually attended home games at Goodison Park, though never together. For Irish, going to the match was strictly a family affair and he normally accompanied his father Callum, his older brother Dermot and met up with some of his cousins, who still lived in the decimated Scotland Road district of the inner city.

Blue attached himself to whoever was going to the match on the day, from any of the Crown Estate's crews. Sometimes this would include Macca (G) and the psychopathic Weaver, though the latter tended to merge with the Gwladys Street Skins and seek out the nearest possible trouble, Yad never bothered with football and expressed no interest in, or loyalty to, either of the city's two prestigious clubs. Consequently Jay Mac and Johno were providing their Eagle crew friends with a brief summary of the events of the day, both on and off the pitch.

"That Crusher is one strong fucker; he was just pickin' up Breck cunts and lashing them right over the tops of cars and vans." Johno was as usual embellishing the tale, stretching artistic licence beyond reasonable limits and thereby removing any credibility for the actual details.

For the sake of historical record Jay Mac felt that he had to interject, "Johno, that'll be a great tale to tell y'grandkids mate but let's have a bit of fact in there, yeah?"

Johno, who was about to be served next, decided to concentrate on ordering his sausage dinner with extra gravy and peas and to allow his team mate to elucidate. Jay Mac then retold the tale briefly and as truthfully as he could from his perspective, though he too concurred with Johno's assessment of Crusher.

"That is one strong cunt, whichever crew he joins, the Crown Team is goin' to get the benefit of havin' their own Hulk on board."

Once they had all paid for their meals, they exited the Golden Diner, deciding to eat their food at once, either leaning against the shutters of the other shops, or seated on the low wall outside the Heron. Unfortunately, Yad, Weaver, Macca (G) and at least half a dozen Juniors were already occupying these positions, in addition Jay Mac saw to his dismay that standing between Yad and Weaver was the aforementioned super powerful Crusher. Surprisingly Yad did not bother goading Jay Mac on this occasion and began speaking to Treky instead.

"Good to see yer back from the Isle of Man mate, how's your little Peter, we haven't seen him in a while?" he began in his usual seemingly inoffensive but totally insincere manner.

"He's alright now Yad but no fuckin' thanks to you. I've told him to keep away, y'know what I mean?" Treky replied sharply.

Yad, who was part way through his curry and chips, reacted in mock surprise, "I don't know what y'mean lad, didn't he tell yer how we rescued him from the Kings twats. He probably wouldn't be 'ere now if it wasn't for me, he should be fuckin' grateful."

The powerfully built Treky moved in front of Yad and stared at him whilst stuffing pieces of steaming white, golden-battered cod into his mouth. He paused for a moment, then spoke, "Don't push your fuckin' luck with me, cunt. I know what happened on the night and I know you're right, he wouldn't have been 'ere now if it had been down to *you*."

Yad smiled then carried on eating but made no response, Weaver had reached inside his denim jacket for his toffee hammer.

"Leave it Terry, it'll keep." Yad said quietly with a grin, then continued, "You're goin' back away on the boats soon, aren't yer, Treky? Don't you worry about yer kid brother while yer gone, we'll keep an eye on him, wont we lads?" He turned to his crew and they all laughed in agreement.

Treky leaned closer to Yad, "You even speak to our Peter and it's over for you. I'll forget who your brother is."

Yad had tired of this sport and focused on a new target, "Hey Johno, not the strongest cunt on the estate anymore." he said without looking directly at the farm-labouring youth, who had just finished devouring his meal.

"Still strong enough to put you through the fuckin' chippy window, Yad." he replied casually.

"Shall we 'ave a little contest then, hey, between you and Crusher?" Yad smiled in triumph knowing Johno could not now back down without losing face.

Both of the powerful youths also understood that they too had to play his game and agreed.

"Right come here Tommo, you're the heaviest Junior," Yad the master of ceremonies paused, gathered everyone together and made sure he had their attention. Some camp followers had arrived and they also waited expectantly for the show to begin.

"Johno, heads or tails?" asked Yad.

The youth chose tails and lost the toss, which meant the showman decided he would be put to the test first.

"Grab this fat cunt any way you like and lift him above yer head. Ok, off y'go."

On receiving Yad's instruction, Johno caught hold of the protesting heavyweight Junior by the throat and between the thighs then turned him horizontal, bringing him to waist height, as he prepared for the dead lift. After some heavy breathing and gulps of air, with a loud groan, he lifted the youth to his shoulders then paused before attempting the final thrust.

"C'mon Johno, c'mon man, do it!" shouted Jay Mac followed by Irish, Treky, then Blue.

Raising the dangling Junior just above his head, Johno was struggling desperately, with his scarlet face showing beads of perspiration and his powerful hands revealing a network of engorged veins and sinews. Try as he might, despite his best efforts and shouts of encouragement from his friends, he stood frozen with the bloated boy suspended just inches above him.

"Give it up Johno, yer can't manage it, put the cunt down," said a beaming Yad.

"Fuck you!" Johno bellowed as, with a loud groan and one last tremendous effort, he thrust the Junior clear above his head and locked his arms out for a count of two agonising, muscle tearing seconds.

Almost dropping the terrified Tommo onto the hard pavement, the triumphant Johno put him down, stepped back and collapsed against the steel shutters behind him, sweating profusely and breathing deeply.

"Well in Johno, good effort mate," Jay Mac and company shouted in congratulations, then Crusher approached the still shaking Tommo.

"Why has it got to be me? No, am not doin' it." the chubby Junior said, rubbing his reddened neck.

"Shut up you little tit, go on Crusher, lift him." Macca (G) shouted, anxious to watch the sport.

In one deft movement the powerful youth grabbed Tommo, using the same hold as the previous contestant and immediately lifted him to waist height. Planting his parted legs firmly on the ground Crusher paused momentarily, then hurled the youth up to his neck before pressing him fully above his head. Standing firm as a mighty oak tree with his arms like thick sinewy branches, he held the captive Junior for a full thirty seconds, then to reinforce his total victory, began repeatedly lowering and raising him above his head, as if he were exercising with a living, flesh and bone barbell.

Yad, Macca (G) and Weaver and the rest of their crew and the recently arrived camp followers, looked on with astonishment at Crusher's awesome display of strength, then began cheering and shouting with delight. After he had returned the shaken Tommo to the ground once more, Crusher walked across to the defeated Johno and offered him his hand.

"Good lifting mate, it's all in the technique."

Johno shook his hand and laughed magnanimously. "Yeah, technique and raw fuckin' strength, good effort."

Yad was pleased with the result of the contest but unhappy with the sportsman-like way matters were proceeding and decided to change tactics.

"Well, we all know who *really* is the strongest now, don't we?" he said smiling, then quickly called to one of the girls nearby, engaged in scrounging chips and cigarettes. "Molly, come 'ere girl."

Yad's order was directed towards a dishevelled looking female of about fifteen years of age at most, she was wearing a grubby denim jacket over an off-white thin blouse tucked into a short checked mini skirt, her dark tights were laddered and her faded red Cuban healed sling back shoes were well worn and scraped. Molly 'skank' Brown did what she was told and presented herself to the waiting Yad, who grabbed hold of her roughly, forced his tongue into her excessively red lipsticked mouth and pushed his right hand up her skirt and began groping her forcefully.

Breaking away from his violent kiss for a moment but still keeping his right hand between the girls' thighs and using his left to snatch a handful of her unkempt shoulder-length fair hair, he pushed Molly's head forward towards Crusher, "See that, yeah? That's what you can have if you join the Heron crew, all the birds come down 'ere, where the real men are."

As if to reinforce Yad's grotesque recruiting advertisement, Macca (G) and Weaver pulled one of the other girls towards them and began jointly molesting her.

Macca (G) then spoke, "We've got it all down 'ere lad, the best chippy, the best birds and the best crew."

Jay Mac looked at the sad tableau in front of him primarily displayed for Crusher's benefit but also for that of the Crown Team members and said, "Well, yer partly right I suppose, Mr Li's place is the best chippy. One out of three's not bad."

Weaver who had been silent throughout the proceedings and was now casually engaged in attempting to remove the underwear of his struggling female captive, who was desperately trying to fend off Macca (G)'s attentions also, stared at Jay Mac then warned "You better shut that fuckin' smart mouth before it gets yer badly hurt."

There was no further conversation as two police patrol cars suddenly swerved into the lay-by immediately in front of the pavement outside the shops where the youths were standing. A lone police officer got out of the first vehicle and approached Yad, placing his hand on the boy's shoulder.

The officer turned and faced the second car, making the stunned Yad take two paces forward, "Is this the one you described sir, are you sure?" he asked a large male, seated in the rear, who leaned against the glass window panel revealing a fresh medical dressing on his injured forehead.

"That's the fuckin' little shit alright, I saw him clear enough, standin' on top of hill, he threw it at me."

Smiling with satisfaction the tall, young officer, whom Jay Mac recognised as being one of those, who had questioned him and his friends about the Tommy (S) merchant seaman incident, firmly grasped Yad's right arm and led him to the front vehicle while saying;

"I'm arresting you for assault; anything you say may be used in evidence against you…"

His words brought a smile of delight to Jay Mac and his friends, which they did not even pretend to hide.

Yad screamed and protested "It wasn't me, it's that cunt over there! I can't even throw straight and I don't know anythin' about any coaches!"

It was now the arresting officer's turn to smile, "Thank you very much lad, I haven't mentioned anything about coaches but I'll make sure I include that in your statement." With that he pushed the indignant Heron leader into the back of the first police car.

As the police vehicles drove off, the Eagle crew waved to Yad and Jay Mac shouted "Have a nice time in the cells, don't drop y'soap in the shower," then turning to Crusher he said, "See what y'get if you join the Heron crew?"

Jay Mac, Irish, Blue, Johno and Treky walked off up the central road to their own territory. Shouts of "Fuck off wankers" and "Don't come back down 'ere, you cunts," plus other assorted threats, followed them long after they had progressed beyond audible range.

Just past the mid-point of the main road Treky stopped and made to leave the group; his parents' house being located across on the eastern side of the estate.

"I'm not going back to the Isle of Man for a while. The landlady's husband is in the Merch and he's just come home from a trip 'Down Under', so I'm gonna let them have a bit of time to themselves before he gets off again." said a smiling Treky.

"He'll probably be going 'Down Under' every night, now that he's back", Jay Mac noted with a wry grin.

Johno then asked the temporarily exiled Treky a question, "Are yer still makin' a few bob on the side doin' that dodgy boxin' stuff?"

Everyone knew about Treky's source of additional income and had heard tales from some of the older crew members, about how the promising young amateur boxing champion threw away his legitimate career chances, for the lure of prize money on the unlicensed circuit. A number of older punters had made enough to keep them in drink for some time on his last fight, which Treky had won in the ninth round by a total knock-out of his opponent.

"Let's just say, I'm in-between bouts and doin' a bit of trainin' at the moment."

His reply was of particular interest to Jay Mac and when his longstanding acquaintance spoke directly to him before walking away, saying if he needed anything, he only need ask, Jay Mac replied, "Thanks mate, I might just take you up on that."

Johno departed not long after Treky, heading in the opposite direction towards the western edge of the estate, leaving only the three Eagle crew members standing by the library and considering their plans for the evening.

"I think we should pay young Glynn a visit, we haven't seen him since he got out of hospital, then we can get a few beers in the Eagle after, what d'yer think?" Jay Mac asked speculatively.

In the absence of any other more stimulating possible ventures Jay Mac's proposal was seconded and carried. Whilst he was on a winning streak, Jay Mac decided to ask Irish if he could sleep at his house that night, as he did not particularly wish to return to the Kings Estate.

"I'll ask me Ma but yer'can't come round lookin' like that, yer'll need to clean yerself up first." With that Irish left Jay Mac and Blue on the corner of the road, where the two Crown Estate youths lived.

"D'yer want to get a wash in ours Jay Mac? Yer look like shite, with all that dried blood on y'neck and face. I'll see if I've got a spare T-shirt that'll fit yer, while me mum does us a bit of food."

Jay Mac was tempted to observe that if one of his corpulent friend's tee-shirts did fit him, then he would be worried but instead he merely thanked his would-be host and followed him through the small metal gate, up to his neatly painted front door.

Just before eight o'clock, the three companions were standing in front of another well-painted front door, outside Glynn's house. Jay Mac and Blue looked presentable, having been fed and watered with a huge evening meal of fried eggs, chips, beans, sausages, several rashers of bacon and numerous slices of fried bread, all accompanied by almost the entire contents of a large brown family sized tea-pot. Once they had devoured the selection of Mars bars and Milky Ways, *'the snack that you can eat between meals'*, or after or during in Blue's case, that Mrs Boyd had generously placed before them, the two Skins set about polishing their red Airwair with true competitive zeal.

With Jay Mac scrubbed clean and wearing one of Blue's smaller white tee-shirts, both he and his friend had collected Irish, who was his usual scruffy self, still yet without passing a comb through his hair, which had grown out considerably since the group's last communal crop.

"Who's gonna knock?" asked Blue, "What if fuckin' nut job answers the door and starts goin' all mental on us?" he continued, worried that Mrs Glynn may now also have returned home.

"Blue, just cos someone tries to do themselves in after a real shite experience, doesn't mean they're fuckin' loopy, now knock on the friggin'door will yer?" Jay Mac instructed his ever-tactless associate.

The door was opened by a tall man in his mid-forties wearing horn-rimmed glasses, a brushed cotton tartan shirt, baggy old dark blue jeans and a pair of brown sandals with odd socks.

"Who might you be?" he asked, trying to pat down his lengthy combed over, trailing light brown hair after an unkind light breeze, suddenly lifted and rearranged it in a less than convincing configuration. To make matters worse, the man spoke with a distinctive, broad Bristolian accent.

"Yes, we are Daniel's friends and we have called to enquire about his state of health," Jay Mac replied, successfully suppressing a laughing fit, that had threatened to engulf him and then spread to his team mates.

"I'll see if he is receiving visitors. Wait there, he's already got company." With that he shut the door and left them waiting outside.

Several minutes later the man returned, admitted them into the house then opened the living room door and issued a warning statement,

"Now Daniel is not to be excited, he gets tired easily and when I ask you to leave, you must go at once, is that clear?"

Jay Mac turned to their usher and said, "Crystal clear sir, you just give us the nod and we'll disappear sharpish."

When they entered the living room, they were shocked to see the physical condition of their friend and even more surprised by the presence of a petite bespectacled brunette, who was soberly dressed and they estimated, about eighteen or nineteen years of age. Despite her initially stern appearance, with hair neatly tied in a short pony-tail and unflattering heavy black rimmed national health glasses, the boys could see that she was quite pretty and had an attractive smile. The frail-looking pale-skinned Glynn sat at one end of the couch wearing an old woollen dressing gown over his striped pyjamas. On his feet, instead of a pair of gleaming red Airwair, he now wore a pair of tartan slippers.

Leaning heavily on the arm of the couch for support, Glynn introduced his comrades by their given first names. "Mary, this is John, Patrick and Billy. Lads this is Mary."

An uncomfortable silence followed for a few moments and then Mary spoke, "Nice to meet you boys. Remember what we've discussed Daniel and don't tire yourself, I'll be off now, see you tomorrow."

She stood up, leant forward and kissed Glynn on the forehead. Then she moved towards the door passing Jay Mac and said quietly, "Don't overstay your welcome boys."

When she had left, Blue and Irish sat down next to Glynn and Jay Mac sat in one of the comfortable arm chairs of the three piece suite.

As usual Blue began speaking before thinking. "Who's that bird, are you knobbin' her... and who's the fuckin' weirdo who answered the door?"

Glynn looked at Blue like a parent might at a child who had not yet learned when it was impolite to speak and what questions were improper. "Her name's Mary Edwards and no, I'm not knobbing her, as for me Uncle Ken, he's me mum's older brother and he's not a fuckin' weirdo, he just comes from Bristol."

On hearing this Jay Mac quickly interjected "That explains it then, poor cunt, that's why he's such a snappy dresser." The three visitors laughed but Glynn barely raised a smile.

Irish was clearly curious to know more about Glynn's relationship with the mysterious Mary. "So this Mary bird, she's a bit old for you, isn't she, and where's she's from anyway?"

Glynn explained that he had met the girl whilst in hospital, when she was visiting a relative with her family. He then astounded them by saying she was from the Crown Estate and furthermore was actually only fifteen years old.

"Mary will be sixteen next month, so she's a year younger than me and she's goin' back in the fifth form to do her GCEs. She wants to be a nurse."

Blue again spoke out, "I know all the decent birds, how come I've never seen her on the estate before?"

A tired Glynn replied, "That's where y'wrong Blue, yer probably have seen her but because she's one of the decent birds, you've never noticed her, she keeps herself to herself and gets on with her studies. Anyway, look at Irish's two sisters, they're decent girls and no one would give them a second glance."

Once more Jay Mac had to interject, "Yeah but in their case, thee look like Irish, so there's nothin' down for them anyway."

Glynn managed a smile on this occasion, then Irish changed the subject after telling Jay Mac where he could go.

"So how are yer mate? When are y'gonna be strollin' about with the crew again?"

Finally Glynn found something that made him laugh.

"I'll tell you how I am Irish and you two. I had a blood clot on me brain, I nearly fuckin' died. When I came out of the coma I was told me mum had tried to kill herself and why did she do that? Because she'd been gang raped by three shits who were supposed to be my team mates."

Glynn paused and took a few sips from a glass of water which was standing on a small table, with his collection of medication, next to the couch. Nobody else spoke. Glynn then resumed his scathing assessment of their lifestyle, environment and his present situation.

"I finished school last summer but I'm still runnin' around like a fuckin' kid with a gang of other kids, playin' a game that could cost someone their life. Look at you Jay Mac, Quirky beat you up and was goin' to cut your dick off for having it off with his sister. It was her fuckin' choice, nothin' to do with him. It's this friggin' place, if yer don't get off this shitty estate, it *will* kill yer. School's fuckin' over; it's time to grow up."

Just then there was a knock on the door, "Is everything alright in there Daniel? Do you want your friends to leave now?" asked a concerned Uncle Ken.

Glynn shouted back that he was fine and told his uncle to go away. His three visitors were uncertain whether to leave or not, Jay Mac decided to delicately enquire how Glynn's mother was faring, hoping not to further agitate his friend.

"She's about as well as you could hope for. I haven't seen her meself but they say she doesn't cry so much now and she's been sleepin' a bit better. One thing I know is, when she gets out of the rest home she can't come back here, not with those three fuckers still breathin'." Glynn stopped talking and it was clear that he was close to tears.

"Don't think about them gobshites, Glynn, their time will come." Jay Mac said trying to console the distraught youth.

Glynn put his hand over his eyes and then said, "Would yer go now please?" The three Skins stood up, said goodbye to their friend and let themselves out. Darkness had now fallen.

"Fuck me." said Blue, "I need a drink, let's get up to the Eagle."

As they were about to walk away from Glynn's house, their attention was drawn to some noisy activity occurring across the road. Standing crowded into the doorway of the flats, where Yad and Weaver had waited for their signal from Macca (G) on the night of their attack on the unsuspecting Sylvia Glynn, were a large number of male youths. To their surprise and horror they saw that amongst them was not only Weaver and Macca

(G) but also the ever-grinning Yad. Even as they spotted the Heron crew, so too were noticed leaving Glynn's house.

Yad was clearly delighted. "Hello girls, see I'm back. bizzies couldn't charge me, when me dad showed up thee shit themselves. Have yers been to see y'boyfriend? Tell him it's still not over, next time yer see him."

The beaming crew leader was momentarily interrupted by some loud screams from just inside the entrance.

"Get in there Crusher, give it to her good." Macca (G) was shouting enthusiastically.

Yad then recommenced his tormenting, "We're just givin' Crusher his present for joinin' our crew. He's gettin' first go on Molly 'skank', then we're all gonna jump her. Hey if Glynn's ma's home, she's welcome to join us."

"Fuck off and die you cockroach!" shouted Blue, surprising his two friends and momentarily silencing the astonished Yad.

"Let's get that drink," said Irish.

A few moments later, as they walked into the Eagle, two young girls standing outside near the door, called over to them, "Have y'got any ciggies lads? We'll give yer somethin' nice for them."

None of the three youths replied. Jay Mac glanced at the next generation of Molly 'skank' Browns and thought how, in the six years that he had been visiting the estate, their names may change but their faces always stayed the same.

Chapter 10

Lean on Me

Friday 22nd September 1972

"*Arse-holes are cheap today, cheaper than yesterday, large ones are two and six, small ones are…*, hey, who threw that?" The aged singer stopped midway into the opening lines of yet another of his vast repertoire of classic military parodies. Jay Mac and his fellow office junior Timothy Murphy, where sat at their old well-worn desk on their equally shabby chairs like two young clerks in a novel by Dickens. Neither of them admitted throwing the crumpled paper ball at the back of the head of their veteran boss.

"Alright Stan we give up, no more fuckin' songs and Tim will make the coffee," Jay Mac the paper throwing culprit announced.

This launched the seventy-year old ex-Battery Sergeant Major Stanley Atkins, into another of his favourite hackneyed expressions.

"You fuckoffee? Me fuckoffee," which he repeated almost constantly, only interrupting himself with appreciative observations, regarding the anatomy of the varied female forms that he was carefully studying, in a magazine from his extensive, well-thumbed and used library. Finally when the nervous tousle-haired Timothy returned with a large mug of hot coffee for Stan and two smaller vessels for himself and Jay Mac, the old soldier re-lit his pipe and fell silent, for a while.

At six foot two and eighteen stone with his thick silver grey hair and moustache, the lively septuagenarian was still an imposing figure. His role within the shipping and forwarding agents, by whom Jay Mac was employed was multifaceted. Located and isolated in their own dowdy, sparse office with Stan, the two juniors were theoretically subject to his commands but he was also head of security, responsible for the movement of mail and, front entrance reception duties.

Jay Mac had grown up in the household of one old soldier and now every day, he worked with another even older veteran.

Stan was ten years his uncle's senior and by coincidence had served in the same regiment from a decade earlier, right until the end of the Second World War. Well used to the humorous songs, ditties and anecdotal tales of military life, both during peacetime campaigns and periods of combat, Jay Mac was comfortable with Stan's particular brand of ribald soldierly banter and brusque demeanour. Timothy was never sure how to read the old campaigner, or how to react particularly when he barked orders at them, as if he was instructing raw recruits. When any of Stan's colleagues, other former members of the Royal Artillery Regiment, now part of an organised ex-military concierge group and all of similar stature, called to see him, Timothy became more nervous than usual and would often make an excuse to leave the room.

Today, a few moments after the shy boy had finished making one of their regular rounds of strong coffee, there was a sharp tap on the frosted glazed panel of the door to their dingy room.

"B.S.M. Cyril Hughes, reporting for duty sir, permission to enter madam?" Stan's cheery friend shouted in a stentorian voice, before briskly marching in and then coming to a formal, precise halt. "Stand by y'beds, ready for inspection ladies," he continued, before saluting Stan who returned the gesture and told Jay Mac to get a chair for his friend.

Jay Mac sprang up, mimicked B.S.M Hughes' movements and said "One shitty chair for the use of sir. You fuckoffee sir?"

Old Cyril was even larger than Stan and bore a badly broken nose, as a souvenir of his regimental heavy-weight boxing champion days. He lunged towards Jay Mac feigning a combination of skilled punches. The youth knew the drill and engaged in a swift mock bout with the powerful veteran, finally pretending to have been knocked out.

Once Cyril was comfortably seated alongside his comrade and supplied with a steaming mug of black coffee, he lit a cigarette, opened one of Stan's magazines and began comparing form with him.

"Nice big tits on this one Stan but a bit sparse down below, still I'd probably give her one, if she asked me nicely."

Stan didn't look up from his arduous assignment but said "You'd bang her if she had a glass eye and a wooden leg, you old bastard."

Turning to the next page of his volume Cyril replied "Aye y'probably right, I wouldn't want the girl to feel left out, y'cunt."

They carried on in their usual fashion for several minutes, totally oblivious to the presence of the two youths. Eventually Stan remembered the purpose of Cyril's visit and asked him for a small collection of invitation cards which he had previously had printed. Once he had checked their specific details and quality, Stan called Jay Mac over to him.

"Right John, you know where all the lads work, so nip round and make sure they all get one of these. Don't take too long about it, or its coming off your lunch hour."

The youth took the Remembrance Day Cenotaph Parade invitations, saluted the two N.C.O's and briskly marched out of the confined space of their small office.

He always gladly accepted any mission that gave him the opportunity to be out in the fresh air and away from the mind-numbing tedium of his menial employment. Having spent the entire morning filling envelopes with shipping cards and then sticking gummed address labels on to the front of those envelopes, strolling through the city's business sector on a sunny early autumn day, with a sharp cold breeze blowing off the river was, Jay Mac thought, about as good as it got.

The youth delivered each of his twelve invitation cards in turn to their specific destinations at his leisure, he was in no rush to return to Stan the porn scholar and Timothy the nervous wreck, to resume the stimulating task of envelope filling and label fixing. Whilst travelling between destinations, he admired the eclectic architecture of some of the city's classic office structures, from the art deco splendour of India Buildings to his last port of call, the elegant Mersey Docks and Harbour Board, topped with its magnificent cupola. Apart from studying these manmade works of art, he also observed and appreciated some of the natural beauties, as they wandered by in their colourful mini dresses, or smart business suits and stilettos. Jay Mac wondered if any of these assorted vibrant women and girls had ever known a Molly Brown, or could possibly imagine the dunghill world in which she lived.

Reluctantly making his way back to his place of employment in Water Street, he mused at how life hadn't really turned out the way he had niaively hoped it would when he was younger. From an early age he had spent every possible free moment sketching everything around him and particularly copies of American comic book characters. By the time he was sixteen, the one teacher who took any interest in him during his five years in the Cardinals' hell hole, Mr Welch, recognised his prodigious talent and wrote to Jay Mac's uncle and guardian, to urgently recommend that he be allowed to attend Art College after leaving school. Jay Mac stood and watched in dismay as the old soldier carefully tore his teacher's impassioned letter to pieces, saying, "There's no money in drawing daft little pictures. Forget that nonsense and fucking grow up, its time you started earning your keep. Besides they're all bloody puffs in that game."

Stepping in from the bright sunlight and walking up the well-worn stairs to his dull clerical cell, Jay Mac contemplated the dreadful prospect of spending the next half century walled up alive in this room, engaged in the same soul-destroying, mindless labour.

"Where the fuck have you been?" asked an angry Stan, who, like Jay Mac's uncle, could change moods dramatically at the slightest perceived provocation. Before Jay Mac could answer, Stan continued, "I bet you've been wandering around looking at all the nice young 'Judies' and playing with y'self, haven't you?"

Jay Mac stared at the old porn collector and replied, "Sorry, I forgot you were scared of real-life birds, cos they might say somethin' when you're wanking off over them."

Stan was furious and stepped forward as if to slap the youth across the face but Jay Mac quickly dodged out of his range.

"You cheeky pup! I fought in the war for the likes of you."

Jay Mac acknowledging the partial truth of Stan's statement, out of respect did not reply and said nothing further.

"...and another thing, this is a place of business, not a fucking 'friends meeting house'. Some lanky prick called 'ere

Something to Do 1972 • **223**

for you before and told me to give you a message." Stan announced.

"What was that message?" Jay Mac asked curiously.

"Fucked if I can remember, not my job to be giving *you* messages," Stan replied peevishly then sat down with a smug grin of satisfaction on his wrinkled face.

When he thought it was safe to do so, Timothy sidled over to the frustrated Jay Mac and delivered the vital information, "It was that tall lad you call Floyd. He said he's got some stuff for you and to meet him in town by the Victoria Monument, at one o'clock."

Jay Mac thanked Timothy and looked across at the old brown clock with its yellowed face, staring down from the opposite wall, it was nearly quarter to one and he knew there was no possibility that Stan would let him go for his lunch early today.

"I'm dying for a 'Turkish', so I'm just nippin' upstairs to the gents, is that ok Stan?"

The old veteran was once again busily engaged in studying another volume from his extensive library and didn't bother to look up.

"Aye, go on, drop a few for me while you're in there." he said, returning more to his usual self.

Jay Mac told Timothy to cover for him, intending to slip out of the room, on the pretext of using the toilet and commence his lunch hour early, to enable him to keep his rendezvous with Floyd. With Stan engrossed in his 'studies' Jay Mac carefully took his Crombie off the coat-rack by the door, folded it over his arm and was about to leave when Timothy spoke quietly to him.

"Could I borrow some money please John, to buy my lunch?" the nervous youth asked, then added by way of explanation that the cowardly bully Josh had got onto his morning bus and forced him to hand over all his money and last remaining luncheon voucher.

The incensed Jay Mac gave his workmate some loose change and said, "Get yerself somethin' to eat and don't worry about that bag of shit. If yer 'ave any trouble, I'll be standin' by the Victoria Monument in Derby Square waitin' for Floyd, come and find me, ok?" then he made his stealthy departure.

He wished he could tell Timothy that the solution was to stand up to the bully and everything would be alright but he knew that in the real world that was nonsense. Practical experience had taught him that the only effective resolution was to use the threat of a greater menace and if that failed, resort to extreme violence. His view was that usually history had shown the man with the biggest stick always wins the argument, although as a keen student of the contemporary course of events in the Vietnam War, he accepted that his contention may appear flawed. Jay Mac knew in this instance, even if Timothy tried to resist his bully he would take a painful, humiliating beating. He himself had been on the receiving end of a number of such reprisals, all he could do for the present was to look out for the nervous boy whenever possible; Jay Mac had enough demons of his own to deal with.

Once he was outside again in the busy sunlit thoroughfare, he threw his Crombie on and raced up to Castle Street, then along to the site of the monument meeting place. After standing there for a quarter of an hour admiring the distracting female passers-by and at the same time searching for any sign of Floyd, Jay Mac began to think that Timothy had got the message wrong, as this was not the place where he usually found his Crown Estate team mate. Looking first down Lord Street, into the bustling crowds of shoppers and then back across Castle Street, in case Floyd was approaching via a circuitous route, his attention was caught by some commotion amidst the mainly office-worker pedestrians. Then he saw clearly the terrified Timothy running desperately towards the junction in Jay Mac's direction, pursued by the vile Josh and one of his craven henchmen.

Almost at the corner of Castle Street, Timothy was caught by the flapping, upturned collar of his R.A.F greatcoat and pulled to one side by the evil grinning Josh. Whilst Jay Mac watched from across the busy road, he saw the bully snatch a paper bag containing Timothy's recently purchased lunch from the shaking youth, then slap him hard across the face, whilst his equally amused accomplice held on to the boy.

'It's not my business,' Jay Mac thought, as countless passers-by did just the same and ignored the clearly distressed boy's plight.

Josh opened the paper bag took out a bread roll and began eating it, then with his free hand he searched the pockets of Timothy's oversized coat for anything else of value.

'Fuckin' shit,' Jay Mac thought to himself, he knew what any of the super heroes of his childhood and adolescence would do; then he found himself deftly weaving through the fast moving traffic, as he had done so many times on the highway battleground between the Estates.

"Hey shit bag, I've just paid for that!" he shouted, when he arrived in front of a stunned Josh.

The tall albino Skinhead fixed Jay Mac with his small reddened eyes under his heavy white-blond eyebrows and a cruel smile spanned his narrow, pale, weasely face.

"D'you even know who I am?" he began, "I'm Josh, I run the fuckin' South Klan, right?"

Jay Mac turned his back to Timothy who was still being held by the equally tall, dark-haired crony of the bully and stood squarely facing Josh.

"Sorry lad, I didn't realise that *you* were the leader of the South Klan. No wonder I've never heard of them, or you, yer fuckin' tit."

Josh at first, seemed unable to comprehend what had just been said to him, then exploded in a paroxysm of rage.

"Grab this cunt Mugga!" he screamed.

Jay Mac didn't resist but let the Skinhead behind him seize his arms. Then just before Josh hit him hard in the stomach, with two quick successive punches, Jay Mac shouted "Run Tim, get away!"

Freed but badly shaken, the unthinking boy darted out into the traffic, only narrowly missing being struck as he ran towards the stone sculpture of the once dowager Empress.

"Get this cunt into the alley now." Josh instructed his minion, motioning towards Lower Castle Street, immediately behind where they were standing.

Looking over his shoulder to check there were no nearby police, or other upright citizens who might interfere with his planned beating of Jay Mac, Josh was standing directly in front of his intended victim with his legs apart presenting a perfect unmissable target. Jay Mac's polished left boot connected violently with the bully's unguarded testicles and he bent double with the gut wrenching spasm of pain that tore through him.

"Do somethin' Mugga, don't just stand there." he managed to gasp in a hoarse pained voice.

His accomplice, however, could now clearly see what Jay Mac had thought he had glimpsed just as he had lashed out at Josh. The traffic lights had changed to red bringing all the vehicles to a stop and there weaving through them, was Floyd leading his four apprentice chef associates, with their dark leather coats flowing behind them in the stiffening breeze, like a quintet of avenging angels.

"Fuck me!" said Jay Mac aloud, "Sometimes the cavalry *do* arrive."

Floyd grabbed hold of Josh with one arm around his throat and stood him up forcibly. The craven Mugga was already sprinting along the broad passageway, when Kenny (D) overtook him and struck out with a tremendous back fist blow which caught him on the side of the face. Kenny then returned with his frightened prey, Floyd held on to Josh; Kelvin, Delroy and Jay Mac formed a small arc around their captives with Timothy standing behind them and Frenchy stood at the entrance to the alley to discourage any would be passers-by.

"Sorry about that Jay Mac my man, got held up bringing the goods out of work," said a smiling Floyd.

"Good to see you man," Jay Mac replied then turning to a shaking Josh, he said "Now tell these gentlemen who you are again, I think they'll find it really interesting."

Josh was reluctant to speak and Floyd who had slipped on his heavy knuckle duster struck him hard in the kidneys to urge him further.

"I said I'm Josh and I know people in the Klan, that's all."

A surprised Jay Mac looked at the bully then at his quaking assistant. "No, that's not right, is it Mugga? Didn't this lump of shit say *he* was the leader of that team of wankers?"

Mugga nodded towards the smiling Jay Mac then said "That's right, he is, I don't even hardly know him, I just went to school with him that's all."

Jay Mac then turned to Timothy "Is that true Tim, is our shitty Mugga an innocent little boy?"

The smiling Timothy said that both Josh and Mugga had been original founding members of the South Klan Team and they had been responsible for its specific agenda.

Kenny (D) then spoke, "You're the fuckers who sneak around our area at night, paintin' your Klan hate messages everywhere aren't yer? Now tell me what it is that you write."

Mugga looked as if he was going to cry, when Josh said "We just put 'blacks out' or 'blacks go home'." he lied nervously, keeping his head lowered.

"No, I don't think that's right is it? I think you use another word that starts with 'N', don't yer?"

Josh appeared to have lost the power of speech, when the angry Kenny (D) stood in front of him; Mugga wanted his mother.

"Let go of him Floyd." Kenny said to the grinning Crown Team player, who instantly released the shaking Josh.

"Now that it's just you and me, do you want to tell me to get out, to go home?"

Kenny paused and stood staring at the terrified Josh, who mumbled "Sorry, I'm sorry," then fell silent while Kenny addressed him once again, "I'll tell you boy and any other fucker who wants to argue about it, I am home. Don't you ever forget it?" Then he slapped Josh hard across the face with the palm of his heavy hand.

"Empty your pockets," Floyd ordered. When the two captives had done this, Floyd handed all their loose cash to Timothy, then spoke again, "You're both wearin' watches, they're mine now."

Again both of the subdued bullies did exactly as instructed.

"I'll let you keep your Crombies and boots but I fancy them laces, so take them out quick."

Finally when their money, watches and boot laces had been taken from them, Floyd gave them both a serious warning, abandoning his usual faux American soul singer's voice,

"We're gonna let you go now but if you ever come near this lad again, or speak to him, it better be to give *him* some money. If me or the brothers ever hear different, you *will* be sorry you were born, now fuck off."

Jay Mac was surprised to hear his friend speaking with a heavy Scouse accent for the first time since he had made his acquaintance. He watched with amusement as the two pathetic figures shuffled away, their open boots flapping with each step.

Timothy actually stood up straight, dropped his usual nervous demeanour and smiled confidently, as he said "I'll go and get some food and a drink from Cubbon's shop, I'll see you back at the office later John, thanks lads." Then he casually strolled away.

'A new day had dawned for Timothy,' Jay Mac thought.

"Now Jay Mac my man, back to business," Floyd quickly and smoothly resumed his familiar character. "Look into this bag of tricks."

The Skin looked into the open large, heavy-duty canvas bag and saw the usual dozen or so bottles of aftershave lying on top of various gleaming stainless steel chefs' knives.

"What the fuck am I supposed to do with these Floyd?" he asked his business associate.

"Jay Mac it's not long until Christmas, think of all those stuffed turkeys that need carvin'. These are top of the range blades, no home should be without one. So my man, I will see you later tonight with my money. I'll have a nice little bonus waitin' for yer."

Then he turned to his colleagues and said, "We've wasted enough time playin' with those two Klan pussies, let's go and find the real thing." With that and a brief acknowledgment from each of the crew members, the quintet of smooth operators departed into the crowd.

When Jay Mac arrived at the Crown Estate that evening, the sun had already slipped below the western horizon and darkness had fallen. Quickly making his way through the bleak streets, he soon arrived at his destination, Glynn's house, just off the central road that bisected and separated the eastern and western halves of the grey ghetto. Since that night in August, after the football coach incident and the subsequent impromptu weightlifting contest organised by Yad, Jay Mac had been considering his friend's words and replaying them in his mind along with disturbing, imagined grotesque pictures of the blinded driver. He too knew full well that the game they played and their lifestyle carried a high risk of serious injury, both for the individual player and the innocent spectators around him.

This was not the first time Jay Mac had visited Glynn after receiving his cautionary warning. In fact he had been calling on a regular basis in an attempt to cheer his friend and aid his recovery, accompanying Glynn on short walks whenever possible but always keeping close to his home and away from any crew members. Tonight he had reluctantly agreed to meet one of Mary's school friends at Glynn's house, after repeated assurances that this was not a date as such but purely a pleasant, casual interlude, where one of Glynn's acquaintances could meet with one of Mary's.

Dressed in his dark Crombie, white Ben Sherman, Prince of Wales checked twenty-two inch parallels and new red Airwair, Jay Mac rang the recently fitted bell outside Glynn's front door. As had now become the norm, he was admitted by Glynn's Bristolian uncle Ken, who was apparently a keen D.I.Y enthusiast and had been busy making alterations and adding 'improvements' around the small residence, in particular secure locks and bolts. Entering the living room where Glynn was seated on the couch, Jay Mac was pleased to note that his team mate looked more like his former robust self, although he was dressed in casual, civilian style clothes of a woollen jumper and jumbo cord trousers with ordinary sensible shoes on his feet.

"Nice kit mate" Jay Mac said smiling, "You look like a twat" he added.

"Yeah, thanks Jay Mac, Mary picked it all for me." Glynn replied dryly.

"I'd never have guessed that, I just thought yer'd gone mental," Jay Mac continued, then sat in one of the armchairs facing Glynn.

"What's with the fuckin' hand bag, is there somethin' you're not tellin' us Jay Mac," Glynn asked noticing the folded canvas bag that his friend was carrying under his arm, which contained two of Floyd's chefs' knives that he had not been able to sell.

"Shit you've caught me out, it's that time of the month and I don't like to leave the house unprepared." Jay Mac responded quickly. "When are the two sexy nympho's gettin' here?" he enquired wearing a facial expression that suggested this was a genuine question.

"Don't start Jay Mac," Glynn warned, "they'll be here in a bit, ok?"

A short while later there was another ring of the doorbell and Glynn's uncle announced the arrival of two new visitors, Mary and her friend. Jay Mac had been mentally speculating what Miss Edwards' friend may look like. He hoped that as he was expecting the worst, whatever actually happened, he would be pleasantly surprised. All such hopes quickly dissipated when Mary entered the room and introduced the heavily built Niamh with her flame red, curly hair, dressed in a traditional beige Argyll woollen jumper, contrasting dark brown maxi skirt and barely visible black shoes with large silver buckles.

'She certainly likes her food,' Jay Mac thought, unkindly, while Glynn the host dealt with the formal introductions, before they all took their seats.

"Well this is nice." said Jay Mac looking across at his friend, trying not to grin too much whilst unsuccessfully sending telepathic messages of 'You cunt, first chance I get, I'm off.'

Glynn and Mary sat together on the couch, Jay Mac remained where he was originally and Niamh occupied the other armchair, fully.

"So what do you do exactly, John?" asked Mary hoping to start the stalled conversation moving.

"Well, that's a good question, I'm glad you asked me that." Jay Mac replied without expanding any further.

Both girls waited in anticipation while he paused and prepared for his response. A worried Glynn wondered what was coming next.

"Yes, I'm in shipping myself, you might say I'm a shipping facilitator actually." Jay Mac paused again.

Something to Do 1972 • **231**

Niamh who was clearly intrigued asked "That sounds very interesting, what is it you do exactly, what's your role in the business?"

Jay Mac looked to his right at the sizeable female, "Another good question. I tend to be heavily involved in caffeine preparation, transportation and distribution, although I do have an assistant and he sometimes fills in for me, while I convey important shipping information to other interested parties."

Mary looked at Glynn who was trying to remain expressionless and then she scowled at Jay Mac. "So you make the coffee and deliver the mail, is that it?"

Jay Mac gave up the game. "Yeah, that's about it, although sometimes I help the old perv that I work for put his porno collection in order, dependin' on how busy we are."

Mary and Niamh were not amused, so Jay Mac tried a new approach.

"So you're both still in school, how's that workin' out?"

Both girls said they enjoyed their studies and that the Sisters were excellent teachers. This prompted Jay Mac to ask if they attended Our Lady's, the local Catholic girls' school, which they confirmed they did.

Quickly thinking of any girls' names that he could remember, who were also pupils there, he asked "So do you know Dymphna O'Hare and her younger sister Geraldine?"

Mary replied "Yes we do, they're both very good girls, very bright."

Then Jay Mac asked, "Do you happen to know Julie Quirk, I think she might have left your place now?"

The two girls looked at each other in horror, then Niamh replied for them, "She has left, thank goodness, an awful tart of a girl that one!"

Now the tone of the evening was set and Jay Mac knew which way the rest of their conversation was likely to proceed.

"So what are you hoping to do when you leave school Niamh?" he asked.

"I'm going to be a police officer," she answered proudly.

"That'll be good, you can never have too many police officers, can you Daniel?" Jay Mac asked, winking at his silent friend who nodded in agreement.

Mary was clearly unhappy with something that had been said and decided to ask her own questions of Jay Mac.

"You mentioned that tart Julie Quirk, John, did you happen to know her y'self?"

Jay Mac looked directly at Mary and replied honestly, "Only in the Biblical sense."

Niamh gasped and the red faced Mary pressed on, "That's not the sort of girl that Daniel would have associated with, I'm sure."

Glynn tried to interject, "I'll get me uncle to make some tea, hey? Everyone likes a good cup of tea, would anyone like toast?" His diplomatic gesture failed woefully, when Jay Mac responded to Mary's assertion,

"No yer right, Daniel's in line for the next Pope I believe."

Niamh now threw her weighty opinion into the ring, "I don't think you should be using The Holy Father's name like that, do you?"

Jay Mac felt the conversation was nearly over, "Listen girl, I'm a Catholic meself, so you can drop that shite," and with the loud gasps that followed from both Mary and Niamh, he knew that it was.

"I'll have to ask you to leave now. I don't really think you should call to see Daniel again," Mary announced firmly.

Jay Mac stood up and looked across at his friend, waiting for him to correct Mary and say that *he* would decide who his visitors should be but Glynn remained silent.

"I'll be off then mate, take it easy. Watch you don't wear y'self out with these two hot birds," Jay Mac said as he walked out of the living room and left Glynn's house for the final time.

After a short walk further up the central road, he turned into the street where both Blue and Irish lived. He first called to see if Blue was at home but Mrs Boyd said her son had already gone out and so Jay Mac moved on to Irish's house, hoping that he would not also have departed for the evening.

"What d'yer want Jay Mac? I'm just watchin' the box, havin' a sarnie and a fag." Irish stated in his usual surly manner.

Jay Mac tried to convince his long-time friend that a few pints in the Eagle, would be a better option than sitting at home all night like an old man.

"What's it to you? I might like bein' an old man. Anyway it's better in 'ere than that shit hole. Like Glynn said, we all need to grow up."

Faced with the irrefutable logic of Irish's response, Jay Mac was almost about to give up when the firm tone of Mrs O'Hare's voice was heard calling loudly from the kitchen, at the rear of the house, "Patrick, get out here and clear these plates. Y'know it's your turn to do the dishes. Patrick, can you hear me?"

Irish moved with surprising alacrity for an 'old man' who had just been relaxing in front of the fire, watching the television.

A few moments later both youths had already reached the front gate, before another sonic boom from the kitchen overtook them, "Patrick, get back here now, or I'll give you what for!"

By the time the physical presence of Mrs O'Hare had caught up with the advanced warning sound of her bellow, both youths had disappeared past the reeking alley and around the corner to the front of the shops.

Irish had thrown his grubby-looking Crombie on over an old jumper and a pair of highly creased jeans that desperately needed ironing. They had to stop by the library to enable him to tie the laces of his unpolished black Airwair, before approaching the Eagle.

"The nights are really drawin' in now and its goin' fucking cold." Irish observed as they crossed the road then stepped into the graffiti covered porch of the pub.

Two girls of about fourteen years of age were standing outside near the entrance and pressing their faces up to the frosted glass windows of the lounge bar. They were dressed in blue-green Travera suits, borrowed unofficially from older sisters, the skirts of which had been altered to a ridiculously short length, white tights with patterned holes up the side of each leg and brogue shoes.

"Giz a ciggie!" one girl shouted to Irish, who was casually lighting another of his usual twenty-a-day quota.

"Piss off!" he replied curtly.

"Buy us some drinks and bring them out here and y'can 'ave a feel." the first girl's companion offered by way of a reasonable exchange.

Jay Mac stopped for a moment and looked at them both then said, "I dunno how old yer are but yer look like a pair of soft kids, wearin' too much make up, go home before somethin' bad happens to yer."

The bartering girl looked up at Jay Mac standing in the doorway and shouted in a shrill derisory voice, "Ooer, he wants to take us home, says somethin' bad's gonna get done to us, dirty git."

Her friend screamed with laughter and then the two of them linked arms and danced about, much amused with their witty riposte.

When Jay Mac joined Irish at the bar he thought about the polarised contrast between the studious Mary and Niamh and the two young girls loitering outside the pub, offering to exchange sexual favours for cigarettes and ale.

"I wouldn't bother wastin' y'time Jay Mac, there's no hope for them, they've already been fucked by the system."

Jay Mac wasn't prepared to argue with Irish's contention but neither did he fully accept it.

They got their drinks and joined Blue, Brain, Johno, Tank and several other crew members seated at the tables nearby, Cream's *Sunshine of Your Love* was playing on the juke box by the door. Jay Mac and Irish soon realised that their friends were excited by events that had apparently occurred only a few hours earlier. Ant One, the marginally elder of the two boxing twins, who worked as a building labourer with Tommy (S), was presently holding court and delivering an eye-witness account.

"Yeah, so like I said, we'd got an early dart off the site with it bein' Friday, anyway one of the drivers takes us all for a few bevvies, before dropping us off at the Lancs Road." The story teller paused, took a lengthy drink from his pint and ensured that his audience were all listening before he recommenced.

"So we're in this fuckin' ale house, right, havin' a drink and a laugh, next thing is who walks in but 'One Eye' with five Kings Team cunts. Tommy (S) is at the bar waitin' to get the ale in when he turns round and sees them. I said to the driver 'I think we'll be gettin' off now and then 'One Eye' clocks Tommy (S)."

Again Ant One paused and took another drink, this time he knew everyone was listening.

"Tommy (S) goes straight in but two Kings players dived on him. I got up with me brown ale bottle and jumped in and some of our lads off the site had a go as well, otherwise we might have had a problem. We ended up fightin' our way to the door and then fell out into the car park. That's when it happened. Tommy (S) is fuckin' batterin' one of these Kings cunts and as he goes down another one jumps on Tommy but y'know what a strong bastard he is, next thing Tommy's lashed the cunt out into the road and bang a car twats him, just like that, it was all over. We got off sharpish but that Kings prick didn't get up."

Ant One finished his tale and then his pint, before he downed his whiskey chaser. Jay Mac wanted to ask him some questions.

"Where had yer been workin' Ant?"

The amateur boxer replied "Over in that Maghull place."

Jay Mac continued, "Did yer notice the name of the ale house?"

Ant One thought for a moment then said, "Yeah it was called the Coopers Arms, I think, why?"

Jay Mac knew exactly where this particular public house was located and announced "That's right at the north end of the Kings Estate, not fuckin' Maghull, the North crew always meet up there."

Ant One was suitably surprised and silent for a moment, then said "There's one more thing, as we were drivin' off, 'One Eye' is kneelin' in the road tryin' to pick the other lad up shoutin' 'Me brother! Those Crown cunts 'ave done our Gerard'!"

Everyone laughed appreciatively when the tale and epilogue finally ended but Jay Mac knew that the stakes in this game had now been raised beyond house limits and someone would lose everything when the final cards were played.

The next couple of hours passed quickly while the crew joked about possible retaliation attempts by the Kings Team and how they would deal with them easily. Not long before closing time Brain was being served at the bar, when the entrance door opened slightly and one of the earlier bartering females poked her head into the room and shouted to him "Gerrus some drinks mate and a packet of ciggies and bring them to us please. We'll pay yer out here, go on."

An unusually animated Brain returned to the crew with some drinks for his immediate group and said "Hey, those two little prick teasers are still hangin' around outside and they're still tryin' to cadge fags and drinks for a feel. I think I'll have a little go meself, anyone else interested?"

Jay Mac caught what his team mate was saying and was concerned with the generally approving responses that he was receiving. "Brain lad, they're only fuckin' kids, y'know what I mean?"

Jay Mac tried the voice of reason approach first but an irritated Tank then joined in "Who gives a fuck? I'm not gonna ask them how old thee are when I'm pokin' them."

Jay Mac looked at Irish and Johno who both had younger sisters but they made no response, as he tried once more "Yeah, that's great that Tank but y'know when yer gettin' *your* arse popped in the nick, because you've knobbed some under-age jail bait, yer'll be sorry yer didn't ask their age then."

All further discussion was suspended, when from behind where they were sitting they heard a loud tapping on the window. Turning around the youths could see two hazy images of the girls' faces pressed up against the frosted glass pane.

"That settles it, I'm doin' one of them, who else is up for it?" shouted Brain standing up from his seat. "I'll get them a packet of fags and someone get them a couple of bottles of brown ale or somethin'."

With that Blue, Tank, Ant One and three other crew members stood up, keen to join the party. Finally to Jay Mac's surprise and regret, Johno followed the seven-strong group towards the door.

As if sensing the disappointment of his two remaining seated friends, Johno turned and said "C'mon Irish, Jay Mac, it's only a laugh for fucks sake, things don't always have to be so bleedin' serious."

Jay Mac looked up at Johno and replied, "That's just it, nothin's ever serious until it's too late and some fucker's been hurt."

Johno said no more but caught up with the others as they left the lounge bar; Hendrix's *Voodoo Child* was now playing on the juke box in the corner.

A few moments later the screaming began outside and as it increased in volume and urgency, so too did the laughing and cheering. Jay Mac and Irish finished their drinks and walked out though the exit and into the cold night air. When Irish stopped to light another cigarette, both he and Jay Mac glanced to their right, the two struggling girls were being carried around the ever-empty car park and about to be taken to the filthy litter-strewn waste ground which ran immediately behind the rear of the public house. With their underwear fully on show and their blouses already opened, they screamed to Jay Mac and Irish for rescue, "Please lads, please help us."

Irish turned to Jay Mac and said, "D'yer fancy a cup of tea in ours and some toast before y'get off?" Jay Mac nodded his acceptance and the pair walked away without saying another word.

When they arrived at Irish's home, everyone had already gone to bed and they entered as quietly as possible so not to disturb the silence. Only Toby, the old black mongrel with his grey beard, was aware of their arrival and he lazily wagged his stick of a tail, stretching out in front of the two bar electric fire, convinced by the undulating red and orange flame effect that some warmth may still be obtained, from the switched off dark grey horizontal element rods.

"You make some tea Jay Mac; I'm goin' for a slash".

Whilst Jay Mac was standing in the small kitchen lighting the gas ring under the steam kettle, with a match and looking around to see where the tea caddy was located, he could hear his friend talking on the telephone in the hall, using a heavily disguised elderly voice.

"Yes, that's right officer, sounded like a couple of girls getting attacked outside the Eagle pub, near the fields…

terrible screams officer… very worrying, I wouldn't want my granddaughter going anywhere near that awful place… So you'll send a car as soon as y'can? No, need to thank me, just doing what any concerned parent would do." Irish finished his conversation and dropped his creaky old voice act before entering the kitchen.

"Took yer long enough, havin' a piss I mean" said Jay Mac,

"I could have been havin' a Turkish while I was in there for all you know. Pass us that bread an I'll make some toast." Irish replied in his dry acerbic manner.

After they had finished their late snack and discussed the way to solve society's major social inequalities, Jay Mac got up to leave and put his rolled up canvas bag package, back under his arm. Irish sat in an armchair smoking his final cigarette of the day, with his grubby boots positioned next to his seat and well-worn sock covered feet resting on the back of Toby, now fast asleep enjoying the genuine heat from the fire which Irish had switched back on.

"Goin' round to Floyd's next Jay Mac?" Irish asked knowingly.

"How did yer work that out?" a surprised Jay Mac responded.

"Easy really, I just opened that bag when yer went to the bar. When I saw those fuckin' big knives, I thought there's only one prick round here who'd be gettin' hold of stuff like that." He paused and blew a large blue-grey smoke ring then continued, "You been sellin' for that cunt again?"

Jay Mac was moving towards the front door and said "Well until the fuckin' revolution comes, we all need money; I'm off, see yer."

Jay Mac let himself out and carefully closed the front door as quietly as he could behind him. His stealthy exit still did not escape the attention of Mrs O'Hare and Jay Mac smiled when he heard a shrill shout coming from inside the house "Patrick, is that you? Don't you go to bed until you've done all those dishes, d'you hear me?"

After a brisk march across the estate to its Eastern perimeter with his Crombie collar now turned up against the cold and his hands tucked into his pockets, Jay Mac arrived at Floyd's residence just before midnight. When he had rang the bell and been admitted by Floyd, Jay Mac was soon ensconced in one of the comfortable chairs in his associate's stylish room. Sly and the Family Stone's *Family Affair* was playing on the stereo record player on top of the small cocktail cabinet. While he sat drinking a cold beer which Floyd had passed him, Jay Mac admired some of the new posters of nubile females on display. Floyd counted his receipts from the knife and aftershave sales then placed the remaining knives wrapped in their bag, inside the cocktail cabinet, behind his selection of exotic-looking bottled drinks.

"Good work Jay Mac, here's three notes man, don't spend it all in the one place."

Floyd laughed, as he passed Jay Mac his three pounds commission, which the office boy would have had to fill and address envelopes, make coffee, deliver mail and put up with Stan's humour for the best part of a week to earn legitimately. Reaching into the inside pocket of his dark leather coat, Floyd took out a small paper-wrapped package and handed it carefully to Jay Mac.

"Here's a little bonus, my man, try some y'self and then sell the rest for what you can get, thirty percent is all I'm askin'."

Jay Mac opened the small parcel and looked at the pale green leafy mixture; its distinctive pungent aroma permeated his nostrils. "No thanks Floyd, this is not for me. I don't even smoke and I wouldn't touch this stuff."

Floyd stopped smiling, took the unwanted goods from Jay Mac and placed a small amount of the contents into a cigarette paper, which he had just removed from an orange Rizla packet. After rolling his home-made joint and lighting it, Floyd sat back in his chair taking a long drag, then resumed his usual trade mark relaxed manner.

"Listen Jay Mac, I'm lookin' out for you man. Y'see this shit, it's gonna go big, yeah? This is the way forward." he paused and inhaled again deeply, "A few years from now this shit-hole of an estate, the one you live on and all the other forgotten dumps across this city, are gonna be crawlin' with the herb and that's only the start, droppin' acid will be like havin' a bit of speed, soon every fucker will be on to it. If you want real money, this is gonna be the only game in town."

Jay Mac looked at his lugubrious host as he stretched out and chilled in his comfortable chair, letting the fumes of the weed intoxicate him, listening to the smooth haunting sounds of the Chi-lites, whilst they delivered their perfect rendition of *The Coldest Days of My Life.* He knew that this was probably the last time he would do business with the uber-cool apprentice chef and that Floyd's way forward was not his.

"Any chance of that lift home Floyd? I'm fucked an' I wanna get some kip."

Floyd laughed to himself at some private joke, then pinched the glowing end of his half-smoked herbal remedy.

"Yeah Jay Mac, of course my man. I'll save this little spliff for later, c'mon".

Soon after, they were riding out of the Crown Estate on Floyd's magnificent Lambretta SX200. As they approached the flyover construction works, Jay Mac realised it was nearing completion with the middle stanchion pillar in place and the huge precast road sections almost joined. Even though he passed that way every day on his journey to and from work, he was surprised at how far the work had progressed.

"Fuckin' hell Floyd!" Jay Mac shouted, "Have you seen them? Look over there."

Passing through the tall, concrete-slab walled tunnel, now created by the enclosing motorway roof above, both driver and passenger's attention was drawn to a group of five Crombie clad Skins, one of whom Jay Mac thought he recognised as Danny (H).

Working away feverishly like industrial painters, they had already completed a giant black message on the left hand pillar and were now adding the finishing touches to that which had recently been erected on the central reservation. The grim, still wet prophecies both read "TOMMY (S) WILL DIE 31-10-72" and bore the Kings Skins logo underneath.

Looking back over his shoulder at the 'workmen' who carried on with their task, Jay Mac knew the game was nearly ended.

Chapter 11

War

Tuesday 31st October 1972

Craig 'Crag' Griffiths marked the passing of one more day on his calendar, then hung it back onto a small rusty nail which protruded slightly from the rough old plaster that covered the walls of the room. He gazed at the more than ample breasts of the naked female model in the photograph, then followed her slender arms down to where both her hands were simultaneously exploring between her parted thighs, kneeling on the satin bed sheets with a curiously surprised look on her face, as if discovering her most private parts for the first time.

"Sorry girl, I won't be needin' you much longer, that's the way it goes, no more 'hard' feelings," he laughed to himself, then took a final drag of his small hand-made cigarette before climbing back up to his top bunk.

The sleeping occupant of the lower tier turned restlessly in his sleep and let out a noisy protracted fart.

"Fuckin' charmin'," Craig said out loud. "That's somethin' I won't miss, roll on tomorrer mornin'."

He lay back on his bed and listened to the sound of the warder's boots approach then pass by his cell.

"Lights out, sleep tight!" the gaoler shouted, the same as every night then there was a momentary buzz and darkness filled the small chamber.

Almost at the end of a three year sentence, received for his part in a failed tobacco warehouse robbery, where he had personally, unnecessarily battered an elderly security guard senseless, Crag had his future life outside carefully planned. Extreme violence was his trademark and he had built a terrifying reputation upon brutal foundations.

Many years ago an accidental misspelling of his first name, omitting the second vowel, on the front of his new school exercise book, led to derision from his nearest classmate. The sharp brass fountain pen nib of the awkward writing instrument that the children had been supplied with, made a deep puncture when the infant Craig thrust it with all his strength into the back of the hand of the unsuspecting boy, seated next to him. With his badly injured paw spouting blood, initially tainted with a small amount of blue-black ink, the howling boy learned a valuable lesson, as did the rest of the class on that cold late September morning, when the five year old Crag began his schooling. Now twenty one years of age, Crag had been generously providing similar free lessons to unwilling pupils ever since, his teaching methods may vary but his objectives always remained the same, as did his extraordinarily high percentage of successful outcomes.

The eldest of three brothers and two sisters in a family originally from the old Scotland Road district of the city, in the early 1960s as part of the Diaspora of Liverpool's original heartland residents, they had been shipped out to the distant Kings Estate. Crag and his siblings quickly established their position in the new frontier town, taking on and despatching all challengers. Having subsequently founded the North Kings Mod's crew with other like-minded individuals, the later smooth transition to a Skinhead team found Crag at the pinnacle of his adolescent career in violence. When he branched out and diversified his operations to include robbery with assault, Crag passed the reins of power within the North Kings Skins to his younger brother Steven 'Steg' Griffiths, expecting the 'family business' to find an opening for their junior partner, Gerard, known as Jegger, in due course.

A year ago, in the summer of 1971, almost two-thirds of the way through his sentence, he had heard with horror of Steg's blinding in an incident outside a club on Mathew Street, in the City centre, during a fight with members of the Crown Team. The monocular Steg had been unimaginatively renamed 'One Eye' on his recovery and resumed his duties as best as he could, with the proud family tradition of terror ready to be fully upheld by the young Jegger.

This September, just one month previous, even before the warders brought official news of young Gerard's terrible injuries, sustained in his road traffic accident, outside the Cooper's Arms Public House, Crag had been well informed via the prison grapevine, of all the essential details. On two separate occasions Crag's brothers had been on the receiving end of severe physical damage at the hands of one particular member of the hated Crown Team rivals, Tommy (S). Ridicule was not something that Crag would ever tolerate, banter was not for him but now even some of the old lags were whispering uncomfortable asides, as he passed in the prison canteen, that suggested this upstart, Tommy (S), had a personal vendetta against Crag's family and that he was probably safer staying inside where he was.

His planned career move to drug sales, distribution and enforcement, which had been nearly three years in the forming, encouraged by new contacts Crag had made during his incarceration, would have to be temporarily put on hold. While he lay there in the semi-darkness with his eyes adjusting to the gloom staring at the cracked plaster ceiling, after saying his fond farewell to Miss October, Crag imagined the details of the fatal beating he intended to deliver to his personal enemy Tommy (S). Tomorrow morning the 31st of October would bring Crag's long awaited release, by the close of that day he knew only his rival's bloody demise, would be a sufficient message to restore him to his rightful position at the top of the heap.

Tuesday 31st October 1972

It was a cold grey morning when the still half asleep Jay Mac pushed his way along through the lower deck of the bus and finally managed to squeeze into a corner seat by the window at the rear of the vehicle. A short time later the crowded double-decker left the Kings Estate and crossed under the nearly completed flyover. While the teams of road workers above laid and rolled the steaming black tarmac surface, adding the finishing touches before its formal opening for use by the motoring public, Jay Mac glanced once more at the stark supposed prophecy of Tommy (S)'s impending doom. Various attempts had been made by Crown Team members to alter the two large menacing black slogans and the one daubed on the central reservation pillar now read, "TOMMY (S) WILL RULE 31-10-72" with the new more positive verb added in bright red above the original which had been crossed through by the latest writer. This act of defiance only resulted in dozens of duplicate warnings being scrawled, painted, sprayed and scratched onto every conceivable surface by the Kings Team publicists, not only on the estates but also randomly around the city.

A loud bang on the window where his head was resting woke Jay Mac from a light sleep that he had drifted into, after the warmth from the engine had sufficiently seeped through the worn leatherette seat covering and his Crombie, into his tired frame. The bus had stopped at the industrial estate on the edge of Crown territory and a horde of manual workers in their blue overalls and heavy boots were alighting from the vehicle, mostly from the upper deck. Jay Mac peered through half closed lids at the alarm provider and saw a stocky Skinhead youth grinning at him, with the thumb of his clenched right fist standing erect.

"Tonight, yeah!" was all that he shouted to Jay Mac, who was at first bemused but then smiled back and returned the gesture, when he realised what had just occurred.

The satisfied youth turned his denim-covered back, revealing a large Kings Skins motto written in black indelible ink, then moved away with his similarly attired and marked colleagues, heading towards the beckoning dark iron gates of the sprawling washing machine factory, which had temporarily opened to release one set of exhausted drones and admit a replacement batch. Because the Kings Estate was so vast, being comprised of three massive sub territories, Skins from the North and West sector, did not necessarily recognise their peers from the South area, therefore the youth who had noticed Jay Mac's 'uniform' had mistaken him for a Kings Team player and thought he was delivering his message of 'goodwill' regarding the planned evening attack on Tommy (S), to one of his own.

The passenger facing Jay Mac had also departed and as he stretched out placing his feet onto the vacant seat, he smiled at the industry of the Kings propaganda teams, for here facing him across the whole faded red leatherette seatback, was another version of the ever-present message but this time, it appeared to carry an official endorsement, "TOMMY (S) WILL DIE 31-10-72 BY ORDER OF THE KINGS SKINS, OK!"

Forty five minutes later at almost half past eight, Jay Mac arrived at his place of work, ready to open the mail and hear old Stan's first questioning plea of the day "me fuckoffee, you fuckoffee?" At the same time across the city in the grim prison situated on the edge of the old Victorian suburbs, Crag was signing for the return of his personal property before being formally escorted to the small, heavy iron reinforced door, to be released from Her Majesty's custody.

By the time Jay Mac was strolling through the shopping district with Timothy during their lunch hour, admiring the variety of females on offer and making speculative assessments of how much certain ones may 'cost to purchase,' Crag was seated in the midst of a packed Cooper's Arms public house in the North territory, chairing a meeting of the allied generals and chiefs of staff of the temporarily unified Kings Estate teams. Nothing was to be left to chance, they all knew the terrain and were familiar with its topographical features, including the strategic value of the newly joined and surfaced flyover.

After several hours of careful planning, Crag sat back in his comfortable chair, enjoying an amber pint of bitter, one of several he had downed during the morning's battle conference. The general good humour and atmosphere of positive expectation was further underscored, when some witty individual included Edwin Starr's anti-war classic *War* in his selection on the juke box, in the crowded lounge bar. Numerous members of the crews joined in spontaneously, with their own aggressive versions of the lyrics.

"That fucker Tommy (S) is as good as dead!" Crag shouted above the din to an appreciative audience, then he stood up adjourned the special general meeting and returned home with the intention of sleeping for the rest of the day, in preparation for the evening's combined assault on the Crown Estate.

"Any plans for tonight Jay Mac with it being Halloween, like?" Timothy asked his friend, while they made their way back towards the shipping office in Water Street.

"Yeah, I'd like to survive it." replied Jay Mac who had growing concerns about the impending evening celebration of ghouls and goblins, not because he feared the deceased but more the actions of the living.

For the past month there had been an almost eerie lack of gang activity on the part of the Kings Team, except for their sterling propaganda campaign efforts. Even at Liverpool FC's most recent home fixtures against Stoke City and A.E.K Athens, where the Kings Kop, as they styled themselves, had been present in large numbers and where Tommy (S) was clearly visible amongst the Crown Team Kopites, all they had done was chant "Dead, dead, you're fuckin' dead!"

While he prepared an afternoon round of coffee for Stan and another of his old soldier comrades, who had called in for a warm drink and to exchange a couple of soft-core porn magazines, Jay Mac considered how the Kings Skins may set about achieving their objective. Equipped with a full change of clothes, he had no intention of returning to his own estate after work and instead had arranged to have his evening meal at Irish's house, before getting ready for whatever the enemy had been planning. Jay Mac did not doubt that something major was about to occur and there would be casualties on both sides.

At six o'clock that evening, Jay Mac was just finishing his second helping of Mrs O'Hare's own brand of hot, tasty Scouse and began wiping his plate with yet another round of heavily margarined bread, having consumed four similar slices already.

"Did you enjoy your tea John?" asked Mrs O'Hare.

A smiling Jay Mac nodded his approval, then after he had managed to swallow his food replied, "Brilliant that, Mrs O'Hare, thanks very much."

Once the table had been cleared and both he and Irish were seated in the living room engaged in demolishing a selection of biscuits, removed by the handful from an old dented circular tin, Irish's two younger sisters immediately took their places at the now vacant all-purpose piece of kitchen furniture and began diligently working on their copious amounts of homework

With Mr O'Hare working a late shift in the furniture factory where he was employed and Dermot, Irish's older brother away at university, only the infant Sean was present in the living room watching television, while the two youths were discussing the possible course of the evening's events.

"I don't think they'll even bother to show up, it's just a bluff," said a sceptical Irish.

"No Irish, there's somethin' goin' on, on the Kings Estate, I've lived there too long not to pick up the vibes." Jay Mac paused and took a sip of his mug of stewed tea, then continued, "Yeah mate, those pricks aren't jokin' they'll be here tonight in force, I'm sure of it."

Just then Mrs O'Hare entered the room and asked "What are you two young fellers going to be doing this evening, are you meeting up with your friends for duck-apple night?" She looked first at Jay Mac then at her second son waiting for a suitable reply.

"Well, Mrs O'Hare we might just have a glass of shandy over in the Eagle with some of the other boys, then we'll probably go round to one of their houses for a few party games."

Jay Mac's response appeared to satisfy Irish's mother and put her at ease and she turned her attention to the young Sean, who was presently rolling on the floor with Toby the old dog.

"Nearly time for bed for you, Sean, c'mon let's get you bathed and ready before your Da gets in."

With that she left the room taking the protesting boy with her and shouted back to Jay Mac and Irish, "Whatever you do decide to do tonight, be careful, I've never liked Halloween meself, there's mischief about and that means the Other Feller's not far behind."

Jay Mac turned and glanced over his shoulder in the direction of the disembodied warning, "Thanks Mrs O'Hare, we'll keep an eye out for him."

For half past seven on a bitterly cold Tuesday night, the Eagle lounge bar was packed to capacity when Jay Mac, Irish and Blue joined the assembled crews of the Crown Team. Tommy (S) was seated at the far end of the stuffy room surrounded by his old guard companions, apparently unconcerned by his supposed impending demise. The hazy atmosphere was a mixture of thick blue-grey cigarette smoke

Something to Do 1972 • **249**

and testosterone fuelled boasts of how the Kings Team would be easily despatched, if they even dared to encroach on their territory.

Within half an hour of Jay Mac and his companions' arrival, just as *Bad Moon Rising* began playing on the juke box, the door to the lounge bar swung open and rather than Nat, Tomo or Peza, the usual message bearers, an excited anonymous Junior burst in. He quickly made his way through the throng towards Tommy (S) and, except for the sound of Credence Clearwater Revival, the room fell silent.

"They're here, it looks like the whole fuckin' Kings Team have turned up," the Junior announced, not realising how near to the truth he actually was.

"Does it now?" Tommy (S) replied calmly, "Well there's no rush, if there's that many they'll be here in no time."

The whole team waited for direction from their leader, as he sat drinking his pint and staring into the distance, without revealing the slightest hint of emotion.

"Anyone who wants to go down and meet the Kings twats in the field is welcome to have a go. Anyone who hasn't got the bottle can fuck off home. I'll be waitin' here, so thee won't have to look hard to find me." That was Tommy (S)'s final dismissive comment, then he continued his own conversation with his immediate peers, who all seemed to have adopted the same resolutely defiant nonchalance.

Faced with the options of meeting the enemy threat at once, or waiting for them to storm the Eagle, the vast majority of the team chose the former and stood up preparing to leave en masse, following the usual routine of stuffing every available pocket with glass ale bottles. It appeared that no one even considered Tommy (S)'s offer of fleeing, if they did, they confined it to their own thoughts.

"Jay Mac come over 'ere mate," shouted their leader, while the stream of Skins was pouring through the lounge exit.

When Jay Mac approached him, Tommy (S) spoke quietly to him, "Later on I might need you for somethin' so be ready if I give you a shout, ok?"

Jay Mac nodded in agreement and then left the pub quickly to join the team, as they marched at a rapid pace down the main central road toward the bottom row of shops and the fields that lay beyond. The youth considered Tommy (S)'s style of leadership; hiding in plain sight; giving his troops the option of fight or flight; and then waiting calmly without any trace of fear to meet his inevitable fate. He was, Jay Mac thought, an honourable character and the loyalty of the entire team was insured by this principal characteristic.

When they reached the old uncultivated fields of the north western boundary of the Crown Estate, facing the dual carriageway that divided both territories, Yad and the entire Heron crew were already present, a light rain was falling and this was carried on a chill wind. A section of the old metal railings had been forced free and was lying buried in the long grass at the edge of the field, providing a wider entrance point for the Skins rather than their usual method of ingress by squeezing through gaps in the fencing.

"Took you's fuckin' long enough!" Yad shouted while the Crown Team began assembling in the tall grass and weeds, with the river in front of them.

"They've been turnin' up there for about an hour and lightin' their fires all over the fuckin' place, it's like they're waitin' for someone," Macca (G) announced while continuing to observe the movements of the enemy.

Jay Mac too studied the positions of the Kings Team, while they gathered around numerous rallying bonfires that they had lit. He could see that they spanned their fields from the boundary walls of the bus depot on their right flank, all the way to the flyover former artillery tower on their left.

"Fuckin' hell, Jay Mac, there must be over a hundred of them standin' there," Irish said coolly to his friend and team mate.

Blue also had his views on the numbers present and expressed his concerns about the glaring disparity, "Shit! There's easily two hundred there and what 'ave we got? Forty to fifty at the most and that's countin' Tommy (S) and his crew in the Eagle. We might as well fuck off now before thee come over."

Turning to his worried friend, Jay Mac said, "Keep it down mate, we don't want any of the Heron crew to think that we're flappin' yeah? Anyway, when they do charge us we'll do a bit of distance throwin' then fall back by the bottom shops. We can bottle-neck them there and twat those who try to get through, with everythin' we've got."

Yad, who was standing close by looked at Jay Mac, "Who the fuck said you were givin' any orders? It's me, Weaver and Macca (G) down 'ere, where's yer great Tommy (S) now then? Hidin' in the fuckin' Eagle I heard."

Jay Mac ignored the glowering Heron leader and waited for the opening move of the Kings Team.

A huge roar suddenly arose from the different Kings cohorts, ranged across their expansive terrain, a new name replaced their usual one-word chant and they shouted in unison "CRAG, CRAG, CRAG!"

Jay Mac had heard and seen the name of the North Kings leader many times since his aunt and uncle were moved to the Kings Estate at the beginning of 1964 but he had never personally encountered Crag and would not be able to recognise him. Clearly his arrival was the signal for the attack to begin and moments later, after resuming their usual repetitive Kings anthem, the first wave of Skins charged forward through the screen of tall grass and weeds, across the outbound carriageway of the main road. The rain had stopped but the bitter easterly wind picked up in intensity, when the first volley was released high into the air, whistling as the long steel missiles cut an arcing path which ended in the soft earth of the Crown Team's field, just in front of the river.

"Javelins, they're throwin' fuckin' javelins at us!" shouted a keen-eyed member of the Crown Skins, looking in disbelief at the half-dozen steel spears stuck in the ground, like a fence of metal porcupine quills. Having raided the huge Kings North Estate comprehensive school sports' department on Crag's orders, this collection of stolen deadly athletics equipment was designed to initially frighten and intimidate their opponents, striking any Crown Team member would have been an accidental bonus in this opening round.

"Stay where y'are, don't go forward, keep the river between us and let them come to us!" Macca (G) shouted, actually using his intelligence in a positive capacity for once and acting as a real general directing his forces.

"Yeah that's right, fuckin' do that," Yad followed up quickly not to be outdone.

Weaver said nothing but stood still, grinning wickedly, holding his toffee hammer in one hand and a gleaming bus pole in the other.

The javelin throwers sprinted across the inbound carriageway stopping at the spiky barricade that they had previously launched and retrieved their weapons; another group ran out from the Kings field and crossed to the central reservation. Once this second wave had joined their colleagues, they advanced towards the river boundary and stopped, forcing their javelins into the soft ground at the very edge of the bank.

"Let these cunts 'ave some!" Yad shouted, trying to assert his authority, before anyone else gave the command to open fire.

A shower of stones, pieces of brick and glass bottles landed either near the enemy or falling short into the stinking, polluted stream, only a few missiles actually reached their intended targets. Two more waves of Kings troops had now arrived behind their lead pathfinders and began throwing a selection of lighted bangers towards the Crown Team lines.

Jay Mac turned to Irish, who was standing on his right "Those bastards aren't gettin' ready to take us on; they're just findin' our range. Someone's planned all this mate."

At that moment Johno joined Jay Mac on his left side and passed him a handful of similar fireworks, "Here y'are Jay Mac grab these, I've just got them off a couple of Juniors. Let's give these arseholes a little shock. Irish do the honours will yer?"

With that he held out a couple of bangers for Irish to light, before Jay Mac did the same then they both sprinted toward the river boundary.

"Check these out!" Johno shouted, as he and Jay Mac threw the fizzing fireworks into the middle of the tightly packed Kings ranks, which landed with devastating effect.

Anguished shouts of pain could be heard erupting behind them whilst Jay Mac and Johno raced back to their own crew, closely followed by a hail of stones which struck them both on the head and back. Once they had recovered from the 'banger' assault, the Kings Skins formed up again and resumed their static position facing the Crown Team across the meandering river.

"Look at those Kings shithouses; see I told yer, they're all like that on their estate. Comin' down 'ere pretendin' to look for a fight and then packin' in before it gets goin'." a delighted, if incorrect Yad was shouting at the assembled Crown crews.

Over on the Kings territory, on their left flank, rockets began to be launched which exploded harmlessly in the sky close to the newly surfaced flyover.

This action amused Yad even more, "Fuckin' dickheads, we haven't even got anyone standin' where they're shootin' their rockets."

A curious Jay Mac was also watching the airborne missiles, while they burst brilliantly away to his right, "Somethin's wrong here Johno, they're not tryin' to hit us, thee must be usin' them rockets as some kind of signal," he said keeping his gaze directed toward the flyover sector of their field.

A few moments later the strengthening bitterly cold wind temporarily parted some of the heavy clouds, that had been obscuring the light of a full moon which was struggling in vain to reveal its cold radiance and suddenly the grey concrete overhead structure to the far right of the Crown Team was bathed in a pale glow.

"They're on the fuckin' flyover, loads of them!" an observant Tank shouted as loudly as possible causing the whole team to quickly glance to their right.

Jay Mac turned to Irish and said "Looks like they're tryin' to get behind us, we need to gerroff while we can; otherwise they'll 'ave us trapped. We can't go forward; they've got the river covered, the only way out is goin' to be through the alley between the Heron and the flats."

Irish had reached the same conclusion himself and passed on the information to Blue who was next to him on his right. Everyone looked to Macca (G) and Yad to give an urgent order to withdraw but both leaders froze and failed to direct. Then before anyone could make a move toward the escape route, the

Kings javelin crew, sprang forward to the river's edge and other members from the rear ran up to join them appearing to point their hands horizontally at the Crown Team formation.

"Ow! Fuckin' hell! What's that?" Johno shouted in agony when one of the first ball-bearings fired by the Kings Team airgun troops, took off the lobe of his right ear and smeared its fleshy pieces, mixed with a splash of warm blood, across the left side of Jay Mac's face.

Further along the line Brain screamed out, "Me eye! Me eye! I can't see!"

Simultaneously, Jay Mac was struck in the forehead and chest, as were numerous other Crown Skins who were peppered with the tiny round metal shots from their rivals' pistols, before the rout began. Almost as one, the whole team turned and raced toward the exit gap in the iron railing fence behind them. Now the Kings Team launched their javelins in earnest, hoping to strike a fleeing victim in the back, leg or arm.

Jay Mac and Johno being the acknowledged fastest runners in the team were usually amongst the last to take to their heels. On Jay Mac's part he acknowledged that this was not out of bravery but that he personally enjoyed the chase and outrunning his pursuers. So it was on this night, while the two friends waited, curiously watching to see what the Kings Team next move would be.

One by one the lead members of the enemy crew were leaping across the river at the narrowest point between both banks where the Crown Skins normally crossed.

'They must have studied the ground beforehand,' Jay Mac thought concluding that the initial javelin throws had been specifically aimed to land at this point, as a marker for the first wave of assault troops. The first two Kings runners had landed on the nearside of the riverbank and were intent on racing toward their javelins to retrieve them. Jay Mac and Johno had the same idea and sprinted the short distance to where the two metal spears were stuck in the soft soil of the overgrown field.

Suddenly they heard a familiar voice behind them, "Go on you cunts, get them javelins before those Kings shits do!"

shouted a wildly grinning Weaver, running up to join them, armed with his toffee hammer and bus pole.

The crossing point was only of sufficient size for individuals to attempt the leap; anyone else who tried on either side of it usually ended landing on the muddy sloping bank and then having to scramble to the top. Because of this only two other Kings runners had successfully crossed so far and they too were racing towards the protruding javelins. For Jay Mac and Johno it was no real contest and they seized hold of the nearest weapons then turned to sprint back towards the exit and safety.

An abandoned car, which was situated on their right, near the high wall that acted as a boundary to the field on its south-western side, appeared to have an 'occupant' Jay Mac thought, glancing at it during his return run.

'Maybe it's a Guy for Bonfire Night and the kids are gonna burn it and the car at the same time,' he mused to himself, leaping like a fleeing antelope across the felled iron railing section buried in the tall grass and weeds. Johno landed an instant behind Jay Mac carrying his 'trophy' in one hand and cupping his bleeding mutilated ear with the other.

When they reached what they believed to be the relative safety of the alleyway formed between the gable wall of the Heron and the back of the burned-out garages below the tower blocks, they heard a tremendous noise composed of shouts and cheers, mixed with the clash of metal poles, dull thuds and breaking glass.

The retreating Crown Team had ran straight into a classic pincer movement trap and were now fully engaged with the majority of the Kings Team forces, who had furtively climbed into the bus depot and rapidly crossed to the Crown Estate, in a reversal of the route that the Crown Team had used earlier in the year to rescue the hostage youth, Treky (P). Jay Mac and Johno prepared to join the melee, wondering whether their captured javelins would be of any use at such close quarters. Even as they considered abandoning their prizes, they heard desperate shouts coming from the rear.

"I'm fuckin' stuck, gerrus out will yer?" a trapped Weaver was calling, having not quite cleared the hidden section of railing and landing heavily between two iron rails, with his left foot wedged firmly in place.

Both Crown Team players looked back at the pathetic sight of the crazed psychopath, down on one knee frantically trying to pull his trapped ankle loose, with four rapidly approaching, javelin-armed Kings Skins only a short distance away.

"Fuck him." said Johno, still clasping his right hand to his wounded ear.

"Yeah, it's about time he took a good beatin'." Jay Mac replied.

At that moment a couple of fleeing anonymous Juniors ran past Jay Mac and Johno in the opposite direction and one of them seeing Weaver's predicament shouted, "Weaver's fuckin' down! He's stuck in the railings!"

If any incentive had been necessary to encourage the Kings front runners to redouble their efforts, this was it, now all those who had crossed the stinking river and heard the ill-timed shout from the unwary Junior, raced to claim Weaver's scalp.

"For fuck's sake help me!" Weaver shouted urgently once more.

Their dilemma was resolved, Jay Mac and Johno both knew that they could not leave a fallen comrade in these circumstances and without another word, ran as fast as they could, back to where Weaver was trapped.

"Take y'fuckin' boot off!" Jay Mac shouted as he and Johno leapt over the buried railings and ran towards the two leading Kings Skins.

"I can't undo the friggin' lace!" Weaver replied to Jay Mac's hurried advice.

"Use y'Stanley knife for fuck's sake," Johno called out before confronting his opponent, who was now only yards from Weaver.

Jay Mac was in a similar position when the Kings Skin facing him, thrust his javelin forward with both hands, like a lance, catching Jay Mac's open Crombie and penetrating the material by a foot length of pointed steel. Before he could withdraw his ensnared javelin from the coat, a one-handed downward-angled spear strike from Jay Mac burst into the right thigh of the horrified Kings youth and he collapsed screaming in agony onto the ground. While Jay Mac tried to pull his downed opponent's weapon from his damaged Crombie, a second thrown javelin narrowly missed him and passed over his right shoulder out into the road beyond. Johno was engaged in a wild fencing contest with his principal adversary and the loud clang of their javelin-swords could be heard echoing across the field, as another opponent arrived alongside him.

"Give us a hand will yer!" shouted the one-booted Weaver, who had extricated himself and was trying to pull his trapped footwear free.

"Leave it y'friggin' maniac, Johno needs help!" Jay Mac shouted back angrily, looking over his shoulder at Weaver, then turning just in time to see his friend struck across the back of the skull and dropped to the floor. A dozen more Kings Skins were racing towards the three Crown Team mates, when suddenly the 'abandoned' car roared into life and began trundling in the direction of their enemy.

One by one, the stunned Kings runners were struck glancing blows by the passing vehicle as it ploughed its circuitous journey around the overgrown field. The three Skins who were kicking and striking the fallen Johno, abandoned their victim and ran towards the car, then threw their javelins, including the one retrieved from Johno, at it hoping to strike the driver or at least slow its progress. Jay Mac and the hopping Weaver took advantage of this diversion and quickly recovered their dazed comrade from the long grass where he was lying.

"Who the fuck's drivin' that car?" asked a curious Weaver.

"I bet it's that theivin' nutter, Spark, y'know what he always says, 'show me the car and I'll 'ave it away'." Jay Mac replied.

With the front passenger door punctured by one of the steel javelins and both windows on that side shattered by the other two, the car picked up speed and then turned in a large circle back towards the improvised entrance in the metal fencing, where it had crashed through earlier in the evening. It was driven, as Jay Mac correctly surmised by the most infamous car thief in the area, the homeless itinerant, Spark, who was reputed to 'live' in a large refuse container behind the shops in the Meadow Green district, just two miles from the Crown Estate.

While Jay Mac and Weaver ran and hopped along dragging Johno towards the rear of the Heron, in front of which their team mates were receiving a ferocious beating from the victorious, numerically superior Kings Team horde, Spark successfully drove across the fallen railings and abandoned the stolen car, before escaping into the night. His action had effectively blocked the path of his pursuers and the remainder of the enemy Skins, who were approaching via the field route.

When Jay Mac, Johno and Weaver reached the alleyway between the pub and garage wall, they found a number of Juniors, including Nat and Tomo, sitting on the floor bleeding from a variety of head and face wounds.

"Don't bother goin' that way, it's too fuckin' late, everyone's been twatted and now they're doin' the shops," said a clearly distressed Nat.

Even as he spoke a tremendous cheer greeted the explosive sound of the not long repaired, Heron saloon bar huge plate-glass window, being smashed to pieces, when a hail of bricks struck it in several places.

"Let's get on the roof of the garages." Jay Mac suggested, as there was clearly now no point in them running into the enemy and joining the list of casualties.

Weaver gave Jay Mac a lift by cupping his hands, which Jay Mac stood on and scrambled onto the flat roof above the eight foot rear wall of the tower block garages, before assisting Johno, followed by Weaver in reaching the summit also. Crawling forward over the sodden, worn roofing-felt covered surface, the three Crown team mates peered from their vantage point and observed the carnage all around in the road not far below.

Those fortunate members of the Crown Team who had remained standing during the mass brawl with their numerous rivals, had managed to make their escape but the unlucky fallen were now captives and at the non-existent mercy of the jubilant Kings horde. From their vantage point, the three Crown Skins could see other team mates being repeatedly booted, stamped, punched and spat on, whilst the Kings Team celebrations continued, with angry shouts and pained screams filling the air. Molly Brown and her associates had arrived at the bottom row of shops drawn by curiosity and the hope of finding new customers to barter their favours with, though they would soon be painfully disappointed, as these victors claimed their spoils of war gratis.

Some of the old veterans were standing at the door of the Heron clutching their pints and loudly remonstrating with the Kings youths, applying the same scathing criticisms to them as they did to those of their own estate.

"Go home yer fuckin' Jessies, no one round here is scared of a bunch of kids," shouted one old curmudgeon, followed by an equally unimpressed colleague.

"Queers, that's all yer are, y'lucky I'm not ten years younger, I'd 'ave the lot of yer."

Standing in the middle of the excited Kings Team was a tall athletic-looking Skinhead dressed in an expensive well-cut Crombie, twenty inch parallel baker's trousers and the usual red Airwair. He had his back to the three Crown youths who were watching from the garage roof and they could not see his face whilst he gave orders and directions, it was clear that he was totally in control of the situation.

Crag was determined to maintain order and was anxious not to let the mob follow their own desires. Knowing that this was a unique event with the biggest Kings Team ever assembled, Crag wanted his primary objective achieved, Tommy (S) must be removed in a brutal fashion, on his home ground with his team thoroughly beaten and decimated, only then would his future drug smuggling prospective employers, acknowledge his ruthless credentials and suitability for the position he sought. Above all he did not want anyone from either estate to ever forget this night.

"Wreck this fuckin' shit hole make it worse if y'can, let them know the Kings Team have been here." Crag shouted before calling for a pre-selected group to follow him up the main central road, towards the Eagle.

"My crew of top boys with me in the lead, the rest follow on when yer've done every fuckin' window in these houses. Remember, smash everythin' on yer way." With that destructive exhortation he set off leading a vanguard of his chosen men.

"*He* is a worse nutter than *you* Weaver." Jay Mac said, turning to his prone team mate, as they watched Crag's departure.

Johno was clearly worried that the rampaging team would spread their activities to his own home and asked "Someone's bound to ring the bizzies, with all this goin' on, don't yer think?"

Jay Mac tried to reassure his friend, "Yeah mate, they'll be here with their own crew any minute now."

Weaver had his own concerns, "I fuckin' hope not, I've not even used me hammer yet, I don't want those cunts ruinin' it before I get a chance."

He did not need to worry, Jay Mac was completely wrong. This was a particularly active Halloween night for the gangs across the whole city and the police were stretched to full capacity. Back on the huge Kings Estate a coordinated attack on the town centre shopping precinct, previously arranged by Crag and his generals earlier in the day, was keeping all available officers fully occupied. No aid or useful intervention would be available to the beleaguered Crown Estate for some time to come.

"I'm gettin' up to the Eagle as fast as I can." Jay Mac said to Johno and Weaver, preparing to lower himself from the roof.

"Me too, we'll go up the side streets, it's longer but me and you can easily sprint it. What are you gonna do Weaver with yer one friggin' boot?" Johno asked.

"Don't you fuckin' worry about me lad, I'll keep up with you two pricks anytime, just watch me."

Without another word all three dropped to the ground and while the Kings Team members were happily engaged in smashing every window, of the small terraced houses in the vicinity of the bottom shops, they darted across the road, ran through a nearby alleyway and began their race to the Eagle.

In the midst of the madness, with the horde swarming around the shops battering the steel-shuttered fronts with poles and bricks, one establishment remained conspicuously untouched, The Golden Diner. Mr Li stood silhouetted in the lighted doorway with two male relatives, meat cleavers clearly visible, like three fearsome human lion-dogs guarding the entrance. They were unperturbed appearing oblivious to the roaming Kings Team, who wisely chose not to engage the unmoving trio. When he was their age, Mr Li had fought as a member of the People's Liberation Army in a real war, these children held no fear for him.

On arriving at the Eagle, Jay Mac, Johno and Weaver were greeted by the sight of their battered team mates, who had escaped from the Kings Team trap, most of whom were displaying head wounds of varying degrees of severity. Brain, who had been blinded in one eye by a metal pellet fired earlier in the evening, had been taken to hospital by taxi, which had been ordered by the head barman of the Eagle. While telephoning for the taxi, he had also taken the opportunity to make a repeat call to the police, primarily through fear of what may happen to his public house when the rampaging Kings mob arrived.

Having received the same reply as most other concerned callers, that a patrol car would be despatched as soon as one became available, he had decided to opt for a more practical immediate solution, offered by Tommy (S) and his crew; they would defend 'their' pub, all he needed to do was provide the ammunition. Consequently when the three runners had made their way through the walking wounded, they found their leader and several members of the old guard stacking crates of empty brown glass bottles near and inside the front entrance porch.

Jay Mac was pleased to see that Terry (H), the school friend of Irish and himself was now present, as was Dayo (G) the older brother of Yad but he was completely surprised by the sight of Floyd dressed immaculately as usual, with his dark brown calf length leather coat flapping in the stiffening wind, whilst he worked on the munitions task with his peers.

"What the fuck are you doin' here man?" Jay Mac asked with a smile.

"Givin' the ladies a night off my man, to build up their strength for our next session."

Tommy (S) placed another crate inside the porch then walked over to where Jay Mac was standing by Floyd with Johno and Weaver.

He looked at the three recent arrivals then addressed them in turn, "Johno, you look like shit why don't you get off home, this could get nasty."

Johno cupped his damaged ear, as if straining to hear what Tommy (S) had said. "Sorry Tommy, I can't *ear* yer." was his reply to the stone-faced leader, who turned next to Weaver.

"You always look like shit, what's happened now? Did yer get tired of hittin' people with yer toffee hammer and decide to use yer fuckin' boot instead?"

Weaver responded with one of his usual wicked grins. Then Tommy (S) spoke to Jay Mac who was bearing a single thin strip of dried blood, also as a result of being struck by a metal pellet earlier, which ran from his forehead to his chin.

"Ok Jay Mac I don't know what the fuck the red stripe's all about but I'm not happy with yer turnin' up wearing a Crombie with a fuckin' big hole in it," he almost smiled momentarily while speaking then continued, "Right, they'll be 'ere any minute so you've got to run like fuck up to the 'Hounds'."

Jay Mac interrupted and said that he did not want to run off anywhere with the whole Kings Team almost upon them.

"Jay Mac, I'm askin' you to do one thing, ok? You've got to find Quirky, he'll be waitin' with his crew for this message. Tell him 'Tommy (S) says... it's on,' that's all. Can y'do that?"

Jay Mac knew this was his mission and said, "I'm on me way Tommy and if Quirky doesn't fuckin' kill me, I'll be back as soon as I've given him the message."

With that he ran through the car park, leapt over the low wall and sprinted up the continuation of the main central road in the direction of the Hounds' Public House, at the north end of the Crown Estate. A bloodied Irish and Blue were standing not far from the place where Jay Mac cleared the car park boundary; Yad was also nearby, "Look at that, it's fuckin' sickenin' what 'ave I told all of you's? The little shit bag's runnin' away just when the trouble's gonna kick off."

Irish was looking curiously at Yad and asked "How did *you* get back 'ere Yad, I thought the Kings twats had gripped yer?"

The Oyster leader turned towards Irish and replied angrily "Yeah, thee did but thee shit themselves when thee realised it was me, an I just battered me way through them, ok?"

The all too familiar chant of 'Kings, Kings, Kings' announced the arrival of their team led by Crag and his chosen vanguard. A number of empty metal beer kegs were also positioned by the pub entrance, for use as heavy artillery and Tommy (S) leapt onto this improvised rostrum.

"Alright lads, the knobheads are here and this is as far as they're goin'. We'll drop the fuckin' lot. Remember this is *our* estate, so let's have them."

The leader jumped down from his platform and stepped into the centre of a small arc of his personal crew, like a medieval Japanese daimyo in the midst of his loyal Samurai, then gave the order to open fire. "Let them 'ave some."

Every member of the Crown Team, who were all positioned within the low perimeter walls of the Eagle, instantly discharged an awesome volley of glass bottle projectiles. The huge Kings Team were too close, too tightly packed to escape unscathed and despite trying to seek shelter by the library and shops, many were struck by this first salvo; another followed almost immediately. This was not what Crag wanted to see and with his own generals, he exhorted the Kings Team to return fire with all the ammunition that they still had, including some remaining airgun pellets and darts. Now it was the Crown Skins turn to take cover, as numerous new casualties were created. In those few moments, while their Crown rivals absorbed the impact of the Kings return fire, Crag urged his crew forward.

"Take that fuckin' ale house, all in, all in, Kings!"

A dozen or more determined runners sprang forward and tried to make the short distance from the shops, to the low walls outside the Eagle.

"Johno, Crusher, now's y'time lads." Tommy (S) shouted to signal the launch of the heavy duty 'shells,' while both Crown Team strong men each seized a steel keg and lifted them above their heads, before heaving them at the enemy assault troops.

Struck hard in the shins like human skittles, two front Kings' runners collapsed screaming in agony, clutching their broken limbs and rolling into their companions. Yet another volley of ale bottles followed and no one else braved the run, even with Crag's angry encouragement.

While the dull steel kegs lay in the middle of the road on a sparkling carpet of a thousand glass fragments, a livid Crag held a brief conference with his generals, then he stepped forward from the mob and left the relative safety of the shops, "I'm Crag, which one of you fuckers is Tommy (S)? Show y'self if you've got the balls."

Tommy (S) shouted back "I'm here Crag, this is me but I've got to tell yer, if you're surrenderin' we haven't got enough room in the Eagle for all your girls."

Crag smiled walking forward a few paces and became clearly visible, for most of the Crown Team this was the first time they'd ever seen the notorious Kings Team leader. With his androgynous, clean-shaven face, neatly cropped hair and pleasant smile, dressed in his immaculate tailored Crombie, except for his white baker's trousers and red Airwair boots, he was another who could easily have been mistaken for a young city executive.

"Alright Tommy? I didn't know you were such a comedian, must be with you leadin' this team of clowns and bein' a short-arse cunt." Crag paused to let his observations be fully absorbed then continued, "Listen mate, there's no need for anyone else to get hurt tonight; this is between you and me. Why don't you stop hidin' over there and step out into the road and me and you will have a go".

Tommy (S) stood perfectly still and shouted his reply. "It's sad that you couldn't find any hard lads on y'whole estate and have had to bring these tarts instead. These Skins here have been takin' it easy on yer so far, I asked them to lead yer up 'ere and now yer fuckin' trapped."

As his words echoed across the otherwise silent debris-strewn road, a number of the Kings Team considered their content and reviewed their position. They were in the heart of the Crown Estate, a long way from home or even the escape routes on the main highway; several of their number had been badly injured and no reinforcements were on the way to replace them; in addition the defiant Crown Team were positioned in a secure redoubt with a readily available supply of ammunition.

If Tommy (S) refused to accept Crag's challenge, they would be faced with a stalemate and wondered how long they could hold on before either the Crown Team's local allies, or the police arrived.

Looking around at his wounded battered Crown team mates dishevelled and bleeding with their numbers reduced, for their leader there was only one honourable option. Whether Jay Mac had managed to deliver his vital message, or even if Quirky was eventually to arrive with his 'cavalry,' his decision was already made, he would not expose a single member of his team to another assault by the Kings mob, if there was any chance that he could settle the score himself. Removing his Crombie and passing it to Gaz, one of his senior crew, he stepped forward dressed in his denim jacket with Crown Team symbol on the back, his twenty four inch parallel Flemings jeans and gleaming red Airwair. No one tried to stop him, or suggest another course of action; they all knew Tommy (S) was his own man.

Holding his empty open hands at shoulder height with his palms facing the Kings Team he shouted "No weapons! Fists, head and boots only!"

Then he stepped out of the relative safety of the Eagle car park, through the entrance opening between its low walls.

A delighted Crag beamed as he held his own hands up in a similar gesture, "No weapons, agreed!" he shouted in reply, before removing his Crombie and handing it to his partially sighted brother, One Eye.

As he passed his coat to his smiling sibling, he furtively reached into one of the side pockets and removed two small, heavy solid steel bars, concealing them inside his clenched fists. Crag then turned to face his hated enemy and stepped forward in his well-scrubbed Levi's denim jacket with bleached collar and Kings Skins emblem on the back, white twenty inch baker's trousers and equally well-polished red Airwair.

The two fighters moved around each other watching for that vital first opening. At six foot one, the athletic looking Crag had both height and reach advantage over his stocky five foot eight rival; his first lightning-fast punch, which caught Tommy (S) on the left side of his forehead, revealed that he had speed also. Tommy (S) felt the weight of the blow and being an experienced scrapper, he knew something was amiss but carried on gamely throwing a tremendous rising right-cross of his own, which only narrowly missed his opponent's jaw. Crag moved around on his toes dancing like a professional in the ring, and then darting forwarded feinted with his right and smashed Tommy (S) with a powerful left-hook into his right temple. Again the Crown Team leader felt the blow and was clearly dazed but Crag stayed back waiting once more.

For the next three minutes Tommy (S) was out manoeuvred and continually on the receiving end of his opponent's ferocious blows, the fighter was being bled by the boxer. Cheers of encouragement rose in volume from the Kings Team spectators, while a stunned Crown Team home crowd remained silent, until Dayo (G) shouted "Go on Tommy, you've got him on the ropes," which triggered other members into adding their vocal support.

Crag changed tactics for his next attack delivering a solid boot to Tommy (S)'s unprotected gut, demonstrating his capability with either fists or feet.

"Y'not much fuckin' use without y'dog lead, are yer?" a grinning Crag asked, clearly aware of his opponent's usual weapon of choice.

Tommy (S) did not reply but instead darted in close to Crag before he could move away and pounded his ribs on both sides, first with a left-hook then a right, in rapid succession. Crag now felt the devastating force and strength of Tommy (S)'s unaided blows and found it difficult to breathe for a few moments after receiving his double body punches. Knowing that he had hurt his no longer grinning adversary, Tommy (S) waited for a split second then leapt in with a jumping head butt to Crag's mouth, which immediately split his lips and drew blood, the sight of which raised an audible gasp from the Kings watchers. Having experienced these few brief samples of Tommy (S)'s strength, Crag realised he was dealing with an incredibly powerful individual, who could focus that power either into his fists, head and no doubt feet when required, he decided that he did not want any more proof.

When Tommy (S) came forward again for his next attack Crag accepted the blow to his stomach, to enable him to close with his enemy and seize hold of him, dropping his metal bars in the process. Both leaders fell to the ground with Crag struggling to hold onto the crazed bull that he had ensnared.

"Now! For Fuck's sake, now!" he shouted desperately, while continuing to deliberately manoeuvre Tommy (S) nearer to his Kings Team senior crew.

Realising his position only a few yards from Crag's chosen Skins, Tommy (S) punched and kneed his rival wildly, managing to break free just as One Eye's left boot caught him fully in the face, Yoz and the remainder of Crag's personal retinue eagerly leapt upon the Crown Team leader, as he struggled to rise to his feet.

For a moment the stunned Crown crews were frozen in disbelief, then they raced forward as one. It was too late, the entire Kings Team swept around their generals allowing them to drag their prize away from the library and into the reeking alleyway behind. Dayo (G), Terry (H) and Floyd fought like men possessed, leaping into the front line of the enemy, followed by the whole Crown Team when the crazed melee began.

Although greatly outnumbered, a desperate, dynamic urgency drove the Crown Skins on. Weaver smashed faces with his toffee hammer as fast as they appeared in front of him, Johno and Crusher pounded then threw battered opponents in their wake whilst ploughing into the Kings mob, Irish unleashed years of pent up rage and Blue finally fought for something other than himself but they could not break through to their captured leader. In the alley behind the shops, Tommy (S) would not go down despite being reduced to his knees and being battered by a dozen Kings Skins enraged with bloodlust, exhausting themselves in their efforts to beat him to death; they did not know that their time was nearly up.

"Crown Team, gerrout the fuckin' way!" shouted a wild Quirky, as multiple blasting air horns signalled the arrival of fifteen scooters, each with a driver and passenger, including Jay Mac on the back of Tony (G)'s LI175. The lead scooters almost crashed into the brawling teams and then when all fifteen came to a halt, led by Quirky, the thirty Centurion helmet-wearing Crown Skin reinforcements dismounted and charged into the action.

"They've got Tommy round the back!" Dayo (G) shouted to Quirky, whose usual psychotic rage suddenly escalated to frenzy level on receiving this shocking news. With his bone-handled cut-throat razor fully open for business, he literally cut and slashed a path through the Kings Team lines, allowing a phalanx comprised of old guard and recent arrivals to follow behind, Jay Mac made sure that he was in their midst. The sound of coarse laughter accompanied by jeers, led them directly to their target half way along the dark alley, where they found a triumphal Crag standing over their battered, motionless leader, enjoying a celebratory urination directed onto Tommy (S)'s scarlet pulp of a face. Other members of the Kings' snatch squad were casually kicking the limp figure, as he lay on the filthy floor.

"This'll wash some of that blood off y'face there, Tommy lad." said Crag, then he looked up and immediately froze at the sight of the Crown Team rescue party, led by the wild Quirky. No words were exchanged by either side and no quarter would be expected as they leapt into each other. For Dayo (G) and Yoz it was round two of their personal duel, while Floyd smashed his brass knuckle duster encased fist hard into One Eye's face, closing his remaining orb, Terry (H) and Jay Mac grappled with two unknown opponents from Crag's seniors, as did the other members of their squad, leaving Crag to meet the full insane fury of Quirky.

Brandishing his razor the Crown Skin swung his blood stained weapon in a series of wild arcs; the dodging Crag reached inside his denim jacket and produced a pearl-handled flick knife, with which he had been planning to remove one of Tommy (S)'s eye's, as a fitting retribution, for his own brother's earlier blinding. If he expected Quirky to back away or assuage his anger, Crag was soon disappointed when the helmet-wearing psychopath charged into him delivering an unstoppable explosive head butt, which caught Crag on his previously undamaged nose and already split lips.

For the first time since he was a child and subject to regular ferocious beatings from his belt-wielding alcoholic father, Crag felt the icy grip of fear and knew that total liver failure was unlikely to save him from *this* terrifying attacker. He plunged his blade into Quirky's left side cutting through his Crombie and denim jacket but Quirky's frenzied attack continued unabated and an excruciatingly painful razor slash across the clean-shaven, unblemished skin of Crag's right cheek, cut a deep scarlet spurting gash almost from his ear to his lip, matching Quirky's own distinctive scarring. The game was nearly over for Crag and he turned and ran slipping in the damp refuse that covered the alley's floor. The shame of defeat and reckless flight abandoning all his loyal team mates to their fate, meant nothing to him, self-preservation was all encompassing, he must escape.

A smiling Quirky turned and rejoined the fight, calmly walking up behind a tall Skinhead, who was trying to throttle Jay Mac and slashing him across the back of his neck, then moved on. Jay Mac watched unsympathetically, when his former opponent dropped to his knees, frantically trying to cover the open neck wound with his right hand and shrieking in pain. He now recognised him as Yoz's limited conversation companion from their bus meeting earlier in the year then he booted him as hard as he could manage in his agonised face. Jay Mac's kick was one of the last acts of violence on that night of madness. Crag's inglorious flight was almost sensed before it became commonly known and then officially verified, by the spectacle of the Kings seniors running from the alleyway desperate to escape from their assailants, seeking any safe route off the Crown Estate.

"What the fuck is goin' on here?" said the driver of the small police patrol car, sat in the parked vehicle with his fellow officer, facing the opposite end of the alleyway behind the shops, where Crag was presently running through.

"I tell y'what, I'm not gettin' out of this fuckin' car until some backup arrives," his colleague replied with a wry grin.

They had been making their way to investigate reports of rowdy youths damaging property, when they had spotted the fifteen-strong scooter team turning down the main central road at some speed. Deciding that their destination must be the middle row of shops and the Eagle, the police officers had driven along one of the old narrow lanes on the western edge of the Crown Estate, hoping to arrive as their quarry were in the act of whatever mischief they had planned. On seeing the mass brawl raging across the road between the shops and the public house, the empty dented beer kegs and the countless glass fragments now fully illuminated under a cloudless sky, they wisely decided to call for assistance, remaining safely seated within their vehicle.

Suddenly a lone, bleeding, stumbling Skinhead in a grimy looking Crombie and filthy blood-stained baker's trousers emerged from the dark alley, almost immediately opposite them.

"Let's have this one, he looks like he's fucked." said the driver, turning to his partner before opening the door.

"Yeah and he's on his own, so let's get him in the car quick."

Running forward truncheons at the ready, neither officer expected the ferocity of Crag's resistance, until he leapt onto the driver pummelling him with an array of punches delivered in a blur. Even after the officer fell to the ground, Crag made sure that his boots struck their target with as much force as he could now muster, before he was repeatedly cracked across the head by the second officer's truncheon. The wounded Skinhead turned snarling towards his lone assailant and grappled with him, while he sought to apply a restraining wrist lock on Crag, both males stumbled and crashed to the floor.

At the library end of the shopping boulevard, the Kings Team were in total disarray. Deprived of their leader who had chosen to make an ignoble flight, rapidly followed by his battered, bloodied generals, they had become the lost souls on this particular Halloween, running in every direction without guidance. In the alleyway itself, Jay Mac stood for the second time in three months looking down on the almost unrecognisable face and unconscious, motionless form of a fellow team mate and friend, Dayo (G), Quirky and Terry (H) were also standing alongside; Floyd had already departed.

"Jay Mac, Terry, you two might as well gerroff, me and Quirky will take care of this." said Dayo (G), staring in disbelief at his long-time friend and fellow founder of the Crown Team.

Just then a desperate warning shout rang out and was repeated like a Victorian felon's urgent nursery rhyme.

"The bizzies are here, the bizzies, they're fuckin' everywhere."

Now the Crown Team scrambled for safety with youths running for their homes or nearest secure bolthole. Irish and Blue lived closest in the road just behind the shops and they both sprinted to the latter's home. The Heron crew ran along the main central road or through the side streets, back down to their own devastated territory, the scooter team leapt onto their machines, then mounted the pavement in a desperate bid to elude their uniformed pursuers.

"Jay Mac for fuck's sake, jump on quick!" shouted Tony (G) pulling up at the mouth of the alley where Tommy (S) lay.

Suddenly brought back to immediate reality, Jay Mac nodded to Dayo (G) and Quirky then jumped onto the back seat of his friend's Lambretta.

"We'll get over to the Westside and hang out in ours until it all goes quiet" Tony (G) shouted back to a silent Jay Mac, who was watching over his shoulder, while the now numerous police officers tackled fleeing Skins to the ground. In particular Jay Mac was straining his helmet-covered ears to listen for any sound of an ambulance but all that he could hear and see in the vicinity of the alley, were four burly constables dashing into the entrance with their truncheons drawn.

It would be a long time before the eighteen year old famed leader of the Crown Team, would receive any medical attention. While his unconscious body lay in the filth with his life hanging in the balance, his two old guard comrades were being viciously beaten for 'resisting arrest,' as their appeals for assistance for their fallen friend were totally ignored.

"Let's 'ave it then!" shouted the incensed Quirky, who had only recently unwisely removed his helmet and thrown it to the ground, in desperation at the lack of response to his and Dayo (G)'s requests. Pulling out his handsome cut-throat razor he delivered some police brutality of his own and in so doing, doomed them both.

Chapter 12

Living in a Broken Dream

Tuesday 31st October – Saturday 4th November 1972

During their race across the west side of the estate, on Tony (G)'s Lambretta, they passed random groups and individual stragglers from both teams, who were themselves desperately trying to evade capture by the pursuing police. Finally they reached the small end-terrace house where Tony (G) lodged with friends of his parents, since their move to the town of St Helens beyond the city's boundaries.

"Can yer get the gate Jay Mac?" Tony shouted, then bumped the machine up onto the pavement and drove towards the metal fence which enclosed the tiny front garden.

Jay Mac dismounted and opened the gate quickly to enable Tony to drive up the short path toward the shared alley, which ran between each pair of adjoining properties in the terraced row. Once a tarpaulin had been securely placed over the LI175, hiding it from the view of any passer-by who may be tempted to 'borrow' the highly desirable ultra-cool vehicle, they entered the property through the front door.

"Can't be too careful Jay Mac, there's some robbin' gits round here." Tony (G), the apprentice electrician and part time car thief said, with a smile.

Even as they stood in the small hallway, while Tony opened the kitchen door and turned on the light, the sickly sweet smell of incense filled their noses and the dull pounding, rhythmic beat of a repetitive musical chant, could be heard from the main front bedroom above. Jay Mac was already feeling uneasy about returning once more to the home of Mal 'the Pig'.

"Is that you Tony love?" shouted Mrs Chadwick, who was watching the television with her husband in the lounge at the rear of the house. "Your dinner is in the oven on a plate, so watch you don't burn your fingers, it'll be hot."

Then Mr Chadwick added, "Been a lot of noise outside tonight Tony, has there been some trouble on the estate?"

Tony paused for a moment, then replied, "No everything's alright, it was just a load of kids tryin' to scare each other with it being Halloween like."

Both he and Jay Mac went into the kitchen and sat by the small rectangular Formica topped table.

"I'll have a look for some ale mate, d'you wanna bit of toast while I scoff me tea?" Tony asked, then stood up and began searching for any alcoholic fluid that he could find. "'Ere we go, four bottles of Guinness, how's that for a bit of luck?" he announced, pleased with his find and passing Jay Mac two of the dark stout beers for his consumption.

"Don't they mind you havin' their booze, Tony?" Jay Mac asked curiously.

"No, they're both alright, as long as I don't start on Maureen's brandy," he replied then returned to the table with his food and a couple of golden slices of toast for Jay Mac.

While they sat eating their food and drinking their ale they discussed the events of the evening.

"Do yer reckon Quirky and Dayo will get done bad by the Pigs, when they get them back to the Nick?" Jay Mac asked, unaware of what had actually occurred in the alley.

"I don't know about Dayo but Quirky is only out on bail, waitin' for sentencing after his last scrap with the Mancs, so he is well and truly fucked," Tony replied, equally without knowledge of Quirky's razor attack on the police officers.

The pounding beat and rhythmic chant from upstairs increased in volume as they were talking and Jay Mac asked, "Still playin' Black Widow is he? He never changes, how d'you stand livin' here with that fuckin weirdo?"

Tony took a swig of his Guinness and belched loudly, "He's alright, just a bit strange that's all."

Jay Mac looked at his friend and raised his eyebrows, "Tony, you are the master of understatement, mate. That cunt is seriously fucked in the head."

Suddenly the music stopped and the sound of footsteps descending the stairs could be heard, the door to the kitchen swung open and Mal entered the room.

"I knew you were here, Jay Mac," he announced, fixing the youth with his small blood-shot eyes.

"Did yer now and how did y'manage that? Was it a bit of the old psychic powers, or did yer just take a little peek out yer bedroom window?" Jay Mac replied sarcastically.

Mal ignored Jay Mac for the moment and stood perfectly still in the centre of the room, staring vacantly into the middle distance.

Jay Mac, who hadn't been in Mal's company for almost a year; studied his appearance and was shocked to see how pale, drawn and thin he had become. His mousey-blond hair was longer, almost reaching to the centre of his back but it was sparse and wispy and his acne-scarred skin appeared grey with dark furrows etched into his forehead and cheeks. What struck him most, was not Mal's mutilated nose, or his rotting teeth, instead his gaze was drawn to Mal's sunken red bead eyes, which almost appeared to glow in the dark hollows of their deep sockets, he had assumed the ghoulish appearance of one of the tormented souls that he so desperately sought to contact. Jay Mac noticed that over his black woollen, skinny-rib, polo-neck sweater, Mal was wearing an inverted silver crucifix and decided to ask him a question.

"Are you still doing a bit of dabblin' mate, tryin' to get through to the other side?"

Mal grinned at Jay Mac fully exposing the pointed, decaying remnants of his teeth and replied, "More than you'll ever know, Jay Mac. I see things you've never dreamt of."

Although a little unsettled, Jay Mac responded, "Well good luck with that Mal. Let me know when yer start seein' next week's Pool's results will yer?"

Mal who had been carrying his heavy R.A.F great coat, draped over his left arm and now began putting it on, laughed loudly at Jay Mac's sarcasm then said, "I've got somethin' for you here in my pocket, here y'are."

He finished putting on his coat, fastened the double-breasted front and reached into the deep right side flap covered pocket, then threw a playing card to Jay Mac. It was one of Mal's tarot cards and bore the image of a grinning skeleton, printed in heavy black ink like a medieval woodcut, standing out starkly against the off-white background.

Jay Mac took the card, glanced at it then looked back at the grinning Mal. "Bit early for Christmas cards and it's not very festive is it? Still I suppose it's the thought that counts."

Tony (G) couldn't help but laugh and Mal turned angrily towards him. "Don't be misled by this unbeliever, he doesn't know real power."

Jay Mac was getting tired of this exchange and reached inside the open neck of his Ben Sherman shirt, then produced a small silver crucifix of his own, which he always wore over an even smaller oval medal depicting St. Michael and said, "Hey Mal, I'll match mine against yours anytime."

Mal turned back to face Jay Mac but averted his gaze from the objects he was holding out on their chain, between his right thumb and forefinger.

"I'll tell you this... fool. Death is following you around, it won't be long now." Mal almost spat his words at Jay Mac, as if he was uttering a curse.

It was Jay Mac's turn to laugh now, "Is he? Well if that's true, he must be bored out of his fuckin' skull."

Making no further response to Jay Mac, Mal turned up the large collar of his coat and spoke finally to Tony, "I'm gettin' off to Ravens Hall Cemetery, it's nearly time, any chance of a lift?"

His lodger was clearly uncomfortable and replied, "Sorry Mal, I would do but I've already promised I'd take Jay Mac back up to the Kings Estate, is that ok?"

Mal turned his back on them both, opened the kitchen door and left the room, "I'm goin' out now, keep out of my room." he shouted and then picked up his old army surplus canvas bag, containing the assortment of items that he required to perform one of his periodic midnight graveside rituals.

"Be careful dear, there are some very nasty people going about nowadays," his concerned mother shouted from the living room, where she was engaged with her knitting, as Mr Chadwick snored loudly in front of their new expensive colour television.

Jay Mac turned to Tony and said, "She's dead right, and her son's one of them."

Mal shuffled off into the cold sharp night hunched over with his hands plunged deeply into his coat's spacious pockets, muttering unholy curses to himself. Even while the macabre figure wandered on, darkly silhouetted against the drab grey concrete structures of the estate, casting a long black shadow, his mother prayed silently for him.

Nineteen years ago, after several miscarriages, she and her husband Bert, were delighted when they were informed that she was expecting twins. Their elation turned to grief after the elder of the twin boys by twenty minutes, stopped breathing shortly after birth and could not be resuscitated, leaving Malcolm as their only surviving child. Excessively spoiled from the moment he was brought home from the hospital, the infant Mal could have anything his two hard-working parents could provide for him and, he could do no wrong. As he grew to adolescence, the boy who preferred his own company and was regularly found in deep conversation with an imaginary friend, began to have increasing problems at school, often described as anti-social and strange.

By the time he was seventeen, his interest in the occult had become an obsession and his parents were horrified when he tore all the expensive wallpaper from his bedroom walls and began covering them and the door to the room with strange symbols, obscenities and figures. Mal smashed his bed preferring to sleep on a mattress on the floor, took out the light bulb from the ceiling pendant holder and lit the room by a low watt, purple-shaded lamp, supplemented by flickering candles. His distraught parents consoled and deceived themselves by constantly saying to each other "He'll grow out of it, it's just a phase he's going through."

It was in this room and in this environment that one year previous, at the beginning of November 1971, Jay Mac, Irish, Blue and Glynn had found themselves participating in a sinister Ouija board session, which Mal the organiser, had first claimed would be 'harmless fun.' Jay Mac refused to take part but finally agreed after peer pressure, to write down each letter as they were supposedly revealed, by the unseen presence. After he had recorded a dozen or so letters, he noticed the sudden drop in temperature in the room and, that except for the wickedly grinning Mal, his friends, in particular Irish, looked terrified.

When the latter asked Mal if he could stop and he responded by rolling his eyes and cursing, Jay Mac took matters into his own hands, jumping up and kicking over the small table with its board and upturned glass tumbler. The crazed Mal leapt onto him with his hands about his throat and his thumbs pressing heavily into his trachea, they both fell to the floor upsetting some of the lit candles and the small lamp which rolled about erratically, until it settled in a corner of the room. Despite repeated hard punches from the struggling Jay Mac, the screaming, cursing Mal hung on with an almost unbreakable grip, until finally Irish and Blue managed to drag him off and temporarily restrain him. One of the flimsy purple Bri-nylon net curtains caught fire and Glynn was trying to put it out, when the window blew fully open allowing the night air to rush in. Mal stood up and spat at Jay Mac who was now also standing.

"You've ruined it, you've ruined it! Get out of *our* house, never come back!" he screamed in a low guttural voice.

The stunned Jay Mac stared at Mal for a moment before he and his friends left the room then he said "It was a shit game of cards anyway, be careful what you're doin' Mal."

Just two weeks later both Jay Mac and Irish would find the unconscious, bleeding Mal, lying on the bonnet of the crashed, smoking wreck of a stolen car that he had been driving and in which, only a short time earlier, they had been passengers.

This night, while Mal was wandering about in the moonlit local municipal cemetery, reading gravestones by the light of his small torch and searching for specific residents to perform his incantation upon, Tony (G) and Jay Mac were speeding along the main highway on the former's Lambretta scooter, heading for the Kings Estate.

"Looks like Danny (H) and his team of painters have been busy again," Jay Mac shouted to Tony (G). "That's disturbin'," he continued, reading the freshly re-altered slogans on the main concrete supports of the recently completed flyover. 'TOMMY (S) DIED 31-10-72' had now replaced the original prophecy, with all other subsequent additions effectively obliterated in heavy bands of black paint.

Turning eventually into Jay Mac's road and then stopping in the lay-by immediately outside the row of shops, with their two stories of flats above, both Crown Skins looked about for any sign of their enemies.

"No one's around, Tony, they must have all gone to bed, thanks for the lift" a relieved Jay Mac said.

"Alright Jay Mac, take it easy mate, I'll see yer." said Tony (G) before racing away out of the estate.

Studying the damage to his Crombie, Jay Mac walked towards the sheet metal-fronted entrance door, between the radio and TV shop on his right and the shoe shop on his left. Everywhere was still and silent, even the earlier strong easterly wind had completely subsided. He reached into the inside pocket of his denim jacket and retrieved his keys; lost in his own thoughts about how the previous evening's events had developed into a major landmark engagement, between the two rival warring teams. It was nearly half past midnight; he was tired and ready for bed. Suddenly and unexpectedly just as he was about to put the key in the lock, the heavy door swung open and he was caught by his outstretched arm, captured by Danny (H) and his crew.

"We've got the Crown cunt." Jay Mac heard them shout before a tremendous head butt struck him fully on the bridge of his already broken nose, sending shockwaves of pain reverberating through his skull and opening the floodgates for another scarlet stream to issue forth. Punch after punch struck him in the face and body, as he was dragged into the entrance by the delighted howling crew. Thrown violently against the metal railings, then down onto the stone stairs, Jay Mac received a torrent of kicks while excited individuals competed to make their own contribution count. He knew the drill; five years of brutal training in his secondary school had at least ensured that this aspect of his education was well attended to. When the opportunity momentarily occurred, he curled up into a tight ball, pulling his knees to his chest and clasping his head with his hands, protecting his face with his closed forearms.

"Fuckin' do him, do this cunt!" Danny (H) screamed incensed on realising that the victim had denied him some of his much anticipated pleasure.

Everyone who could reach the downed target booted and stamped the rolling Crombie-covered football. Locked inside his mind, after retreating from the pain, as he had learned to do from an early age, Jay Mac thought that above the wild noise of the cursing and cheering youths, he could hear other familiar voices.

"I've called the police!" shouted an anxious elderly female, then repeated, "I said, I've called the police."

Jay Mac recognised his would-be rescuer, Mrs Ashworth, who lived in the flat above his aunt and uncle and was the only resident of the four families within their block who actually owned a telephone.

Then he heard his aunt shouting "Jack, get the dog, they've got someone down by the bins, hurry up!"

She hadn't realised that the victim was her nephew but she was not prepared to see a defenceless individual, whoever they may be, being subjected to a brutal attack from a vicious gang. Mrs Ashworth who was a few years older than Jay Mac's aunt was of a like mind and, she also called to her ex-Royal Navy and now long-distance lorry driver husband, to assist in the rescue of the battered youth. "Eric, get y'belt, there's a lad gettin' done over down stairs!" she shouted at the top of her voice, to ensure that the youths below could all hear her words.

Mixed within the cacophony of sounds were the giggles and excited screams of the Anvil crew's own camp followers, who urged on their male 'heroes'.

"He's covered his fuckin' face, that's no good, y'need to do his face," one particularly enthusiastic female spectator shouted, expressing her disappointment at the limited bloodshed on display.

"Shurrup girl, I say what we're doin' here!" said an increasingly exasperated Danny (H). "Now get y'Stanley's out and slash the cunt, he'll soon open up then."

The keen-eyed Mrs Ashworth who was looking over the railings on the top landing, thought that she recognised the victim

"Eric! Hurry up, I think it's young John they've got!" then shouted down to Jay Mac's aunt, who was occupying a similar vantage point on the floor below, "Mrs Palmer, I'm sure that's your John they've got there and they're shouting something about getting someone to slash him!"

Although her hearing had been rapidly deteriorating for years and without her aid she was virtually deaf, Jay Mac's aunt still possessed excellent eyesight and she too was now convinced that the gang's victim was indeed her own nephew.

"Jack! It's John they've got, they're holding them craft knives and I think they're going do something bad!" the desperate woman shouted.

While the crew set about their task with relish, slashing Jay Mac across the arms, back and legs the furious Danny (H) exhorted him to cry out in pain. "C'mon you fucker, shout out! Come on, just scream, beg us to stop and we'll let y'go." he lied, whilst watching and listening for any sign of pleading from Jay Mac.

Although he could feel some of the sharp stings as their blades cut through his layers of clothing, his slashed Crombie and denim jacket absorbed much of the force of their wild strikes, he was determined to deprive Danny (H) and his crew of any additional pleasure. Once again earlier experience had taught him hard lessons and he knew for the sadist inflicting the punishment was only part of their enjoyment; true ecstasy was only achieved when the victim yielded and begged for mercy.

A panting Danny (H) stood back and admired his and the crew's work. Jay Mac lay on the floor in the corner facing the bottom steps, with his prized Crombie cut and gashed in dozens of places, his Flemings' jeans were in a similar state with thin trails of blood trickling down his legs and staining the material.

Still not satisfied with the results of their efforts, Danny (H) stopped any further activity and stood back for a moment saying "Not bad but we need to do his face, then we can all have a piss on him, like Crag did when they killed Tommy (S)." he paused for a moment then continued "Right get hold of his fuckin' arms and drag them apart."

Having heard what they had said, Jay Mac realised that the legend of the attack on Tommy (S) had already been spread and added to by those members of the snatch squad, who had escaped from the alleyway. Even as these thoughts where passing through his mind, he could feel the firm grip of several hands, when four of the Anvil crew seized his forearms and began to wrench them apart, exposing Jay Mac's face ready for the final assault.

"Hold him stil... that's more like it," shouted a delighted Danny (H) standing above Jay Mac with his back to the stone stairs and holding his Stanley knife in his right hand dramatically raised above his head, poised for the coup de gras.

"If y'ever do see Yad again, tell him thanks for the info, we never knew just where y'lived until tonight. Okay, I think we'll have an eye first." he said smiling while staring down at Jay Mac's already bloodied face.

His hand never moved from its raised position.

A grip so powerful that he felt his wrist bones would snap, now held Danny (H)'s motionless hand behind his head, then he heard the accompanying deep voice.

"You won't be cuttin' anythin' else tonight boy. Drop that fuckin' toy knife before I break yer wrist."

Jay Mac looked up from where he was sat upright on the hard floor and saw his uncle standing on the bottom step, immediately behind Danny (H) with Mr Ashworth only two steps above. Turning round sharply to see who his captor was, the Anvil crew leader was desperately trying to hold onto his craft knife but the pain in his wrist was almost unbearable. He looked at the two men standing behind him in horrified disbelief, there was Jay Mac's sixty year old uncle with the bull-like Mr Ashworth two years his senior, both dressed in almost comic parody of the Skins.

Jay Mac's uncle roused from his sleep and due to be up for work at four a.m., to travel into the city centre head post office and start sorting his morning mail delivery round, had pulled on his dark uniform trousers with their black braces, over his pyjama bottoms and slipped his parade ground finished black army surplus boots onto his bare feet. Mr Ashworth was similarly attired except for an old rugby shirt that he was wearing inside out over his string vest.

"Listen granddad you and your boyfriend better fuck off back up them stairs before you get really hurt, right?" Danny (H) said unconvincingly in a wavering voice.

Both Jay Mac's uncle and Mr Ashworth stood looking nonplussed at the skinny youth, the former having faced the might of the German Wermacht and the Nazi Waffen SS throughout the Second World War, being captured and subsequently escaping on three occasions from brutal Stalags and, the latter surviving in the deadly ice cold waters of the North Atlantic, after twice being torpedoed whilst escorting Merchant Marine convoys, they were incapable of being afraid of a boy threatening them with a craft knife.

The powerful straight left jab that struck Danny (H) fully on the left side of his face dislocating his jaw, spun his head around and as his wrist was released from the vice-like grip, he involuntarily dropped his knife to the floor, closely followed by his unconscious body.

"Shit! Fuck this!" shouted one of his nearest astonished accomplices and with that the desperate scramble for the front door and escape began.

Chased out into the road whilst being booted in the backside by both Jay Mac's uncle and Mr Ashworth, the dozen members of the crew including their three female consorts, were too tightly packed to avoid the kicks and slaps that they each received while scrambling from between the shops, pursued by the two smiling veterans. When they returned inside the entrance area, they found Jay Mac being assisted to his feet by his aunt and Mrs Ashworth. Danny (H) had been sat up against the wall nearest to where he had fallen, Jay Mac's aunt liked to keep things neat.

"Wake up lad, you've only had a tap," Jay Mac's uncle said giving Danny (H) a sharp slap on his right cheek.

He opened his bleary eyes and looked about, still unable to fully comprehend what had happened to him, placing his left hand on his throbbing jaw. Before anything else was said or done, a police patrol car arrived in the lay-by immediately outside the open door of the two-storey block.

Whilst the driver remained in the vehicle, a mid-thirties stocky police officer stepped in through the entrance and said "We've received a report about an assault by a gang of youths, are these two of them?"

He looked at Jay Mac standing close to the far wall trying to staunch a steady trickle of blood running from his nose, with a handkerchief his aunt had passed to him, wearing the tattered remnants of his black Crombie over his denim jacket and Flemings jeans also displaying gashes in several places. Next he turned his attention to the dazed Danny (H), sitting on the floor with his back to the wall opposite the stairs, rubbing his swollen jaw with his hand.

"Well, has anyone got any answers? Does someone want to tell me what happened to these two for a start?" the officer asked, expecting one of the four sixty-something adults to offer some insight.

Sensing that the wrong answer could possibly lead to his uncle facing a criminal charge, Jay Mac quickly provided a suitable response, "What happened officer was, that me and me mate here, were just standin' talkin' outside these shops when a gang of lads ran up and started hittin' us for no reason."

The police officer waited a few moments while Jay Mac paused, considering what to say next. "Go on, I haven't got all night" he said impatiently.

"Yes, as I was saying, the door to these flats was open and the gang pushed us in here an' started beatin' us up. One of them had one of those terrible craft knives that y'hear about an' another one punched me mate hard in the face. Anyway these very kind people here came down an chased them off."

When Jay Mac had finished his tale, the officer looked at the adults and said, "Is this true, is that actually what happened?"

They all agreed with Jay Mac's statement, adding comments about the general decline in the behaviour of contemporary youth.

"What about you lad, did you see who hit you? Is your mate right in what he's saying?" asked the officer of the seated Danny (H).

Everyone stared at the subdued Anvil Team leader, waiting for his response.

Danny (H) looked at Jay Mac then directly at the officer, "Yeah, that's exactly what happened and no, I didn't see who hit me. I just wanna go home now."

Reasonably satisfied but not entirely convinced by what he had heard, the questioning officer's attention was suddenly diverted by his driver colleague who announced, "We've got a shout Davey, some trouble up by the Brow, and we're the nearest unit."

Having confirmed that no one wanted to make a formal complaint and, leaving his police station contact details, PC Davey dashed out of the doorway shouting "Bloody Halloween! What's wrong with them all tonight?"

After being thanked by Jay Mac, Mr and Mrs Ashworth went back up the two flights of stone stairs to their flat. His uncle helped Danny (H) to his feet and steadied him then departed, hoping to get some sleep in the three remaining hours, before the insistent alarm clock woke him for his work.

Jay Mac's aunt remained for a moment and said firmly "Is everything going to be alright here, there won't be any more trouble will there?"

Both youths assured her that for the present matters were resolved and she too returned to her flat to continue reading one of her Agatha Christie novels and enjoy another Embassy filter-tipped cigarette, before finally retiring for the night.

Danny (H) was studying his bloodied rival, he had been carefully considering what had occurred and, what had been said, "It's a pity you're playin' for the wrong team lad." He paused for a moment and stepped out into the cold, still, brilliant moonlit night, then turning back to face Jay Mac, he added, "You wanna watch that cunt Yad, he's a fuckin' snake. When we had him by the Heron tonight he gave you up straight away to save himself."

Jay Mac watched as Danny (H) turned up the collar of his Crombie and, once again rubbing his aching jaw, walked away in the direction of the Anvil public house. "Thanks for tellin' me, I'll take care of that cunt meself, he's finished, his time's over."

Jay Mac did not go to work the next day and, after convincing himself of the cogent argument in support of taking the rest of the week off, he decided to remain absent without leave until the following Monday. His uncle reluctantly agreed to advise Jay Mac's immediate boss, old Stan of his 'illness,' when he had finished his morning delivery round, which happened to bring him close to the shipping office where the youth worked.

Sitting in his aunt and uncle's small flat, waiting for his injuries to heal sufficiently to enable him to undertake the task, that he always knew would inevitably fall to him, Jay Mac constantly reviewed possible ways that he would issue his challenge and more importantly defeat his wily, skilful enemy.

While his aunt wandered in and out between the living room and kitchen, engaged in her daily cleaning and polishing routine, continually singing a selection of 1930s and wartime favourites, Jay Mac lay on the temporarily vacant couch or, when required to move, sat in one of the well-worn armchairs, trying to listen to the radio and gather his thoughts.

Although Jay Mac did not know the exact fate of Dayo (G), he expected that he had been arrested and hoped he may not currently be socialising in the Heron with their crew, or at least, would be reluctant to get involved in another major incident. Either way he determined that now was the optimum moment to finally deal with Yad.

Patch the old mongrel dog remained virtually in the same position, throughout Jay Mac's three-day convalescence, stretched out in front of the electric fire listening to the youth's restless disturbed sleep each night, barking on every occasion that he cried out in the midst of his recurring nightmares.

Saturday 4th November 1972

"Bit cold for that haircut now, isn't it?" Jay Mac's uncle asked casually commenting on the youth's latest number one crop, with obligatory razored trench that he had asked the local barber for earlier in the day, as part of his preparation ritual.

"Thought I'd give it one last go before the winter sets in, any chance you could iron me baker's strides?" Jay Mac replied, forcing a painful grin and receiving feigned protestations from the old soldier.

Leaving the living room, Jay Mac crossed the tiny hall and entered the bathroom where he remained for some time soaking in a hot bath, listening to the small transistor radio and trying to ease some of the aches from the extensive bruises that covered his back, arms and legs in a patchwork of varying purple, black and yellow hues. Whilst he lay there in the steaming soapy water, he placed a hot wet flannel over his pained face, across his damaged nose and two swollen dark-ringed eyes. The Doors, *Riders on the Storm* one of his favourites was playing on the radio, which he had precariously balanced on the nearby sink and he laughed to himself visualising his own brain 'squirming like a toad,' whilst contemplating his forthcoming battle with the sadistic Yad.

An hour later a cleansed and suitably attired Jay Mac had just finished his evening meal of fried sausages and mashed potato and was sitting on a hard backed chair in the kitchen, working away on his boots with his polishing kit, striving for the ultimate shine.

"Anything special going on tonight, with it nearly being Bonfire Night?" Jay Mac's uncle asked curiously, whilst rinsing his false teeth under the cold water tap at the kitchen sink, before immersing them in their plastic beaker filled with Steradent solution.

"No, am just goin' to meet some of the crew in the Heron and then see what happens," Jay Mac replied honestly.

His uncle reached into his trouser pocket and passed Jay Mac some loose change, "Here's a few bob for drinks. Just make sure you keep out of trouble, there'll be enough fuckin' fireworks going off all over the place without you adding to the commotion, right?" With that he left the kitchen and returned to the living room to relax with his pipe and watch the 'Black and White Minstrels Show' on the small rented television.

After putting away his polishing equipment and leaving the kitchen, Jay Mac stood in the doorway of his aunt and uncle's bedroom admiring his gleaming red boots in the dressing table mirror, which contrasted starkly with his immaculately ironed white baker's trousers. He fastened his Levi's denim jacket with bleached collar and slipped on his black Harrington jacket in place of his now useless, discarded Crombie, then he pulled a black woollen tight-fitting skull cap onto his head, shouted a brief goodbye and left the flat.

Quickly descending the stone stairs, he passed the scene of his recent attack by the Anvil crew, opened the sheet metal covered door and stepped out into the bitterly cold November night. A squall of sleet suddenly broke and danced around him, whilst he briskly marched towards the battered old shelter. Standing silhouetted in the opening space under the flats which spanned the chip shop on the left side and, the newsagents on the right were Danny (H) and his gang. They watched Jay Mac with casual interest, blatantly standing at the front of the bus stop, clearly visible in his white trousers.

Danny (H) walked forward a few paces while eating his chips out of their newspaper wrappings and stood in the cold rain that was now falling steadily, staring at his former rival, then shouted "You look like yer dressed for bovver, lad! Anyone in particular that yer after tonight?"

Jay Mac stepped out fully, he could see his bus approaching and replied, "Only a fuckin' snake, am goin' to tread on him permanently."

Danny (H) watched as Jay Mac got onto the bus and mouthed some final words of warning, which he did not hear. "Watch he doesn't bite *you*, he's a slippery cunt."

Fifteen minutes later after leaving the bus at the corporation garage stop, instead of following his usual route from the Western perimeter of the Crown Estate, past Mal 'the Pig's' house, over the waste ground and along the central road towards Irish's residence, Jay Mac turned to his left and walked along the bottom edge, heading for the Heron public house.

On approaching the drab graffiti covered building with its recently reboarded windows; he could smell the acrid smoke which, despite the ice cold drizzling rain, was billowing from a crackling bonfire on the field to the rear, where the last major engagement between the two estates' teams had taken place.

Sitting on the low wall outside the pub were a new assortment of anonymous Juniors, who were all unknown to Jay Mac and busily cackling away to each other like a murder of crows in their long, wet, black coats. Clearly they recognised the lone Skin walking through the entrance gap in the car park boundary wall, as one of them shouted "I wouldn't go in there Jay Mac, not on yer own. Yad and the crew are all havin' a drink and he's really pissed off about their Dayo!"

Jay Mac ignored this well-meant warning and stepped up into the entrance porch, where two of Molly Brown's younger associates were sitting on the cold floor.

"Penny for the Guy lad?" one of them called out, gesturing towards her associate, who, on seeing the scowl on his face, continued "Or two pence for a wank if y'want." Both girls howled with laughter at the spontaneity of their wit.

Passing through the battered full-length swing door, which now also had a wooden panel nailed in place where previously the glazed one had been, Jay Mac stood perfectly still just inside the blue-grey smoke filled room, letting the blast of freezing night air, that had used his entry to gain momentary ingress, announce his arrival. Yad, Weaver and a dozen other members of the Heron crew, including the newly promoted Tomo, Nat and Peza trio, who were no longer ranked as Juniors, were sitting at the far end of the lounge bar, occupying several tables; they casually glanced in Jay Mac's direction.

He smiled as he made his way through the crowd of seated civilian drinkers and approached Yad's table. The youth was not amused by his situation or what he was about to do but at a quirk of fate, whereby someone had included his current favourite song in their jukebox selection and, he heard the opening bars of *Living in a Broken Dream*. The rest of the song seemed to fade into the general background din, as he stood smiling directly in front of Yad's table.

"Something amusin' you?" an angry looking Weaver asked but Jay Mac did not reply.

"What's happened to you Jay Mac? One of your boyfriends been gettin' a bit rough, or did Danny (H) finally catch up with yer?" Yad asked, laughing at his own humorous question.

Jay Mac stopped smiling and said, "Outside in the car park now, you bag of shit."

All conversation amongst the Heron crew stopped abruptly and the ripple of silence spread out from the epicentre of Jay Mac's challenge. Only the sound of the record re-emerged to fill the void.

Yad stared up at Jay Mac shaking his head in disbelief, "I'm not in the mood tonight, so am gonna give yer a chance to walk out that fuckin' door while yer still can. Piss off."

Jay Mac suspected that part of Yad's apparent reluctance was due to the possible enforced absence of his brother, which he had deciphered from the Junior's cryptic warning a few minutes earlier. He also knew that he had come too far to walk away; by giving Jay Mac's home details to the enemy, Yad had now endangered his aunt and uncle and that was unconscionable. All the American comic book characters he had ever read about kept their real identities secret for this very reason, the treacherous Yad had broken the last taboo, exposing Jay Mac's guardians to possible attack.

Seizing the nearest resting pint glass, which Peza had momentarily placed down on his table whilst lighting a cigarette, Jay Mac threw its half-filled amber liquid contents into Yad's face, producing the result that he wanted. His enemy sprang to his feet, wiping his drenched face with his hand and unsettling the table he had been seated at.

Yad grabbed hold of the front of Jay Mac's jacket and shouted "You are fuckin' dead lad! You must be mental comin' in here on yer own and challengin' me. I am gonna fuckin' beat you to death!" Then a wave of caution passed over the enraged Heron leader, "Nat, go and check outside. Make sure that this cunt is on his own, an' hasn't got the Eagle crew waitin' in the car park for me."

Jay Mac smiled at his enemy and said, "I'm on me own shitbag, this is between you and me. I'll be outside, don't leave me waitin' or I will drag yer out of here if I have to."

With that Jay Mac turned and walked as calmly as he could towards the door, then out through the entrance porch. Looking down once more at the two young girls still begging for change, he said "The 'Guy' is goin' to follow me out shortly, ask him for some cash, he won't need it much longer." Jay Mac knew they would repeat his words to the already incensed Yad.

Standing in the middle of the dark grey, forlorn car park, bathed in the pale amber glow of the one functioning street lamp atop of its precast concrete perch, he watched another squall of freezing hail and rain which was briefly captured as it streamed through the same broad beam of light. Despite the inclement prevailing weather conditions, the arena was soon ringed by an eager human circle buzzing with expectation. Jay Mac looked at the Heron crowd and realised his own words were entirely true, he was completely alone, with not one friendly face or supporter amongst them.

Yad made his spectacular entrance to the wild cheers of the assembled spectators and he drew reassurance from their reaction, as without his brother, Dayo (G), who with Quirky had been remanded in custody without bail to await trial for violently assaulting several police officers, he was not sure how much longer his reign of terror may go unchallenged. His anticipated total demolition of the foolhardy Jay Mac would be easily achieved, he thought and it would prove to be a suitable bloody reminder of how vicious he could be.

The Heron leader removed his Crombie and passed it carefully to Peza then leaned into the former Junior, saying something that only he could hear. Jumping on the spot, waving his arms and shouting out loud curses, Yad the showman whipped the crowd's carnal desire into a state of frenzy, exhorting them to point at Jay Mac and chant "Your dead, you're dead, you're dead!"

Jay Mac moved his head from side-to-side, then raised his fists and stepped forward to meet his fate.

Yad danced around him for a few moments then threw a straight right to his face which Jay Mac only just dodged, passing his opponent on the right and delivering a powerful back-fist strike to Yad's unprotected temple. Feeling the force of the unsuspected blow, Yad stepped back only to receive this time a spinning back fist from the lightning fast Jay Mac as he weaved in front of him turning like a top, whipping out his arm in a blur.

Yad wasn't sure what was happening, having received two unconventional hits, the type that he thought *he* was the only one to have knowledge of and he decided to change tactics, lunging forward to grapple his enemy while his back was partially turned. He caught Jay Mac around the waist but his grip wasn't secure enough and the lithe youth rotated just sufficiently to bring a tremendous strike, with the heel of his left palm onto the top of Yad's head, which shook his brain making him release his hold.

The cheering crowd had almost all fallen silent, Yad had been stuck three times and his own attacks had been futile, he looked at them with his head spinning and ordered "C'mon keep shoutin', c'mon!"

Some lack lustre cheers resulted and Yad straightened up to launch another assault, moving in close with his raised fists hoping to exchange punches with the fast moving Jay Mac.

"Stand still and fight you fuckin' tart, stop runnin' away." he called to Jay Mac, who was now up on his toes, dodging and weaving about in front of him.

Jay Mac was determined that his recent painful training sessions with Treky, would be utilised to maximum effect and had no intention of letting Yad dictate the pace, or direction of their encounter. Keeping his already badly injured face protected with his forearms and fists, he caught Yad with a powerful snap kick to his stomach, which forced him backwards a few steps winding him in the process.

So far the traffic had all been in one direction in Jay Mac's favour but he did not let this deceive him, knowing that Yad liked to test the best shots from an adversary, before fully committing himself. For his part, Yad felt Jay Mac had some useful tricks, though as yet, he was confident there was nothing that would prevent his total victory.

The now stationary Yad, was holding his stomach as if he had been more seriously injured than he actually had, encouraging Jay Mac to close the distance between them. A tremendous right hook caught him in the gut, followed immediately by a left to his already badly bruised ribs. He winced in pain, lowering his guard from his damaged face and Yad sprang forward intending to deliver a devastating head butt on to his opponent's broken nose. Dodging to one side, Jay Mac threw a short range straight right jab, banging hard against Yad's mouth, splitting his lower lip and drawing the all-important first blood.

Wiping his bleeding mouth with the back of his hand, even before he could recover, Jay Mac's left hook caught Yad in his aching stomach. This was sufficient evidence for the Heron leader, he wasn't badly hurt but he was not going to allow Jay Mac to dominate the action and continue landing blows, then moving out of range. He came forward again, this time with a different purpose in mind and threw a couple of wild punches which completely missed the dodging Skin, who responded with a thundering right uppercut to the jaw, violently snapping Yad's head back, hurting him more than he had expected.

As the genuinely dizzy Yad staggered away towards his now totally silenced supporters and knelt down on one knee, Jay Mac waited, standing still in the middle of the human circle, watching to see what his enemy's next response may be.

Suddenly his attention was drawn by a familiar voice from the crowd "Go on Jay Mac, finish the bastard, don't give him a chance to get up. Remember the Cardinal Boy's rules!" shouted Irish whose urgent advice was joined by several other calls from Jay Mac's Eagle crew mates.

Unknown to Yad, who was still partially kneeling and breathing heavily, next to Peza at the edge of the 'ring', the lone anonymous Junior, who earlier tried to warn Jay Mac, had ran all the way to the Eagle when he saw him exit the Heron followed by Yad and his crew. Irish, Blue, Johno and several others of Jay Mac's friends had raced down to the car park arena and barged their way to the front of the tightly packed spectators.

One other former Eagle crew member had also made his own way to the scene of the fight as fast as he could manage, arriving at the moment Jay Mac's most recent blow connected with Yad's jaw; Glynn. Despite Mary's outraged protestations, after Irish had called enroute and delivered the news, Glynn had quickly changed from his civilian garb into his old player's uniform, told the hysterical girl to be quiet and pushed his well-meaning uncle to one side as he opened the neatly painted front door, to escape for one more evening of madness. Dressed in his Crombie, jeans and boots and leaning on a polished dark wooden walking stick for support, he joined the vocal group who were urging Jay Mac to finish the downed Yad.

What neither they or Jay Mac could see was that while the slyly smiling Yad leaned on Peza, to assist him in standing, he furtively received his heavy brass knuckle duster which the ex-Junior had been keeping safe for him. He returned confidently to the fight with renewed vigour and enthusiasm, keeping his fists raised with left over right to obscure the devastating metal aid.

Both Yad and Jay Mac circled and stalked each other looking for an opening, waiting for an error. Yad dropped his hands almost inviting Jay Mac's swinging left hook that only just missed his enemy's head, as he successfully dodged and thumped a bone-cracking knuckle duster encased right hook into his left side. Jay Mac let out a gasp as the air departed from his lungs and he felt the terrible pain shoot through his damaged ribs, he knew something was seriously wrong. He brought his left arm down to try and shield that area of his body, exposing his face in so doing and receiving a beaming Yad's reward of another tremendous right hook, this time to the left side of his face, just in front of his ear. The metal implement dug deep and a new gash opened up to release its scarlet fluid first in a spurt, then a steady stream.

"Something's wrong." Irish said to Johno, "A normal punch wouldn't have cut like that, has that cunt got somethin'?" he continued, trying to catch a clear look at Yad's right fist, while Jay Mac staggered about dazed from the awesome blow.

"What's the matter 'girl', can't take a real man's dig hey?" Yad shouted with delight, once more encouraging his supporters to show their appreciation.

Jay Mac abandoned all reason, he knew Yad had something in or on his right hand and that he could not absorb many more of his devastating punches. Pouncing like a wounded animal, he grabbed Yad by the lapels of his denim jacket and projected his own skull with all the strength that he could muster, from his inner core through his neck muscles and focused in his forehead at the point of contact; Yad's previously straight, unbroken nose. The audible crack stunned the crowd, almost as much as the tremendous blow did the reeling Yad, whose eyes watered while the dislodged broken bone and cartilage in his nose were swept to one side by the initial torrent of blood that burst forth. Desperately holding on to Jay Mac to steady himself, Yad lost his footing on the wet dark grey surface and both bloodied adversaries crashed to the ground.

They rolled over and over trying to apply a hold, or deliver that decisive punch, until finally Yad brought his heavier weight advantage into play and pinned the struggling Jay Mac underneath him. Straddling his captive's chest, as he had done with Glynn previously, Yad was feeling triumphant and looked about at the wildly cheering crowd until he spotted his former victim, then shouted, "I'm glad you're here, dickhead! Now you can watch this fuckin' tart gettin' done proper, just like I done you and yer slag of a mother!"

Then as an anguished Glynn cried out, "You bastard, you fuckin' bastard!" Yad struck Jay Mac twice more with his right metal assisted fist, opening his broken nose and cutting his left eyebrow. He leaned forward placing his left hand across Jay Mac's mouth, intending to gouge out his eyes with his thumb and forefinger but the youth was too quick for him, clamping the stretched skin between those two digits with his teeth, biting hard almost to the bone. Yad screamed out in pain, desperately trying to extricate his badly damaged bleeding hand without success, in desperation he punched Jay Mac repeatedly with his right fist but the barely conscious Skin held on tenaciously like his favourite breed of dog, an English Bullterrier.

Turning next to the crowd for assistance Yad shouted, "Peza, now! For fuck's sake, throw me knife over to me!"

The nervous former Junior prepared to do as instructed, drawing the Commando blade from its secure hiding place within Yad's Crombie but as he was about to toss it to his leader, a sharp blow to his arm from Irish made him drop the weapon and it clattered to the floor, sliding a short distance before stopping at the feet of Weaver.

Yad grinned through the pain of his injuries and called to his fellow commander, "Terry, mate, kick it over, quick! I'll cut off one of his ears then you can have a go with yer hammer!"

Stone-faced the psychopathic Heron general looked at Yad dispassionately and focused on his still, outstretched right hand, where even in the driving rain, his blood stained heavy brass knuckle duster could now clearly be seen. Without a single word or hint of expression, Weaver kicked the rain-spattered blade away to his left.

Jay Mac was struggling to remain conscious but through his blurred vision, he witnessed Weaver's act and as warm blood mixed with cold rain, trickled into his mouth, he forced a smile, releasing Yad's left hand and said, "The game's over you fuckin' snake, its full time."

A desperate Yad ignored Jay Mac and erupting in a paroxysm of frustrated rage, like a spoiled child, he screamed "Give me my fuckin' knife, someone! Give it to me now!"

The driving rain increased in intensity as the anonymous Junior message-bearer bent down and retrieved the family heirloom weapon, that had skidded to a halt immediately in front of him, then clasping it firmly he walked forward with a measured tread.

"C'mon yer little fuck, move y'self, give it to me!" Yad screamed once more, while others, including some of the Heron crew cried out "Don't do it lad, don't give him it!"

Drenched with rain and soaked in his own nervous sweat the red-eyed, skinny Junior crouched over Yad and the fallen Jay Mac who had always been pleasant to him, who he admired and who he had tried to warn earlier, then he plunged the knife up to its hilt into Yad's lower back, tearing through yielding flesh, sinews, veins and vital organs. Again and again, he struck at the object of his hatred and pent up rage, how long he had waited for this moment, ever since that February night when the evil Yad had captured his sister, Debbie, and led his cheering Junior disciples in her brutal gang rape.

Michael Gill pulled out the scarlet knife from his final puncture of the gurgling, twitching body of the dying Yad, stood up now perfectly relaxed and motionless, staring down at the seventeen-year old former Heron leader, as he slowly collapsed to one side rolling off the pinioned Jay Mac. All were frozen for a few seconds of eternity and then as if the crowd had been held by invisible, taut elastic strands that had suddenly snapped, they scattered explosively in every direction, save for Irish, Blue, Johno and Glynn.

Lifting their battered friend carefully from the blood stained ground, Irish and Johno raised him to his feet and, supporting him on either side, moved away from the grim scene. The usually loquacious Blue remained silent for once, staring in stunned disbelief at the lifeless body of Yad, while a steady dark red stream poured from his wounds staining the back of his denim jacket, bearing the Crown Skins emblem across the shoulders.

Leaning on his stick, Glynn's urgent shout snapped him back to reality, "C'mon mate, we've got to get away before someone calls the bizzies, leave that piece of shit to rot!"

Both he and Blue crossed the road in front of the bottom row of shops, following Irish and Johno as they assisted Jay Mac in departing from the lower area of the estate.

Only the lone fifteen year old Michael remained unmoving, still tightly clutching the dripping knife, rooted to the wet ground, standing in the pouring rain as it washed dark rivulets of blood around his feet. Yad had never asked his name, he didn't bother getting to know new members, now everybody would know this anonymous Junior, the boy who only joined the crew to avenge his sister. Away in the distance sirens could be heard once more.

Chapter 13

Ghost Riders in the Sky

5th November and 29th-31st December 1972

Sunday 5th November

The day after Yad's demise at the hands of young Michael Gill, was a bleak, grey, wet Sunday and it was the fifth of November, Bonfire Night. On both estates it had been keenly anticipated, for once legitimising the gangs' practice of lighting impromptu fires where and when they saw fit. Normally each year the Kings Team would vie with their Crown Team rivals, in raising the biggest mounds of wood and other assorted flammable debris, on their respective sides of the main highway. Once ignited the objective was to maintain them for as long as possible and keep them blazing long into the night.

This year it was a case of absolute contrast. While the jubilant Kings Team celebrated what they viewed as a total victory, with the death of the Heron leader, Yad and, as they wrongly believed, that of Tommy (S), who despite the best efforts of Crag and his chosen men, was still alive albeit in a critical condition in hospital, the Crown Team bonfires remained unlit. Crag's arrest and re-imprisonment did little to dampen the Kings Team exultation, as far as they were concerned, the enemy was leaderless, both at crew level and at the pinnacle of their high command. Added to this, their territory had been overrun with considerable destruction of property in the lower part of the estate, including one of their key strongholds, the Heron Public House.

In fact to a great extent the Kings Team were correct. For the Heron crew, there seemed to be no way they could recover, at least for the present. Yad was dead; Macca (G) had been badly injured in the Halloween debacle, once again having to withdraw temporarily from his leadership position, leaving only the psychopathic Weaver in charge. The Juniors, whose tutelage Yad had always maintained as his sole preserve, were without direction and acutely aware of the fact that it was from within their own ranks, that the killer of their sadistic mentor had emerged.

For Jay Mac this particular Bonfire Night was just another day spent trying to recover, before returning to work the following morning. He sat on the couch in his aunt and uncle's flat attempting to explain how he acquired his most recent wounds and vehemently denying that he was anywhere in the vicinity of, *'the vicious murder of a local youth,'* reports of which were being widely circulated by both the police and the gossips. Whilst the wounded Skin lied to the best of his ability, comfortably ensconced in front of the two-bar electric fire, reading the *News of the World*'s latest accounts of the American forces position in Vietnam, a few short miles away in a police interrogation room, the terrified former Junior, Michael, maintained his total silence.

Only in the mid afternoon when his older sister, Debbie, finally broke down, during a police questioning session in the company of her distraught parents, revealing all the sickening details of her rape and the names of her attackers, did Michael finally speak. Even as the wildly protesting Nat, Peza and Tomo were being arrested, handcuffed and dragged from their respective houses, the once anonymous Junior was signing a prepared statement where he confessed to being the sole perpetrator of the rape organiser's murder. For the present the local police were satisfied, even if all the pieces did not quite fit, two serious crimes had been committed on their patch and in one day they had all the principal offenders in custody.

Residents' outrage on the Crown Estate finally made the transition from private grumbles to public protests and angry demands were made of incompetent, self-serving councillors, who finally brought to account, had to justify their comfortable civic positions and excessive salaries. A strong visible police presence was promised, at least for the short term and the Crown Estate now had a new uniformed team patrolling its grim streets and dank alleys. Both Eagle and Heron crews abandoned their territory to these organised official rivals, returning to boring 'civilian' life for the moment, until the time was right to re-emerge and take control once again.

Friday 29th December to Sunday 31st December 1972

Time passed, days became weeks, November ended and with the arrival of December, almost on cue, a cold wet autumn surrendered its control of the elements to a bitter, freezing winter. During the first dark week of that season, the funeral of the seventeen year old Yad took place, the police having released the body after obtaining a detailed post mortem and satisfying themselves that any further delay would provide no significant contribution to their enquiries. It was a quiet affair, the Day family where devastated by the loss of their youngest child, with their surviving son Graham (Dayo (G)) only being allowed to attend handcuffed and flanked by two burly warders, then having to return immediately from the graveside to the confines of his prison cell. Both Eagle and Heron public houses remained open for business but neither received much custom, only a handful of drinkers in either establishment raised their glasses, whether the gesture was one of commiseration or celebration, they chose not to reveal.

Now several weeks later, with Christmas just passed, the month and year were drawing to a close, Jay Mac, Irish, Blue and Glynn were sitting with the rest of the Eagle crew at the tables around the semi-circular edge of the lounge bar. Glynn, having established a more balanced relationship with his girlfriend Mary, had been allowed to join his friends for the evening, on the strict understanding that if any trouble began he must return home at once.

He was presently holding court, making the most of his freedom, "Yeah, what I'm sayin' is, if that cunt didn't have that fuckin' knuckle duster, Jay Mac would've done him."

Those drinkers, who were able to hear his remarks over the general din and sound of Lieutenant Pigeon's *Mouldy Old Dough* currently playing on the juke box, agreed adding their own comments.

Jay Mac was anxious to change the topic, becoming increasingly uncomfortable with recent developments regarding his final encounter with Yad. A peculiar phenomenon was occurring and he was acutely aware of it. Only a few years previous he and Irish were trapped with the rest of their long-suffering class mates, in another double period of the subject that they all hated more than any other – Physics, with the singularly most boring teacher in the 'school' and possibly profession, Mr Leonard Wilkinson, whose halitosis breath it was reputed, could stop a charging rhino at a hundred yards. With his deadpan monotone delivery, his tedious lengthy monologues on the revelations to be gained by studying *his* personal favourite, 'the parallelogram of forces,' he had managed to repeatedly switch off successive year groups of previously open-minded boys from this branch of Science. However, on this day, 'Lenny' appeared almost animated about a new topic, "nothing" as he called it and began describing an experiment known as the Magdeburg Hemispheres, which proved the existence of a vacuum. What caught Jay Mac's interest and remained in his mind long after he had served the detention for proving Lenny's theory, with a loud farting noise made with the back of his hand, was that nature abhors a vacuum, something will always fill the void.

Sitting in the positively charged, testosterone filled atmosphere, with his Eagle team mates, he knew he was unavoidably being pushed into the centre of the power vacuum that had now been created within the Crown Team. On one side the Heron crew were to all intents leaderless, with Yad deceased and Macca (G) retired for the foreseeable future, no one wanted to follow Weaver's ill-conceived orders.

Tommy (S)'s condition had only recently been downgraded from critical to comfortable and Quirky and Dayo (G) were both imprisoned, consequently the Eagle crew lacked direction. As the tale of Jay Mac's lone Heron saloon entrance, daring personal challenge and ensuing deadly disadvantaged struggle, which resulted in the bloody death of his hated rival, grew in the telling, so too did the calls for him to assume a caretaker manager leadership role within the Crown Estate Team.

When Irish jokingly said "You've become a real life Lone Ranger," Jay Mac laughed and like anyone else of his generation, who had grown up watching the stirring adventures of the Masked Rider, followed by Wagon Train, Rawhide, Cheyenne, Bonanza and countless other television Westerns, he was greatly flattered by the compliment. An accompanying almost subconscious understanding of the morals, ethics and behaviour pattern expected of the heroes who populated Hollywood's 'Old West,' also warned of the inevitable nemesis that always stalked the successful gunslinger; dangerous up-and-coming rivals, intent on creating a new power vacuum then filling it themselves.

Having had enough of fighting for the present, bearing the physical and mental scars to remind him of the pain of both failure and success, Jay Mac wanted to move on, change course, even abandon ship, not take the helm. His thoughts were on other matters, he had earlier given Irish the specific details, now he wanted to close the discussion concerning the late Heron leader, putting an end to any further exaggeration about his own fighting prowess and speculation about his leadership potential. Glynn provided the beginning of an escape route.

"At least that bastard's back in Hell where he came from" he said, before taking a sip of his whiskey chaser.

Irish and Jay Mac both looked at him sternly and, as if to rebuke him, Irish said, "Don't yer know, it's not right t'speak ill of the dead?"

Glynn nearly choked on his drink then responded, "Fuck him."

Jay Mac then joined in, "Ah well, wherever he is, good luck to him, he can't do any more harm here and that's for sure."

A scowling Glynn was clearly unhappy and Irish decided to lighten the topic, "I'm certain the feller with the pointy tail and the pitchfork has found a new position for him."

To which Jay Mac immediately added "Yeah, on his knees with Old Nick's cock up his arse." All the crew within hearing range laughed at this comment, conjuring up their own disturbing mental images of the sadistic youth vigorously receiving his painful, just reward from his master.

Glynn appeared particularly pleased as he savoured the thought, wishing somehow he could unlock his mother's nightmare prison and if not quite set her free, then at least provide some solace, with the news that one of her evil attackers had been sentenced to an eternity of torment of his own.

Jay Mac then went to the bar for another round of drinks and when he returned, Irish changed the conversation to a different topic. "So this bird you was tellin' me about before, what's so special about her?" he asked grinning, while Blue and Glynn looked at Jay Mac expectantly.

"Stunning mate and that's not even good enough to describe her," Jay Mac began, then slowly poured the bottle of brown ale into the pint glass half filled with amber bitter. He waited a few moments before taking a long draught, knowing that his team mates were waiting for him to continue.

"Fuckin' hell Jay Mac' give us the bleedin' details then." Blue asked looking forward to a full topographical survey from his friend.

"This girl is number one mate. Incredible looks, Hollywood film star smile, a top model's body and I don't mean like a fuckin' Twiggy type and legs up to her … armpits, only wears smart kit, definitely classy."

Jay Mac stopped and took another drink as Irish responded, "Well out of your league then, you've got no fuckin' chance there."

Blue required the answer to one further question to satisfy his curiosity "Yer not givin' much away there Jay Mac, I mean, would I have a go meself? No disrespect like."

Slowly placing his pint back onto the small round table in front of him, Jay Mac stopped smiling then stared coolly at his corpulent team mate, "Blue what sort of recommendation would that be? You'd fuckin' bang anything if it stayed still long enough, why d'yer think Irish's dog, old Toby runs off and hides in his kennel whenever you show up?"

Irish and Glynn both laughed acknowledging the truth of Jay Mac's observation, Blue was uncertain how to react. Then Jay Mac added "Am only jokin' Blue, old Toby likes you really."

Amused himself by Jay Mac's comments, Blue smiled deciding somehow that his friend was acknowledging his sexual prowess, then said "Yeah, I am a bit of a stud I s'pose." The whole crew laughed at this statement.

During the next few rounds of drinking, Jay Mac described how the object of his desire had first come to his attention towards the end of the summer, while he was delivering bills of lading and other office mail, in the business sector of town.

Despite his best efforts and constant vigilance since then, he had only managed to catch fleeting glimpses of this stunning female, until earlier this day when he had been allowed to finish work half an hour earlier than usual as a festive goodwill concession, acknowledging the approaching New Year celebrations. On reaching his bus stop in Chapel Street, he was transfixed on finding his love interest standing in all her glory casually adjusting her long dark hair and causing consternation amongst the male passers-by, both pedestrian and motorist. When her bus arrived, Jay Mac was pleased to see that it would eventually end at the Kings Estate northern terminus and, even though it was not his usual bus, he leapt on determined to make her acquaintance.

After she had taken her seat at the rear of the vehicle, Jay Mac made sure that he pushed and elbowed his way to the one directly facing her. Despite feeling more nervous than on any other occasion, even when he had faced his Kings Team opponents, he managed to summon up the courage to speak and, during the twenty exciting minutes until she left the bus at her stop in the Walton Hall Avenue suburb region, he put forward as many cogent arguments and salient points as he could, in an effort to obtain a date with her.

"So even though she's got a boyfriend on the go, she finally agreed to meet me tomorrow night outside Dickie Lewis at eight o'clock. No fuckin' way am I goin' to blow this. I'm tellin' yer, she's got it all." Jay Mac finished his tale and then his pint.

While Blue and Glynn where at the bar getting another round of drinks and salted snacks, Irish spoke to his long-time friend, "What are y'gonna do if yer get off with this top bird? I bet she won't be happy with yer bein' in a Skinhead team and gettin' into aggro all the time."

Jay Mac waited until his two friends returned with their pints and food, then said, "Listen, things that have happened recently have shown me that this fuckin' game has got to end. It's like Glynn said, we've got to move on, I'll be eighteen in January, an old man. And another thing, the Skinhead days are over, we're the only ones left, who gets a fuckin' number one now?" He paused for a moment, mixing his pint then said finally, "Here's a good example for yer, y'see this new Crombie am wearing? I had to look all over town to find this; no shops stock them anymore because nobody wants them. It's all velvet jackets and fuckin' flares now with long haired twats everywhere."

After Jay Mac had finished his revelatory assessment of current teen fashion, the four friends sat quietly drinking, as if individually considering what the future may hold for each of them, once they were forced to emerge from the collective security of uniformity.

The sound of several Lambrettas arriving outside the main entrance roused the companions from their personal reflections. Flinging open the full length swing door Tony (G) marched in briskly, removing his helmet as he did, then standing close to the table where Jay Mac was seated with his friends, said, "We've just driven in off the Lancs Road by the bus depot and we saw a full crew of Kings cunts runnin' across from there. I think they must be goin' to come round from that side and do the Heron."

Everyone looked across towards Jay Mac except for two of Tommy (S)'s old guard, who were sitting at the end of the room casually smoking their cigarettes and drinking their pints. Jay Mac could almost feel a palpable sense of expectation, while the crew waited for his decision. He knew that if Weaver was 'surprised' his response would be to commit all of his troops, including his novice Juniors, to an immediate bloody reprisal without thought of casualties. He also understood that if they left at once, by using the side streets, the Eagle crew could repeat the Kings Team Halloween Night pincer movement and effectively trap *them*, between both of the Crown Team's forces.

Glynn had almost finished his pint and looking directly at Jay Mac said, "I know what you're thinkin', Jay Mac, 'let's get down there and catch them while they're layin' into the Heron crew,' well if you do that, you are fuckin' mad. I'm goin' home and you should do the same, forget it, Weaver could do with a good kickin' anyway."

He swigged the last of his pint, stood up, put on his Crombie on and left.

Irish now added his comments "It's down to you Jay Mac, Weaver's no leader, those Juniors will get fucked, unless we get movin' and jump in but if you've had enough of this shite, then it's not your problem."

After both surviving five years in their sadistic school environment, Irish knew how to make his friend respond to certain situations.

Jay Mac shouted across to the two old guard drinkers "Any advice lads? D'you wanna step in and lead the crew?"

Raising their glasses, Gaz the elder of the pair replied, "This one's on you Jay Mac, you say what goes and we'll back yer up either way."

Resigned to his fate, Jay Mac finished his drink, stood up and, putting on his smart new Crombie, said, "Fuck it. Like Tommy (S) said, this is *our* estate, let's have them."

A few minutes later, the whole crew, suitably armed with the usual ale bottle ammunition, were rapidly making their way through the side streets and alleys, intent on relieving their Heron Crown team mates and trapping their Kings Team rivals; leading the vanguard was the newly promoted, reluctant general, Jay Mac.

Arriving at the bottom edge of the estate, they emerged from the alleyway that Jay Mac, Johno and the one-booted Weaver had run through, during the night of the Halloween attack. They were positioned to the far left of the Heron public house and could clearly see the Kings Team massing around the front of the building, numbering about fifty strong, throwing bottles, bricks and stones at the beleaguered Heron crew, who had fallen back in front of the shops seeking cover.

"Unload everythin', lash the fuckin' lot!" Jay Mac shouted as the signal to pour a withering fire of their glass projectiles, onto the rear of the Kings Team packed ranks.

Struck mainly on the head, back and shoulders, they turned in surprise to find the jeering Eagle crew about to launch another salvo. Standing in the open ground of the vehicle-less Heron car park, there was no shelter available to them and again individuals were hit by glass bottles, some of which smashed on contact, causing painful injuries. Using the remainder of their own existing ammunition and anything else that came to hand, including some of the unbroken bottles that landed near them, the desperate Kings Team returned fire as best they could.

In the immediate distance, just beyond the Kings position, outside the metal shuttered shops, Weaver was preparing to lead a counter attack of his own, rallying his troops ready for a wild charge. Jay Mac had anticipated this would be his response and asked Johno to sprint around the very edge of the action to tell Weaver to hold back and maintain his fire, keeping the Kings Team constantly under missile attack, wearing down their numbers with increasing casualties.

As Johno raced away, keeping close to the row of terraced houses, Jay Mac was aware that he was out of ammunition and while the remainder of the crew maintained a steady covering fire, he and five other Skins darted across to the nearest doorsteps, reloading with as many empty glass milk bottle 'shells' as they could carry. Suddenly a large piece of masonry consisting of several bricks still mortared together, which had been dislodged from the low walls outside the Heron by determined repeated kicking, flew over Jay Mac's head, as he returned to the crew with their much needed supplies. It crashed and broke loudly behind their lines, announcing to them all the presence of the Kings Team's own strongman, Mono.

"Come on you puffs, come 'ed, stop your fuckin' throwin' and let's get into it, if you've got the balls!" Mono shouted, stepping forward through the Kings Team lines and revealing himself, now wearing not only a bowler hat but also dressed in a white bib and brace visible under his open Crombie, with the trousers tucked into a pair of black Airwair boots. Ever the theatrical, Mono had decided to adopt the full *Clockwork Orange* look, still yet in advance of them seeing the actual film.

"I'll 'ave you then, yer fuckin' knob head!" bellowed the powerful Crusher, charging out from Weaver's contingent, intent on taking Mono's challenge literally and personally dealing with him.

Even as Jay Mac shouted desperately to Crusher "Get back! Stay with y'crew, this is what he wants!" it was too late.

Mono swiftly disappeared back inside his own ranks, which absorbed the Crown Team's juggernaut's attack, opening up to admit him and then closing the trap behind him. Capturing the crazed rhino was one thing, subduing him proved to be something quite different. Leaping onto the wild Crusher, punching, kicking and trying to get a firm hold on his powerful bulk, was almost causing more casualties than the Crown Team's glass fire, until Mono finally managed to place a deadly python's headlock around his thick neck.

Now the die was cast, distance fighting was abandoned; all were to be committed to hand-to-hand combat. Leading his crew, with toffee hammer drawn, Weaver ran forward, leapt a few feet in the air and landed amidst the Kings ranks, striking out in every direction. At the same moment Jay Mac ran to the first Kings opponent that he could close with and struck him hard in the face with an empty glass milk bottle, which to the surprise of both did not break. The entire Eagle crew followed suit, joining the melee en masse.

The struggling swirling mob of Skins moved across the open ground of the car park, then spilled out into the main lower road between the shops and houses like a huge rugby scrum comprised entirely of black-coated players. Shouts of encouragement and cries of pain filled the air in equal measure, mixed with the sound of flesh being struck by punches, head butts, metal poles and glass bottles. Opponents changed, either being dispatched or merely dislodged by the sheer momentum of the combatants. Located at the very centre of the maelstrom was Crusher, who with his arms around the waist of the strangling Mono, was himself squeezing the air out of his enemy's lungs, despite being pummelled by numerous Kings Skins.

Trying to break through to his Crown team mate, Jay Mac raised his right hand preparing to crack another head with his glass milk bottle mace, before it finally shattered. Suddenly he felt a firm grip on his wrist and simultaneously a restraining arm closed around his neck. Staring at his intended victim's horrified face, Jay Mac knew only one phenomenon could induce such a response; the Police. Within seconds his worst fears were confirmed as the desperate warnings rang out once more.

"It's the Pigs, the fuckin' Pigs they're everywhere!" For a wildly struggling Jay Mac and dozens of other unlucky players the alarm was raised too late. Dragged to a nearby waiting patrol car, he was roughly forced inside, handcuffed and had to sit watching from the back seat next to the arresting officer, whilst Skins from both teams were similarly tackled then marched to a variety of police vehicles, that had arrived deliberately without advance warning sirens.

Tony (G) and his scooter companions had not been the only observers of the Kings Team movements that evening. An unmarked police car responding to intelligence reports from their Kings Estate colleagues, drove past them at the corporation bus depot crossing point and parked nearby noting the direction of their progress, then called for urgent significant backup. The residents of the Crown Estate finally got what they had requested so many times previously, a robust police response with sufficient numbers to make significant arrests. Jay Mac looked out of the rear passenger window which was beginning to mist with condensation and began to fully appreciate the scale of the operation, while the huge team of uniformed officers, some leading loudly barking large German shepherd dogs, captured fleeing youths in every direction that he could see.

A sudden bang on the roof of the car that he was seated in, followed by the brief instruction from outside "Right off y'go, Ravens' Lane for this one" was the signal for their driver to depart and join the convoy of vehicles heading to various police stations situated in the northern district of the City.

The young officer next to Jay Mac then spoke, "Well, if it isn't the little smart arse himself, fancy that? Small world eh?"

Jay Mac turned and looked at the speaker recognising him from previous encounters but responded "I don't think I've had the pleasure officer."

His captor laughed, then replied, "That's it lad, carry on like that, the DCs are going to love questioning you tonight."

Feeling sick Jay Mac tried a desperate gambit based on tales that he had heard from other team mates, who had been in this position. "Listen, I don't need any trouble, it would upset me family too much, so what about a kickin' down at 'The Fields', then you can let me go?"

All the Skins on the Crown Estate were familiar with this unorthodox policing method, whereby instead of being formally arrested and charged, they received a sound beating in a deserted wasteland known locally as 'The Fields' and then were released with the matter considered closed by all parties.

The young officer spoke to his driver colleague, "What d'you think Peter lad? Should we take this little shit down to the field and give him a good kickin', you could do with the exercise?"

Peter the considerably overweight driver replied without turning to look in their direction, "Fuck off you cheeky twat, it's freezin' out there tonight and I'm going to have a nice hot brew and a smoke, while you write up your report about this tit."

No more was said and the topic was closed. Not long after they sped past the municipal cemetery, crossed the busy main junction and drove into their allocated parking bay, outside the double storey early 1960s bland utilitarian, grey police station.

"Full house here tonight," said the cheery desk sergeant as Jay Mac was marched through the entrance doors and then positioned in front of the reception counter. "We're going to have to stack them on top of each other, if you lads keep bringing them in at this rate," he continued, taking the top off his new black ballpoint pen, carefully chosen from a colourful collection proudly stored in the breast pocket of his short sleeved shirt.

"Right then, empty your pockets soft lad, then we can have your details and get you squared away for the night." He recorded Jay Mac's name, address and date of birth then spoke to the arresting officer, asking him for the specifics of Jay Mac's crime.

"Offensive weapon in a public place… namely one empty glass milk bottle… assault and affray… public disorder…and we have exhibit 'A', the weapon as evidence."

The beaming sergeant completed his cataloguing of Jay Mac's misdemeanours repeating loudly each one in turn with a brief pause between, while the tall young policeman, who had recognised Jay Mac, read them from his notebook.

"This is very good, excellent," said the sergeant, adjusting his heavily Brylcreemed, combed-over dark hair with his left hand, after it had fallen forward slightly across his forehead, revealing his gleaming bald pate for all to see.

Standing back from his ledger for a moment and sucking his pen with a perplexed look on his pock-marked face, he asked "So your home address is on the Kings Estate but you were arrested, according to this officer's report, whilst engaged in a scuffle assisting boys from the rival Crown Estate gang? Very peculiar, we'll see what the DCs make of this one."

Turning to the two constables who were still flanking Jay Mac he continued, "Take this little toe rag through to the cells, there's just one remaining at the end of the corridor, then have yer break."

A few moments later after passing through a reinforced security door, Jay Mac was briskly marched towards his allocated cell, then once the sturdy metal door to that room had been unlocked and his handcuffs removed, he was forcibly shoved inside.

"Get y'head down boy, it's going to be a long night." shouted the original arresting officer, turning the key before following his colleague 'Peter the driver' quickly away from the cell block and along to the nearby canteen.

Sitting on the narrow wooden bench looking around the windowless cell, with its basic lidless flushing toilet at one end opposite the door and casually reading some of the amusing comments on the graffiti covered grey walls, Jay Mac knew he was in serious trouble. Realising his predicament he was thankful that he had not been carrying his razor sharp, long, slim knife in its lacquered black scabbard which he had not yet retrieved from the lining of his old tattered Crombie, as he felt its presence may have escalated his milk bottle offensive weapon charge into a much more serious matter.

Time passed slowly in the confinement of his cell and his own troubled mind, whilst he tried to gather his thoughts in preparation for the interrogation which he knew must be approaching shortly. He had noticed that the clock on the wall behind the desk sergeant's position had displayed a quarter to eleven when he was brought in and estimated at least two hours had passed since then. Cell doors along the corridor seemed to be opening then clanging shut with some degree of regularity but there was little noise from the other occupants, Jay Mac considered that like himself, most of them were probably exhausted taking any opportunity to sleep, he decided to do the same.

What seemed like an interminable time later, the youth was roused from a dark dream by the sound of keys in the lock of his cell door, then the door opened partially and a uniformed officer leaned into the small room shouting, "Gerrup you little shit, c'mon move!"

Jay Mac jumped up and was roughly pulled through the doorway, then marched the length of the narrow corridor to yet another windowless grey chamber.

"Gerrin and stand fuckin' still," his escort instructed brusquely, flinging Jay Mac into the interrogation room, where for a few moments he was dazzled by the stark brightness of the light from two overhead, shadeless fluorescent tubes that buzzed with the electric current passing through them.

Sitting at a small table littered with files and loose papers were two large jacketless males, whom Jay Mac took to be in their mid-thirties. They were both similarly dressed with open-necked badly fitting plain Bri-nylon shirts, one of pale blue, the other lemon, with large knotted kipper ties hanging at half-mast. Jay Mac could not see what style of trousers or shoes they were wearing at first, as they both remained seated but the overpowering smell of their strong body odour, was visually corroborated by the evidential dark sweat stains clearly visible, radiating outwards from the armpits of their shirts.

"Take that fuckin' rag off and bring it over here now," the pale blue, shirt wearer said in a stern voice.

Jay Mac removed his Crombie, walked towards the table and handed his coat to the speaker.

Whilst he carefully searched the pockets, turning the sleeves of the garment inside out, scrutinising the lining for any rends, his colleague, who Jay Mac could now see had unkempt light brown hair and a deep disfiguring scar running from his left nostril up to the outer corner of his eye, stared intently at the youth.

The detective who had been searching Jay Mac's Crombie completed his task, then threw the recently purchased prized item of clothing onto the floor in front of the table and shouted, "Put your hands on your head, gerrup on your toes then turn round slowly and keep turnin' until I tell you to fuckin' stop."

Jay Mac tried to do as instructed, pirouetting awkwardly for almost a full turn before stumbling and coming to a halt. He was surprised at the speed of the large male who had given him the instruction, as he leapt up from his seat and punched him hard in his unprotected, unprepared stomach.

"I didn't tell you to stop, you little puff. Get on your fuckin' toes and start again," he shouted angrily at the youth, who was doubled up in pain, trying to catch his breath.

Jay Mac attempted the task once more placing his hands on top of his head, even though his aching gut made this extremely painful to accomplish, again he managed only part of the required movement and again received the same punishment for his failure, the only difference this time being that he collapsed onto the hard floor, after receiving this second blow.

"Well, even though you look like a fuckin' queer, yer not much of a ballet dancer are yer?" the officer in the blue shirt announced standing over the stricken youth. "You've got some shitty drawing of a little fairy's crown on yer back with the word 'Skins' inside, I thought you lads were supposed to be hard cases but I've only tapped yer and look at the state yer in. Get up and sit on the 'naughty' chair, in the corner over there."

After giving Jay Mac the instruction he returned to his desk and his as yet silent partner, stood up and walked towards the seated Skin.

"Put y'hands behind the back of that chair and keep them there, if you move them I will personally break your wrists."

Jay Mac complied and waited nervously for whatever technique this new tormentor would employ. He didn't have long to wait as the scar faced officer followed a similar routine, to those detectives he had encountered earlier in the year, telling him to open his legs then placing the pointed toe of his black zip-sided Chelsea boot under Jay Mac's groin acting as a physical lever to assist in extracting information. Making certain that the youth clearly understood who was in charge and the precise methods that he may use; he leaned forward and slapped him hard across the left side of his face.

"You are in fuckin' serious trouble boy, and I'm not just talkin' about you playin' spin the bottle with your boyfriends earlier tonight. Over on that desk are a dozen witness statements that implicate you in the recent murder of one Alfred Day and, three of them statements say you were the actual perpetrator. What do you want to say about that?"

Jay Mac looked up at the sweating, heavily built, scar-faced detective and replied "Sorry sir, I don't think I've ever heard that name before."

Apart from a sharp increase in the pressure under his testicles another powerful slap struck him, further reddening the already glowing left cheek of his face.

"Think again shit head, it's been a long night and we're both gettin' really fuckin' tired of talkin' to you little fruits. We know who *you* are; the only kid who lives on the Kings Estate and plays around with the Crown Estate boys. Some of those lads, who you *think* are your friends, told us that you led them in tonight's game and you gave all the orders. So just to make it clear, you are totally fucked."

After absorbing fully what had been said, Jay Mac decided to co-operate, at least for the moment. "What I meant sir, was that I didn't know that was the name of the lad who got killed, I only knew him as Yad."

His interrogator smiled then said, "That's more like it, now I'll tell you something. We've got a stupid little fucker locked away who was arrested at the crime scene with the murder weapon and we've got three rapist shitbags who have all admitted assaulting his sister, the problem is, they also swear that you stabbed the deceased, then passed the knife to our confessor. On top of all this, Day's other injuries show that he was in some sort of a fight, immediately prior to his death, so think very carefully this time and when y'ready, we'll take your statement".

When he had finished speaking he returned to his seat and lit a cigarette, as did his colleague. They both sat staring at Jay

Mac who remained exactly in the position he had been ordered to assume.

The terrified youth realised that he was in a dire dilemma and considered his next cautious response, "I don't wish to say anything further until I've seen a solicitor, which I believe I'm entitled to."

Almost exploding with rage, the blue-shirted detective sprang across to the seated Jay Mac and threw him off the plastic chair onto the floor.

"Listen you stupid little cunt, we're not playin' a game, you've got no fuckin' rights, nobody even knows you're here."

Lying on the cold lino-covered floor, Jay Mac stared up at the officer and replied, "I've got no further comment."

For the next few painful hours, Jay Mac was stood up, slapped, then sat back down in the required position, slapped again, made to face the wall and thrown onto the floor, all in a constant repetitive cycle. Finally he was returned exhausted to his cell, where he collapsed onto the narrow bench without any knowledge of what time it was, whether it was night or day and fell into a deep sleep.

Jay Mac dived headlong into that dark pool and lay unmoving in a black state of dreamless unconsciousness for an eternity and was totally unaware of the uniformed officer when he loudly burst into the room several hours later, "Wake up you lazy shit! I'm not gonna tell you again!"

Disoriented and dazed, the youth rubbed his eyes as he was yanked to his feet, once more to be marched back to the dreaded, claustrophobic interrogation room.

The overpowering stench of body odour had increased in intensity and been added to by that of stale cigarette smoke, greasy food and foul air, expelled from other orifices. Jay Mac was told to resume his original standing position with his hands on top of his head but for the present was spared from attempting another pirouette. Both officers looked as if they had remained in that room, in the same position since his last session, with the only new addition being two plates of canteen fayre and two mugs of steaming brown tea.

While Jay Mac stood perfectly still the two large males finished loudly consuming their bacon sandwiches then slurped their tea and for a few minutes there were no other sounds within the humid, stale room. After he was completely satisfied that there was not another morsel left to eat, or a drop of liquid in his badly stained empty mug, the scar-faced officer opened the latest round of questioning, whilst his colleague busied himself by picking at his teeth, searching for any lingering remains.

"Right, John Mack, we've been doin' a bit of checkin' on you and here's how we see it," he paused for a moment, belched loudly then resumed his assessment of Jay Mac's predicament and background. "You've already got a suspended sentence hangin' over you from a conditional discharge at the beginnin' of the year for theft, so that's goin' to add to whatever the judge gives you next, dependin' on how well you co-operate with us, that is. Is that clear?" Again he paused and Jay Mac replied. "Yes sir."

Now the officer applied leverage that Jay Mac had no defence for, a direct threat to his guardians. "You live with yer aunt and uncle, a Mr and Mrs Palmer in South Kings Estate and your mother, one Eileen Mack, lives in the Everton district of the city but I can't seem to find yer father's details, so maybe you can provide them? Come on don't be shy." He waited for Jay Mac's reply.

"I never knew him or his name" was all the youth said, which prompted the blue shirted officer, who had completed his dental cavity search, to interject, "So you *really* are a little bastard then?" Both males laughed loudly at this witty observation; Jay Mac remained silent.

The questioner resumed his latest tack, "Ok, so I take it that you don't get on with yer ma but you do like your aunt and uncle. Here's what we're going to do, me and my mate are going to get a bunch of our big, clumsy uniformed lads and go with them to yer aunt and uncle's nice little flat, turn it over, smash the whole fuckin' place to pieces and, if the two old duffers get in the way, they might end up gettin' badly hurt as well."

Jay Mac dropped his hands from his head and sprang towards their table shouting "You fuckin' cunt! Don't you go anywhere near them!"

Almost immediately the officer in the blue shirt leapt from his seat, grabbed Jay Mac by the throat lifting him off the floor and thrust him backwards towards the wall opposite. Whilst holding the struggling youth with one hand, he punched him hard in the stomach twice with the other, then flung him down onto the floor once more.

"Alright soft lad, now that you've calmed down, I'll continue." said the scar faced officer as his sweating colleague returned to his seat.

"Here's your fuckin' choice, come with us and watch while we make a real good job of searchin' your aunt and uncle's flat, or, just give us a signed statement telling us exactly what happened on the night of the fourth of November, when the other little rapist shit got what he deserved. What do you say, it's up to you?"

When he had finished outlining his offer he sat back, lit a cigarette and passed one to his colleague, all the while watching the crumpled youth who remained sitting on the floor where he had been thrown. Jay Mac carefully considered what had been said, he may have deviated from the straight and narrow path of righteousness but he was an intelligent deviant and knew when he was faced with an unwinnable position.

Without being asked he stood up, brought the chair with its plastic seat and back over to the waiting detectives' desk and sat down in front of them, then said, "Where do you want me to start?"

A couple of tiring hours later, surprisingly relieved by his coerced confession, a chastened Jay Mac was once more returned to his cell and eventually provided with a glass of water to accompany a dry cheese sandwich. Again time passed slowly without any means of measuring its progress.

After another eternity of anxious waiting, his cell door was reopened and a uniformed officer told Jay Mac to follow him to the reception area. While he was standing in front of the same desk sergeant who had admitted him on the previous night, signing for the return of his personal belongings, including his black half-inch braces and essential boot laces, he realised it was still dark outside and looking at the clock on the wall, saw that it read five minutes to eight.

"Don't you ever go home?" he asked the chirpy sergeant, who looked at Jay Mac and smiled.

"I've been home this morning soft shite, its eight o'clock at night and I started me shift an hour ago. Now, here's the details of your magistrates' appearance. Make sure you turn up, or there'll be a warrant for your arrest and by the sound of it, when I spoke to Mr Palmer, your uncle, on your neighbour's phone earlier, he sounded totally pissed off and doesn't need any more trouble from you."

Moments later Jay Mac stepped out into the freezing winter's night, he breathed a huge sigh of relief then filled his lungs with the cold, fresh air. Turning up the collar of his now grubby Crombie, he dug his hands into its pockets and began the long trek to the nearest bus stop. A light flurry of snow began to swirl about in the sharp darkness, whilst Jay Mac walked along, lost in his thoughts, hardly noticing that he was passing the ten foot walls that surrounded and marked the entrance to the huge Ravens Hall Estate. Only when he happened to casually glance to his right, just before approaching the main cross-road junction facing the municipal cemetery and saw the slogan announcing that this was the territory of the RAVENS SKINS, painted in black, two foot high letters, did he realise he was in the heart of another rival team's area.

Following the curvature of the perimeter wall around to where he knew an outbound bus stop was located, Jay Mac stopped in his tracks when he saw the dozen or so Skins with their female companions, loitering in the entrance to one of the three tower blocks situated across from the estate and outside its brick boundary. They saw him almost at the same instant, recognising his '' as that of another team's player and raced towards him, hoping to capture an enemy Skin for some momentary, diversionary entertainment on this otherwise night of frozen boredom.

"Come here you fucker!" they shouted, sprinting between the traffic, encouraged by their own camp followers' calls of "Get him lads, bring him over 'ere so we can 'ave a laugh!"

Totally exhausted with aching muscles and tired limbs, Jay Mac summoned every last vestige of remaining strength that he had, taking to his heels with a burst of speed that belied his physical condition. Like a sprinter bolting from the starting blocks he was gone in a second, flying through the blinding blizzard that had now developed, with the pursuing eager Skins also running as fast as they could manage. Roused fully from his state of reflective torpor, Jay Mac relied on raw ability that had been honed through years of hard training both during his school athletics career and more importantly his childhood street adventures, for him this was yet another race that he must win.

Even as he neared the low cemetery walls, after skilfully negotiating the busy traffic junction, he could hear the three lead runners of the Ravens Skins desperately trying to close the distance between him and them; their less able colleagues had already abandoned the chase. Jay Mac cleared the sandstone block boundary wall with a single-handed vault and landing on his feet, immediately continued his sprint with hardly a break in stride. Moments later the first Ravens Skin repeated the action but he was unable to see any trace of his fleeing Crown Team rival in the darkness and the swirling snow storm. His two colleagues now also dropped over the wall but decided that was the limit of their pursuit. They shouted to their team mate to give up the chase too, telling him to 'leave it'; he rashly ignored their advice and picked his way carefully through the maze of differing sized gravestones.

Separated by a few dozen yards from his waiting friends, the crouching Ravens Skin peered about through the eerie, dank atmosphere, sprinkled with a myriad glittering snowflakes, without success. The petrified branch that cracked him hard across the face, only just became visible an instant before impact.

"Happy fuckin' Christmas, sorry it's late." Jay Mac said with a sinister grin, as the stunned Ravens Skin fell with a thud onto the snow covered earth.

"He's fuckin' done Smigger, c'mon." shouted one of the waiting pursuers, then they both ran forward to rescue their team mate. Jay Mac was long gone before they reached the spot where he had struck.

Five minutes later, after emerging from the northern end of the municipal cemetery close to its Crown Estate boundary, he leapt onto a waiting bus temporarily stopped near the washing machine factory gates, while it collected the overtime, twilight-shift drone passengers. Seated downstairs at the rear of the vehicle trying desperately to absorb any escaping heat from the engine, as it seeped through to that region of the lower deck, he wiped the condensation from the window and stared blankly into the snow-filled dark void beyond. His turbulent mind raged with a blizzard of its own, thought after disturbing thought swirled through its chambers each pressing its claim to occupy a predominant position. Jay Mac's immediate concern was what would be waiting for him, when his present short bus journey ended on his return to his aunt and uncle's flat.

When he finally arrived at his destination the youth decided that there was no point in trying to enter stealthily and, his best option was to boldly face whatever punishment his guardians were about to administer. Once inside the small hall, he braced himself before entering the living room where he could hear the sound of the television blaring loudly from within.

"So y'back are you?" asked his aunt coolly, not bothering to raise her eyes from the latest lurid murder mystery she was presently reading.

Jay Mac nodded, knowing when it was best not to speak and stood behind the old worn couch, also keeping his gaze lowered.

"Most of y'clothes are ready for you in those bags, you can collect the rest of your stuff some other time." his aunt announced calmly before taking another drag of her Embassy king-size filter-tip cigarette.

"Its New Year's Eve tomorrow we'll be going for a drink with Reg and Ethel, just make sure you're gone before we get back the next day," she delivered her ultimatum then returned to her novel without another word.

The exhausted youth looked to his uncle to see if there was any possibility of an appeal but the old soldier did not even acknowledge his presence in the room and remained watching the television while smoking his pipe. Jay Mac went into the kitchen hoping vainly that there may be the remnants of an evening meal saved for him. He was sorely disappointed and settled for a bowl of cornflakes, deciding to stay where he was for the rest of the evening, quietly listening to the radio until his guardians had both gone to bed.

Sunday 31st December 1972
The frozen morning of Sunday 31st December began with chill conditions both outside and within the small council flat of Jay Mac's aunt and uncle. Whilst they carried on conversations between themselves as if he was no longer present, he packed any remaining items that his aunt had not yet forced into plastic bags of varying sizes. Breakfast and lunch were prepared, served and ate with the two adults continuing their isolationist routine, discussing recent and forthcoming events only amongst themselves. Jay Mac knew that there was a storm brewing and by the end of their evening meal, the first few drops of the impending torrent began to fall.

"Y'know you brought this on yourself, don't you?" his aunt began innocently enough, appearing to leave him with the option of accepting her contention or arguing his case, though in reality as he well knew, any answer would be the wrong answer.

He decided for acquiescence "Yeah, I know y'right," he replied.

His uncle responded immediately "Too fuckin' right we're right, you've done this to y'self, throwin' your life away before its even started and for what? Absolutely nothin'." he paused, letting the enormity of his words be fully absorbed.

Jay Mac tried to frame a suitable reply, knowing once again that anything he said may be taken down and used against him. "It wasn't for nothin'; I tried to be me for once. No one in here knows who I am but some people out there do, they know my name." Jay Mac stopped and looked at his aunt and uncle, waiting for a comment.

"Yeah, some people know your name alright, the fuckin' police. What were you tryin' to do, every night with those mates of yours, hangin' around on street corners?" his uncle asked, genuinely perplexed, unable to grasp the mind-set or rationalise the thought processes that motivated Jay Mac and his team mates.

The youth then put his foot fully into the snare, "You wouldn't understand, things were different in your day, we're not all working sixteen hour shifts now and thanking the bosses for it. We've got some free time and a bit of money so we're looking for something to do, that's all," he finished speaking and looked at his uncle whose face was turning purple with rage, then the old soldier exploded.

"Something to do! I'll give you fuckin' something to do, you stupid little idiot! Try puttin' food on the table when you can't afford it, or there is none; try keepin' a roof over yer head when you can't pay the rent; try fighting in a war to save your country from fascist bastards! Never mind walking around with a gang of gobshites acting hard, making things worse for your own class, stealing or destroying their property, vandalising the shitholes where they're forced to live!"

He stopped talking then stood up and walked away from the kitchen table, he had said all that he wished to say to the youth.

His aunt also left the room but before closing the door, reminded Jay Mac of his impending eviction, "We're going to get ready to go out, you can help y'self to some drinks and there's some sliced ham in the larder, so make y'self some sarnies. Just make sure that you're not here when we get back tomorrow, or I will personally put your belongings out in the street, ok?" and with those final words, she departed to the bedroom to make her preparations for the night.

An hour later Jay Mac stood by the large one panelled window of the flat and drew back the curtains watching his aunt and uncle hail a taxi, after abandoning any hope of a corporation bus ever arriving on New Year's eve, in the middle of another heavy snowfall. After they had finally left, in a black cab partly covered in white powdery drifts, he remained watching the silent, deserted road and the battered old concrete bus shelter which, now camouflaged in a thick layer of snow, displayed an almost rustic charm as if it were a pioneers log cabin or a lonely hermitage. Jay Mac listened to the sound of silence with every noise lost in the glistening carpet's deep pile. He felt as if he was literally living within the lyrics of Simon and Garfunkel's *I am an Island,* as he closed the curtains, moved away from the window and sat down on the old couch in front of the glowing electric fire.

Only a few short miles away in the more affluent 1930's semi-detached suburbia of the Walton Hall Avenue district, the stunningly beautiful girl of Jay Mac's dreams was also preparing for the evening's festivities. Finally satisfied with her make-up and the style of her thick, luxuriant, long black hair with its blue sheen, she was busily selecting one of her most provocative outfits. Looking forward to the arrival of her latest boyfriend, who was the fortunate one selected from an army of suitors, to have the pleasure of escorting her for the night. She had already dismissed any thought of the forlorn Jay Mac from her mind; he had been given a chance and thrown it away, whatever his reason may have been she did not care. The house party that she would soon be attending, was located only a few roads from that which his aunt and uncle would be welcoming in the new year with older relatives.

Even as the final hour of 1972 was rapidly drawing to a close, the lonely, pathetic, tortured figure of Mal 'the Pig', having made one of his usual random pilgrimages to the municipal cemetery, was kneeling on the snow-covered soil of the relatively recent grave that he had been seeking with his inquisitive torchlight and was desperately trying to communicate with its not quite resting in peace occupant, Yad.

After arranging his peculiar assortment of items, including: hair and nail clippings; bodily fluids and excreta, he placed his inverted crucifix into position and prefaced his occult chant by saying "Not long now brother, my master will let you see and speak to me through this new one, we will be together again soon."

Whatever special powers Mal imagined he had been granted, extra sensory perception was not one of them, as he was totally unaware of the crew of Ravens Skins approaching stealthily towards him, until it was too late and he was completely surrounded. Smigger and his friends were more than happy to take their revenge for the previous night's assault, on this sorry individual. The vicious beating that they administered to the wildly struggling, misguided youth, would bring him closer to his long dead sibling, than any of his regular theatrical graveside rituals.

On the bleak Crown Estate, in both the Heron and Eagle public houses intoxicated revellers were in full party mode. The respective jukeboxes blared out a selection of favourites, that were accompanied by discordant drunken versions from the remaining members of each crew, those who had evaded capture during the concerted police action of two nights previous.
Irish raised a glass "To absent friends and those who are no longer with us."
While spontaneous rousing cheers erupted from the assembled youths, he wondered what fate had befallen his long-time friend, refusing to believe the two latest wild rumours, that the newly promoted general Jay Mac had either been wrongly charged with Yad's murder, or worse still, had been "killed by the bizzies" whilst in their custody.

Stretched out on the old couch drinking the last of his supply of bottled Guinness and eating the final handful of mixed savoury cheese snacks, including the oddly shaped, excessively salty mini pretzels, Jay Mac was considering whether to consume the remainder of his aunt's special reserve port as a final act of madness, whilst he reflected on his present unfortunate situation. Patch, the old mongrel was also relaxing in front of the two-bar electric fire, intermittently glancing towards the flickering black and white television, with its volume control knob turned to its lowest setting by Jay Mac, who was now also simultaneously adjusting the station selection dials of the small transistor radio next to him, desperately trying to find something to listen to as an alternative to watching the 'Andy Stewart Hogmanay Show.'
"Well mate, it looks like this is goin' to be our last conversation, for a while anyway," Jay Mac began, addressing

the recumbent hound with one of his regular rhetorical questions, "What's that y'saying... I've only got meself to blame? Yeah, I suppose y'right."

He paused and continued fiddling with the radio tuning dial, then took another drink of his bottled stout. "Snowin' outside, bloody freezin' as usual, better off in 'ere than walking those streets, anyway mate."

Leaning down to the floor he poured some more dark brown liquid into the small saucer for the appreciative hound, then patted her back as she lazily wagged her brush of a tail.

"Fuck it, 1972's nearly over anyway, what a shit year."

Then suddenly he found one of his childhood favourite records a crackling 78 (rpm) western classic, being played on some obscure foreign station which the receiver could barely pick up. While Jay Mac listened to the lyrics of Frankie Laine's version of *Ghost Riders in the Sky*, he felt that the leader of the relentless pursuing cowboys was speaking directly to him, when he advised the recipient of his wisdom to change his ways if he wanted to avoid eternal damnation.

"That's going to have to be my new year's resolution mate; I've got to turn over a new leaf for '73. You can't argue with a ghostly cowboy doomed to chase the devil's herd across the skies forever, can yer?"

Outside, the snow continued to fall steadily, covering both estates with a soft white, unblemished blanket. For a brief moment in time the stark, inhospitable appearance of the grey, concrete ghettos was masked and replaced by a winter wonderland of tall protective towers set amidst simple houses, all aglow with a thousand twinkling lights. The great arcing flyover that spanned the uncultivated battle zones was now fully open for business but there was little traffic tonight as the clock finally struck midnight, announcing the end of the old and the birth of the new. The events of 1972 passed into history, soon to be forgotten by all involved save for a handful of players, who bore the scars long after the reality faded into myth.

THE END

MUSIC

Chapter 1 (*Starry Starry Night -- Vincent*, Don McLean)
Come to the Sabbath - Black Widow
Sweet Black Angel the Rolling Stones (*Exile on Main Street* album)
Motown Chartbusters Volumes 3 and 4.
Still Waters - The Four Tops
Runaway Child Running Wild - Temptations

Chapter 2 (*All the Young Dudes* – Mott the Hoople)
Swanee River - Al Jolson
Ride a White Swan - Marc Bolan T-Rex
Baby Jump - Mungo Jerry
On the Good Ship Lollipop - Shirley Temple
Gimme Shelter - Rolling Stones
Only the Lonely - Roy Orbison
It's All in the Game - The Four Tops
Little 'Ole Wine Drinker Me - Dean Martin
New York, New York - Frank Sinatra
I Love You Because - Jim Reeves
Oh Danny Boy - Joseph Locke

Chapter 3 (*Everywhere there's lots of Piggies* – The Beatles)
No music mentioned

Chapter 4 (*Ball of Confusion* – The Temptations)
No music mentioned

Chapter 5 (*Instant Karma* – John Lennon)
He's Gonna Step on You Again - John Kongos

Chapter 6 (*Move on Up* – Curtis Mayfield)
Chi-lites - No music mentioned

Chapter 7 (*Leader of the Pack* – The Shangri-Las)
I Can't Help Myself (Sugarpie, Honeybunch) - The Four Tops
Floy Joy - The Supremes

Double Barrel - Dave and Ansell Collins
Have You Seen Her - The Chi-lites
I'm Still Waiting – Diana Ross
Tears of a Clown - Smokey Robinson and the Miracles
Liquidator - Harry J. Allstars
Israelites - Desmond Dekker
My Girl - The Temptations

Chapter 8 (*Rocket Man* – Elton John)
Rocket Man - Elton John
Viva Las Vegas - Elvis Presley
You Need Hands - Max Bygraves
Ruby Don't Take Your Love to Town – Kenny Rogers and the First Edition

Chapter 9 (*School's Out Forever* – Alice Cooper)
Land of Hope and Glory' - lyrics, A. C. Benson (E. Elgar's *Pomp & Circumstance March No1*)
You'll Never Walk Alone - Rodgers & Hammerstein (Carousel)

Chapter 10 (*Lean on Me* – Bill Withers)
Sunshine of Your Love - Cream
Voodoo Child - Jimi Hendrix
Family Affair - Sly and the Family Stone
The Coldest Days of My Life - Chi-lites

Chapter 11 (*War* – Edwin Starr)
War - Edwin Starr
Bad Moon Rising - Credence Clear Water Revival

Chapter 12 (*Livin' in a Broken Dream* – Python Lee Jackson)
Riders on the Storm - The Doors,
Livin' in a Broken Dream - Python Lee Jackson

Chapter 13 (*Ghost Riders in the Sky* – Frankie Laine)
Mouldy Old Dough - Lieutenant Pigeon
I am an Island - Simon and Garfunkel
Ghost Riders in the Sky - Frankie Laine

Printed in Great Britain
by Amazon.co.uk, Ltd.,
Marston Gate.